The Donors

By
Jeffrey Wilson

JournalStone
San Francisco

JournalStone books may be ordered through booksellers or by contacting:

JournalStone
199 State Street
San Mateo, CA 94401
www.journalstone.com

The views expressed in this work are solely those of the authors and do not necessarily reflect the views of the publisher, and the publisher hereby disclaims any responsibility for them.

ISBN: 978-1-936564-46-0   (sc)
ISBN: 978-1-936564-48-4   (ebook)

Library of Congress Control Number: 2012937961

Printed in the United States of America
JournalStone rev. date: June 29, 2012

Cover Design: Denise Daniel
Cover Art: Mike Bohatch

Edited By: Elizabeth Reuter

Endorsements

"With its tight muscular prose and sharp dialogue, The Donors will keep you hooked from the opening page. Wilson has written a novel packed with surprises and suspense, and drawn characters whose every pang the reader feels. This is a novel full of visceral, intense moments. It will keep you holding on until the brilliant end." - Richard Godwin, author of *Mr. Glamour* and *Apostle Rising*.

"Jeffrey Wilson can spin a chilling scene with the best of them, but it's his characters that make his writing so horrifying. These are real people and real families, and Wilson forces us to walk with them on a terrifying journey into the blackest shadows where creatures of primordial evil feed on their darkest fears." - Brett J. Talley, 2011 Bram Stoker Finalist and author of *That Which Should Not Be* and *The Void*

Dedication

For Wendy — as always

Additional titles from JournalStone:

Shaman's Blood
Anne C. Petty

The Traiteur's Ring
Jeffrey Wilson

Jokers Club
Gregory Bastianelli

Ghosts of Coronado Bay
J.G. Faherty

Contrition
Robert E. Hirsch

That Which Should Not Be
Brett J. Talley

The Void
Brett J. Talley

Available through your local and online bookseller or at
www.journalstone.com

Chapter
1

He stayed to the shadows. It wasn't fear that kept him in the dark, wet alley beside the emergency room. Not even remotely. He preferred the shadows, felt comfortable there. They were home.

The people that milled about the entrance to the emergency room held no threat.

Opportunity—yes.

He pulled the collar of his trench coat up around his thin, pale neck and watched. So many years spent watching and waiting, enjoying the scent of powerful emotions. He didn't miss those years. How had he ever tolerated it? To smell the meal, but never taste it? He had evolved for something bigger.

A soft glow appeared beside him and he spoke without turning.

"Is there a space that meets our needs?" he asked.

"Yes," the wet, slithering voice answered.

"We will go to the key people beginning tonight. We mustn't be hasty."

"Of course," the voice replied. It sounded irritated.

Just hungry, perhaps.

"Patience," he said.

The form beside him nodded and then he felt the rustling of wind. A strong odor filled the air. He watched an ambulance pull up to the entrance of the ER. Paramedics dragged a stretcher out of the back and he drank in the delicious wail of a hysterical woman. Leaning out of the alley for a better look, he tugged the brim of his hat lower over his pale face, nearly covering his glowing yellow eyes.

"Omigod… omigod. Please help him. God, please help!"

The screams of the woman made him smile. He felt even more aroused by the fear that emanated from the motionless figure on the stretcher, a bloody sheet pulled to the bare chest. He breathed in deeply.

"God, please. Oh, please!" the woman cried again.

His smile widened.

"God's not here," he hissed and licked a deep, red tongue over his long teeth.

Back into the shadows, he readied for his own journey.

Lots of work to do.

* * *

Nearly two thirty and the lying bitch still ain't home yet.

Steve shifted on the couch and looked at his watch, his face flushed with anger. He hated watching the little brat, although now that he had shown the kid who was in charge, it was a lot easier. When he told the kid to do something nowadays, the brat sure as hell did it. Pleased, the man tipped his Bud longneck to his mouth, draining the last swallow. He looked again at his watch.

Shit.

The game had been over for half an hour so Steve flipped mindlessly through the channels, bored. Down at the Kozy Korner, the guys would be on their second pitcher, without him. Maybe he could find Toby and they might get an hour of fishing in at the pier.

If she would hurry the hell up!

Goddamnit, Sundays were *his* days, the only days he didn't work his ass off. She had fifteen more minutes and then he would leave whether she got home or not. The brat could fend for himself.

Not even my damn kid.

He dragged himself up off the couch and clomped into the kitchen for another brew. Where the hell was that kid anyway? Steve hadn't heard a peep from him since telling him to shut up over an hour ago. Well, the brat better not be fucking with any of his fishing stuff or he'd get a beating to remember. Steve set his empty can on the table and pushed through the swinging door into the kitchen. What he saw did not make him happy.

"What the fuck are you doing, kid?"

* * *

Nathan stood on an overturned bucket beside the gas stove and froze in fear at the man's cursing. His right hand clutched an opened can of Chef Boyardee Spaghetti-O's. He managed not to spill any on the counter, but his throat tightened as he now saw two tomato-spattered "O's" on the floor beside him. He had tried to be as quiet as possible, tried not to bother Steve, because Mommy said if he kept making Steve mad he would go away and there would be no one to help them. Nathan didn't want Mommy to be sad anymore, and anyway, Steve scared him. It had taken a long time to quietly get out the pan to cook his Spaghetti-O's.

Nathan wanted to wait for Mommy to get home, but his tummy growled and felt so empty it kind of hurt. Dinner seemed an awfully long time ago and Mommy promised Steve would make him Spaghetti-O's for lunch. But he definitely couldn't ask. The last time Steve got mad at him, his back had hurt for so long he couldn't close his hand for a long time. Sometimes it *still* hurt. So he decided, when his stomach started to *ache* for food, that he could do it himself. Mommy said he was her little man.

I'm almost six — more than the fingers on one hand!

The sound of Steve hollering made his stomach hurt in a different way and his hand, the one that sometimes ached from the last time, trembled until he thought he might drop the can.

"Jesus Christ, Nathan! Look at this goddamn mess! What the hell do you think you're doing, you goddamn little shit!?" Steve's face looked red like before.

Nathan scrambled off the bucket, stumbled, and fell to his knees. He crawled quickly to the corner of the kitchen and pressed himself into the wall, trying to disappear.

Please come home now, Mommy! Please come home RIGHT NOW!

Steve pounded his fists together on the counter.

"A little kid ain't supposed to be fuckin' around in the kitchen! You tryin' to burn down the fuckin' house? Don't you know what a stove does, you little idiot!?"

Steve smacked the empty can of Spaghetti-O's off the counter. It flew through the air and landed at Nathan's feet, little splashes of sauce dotting the floor and his Winnie-the-Pooh tennis shoes, the ones from Christmas. He started to cry and tried to stop, tried really, really hard.

Hurry, Mommy.

He squeezed his eyes tight and tried to make her walk through the door.

Come home, come home, come home —

Nathan's eyes sprang open at the sound of Steve's heavy boots on the floor. The man's fists were balled up and he hovered over him, his face still red.

"You better fucking answer me, you little queer! Do... you... KNOW... WHAT... A... *FUCKING... STOVE... DOES?*"

Nathan tried to talk, to answer Steve, because you're supposed to always answer grown-ups, but he couldn't. He didn't want to be wrong and make Steve even madder. And his voice just wouldn't work. When he opened his mouth his throat just made a noise like a kitty cat. The sound made Steve's face turn a worse color.

"Well fine! I guess I'll just have to show you." Steve stomped toward him and Nathan shook, tears spilled onto his cheeks. "*COME HERE!*"

Nathan remained still. He couldn't move, almost couldn't breathe. He felt his pants getting warm and wet; he sobbed.

Mommy will be sad if she finds out I wet my pants. I'm supposed to be her little man.

The man grabbed Nathan's right arm so hard he thought the pain would make him pass out. There was a crunching noise and he made a loud moan, then bit his lip, trying hard not to cry.

I'm Mommy's little man. I won't cry! I won't cry!

Tears spilled over his cheeks, but he struggled to stay quiet as Steve dragged him to the stove. He pretended to be somewhere else, pictured himself in a swing at the park, his mommy behind him, pushing and laughing. He couldn't remember where that park had been or if he had ever really gone there.

"I'm gonna show you what a stove does so you'll *NEVER FORGET!*" the man raged, clutching his arm so tight that Nathan felt the little bees buzzing in his fingers like when it fell asleep sometimes. With his free hand the man spun the dial on the stove and the front burner hissed to life. A blue flame ignited. "*THIS IS WHAT A GODDAMN STOVE DOES NATHAN!*"

Nathan gasped as he felt himself lifted into the air by his hurt arm and a new pain shot through his shoulder and back. Then his tingly hand was brought back to life as Steve thrust it into the flames.

"*THE STOVE IS HOT, YOU LITTLE IDIOT! SEE HOW HOT IT IS? DON'T...TOUCH...THE....STOVE!*"

The skin on his fingers turned red, then white. He screamed briefly and squeezed his eyes shut.

But he didn't cry.

Nathan fell to the ground where the man dropped him and curled up in a ball, his burned flesh clutched to his chest. He started to rock back and forth and whimpered softly.

I didn't cry, Mommy. I'm Mommy's little man. I didn't cry, so Mommy won't have to be alone.

* * *

The loud chaos of the ER, mixed with the strong smell of antiseptic and body odor, made Sherry clutch her little boy tightly as he lay in her lap. Nathan's head lay against her chest and his arms wrapped around her. Her son's right hand was wrapped in bulky white gauze which secured a plaster splint halfway around his arm, from his hand to just above his bent elbow. As she rocked, she heard Nathan whimper softly in rhythm. Then his eyes, glazed with morphine, flickered open and he looked quickly up at her, momentarily panicked. When he saw her face he gave a crooked smile and closed his eyes again, squeezing her tight.

"I didn't cry, Mommy."

The woman's eyes filled with tears and she held her boy tighter. Her voice cracked. "I know, baby. You're Mommy's little man. Mommy loves you." Tears dripped off her chin into her son's curly blond hair. She smoothed it back on his head and kissed his cheek. "Nothing will ever hurt you again, baby. Mommy loves you soooo much." She squeezed her eyes shut.

The curtain opened and a tired young doctor came in, his face rough with a two-day growth of beard, his eyes dark and heavy from the never-ending sad stories. Beside him stood a uniformed police officer, a woman, who looked both mortified and angry.

"Ms. Doren, I'm Dr. Gelman." The young man spoke softly.

"I remember," the woman said. She held her boy tightly, afraid they would make her let him go.

The young man's eyes looked kind, despite being bloodshot and underscored with the dark shadows of a long sleepless night.

"Ms. Doren, Nathan has a broken bone in his arm just above his wrist. It's a stable fracture and the splint will let it heal fine. I spoke to the pediatric orthopedist and he doesn't feel it will need surgery, just a better cast." He paused and put his hands into his faded lab coat. Sherry didn't speak and held his eyes as bravely as she could. Her cheeks felt hot and wet and she pulled her now-sleeping boy more tightly to her chest.

The doctor sighed heavily and rubbed his face with both hands. Then he sat down in the plastic chair beside her. He stroked Nathan's hair as she held him and a sad, almost-smile appeared on his face. Then he looked at her again. She felt more comfortable. She decided she liked this doctor.

"Ms. Doren, your son's hand is more serious. The burns are what we call 'full thickness.' What that means is the skin and soft tissues were burned badly and have died. The plastic surgeons feel he will need to have the dead skin removed and then a skin graft placed."

Sherry closed her eyes tightly. She felt a deep vacuous agony grow inside. She thought she might be sick.

"An operation?" she whispered and then opened her eyes to study the young doctor's face.

The doctor looked dejected—or maybe angry? She wondered if he blamed her, thought she was a terrible mother.

Maybe I am, or was, but never again.

"Yes, Sherry. An operation. They'll have to take skin from Nathan's thigh and graft it over his hand so it will heal properly. Hopefully, that will let it regain normal function."

"Will it hurt him?" She choked back tears. She didn't want to see the look on the doctor's face anymore.

"We'll give him medicine for the pain, Sherry." She felt a hand squeeze her shoulder and she looked up, almost pleadingly, with red, burning eyes. "Kids are tough. He'll do fine." She began to sob. The doctor stood again, and there was a long, awkward silence.

"Sherry, this police officer needs to talk to you. They want to make sure your boyfriend never hurts Nathan or anyone else again, okay?" He squeezed her shoulder, gently.

"Okay," she whispered. She felt a strength surge through her at the mention of Steve—and hatred. "He's not my boyfriend anymore." As the police officer stepped forward, she squeezed her boy.

"I have a few questions, Ms. Doren."

Sherry straightened herself up, trying not to wake Nathan as she did. She wanted to wipe the tears from her face, but didn't want to disturb her sleeping little man so she let them dry uncomfortably on her cheeks. The officer did not look as soft or kind as Dr. Gelman, who left the room now and pulled the curtain closed behind him.

"Sherry, I need to ask you a lot of personal questions about Steve Prescott and your relationship with him, okay?" Sherry nodded. "I know it's hard."

"Will he pay for what he did to my son?" Sherry asked. Her voice cracked, new tears spilled out into the drying tracks on her cheeks as she thought of her tortured son. *He might not have normal function in his hand? Is that what Dr. Gelman had said? What did that mean?* She felt a rage inside her that began to beat the fear into submission. "Can you make him pay?"

The policewoman tensed her jaw, as if unsure what to say.

"I don't know, Sherry," she answered honestly. "We'll do our best to build a case, but he has no record, except a few juvenile misdemeanors. There are no witnesses except your boy, and his attorney will have his testimony excluded. All we really have is his story and what you tell us."

"And my little boy's broken arm and burned hand," Sherry said and felt her lip tremble.

"Yeah," the woman responded, softening a little. "Yeah, we have that." She flipped open a notebook and started to ask Sherry about Steve.

Chapter
2

Steve sat in a large vinyl-covered chair in the quiet consultation room just outside the ER. He had been told in no uncertain terms that he was not to leave. He felt more pissed off than scared, but knew he was in some serious shit. The cops had grilled him for nearly an hour. Apparently, Sherry's brat needed an operation for his hand. Christ, he only meant to scare the little shit. He told the cops that the kid had burned himself trying to cook spaghetti and that he'd grabbed his arm to pull his hand out of the fire.

"I guess I grabbed him harder than I thought, but if I hadn't been there he would have been burned worse. A *LOT* worse."

They obviously didn't believe him, because different cops kept asking the same stupid questions. So fuck them! They couldn't prove anything, unless that little shit talked, and that would never happen. The kid knew better than to rat on him, no doubt about that.

A skinny child-cop sat in a chair across from him in the small room. His quiet glare made Steve really nervous. The cop didn't look away, read a magazine, or anything. Steve glanced over at him and then diverted his gaze to the floor.

What an asshole.

Fuckin' cops.

The door to the quiet room opened and an older cop, red-and-gray haired with lots of stripes on his left sleeve, came in. He stared at Steve, who felt his pulse pound harder in his temples. There was something strange about the older cop's eyes, but Steve was unsure what it was, other than that they made him uncomfortable. His eyes looked kind of blank or something. When he turned to the other cop, Steve could swear he saw a kind of little yellow glow in his pupils. The yellow-eyed cop leaned over and whispered something in the younger cop's ear. The young cop looked surprised.

"You're shitting me!" he said and then rose. "What the hell is that all about? Are they Feds?" The young cop seemed pretty pissed at whatever the news was. Steve relaxed a little. Maybe they had to let him go. He knew the little brat would be too scared to fuck him.

The older, yellow eyed cop stared vacantly at the wall. "It's all taken care of, so don't worry about it."

The first cop looked at Steve in disgust and shook his head. Then he stormed from the room. The older cop held Steve's eyes and then a thin, tight smile flashed for a moment on his lips.

"Don't leave. There are some men who want to talk to you." He smiled that hard, mean smile again, but his eyes still looked dead, vacant maybe. Steve looked at the gold name plate above the cop's right breast pocket—Maloney. He tried to remember that in case the asshole tried to rough him up or something. He'd have the shithead's badge. Steve shifted nervously and fought not to look again at the cop's strange eyes, but then the older cop turned and left, closing the door behind him.

Some men? What men? They had to be some kind of cops, he guessed. Something in the cop's icy voice and dead eyes made Steve shudder. Beads of sweat popped out on his forehead and ran down his back under his flannel shirt.

What the fuck?

The man who walked in towered above him. Steve couldn't tell if he was big as well as tall because he wore a long gray trench coat, with no belt, that came nearly to his ankles. A shorter man with a similar coat stood beside him. Both wore gray hats, like Bogart in an old black-and-white movie. The wide brims cast shadows that prevented Steve from seeing their eyes. The shorter man closed the door behind them and then stood behind his boss, arms across his chest. The tall man spoke. His voice was deep and even with no emotion. The voice sent a chill through Steve.

"Mr. Prescott, my name is Mr. Clark. This is Mr. Smith." The tall man indicated his partner with a long bony finger, the skin so pale it seemed translucent. He paused for a long time, like Steve was supposed to say something. Instead, he shifted uncomfortably on the vinyl seat and felt a droplet of sweat trickle down his neck from his face. He wanted very much to see the man's face, but couldn't. Only a thin-lipped mouth, like a purple cut across his white face, and then above that, shadows.

"You more fucking cops?" Steve asked. He tried to seem bored, but realized he sounded small instead. The tall man bent his head forward as if holding his tongue and then spoke again.

"Mr. Prescott, my name is Clark and this is Smith." The same long pause, only this time Steve looked down and said nothing. "Do you know why you are here, Mr. Prescott?"

"My name is Steve and yeah, I do. My girlfriend's rocket-scientist kid burned his hand. I tried to help him and now you cops are trying to fuck me over. I didn't do nothin' wrong, but I get in trouble. I should have let the little shit burn." He wanted to exude toughness, but again his voice sounded different than he intended.

"Mr. Prescott, we are not policemen." The man behind him opened a small notebook. "We need you to answer a few simple questions. What is your full name, please?"

"Man, you guys are killin' me. I already answered all this shit. Ask your fucking cop friends." The tall man tilted his head slightly but his face remained shadowed.

"Mr. Prescott"—the voice was like ice—"what is your full name please?"

Steve sighed nervously and tried to swallow but his throat felt painfully dry. "Steven J. Prescott." His voice cracked. The man with the notebook scribbled in it with a short little stub of a pencil.

"Mr. Prescott, what is your full address?"

"2717 West Brandy Court, apartment 210. I'm telling you, I already told the other cops all of this shit, if you would just ask them. Jesus!" The short man scribbled and the tall man again paused for what seemed like minutes.

"Mr. Prescott, do you have any health problems?"

"Health problems? No, nothing. What the hell do you need to know that for?" His voice sounded more like a bark. God his throat hurt.

So fuckin' dry.

"Can I have something to drink? A soda or something?"

"What is your blood type, Mr. Prescott?" The man's voice had yet to change pitch.

"Hell if I know man. You looking for a donation? You from the fucking blood mobile or something?" Steve tried to laugh but instead choked out a raspy cough.

"Any allergies?"

"No," Steve replied. He felt suddenly too exhausted to be a smartass.

"Thank you, Mr. Prescott. We are through." The man spun on one heel, opened the door and left. His partner finished scribbling, then turned and left also. Before he closed the door he spoke, his voice a deep whisper.

"You may go, Mr. Prescott. We'll be in touch." The shorter man tilted his head back and for a second, beneath the brim of the hat, the light illuminated his face. Coal-black eyes, haloed by a shimmer of orange, stared at him, but looked hollow and unseeing. They were set in skin as white as snow with a single, angry red scar that ran from the temple, up in an arc and then down again, stopping just beside the nose. The man turned and closed the door. Steve sat alone and frightened.

What in the holy fuck was that? It was a trick. Funny light or something. No one could have eyes like that.

"They got me acting like a scared little girl," he choked out to nobody, his throat burning.

It's like a thousand fucking degrees in here.

Steve sat for a moment and fidgeted, wondering what to do next. Then he rose and crossed to the door on wobbly legs. "Fuck this noise," he said. They had said he was done, hadn't they? Those two were freaking him out.

Just trying to scare me. Bullshit, they ain't cops!

He opened the door and walked out into a long hallway; the two men in trench coats were gone. Where could they have gone? A horrible smell wafted through the air, like someone had shit themselves, and Steve wrinkled up his nose. He saw no one in either direction. Steve shook his head and headed quickly for the electric doors at the end of the long hallway. He passed a desk where a nurse impatiently asked questions of an old man who breathed way too loudly. Steve kept his focus on the floor.

Sherry and the brat can find their own friggin' ride.

He went out through the electric door, past a parked ambulance, and headed to his pick-up truck in the lot across from the ER.

* * *

The tall man watched Steve from the shadows at the corner of the building, hands clasped in front of him. As Steve drove off in his truck, the tall man turned his head to his partner and their dark eyes met in the shadows. Then he nodded slightly, turned and walked down the dark street away from the hospital. Several paces later he stopped, and after a pause, he spoke without turning around. "Tonight." His voice sounded hungry. Then he resumed his way down the street. The night air inhaled him as its own.

The man with the scar pulled out his notebook and scribbled in it again with his stub of a pencil. Then he put both in the pocket of his long trench coat, turned in the opposite direction from his boss and disappeared into the night.

* * *

Jason Gelman felt exhausted. He had arrived at the point where he started to feel like he had the flu—super-sensitive skin, muscle aches and nausea. A few hours of sleep and he would be like new. All he had to do was give a quick report to the senior ER resident relieving him and he could get out of here.

He looked at his watch. Six-fifty p.m. Ten more minutes and his shift would be over. Dietrich would be right on time, maybe a little early. He plopped down on the cheap, stained couch in the ER resident lounge and stretched his stiff legs onto the coffee table, which balanced precariously on three remaining legs. His aching back cracked as he attempted to unlock the knots, then settled back and took a sip of his lukewarm coffee.

Jason wondered for the thousandth time whether he had made the right choice for his career. In general, it gave him grueling twelve-hour shifts of monotonous, clinic-style care, punctuated only occasionally with something exciting or interesting. Even then he was involved only transiently, until a doctor from another specialty arrived to assume care and admit the patient.

He had never been a thrill seeker and it wasn't the lack of excitement that wore on him. He enjoyed the trauma patients and cardiac arrests; it felt good when he did his job well, but he was also perfectly content to pass on the follow-up care and move to the next patient. He often joked that he had chosen ER because of his attention deficit disorder. Once the hyper-acute phase of medical trouble ended, he got bored.

No, the level of excitement and mental stimulation seemed just about right. The emotional impact of human tragedy he waded through daily at work didn't bother him either. In fact, what scared him these days was how little that seemed to affect him. A few years ago, as a student and intern, he invested himself completely in the lives of the patients he encountered. He remembered more than a few times lying in bed after work, weeping softly at the thought of a patient he had cared for who had died despite his best efforts. These days he couldn't remember the last time he had felt that way. More than a few times he had turned angry or annoyed when a patient's problems (often from their own stupidity) interrupted an otherwise pleasant—which these days meant quiet—shift.

Jason sipped the bitter coffee from his cup and shook the thoughts out of his mind. He looked again at his watch. Two minutes 'til. Where the hell was Dietrich? The end of a shift was no time to make a big life assessment. He looked at the now-nasty drink in his hand and tossed it with a plunk into the institutional wastebasket beside him. A middle-aged moan—

Where the hell did that come from? I'm only twenty-nine years old.

—hissed out of him as he grabbed and dropped the remote in his lap without turning on the TV, which hung suspended in the ceiling corner.

Jason closed his eyes and reluctantly let his thoughts wander to Nathan Doren and just where he was right now. Probably up in the burn ward, getting his first painful debridement. The thought made his throat tighten. It was no mystery to him why this child brought back his long-absent empathy. He unconsciously rubbed his right thigh, the break long ago mended, and kept his mind on Nathan and his mother, not on his own past.

The patient, the poor five-year-old boy, would get Fentanyl and some Versed, he remembered from his rotation on the Burn/Trauma Service. The Fentanyl would help the pain and the Versed would hopefully keep him from remembering whatever pain the narcotic couldn't dull.

It's not really about the pain though, is it? It's the fear. Fear of the unknown. Fear of being hurt again by a grown up. Fear of letting down my mom.

Jason wiped a tear from his cheek with some annoyance and rubbed his thigh again. He remembered his mother crying beside him while he looked in drug-dazed terror at the large drill they assembled to screw a pin through his flesh and into his bone. He remembered hatred of his bastard father, but mostly, the fear that Mommy would be mad at him had ruled his younger mind.

He shook the thought away violently enough to cause a twinge in the muscles in his neck.

Goddamnit, this is not the time or place.

Five years ago, maybe even less, he would have hated Sherry Doren for letting this happen to Nathan or any other little Jason Gelman clone. He had gotten through that somehow over the last few years. Sherry was a victim, too. They both needed help.

And that lying prick that came in with them needs to bleed and suffer in ways the fucked-up legal system will never achieve.

"You alright, dude?"

Jason looked up at Rich Dietrich, startled. His friend stared down at him with real concern and Jason felt embarrassed.

"Were you dreaming or something?" Rich asked.

Jason tried to play it off and wiped a tear from his cheek as casually as possible. "Yeah, what the hell, huh? Boogeyman almost got me." He tried a half-hearted chuckle which fell flat. "So where the hell have you been? Our little ER didn't interrupt your busy social life again, did it?"

Dietrich laughed and Jason felt grateful he could still turn the conversation and mood so easily. When in doubt, just bring up his girls and you could spin a whole egocentric side of Ol' Rich Dietrich. His legendary prowess with the women of University Hospital remained the only thing that could get him talking of something other than medicine. Rich was a good friend and a great doctor and, to be honest, if Jason didn't love him so much, he would have hated his guts. Seemed everything came easily to Rich.

"Hey, man, it's like two minutes 'till. How the hell am I late getting here fifteen minutes before your best showing?" Rich clapped Jason on the back and laughed. "At least if I'm late, I'm doing something worthwhile."

"Some*one*," Jason corrected and pulled on his stained white coat.

"Yeah," his friend agreed proudly. "More often than not."

They walked together from the lounge and stood in front of the big dry erase board as Jason gave Dietrich the run-down on the patients he had been seeing that remained in the ER. He proudly told his workaholic friend that all but two had a disposition and would need nothing from Rich. The two still in the middle of a workup were stable and would probably need admission to the Medicine Service.

"Anything cool?" Dietrich asked when he had finished his sign out.

Jason felt weird that he wanted to talk about Nathan Doren. What would be the point? No one, not even his close friends (or as close as he allowed) knew anything about his past, of course. What the hell was there to say about Nathan Doren? One more unfortunate kid, fucked up by an uncaring asshole, who would likely never see the inside of a jail cell, much less get the total ass kicking he deserved.

"Just another day," he said.

"Yeah, well bring it on," his friend said and picked up the chart of one of the two patients leftover from the day shift. In moments he looked lost in the record, searching for missing clues, Jason supposed. Jason shrugged and walked away.

He dropped his coat unceremoniously into the bottom of his locker and left the ER. As he passed the elevators, he felt a powerful draw. He stood a moment, contemplating.

What the hell's the point? What am I gonna do? Tell him I've been there?

"Fuck." He sighed and pushed the up button on the elevator.

He hated the burn ward all over again the moment he stepped out of the elevators. The smell brought back the horror he felt every day he'd worked on the Burn Service the year before. It wasn't a bad smell but it was distinctive and brought back a flood of emotional memory: people not only deformed, but in agony. He remembered the screams of dazed and slurred-speech patients when he had scrubbed away dead skin with a surgical brush, scrubbed until they were left with nothing but raw, bleeding tissue. Could he stand seeing little Nathan Doren like that?

"Can I help you?" a fat nurse he didn't know asked. Her tone did nothing to convey a desire to help him in any way.

"Yeah," he said. "I'm Dr. Gelman from ER. I'm just here to check on a patient of mine. Nathan Doren?"

"Oh yeah," the nurse said without much interest. "The kid. We couldn't keep him here. He's down in Pedi ICU." Jason walked away without bothering to offer the customary thank you.

The nurse that greeted him in the Pediatric Intensive Care Unit seemed the total opposite of her miserable colleague. In a different mood he might have been attracted to her. Young, pretty, enthusiastic and eager to help. Today, she just annoyed him, but he remained a good enough person to feel bad about that.

"Oh, the little boy with the hand, bless his heart," she said, touching him on the arm. "It's so nice you came to see him. Not many of you ER guys come up here." She looked at him expectantly and was clearly not giving him the room number until he responded.

"He seemed like a really nice kid," he said awkwardly.

"He's in six-twenty-two," she answered, apparently satisfied.

Jenny her name tag said. Jason decided to remember that for future reference.

"Thanks, Jenny." He headed down the little hall between the large nurse's station and the patient rooms.

Jason peered into the room through the oversized window with its half-drawn shades. The sign on the door read "SMH DOE," the code for a patient with legal issues that should not have any information released. Nathan appeared to be asleep, his eyes closed and his left hand cupped around the bulky white bandage on his right. His mother stretched awkwardly in the chair beside the bed, her head lying across an outstretched arm and her hands across her son's waist. He watched them for a moment and remembered things best forgotten.

There was no point in waking them, and Jason felt glad that he wouldn't have to talk to the mother again. He would visit in the morning on his way in, he decided, just to see how his patient was doing. As he watched, Nathan opened his eyes. They stared at each other. Then the little boy gave a limp wave and smiled. Jason smiled and waved back, just as Nathan's eyes closed again.

Jason wiped a tear from his cheek and turned to leave.

See you in the morning, little buddy.

* * *

Steve laid back in his recliner in front of the TV, a half-finished cigarette in his right hand and the empty bottle from his fourth beer in his left. His eyes half-closed, his near-sleeping brain took in the soft-core porn from the late-night pay TV and turned it into a great dream. The still-conscious part of his brain took a last drag on his Marlboro and stubbed out the butt in the overflowing ashtray beside him. Then his eyes closed the rest of the way and his beer bottle slipped softly to the carpet beside him as his breathing grew heavy.

When Steve opened his eyes again, he saw only darkness. He peered through the black, searched for the light from the TV, but found nothing to break up the darkness, not even the usual hazy glow from the outside lights in the parking lot.

Power's out, his sleepy mind told him.

He closed his eyes again and searched for the seductive dream he had been having, when a soft noise made his eyes snap back open.

The fog of sleep evaporated immediately. He sensed it more than heard it—not a creak or even a "house" sound, but more of a rustle, like someone moving in the dark, the clothes on their skin making the softest of noises. He felt his pulse quicken and suddenly his breathing seemed very loud. He pushed up and out of the chair to search for a flashlight in the small apartment. He still had a big torch in the junk drawer in the kitchen, as good for cracking heads as it was for seeing in the dark. Halfway out of the chair, he felt strong hands grab his arms at the elbows and force him back down again with a painful thump.

"What the fuck?" he hollered. Pain shot down his arms and caused his fingers to tingle. The vice-like grip crushed his flesh above the elbows and secured him to his chair. Steve kicked his feet and thrashed his head. Fear seized his throat more powerfully than the force on his arms. His hands went numb and heavy, and he hollered into the blackness of the dark apartment. "What the hell is going on? WHO'S THERE?" He heard the shrill panic in his own voice but little else.

Wait. What was that?

More rustling. Someone moved past him in the shadows and then he felt something cool and wet on his forearm. He kicked his feet, renewing his struggle, but his arms and upper body remained motionless in the iron clasp of his abductor. Terror rose in his chest and he thought he might scream. For a moment, he worried he would piss himself. Then a voice spoke, a familiar deep whisper.

"Mr. Prescott, are you sorry for what you have done?"

Steve strained his eyes but saw nothing.

"What are you talking about? What have I done? What am I supposed to be sorry for? Jesus, get these fuckin' guys off me, you assholes! *I DIDN'T DO ANYTHING WRONG!*"

"Wrong answer, Mr. Prescott. Okay," the whisper commanded. "Go ahead."

"Go ahead and what? What's going on?" Steve threw his head back and forth, completely at the mercy of his own terror now. He felt a sharp pain stab into his right forearm, followed by a burning that moved slowly up his skin to his chest. He felt his arm get weak and his head grow fuzzy. It felt like being pulled under swirling water by unseen hands. He felt warm all over, then hot and light-headed.

Then he felt nothing at all.

Chapter 3

Jason slept like a rock, but awoke before his alarm rang. He lay in the dark of his bedroom, thinking about Nathan Doren. He realized that he must have thought of him in his sleep as well, because he woke with Nathan's cute little face imprinted on his mind. He'd set his alarm for five a.m., a little earlier than usual, and had intended to see the boy before his shift started. Hopefully, he could visit without having to talk much with the mother. Jason felt bad about the injustice of that, but knew it reflected his unresolved feelings about his own childhood, not any great sin of Sherry Doren.

As he lay in bed, his thoughts shifted, as they often did, to his mom. He wished she had lived long enough for him to let her know he loved her. She had died of breast cancer, and maybe a broken heart. When she'd died he still blamed her for what had happened to him. He was older now, not much wiser, but maybe a little more worldly from his experiences in the ER. He knew that his mother had loved him. He also knew he loved her and missed her terribly.

Not your fault, Mom.

The obnoxious squeal of his alarm clock brought Jason back to his bedroom. He pounded it into silence, sighed and got stiffly out of bed. Man, he felt it these days. No more double shifts for him, no matter what a fellow resident might promise him in return for an unscheduled day off. Outside of the Trauma Service, where it was mandatory, he promised himself no more twenty-four-hour shifts. Too painful. The face that looked back at him from the dirty mirror in his otherwise tidy bathroom agreed wholeheartedly.

A half hour later, Jason headed for the hospital at a brisk walk, hoping that the early morning cool might help him shake the nagging strings of drowsiness. By the time he strolled down the drive toward the ER entrance, he felt pretty good. He forced his mind to the mundane thoughts of his coming shift and the academic conference later that day—anywhere but to the thoughts of his past. Nathan opened a lot of old wounds.

As he crossed the last corner, he glanced down the alley between the ambulance entry-way and the office building and saw two figures engaged in a hushed conversation. What stopped him in his tracks was not just their strange appearance but a nagging sense familiarity that made his heart pound in his chest.

Their coats hung nearly to their ankles and both wore nineteen-forties-style top hats. They looked to Jason like extras in an old black-and-white private eye movie. Then the taller of the two men's attention shifted, turning slowly toward Jason.

From beneath the brim of the top hat, from the shadow that covered the man's face, Jason saw two orange eyes. They looked like dying embers from a charcoal grill and Jason felt them focus on him—through him, really. A sudden chill made him shudder. The man's slash of a mouth seemed to slide apart, and in the grin, he saw rows of impossibly long, narrow pointed teeth. Though the man didn't speak, Jason felt rather than heard a soft voice. It seemed to penetrate him and filled his head with static energy.

Hello, Jason. Remember me?

Jason pulled his light jacket tightly around his chest and darted the rest of the way across the alley entrance in a near-panic. His pulse pounded in his temples and bile filled the back of his throat. With an almost painful effort, he turned his eyes back to the alley as he reached the corner, terrified that he would see the demon-like man only inches from his face, the shark like mouth open and bloody.

But he saw nothing. The alley stood empty except for a grey cat that stopped its slow, arrogant stroll long enough to look at him with indifference, then turn its ass at him, tail upright, and saunter away.

What the holy hell was that?

Jason reached out a trembling hand for the corner of the hospital to steady himself. The chilly air now felt hot and his stomach turned enough that he thought for a moment he would add his vomit to the stench of the alley. He couldn't tear his eyes from the empty alley and fully expected the two figures to magically reappear at any moment. Jason squeezed his eyes tight and felt the swaying sensation dissipate. When he opened them again he saw only the dark blue Crocs on his feet. He never paid much attention to his shoes, but they seemed to realign his thoughts at the moment. He felt his world normalize, his breathing slow, and he stood up straight.

Hallucinations. Nice. Well aren't we the model of mental fucking health?

He had lived with night terrors for most of his life, but he had never felt anything like this. As his breathing continued to slow, his mind went about the familiar work of rationalization. It was okay to see bizarre men in top hats in alleys. Just a trick of light and a leftover nightmare of the boogeyman. Maybe a bad burger or something.

By the time he swiped himself through the doctor's entrance beside the ER triage desk, he had decided to move past the incident completely, though he doubted he could.

And why was it oddly familiar?

Jason took the employee elevators to the sixth floor. He had to walk right past the visitor elevators but he really didn't want to muster, a fake I'm-a-doctor-and-I'm-here-to-help-you smile.

The Pediatric Unit was quiet. The nursing staff had passed out the meds and was, for the most part, catching up on their charting.

"Good morning, Dr. Gelman," a soft voice whispered. He looked over as Jenny waved with two fingers from her seat at the nurse's station. He waved back awkwardly and felt uncomfortable.

"It's Jason," he whispered back, then stood there like an idiot, not sure what else to say. At least she smiled back at him. He wished he had shaved. He waved again and then headed over to Nathan's room.

Jason peered through the large half-window into room twenty-two. Nathan looked wide awake, but lay still and stared at the ceiling as if deep in thought. Jason thought he looked much older than a five-year-old should. In the corner of the room, his mother stretched out on an oversized chair that had converted to a less-than-oversized bed.

Jason managed a smile as he opened the door, but the flash of fear in Nathan's eyes made him sorry he had worn his white coat. The boy's face relaxed when he recognized Jason.

"Hi." His soft voice was overwhelmed by the bed. He waved a shaky hand, an I.V. tube taped to the back. His eyes were sharp and not at all glazed from morphine as Jason had expected.

"Hey, buddy." Jason walked over to the bed. "How ya' doin', lil' man?"

"'Kay," Nathan answered, then raised his arm, wrapped in a bulky dressing over an L-shaped splint. "Hurts."

"Yeah, I know." Jason fought the tightness in his throat. He tried to sound half as brave as the young patient. "Not really fair is it?"

Nathan looked at the ceiling a minute, pondering the question, and Jason felt sorry he had asked it. The little boy turned toward him, his eyes clear and focused.

"No, I guess not," he answered softly. "At least my mommy is all right." Jason realized that he had taken Nathan's hand in his own and that the boy was squeezing tightly. Nathan's fingers felt tiny and frail. He realized the boy had said something else.

"What, buddy?" he asked.

"Do you think Steve is sorry for what he did?" the boy asked again.

"I… well… uh," Jason had no idea what to say. "I don't know, Nathan," he finally stammered out. The boy looked at the ceiling again. How did you tell a kid that the world sucked, that people like Steve felt nothing but anger and hate? How did you tell him that the man wouldn't pay at all for the pain he had brought this brave boy?

"He will be sorry, I think," Nathan said softly, almost to himself.

"Why do you say that?" Jason said skeptically. The little boy turned to him again. He looked frightened.

"I had a dream," he said and looked over at his sleeping mother as if afraid she might hear. "The Lizard Men hurt Steve—hurt him real bad." The small hand squeezed harder now. "The men with the glowing eyes are going to hurt him in really bad ways." The boy's voice quivered and Jason wondered what kind of horrible nightmare all of this had created. Maybe the morphine had made it worse.

"It's okay, Nathan," he said, smoothing the boy's hair from his eyes. "It was just a bad dream."

"No," the boy said in a firm voice. "We should tell Steve to go away before the lizard men get him."

Jason rubbed his fingers across Nathan's head. They were both quiet until Nathan's eyes flickered closed and his breathing deepened. Then Jason pulled the covers up around his shoulders and touched his cheek gently.

Fuck Steve. I hope the lizard men skin him alive.

He had been around long enough to know there would be no such justice.

* * *

Jenny couldn't seem to get Dr. Jason Gelman out of her mind. Maybe it was the way he seemed so troubled. She knew that she tended to be maternal, but she also felt touched that the doctor had come to visit Nathan—not once, but twice. She had never seen one of the ER docs come to the unit to visit anyone.

The way he looked at the little boy the night before, watching him sleep through the window, had been almost as sweet as the way he had held the boy's hand and smoothed his hair this morning. She had been unable to keep her eyes off of the quiet, attractive man. More than once, she had walked past the room just to get another glimpse of him. When he'd left, he seemed very troubled and she felt oddly worried about him as she rode the elevator to the first floor, another tiring twelve-hour shift over.

Don't forget the rule.

Jenny had not been a nurse long, but she already knew enough broken-hearted colleagues who had not followed the simple rule: no dating doctors, especially not residents, who are really just passing through. She had no interest in being a convenient pit-stop for a man who worked long hours and had little time to spend on anyone but himself. Still, something really intrigued her about Dr. Jason Gelman. She blushed as she thought about him touching her arm the night before.

Jenny passed through the sliding doors and into the glass walkway that connected the hospital to the parking garage. She tried to shake her school-girl thoughts from her mind. Better to think about other, more important things, though she couldn't remember any at the moment. She forced her thoughts to Nathan Doren and thanked God for the tenth time in twelve hours for her perfect and protected upbringing. She remained close to her parents and her younger brother. The idea of a grown-up hurting an innocent child seemed foreign and unbelievable to her. She fumbled in her backpack for her keys as she passed through the second sliding door with a familiar "whish."

The garage always made her nervous, but today the feeling was so intense that she briefly thought about turning around. A time or two in the past, when feeling really badly about a particularly tragic patient, she had found someone to walk her to her car. The problem was that the girls she asked usually made her feel silly and the guys always assumed she was flirting then wound up hitting on her. She looked around the garage and saw no one suspicious. In fact, she saw no one at all.

"Stupid," she said with some annoyance. Her voice echoed from the enclosed parking deck. Jenny walked briskly to the elevators, only a few yards from the doorway, and pushed the button for seven, the highest floor, where she seemed always to get stuck. The elevator dinged and she watched the numbers count down from five on the illuminated dial.

A chill swept through the stagnant air, and Jenny pulled her thin cotton nursing jacket around her shoulders more tightly. Her heart raced and she watched anxiously as the numbers counted down above the elevator, waiting for the next ding. Had the number been anything but three she would probably have sprinted back into the hospital.

She glanced around the empty garage, certain she was being watched, and felt for a moment like prey being stalked by an invisible predator. When the doors to the elevator began to open she squeezed herself through without waiting for them to finish, spun around and jabbed her finger repeatedly on seven. Even when her fingernail splintered, she continued to pound the button until the door slid painfully, slowly shut with an anticlimactic thump.

Jenny leaned back against the wall and closed her eyes. Her breathing slowed to normal and again she felt ridiculous. She laughed aloud, her voice a hollow resonating emptiness in the elevator, and pounded the heel of a hand gently on her forehead.

"You dopey girl," she said aloud to the dirty silver doors. "You silly, absurd girl." She laughed again.

By the time the elevator groaned its way to the seventh floor of the parking deck, the feeling of being stalked had evaporated completely. Nathan's story must have settled more deeply in her psyche than she thought.

As usual, her car was one of only a few scattered about the seventh floor, despite the mass of vehicles that had been there when she had come to work last night. Trouble with the night shift was you got there before all the day employees had left, so parking was scarce. She spotted her grey Ford Escape, the closest thing she could afford to a real SUV on a new nurse's salary. It sat several rows over at the end, just beside the entrance to the stairwell. As she got closer, she jabbed the button on her FOB and heard the satisfying chirp of her doors unlocking.

Something felt very wrong though, and Jenny slowed as she approached her truck. She saw no one on the wide-open, well-lit floor. It took her a minute to figure out what her brain was trying to tell her. Then she saw the glow and stopped. She strained to see better into the stairwell, a few yards beyond where her car sat, its lights blinking as if to say, "Come on, hurry up. Get in already."

The stairwell looked empty and dark except for two sets of glowing lights. They looked like slowly dying embers in a campfire and seemed to hang in midair, one pair nearly a foot higher than the other. Jenny stood there, her keys held out in front of her, and strained to see the source. She got the sense that the lights moved ever-so-slightly, as if swaying in the wind, and she felt her earlier foreboding return.

She stopped giving a damn what the lights were and ran to her car, her keys still in front of her like a talisman that might ward off whatever evil lurked in the dark. Jenny kept her eyes locked on the floating orbs, ready to change direction should something leap out of the dark. Another nail tore as she pulled open her car door with such force that it bounced back on its hinges and struck her painfully in the hip.

Suddenly, she felt, more than heard, a pop, like a sudden change in the pressure in an airplane, and a terrible smell filled the garage. The four glowing embers vanished. Jenny stopped, her hip throbbing, and looked deep into the darkness, but the little lights were gone. A static-like crackling made her jump. A random noise came from her throat that in other circumstances would have made her laugh, and then the luminescent, overhead lights in the stairwell flickered twice and crackled to reveal—

Nothing.

The landing stood completely empty. Jenny felt emotionally exhausted, unable to even chuckle or chide herself. She slid heavily into the driver's seat, then closed and locked the door. The seatbelt clicked into place and the engine roared to life, but instead of pulling away, Jenny leaned her head on the steering wheel. She felt so tired that for a moment she could barely move. Then she sighed heavily, shifted into reverse and turned to look over her right shoulder, to back out.

She froze. In the seat beside her sat a strange, terrifying figure with his hands clasped together in the folds of his heavy overcoat. What she could see of his face was white—paler than the handful of dead bodies she had seen in her young career—interrupted by a red slit of a mouth. His eyes were hidden in shadows from his top hat but she thought she saw a pale glow beneath the brim.

"Hello, Jenny," a scratchy voice said, though she was certain the hideous lips never moved.

She heard a horrible scream. Her mind clouded, and the world tilted sharply to the left. It was impossible to tell if the scream was out loud or in her head. She tightened her grip on the steering wheel as she faded out, the world and the horrible creature beside her turning gray.

"I am going to help you remember things better, my dear," the voice said from somewhere behind the motionless lips. "And then you will be able to help us." Now the lips did part, revealing a shark-like row of impossibly long teeth. She realized now that the screaming was actually her car horn and that her head rested on the steering wheel. She couldn't move. She listened to the shrieking horn and watched as thin, sallow fingers reached out and caressed her cheek. The skin on the bony hand felt as cold as ice, rubbery, like a piece of raw fish.

The grey turned black, and far away the sound of the horn abruptly fell silent. She thought that should mean something to her but it didn't. Then she let herself drift away into the darkness.

* * *

If I go crazy then, would you still call me superman?...If I'm alive and well would you be there, holding my hand?...I'll keep you by my side with my super-human might...

Kryptonite!

Jenny slowly comprehended that the sound was coming from her car radio and not from her alarm clock, as her mind had tried to convince her. She peeled her eyes open as the 3 Doors Down tune continued to blare, way too loudly, from her radio. She smelled something, like road-kill, but in the moment it took her to grow disgusted, it disappeared. She raised her head off the headrest and found her neck painfully stiff.

She had fallen asleep in her car with the engine running and the radio on. From her stiff neck she guessed it had been for more than a moment.

Nice. Great way to become a statistic. As if you don't have enough bad shit in your life.

Jenny shook the cobwebs from her mind and looked around the nearly empty garage. She felt like she needed to remember something but had no idea what it could be and discarded the feeling. She twisted the radio down to a tolerable level, put her truck in reverse, and backed out, looking around the lot as she did.

Definitely empty. What the hell is wrong with me?

As she drove carefully around and around the tight turns that wound her down from the nosebleed section of the parking deck, her mind drifted to Jason Gelman for a minute. Very attractive man—a little dark and mysterious. Jenny wondered whether she was (or ever could be) ready for something intimate. She fantasized about kissing him… or more. Another part of her felt terrified of the thought, anxious about the memories it might resurface.

Thanks for that, Dad, you miserable shit.

She shuddered. Why did that feel so wrong?

A sudden vibration in her scrub jacket made her jump, and she fumbled in her pocket for her cell phone. She silenced it as she brought it up to eye level so she could read the caller ID without slamming her budget SUV into a cement wall.

MOM the phone flashed.

She sighed and tossed the thing on the passenger seat.

It's a struggle to talk to that self-pitying woman on holidays. What on earth would make her think I would talk to her at eight o'clock in the fuckin' morning?

She turned the music up, tapping her thumb on the steering wheel to an old Pearl Jam tune as she pulled out of parking deck and turned left toward her apartment.

Chapter
4

Steve watched as the light grappled for life, as if a thin sheet were being pulled slowly off of his face in a poorly lit room. At first it felt like waking from a nightmare. He watched as reality came into focus, white with a black line down the middle. He tried to raise his right hand to his face, to rub his eyes, but couldn't. In the background of his hazy mind, he heard an annoying beeping he couldn't ignore but couldn't pinpoint, either.

Suddenly, his mind was jolted by a loud *HISS* and a rush of air in his chest. He felt his lungs fill, his ribcage expand. It was excruciating. Something forced gas into his chest, followed by a terrible metallic taste. He tried to hold his breath, hold back against the rush of pressure, but he couldn't. God, his body might explode! Then, just as suddenly, the rush of air disappeared and he felt his body deflate. He tried to raise his hands to his face again, tried as hard as he could. He concentrated on moving his arm—nothing. He felt no pull on his limb, no tightness at his wrist. He simply couldn't move it, like it wasn't connected to his body at all—except he could feel it. He felt a distinct prickling in his skin and a burning in his mid-forearm. Farther up his skin felt cold. The panic returned, a breaking force in his head like a hangover, and then—

HISS!

—the hissing rush of pressure filled his chest. Again he struggled to fight it and couldn't. The annoying beeping grew faster and louder.

When the overpowering sensation went away again, he felt his eyes fill with tears. His vision became distorted and fuzzy. He tried to blink but nothing happened. He tried again—strained with all his might, focused as hard as he could, and then he watched as darkness pulled slowly over his vision, like a window blind being lowered. He felt tears, forced from both of his eyes, trickle down the sides of his face and soak into the hair at his temples. Then he relaxed and the blinds retracted, stopping halfway, until he concentrated again and they finished pulling all the way up, out of his field of view. He half-way noticed that the beeping had slowed again until—

HISS!

—the pressure began again and the beep picked up tempo.

He stared at the whiteness with the dark line, unable to look anywhere else, and searched for a reference to the familiar pattern. It looked like white press board panels separated by dark strips between them—a ceiling! Unable to move his eyes, he followed the checkerboard pattern with his peripheral vision, marching the panels out until they ended at an all-white wall. To his left, he saw a large metal saucer of some sort, like a big, upside-down metal bowl, with a handle that stuck out from the middle. Frustrated that his head wouldn't move, he tried instead to move his eyes to the left. They ticked briefly and then snapped back to the center.

What the fuck is going on? Why can't I move?

He felt his stomach tighten in fear and confusion, and again the beeping sound got faster, just as—

HISS!

The pressure and expansion that he couldn't fight eclipsed the fear erupting from his very soul. The sensation didn't bring its own terror this time, as he knew what was coming, but it felt awful.

Have I been in an accident? Am I some kind of cripple now, paralyzed like that guy who played superman in the movies?

He had seen the guy on TV and the idea of being strapped to a chair, breathing through a big tube in his neck nauseated him. He tasted bile in the back of his throat. The beeping got faster again. This time—

HISS!

—he barely reacted to the hissing and rise of his chest.

Wait a goddamn minute. I hadn't been in any fucking accident! He remembered now! He remembered the darkness and the rustling—remembered the strong hands holding him and the deep whisper of a voice. What had it asked him?

"Are you sorry for what you have done?"

What the hell happened after that? Sorry for what? He remembered the burning that ran up his arm and the feeling of drowning. He remembered passing out and then—

HISS!

—nothing, until the ceiling and the awful hissing that made him feel like his entire body would explode. The beeping seemed louder and was definitely faster. He became aware of the burning in the back of his throat and then he felt his stomach muscles contract violently.

He vomited. The warm, thick liquid filled his mouth, then overflowed and ran down both cheeks, pooling behind his neck. His hearing became muffled as the puke filled his right ear. A shrill squealing like an alarm joined the annoying *beep– beep– beep*. He tried to turn his head and raise his hands to his lips, but couldn't. He tried to spit the vomit out of his mouth but couldn't. He was sure he would choke if he didn't and again—

HISS!

—he began to panic. But he didn't choke, for some reason. His eyes filled again, his vision blurred and warm tears ran down his face, mixing now with the vomit he could feel clinging there.

PLEASE, GOD, WHERE IS EVERYONE? WHY WON'T SOMEONE TELL ME WHAT THE HELL HAPPENED? I DON'T WANT TO DIE!

The salty stream flowed down his cheeks and his monotonous view of the checkerboard ceiling cleared when—

HISS!

—he heard a sound like a heavy door opening.

THANK GOD! Someone is coming! A nurse or a doctor maybe.

Finally, someone to help him, tell him what had happened! He felt movement above him, just out of view. He heard a click and the alarms stopped, then the beeping got quieter, like someone had turned down the volume on a TV. In a minute he would be able to see them. The face of a kind nurse, a hand on his arm, and everything would be all right. Above him features came slowly into view. He strained to move his eyes up, to see the peaceful face of his nurse when—

HISS!

—something familiar, pale, thin-lipped bent over him, the eyes hidden by shadows, below the brim of a gray hat.

"Good morning, Mr. Prescott." The thin lips held the hint of a smile and Steve tried to scream.

But of course he couldn't.

* * *

Jason found himself unable to get engaged in the chart he was reviewing (okay, re-reading for the third friggin' time). His mind raced repeatedly away from the elderly man in Chest Pain Two and found its way to either Nathan up in Pedi ICU or Jenny. She would surely be gone by now, her night shift long over, but he found himself hoping that she was on duty again tonight, that he might run into her after his shift when he went to check on Nathan.

Nathan. How quickly that little kid had become real to him. He no longer thought of him as "the burns and fracture in Pedi room number three." Nathan had captured him for certain.

What about the little kid's nightmare bothered him so much? Something about Lizard Men and the terrible things they would do to Steve, his abuser. No reason in the world that should bother him. A dream about that son of a bitch getting what he deserved seemed more of a dream come true. Still, something he couldn't quite remember frustrated him.

Jason noted that the CPK-MB's on Mr. Montoya were normal. Who the hell was Mr. Montoya and why should he care? ...Oh, right...chest pain guy. Normal enzymes so he hadn't had a heart attack. A little angina maybe. Better rule out pulmonary embolism. The man didn't look like he got around much.

"The men with the glowing eyes are going to hurt him real bad."

Nathan's scared, cracking voice from early that morning. Men with glowing eyes...

Jason's mind shot suddenly to the alley beside the hospital and the two figures in long trench coats and top hats. Shadows over their *glowing eyes.*

He felt his throat tighten and his heart race. Had he mentioned that to Nathan? Oh, for Christ's sake... of course not. Why would he tell that eerie story to a five-year-old? Where the hell had it come from?

Easy there, brother. You're getting a little ahead of yourself. You're acting like you think you really saw two dudes in top hats with glowing eyes. Time for a short reality check, man.

Of course he had imagined the men in the alley and for sure he had imagined the glowing eyes. One hell of a coincidence though, huh? He shuddered for a moment, like when you hear a story about a man on a road warning two travelers that the bridge is out, and later find the man died two years ago on that bridge.

This felt different than that, though. There was no ghost talking to people on the side of a road here. Just two people, a man and a child, with similarly bizarre imaginations. Nothing other-worldly.

"Whadya think?"

Jason jumped. He looked up at Dr. Yeatman, the Emergency Room attending and his boss for the day. "Think?" he stammered, still confused.

"MI or no MI?" Dr. Yeatman asked impatiently and stared at him over his half-lens reading glasses that everyone agreed he wore for effect.

MI? ...Oh, yeah. Myocardial infarction. Heart attack. Right, the dude in Chest Pain Two.

"Uh, no MI," he answered, coming back. He flipped through the chart, though he wasn't looking for anything. "Normal enzymes, borderline EKG—I'm gonna rule out PE and then have medicine admit him."

"How are you going to rule out PE?" Yeatman demanded.

"Helical CT," Jason answered without hesitation.

Are you kidding me? You got any tough questions?

"Alright, young man," Yeatman answered, satisfied. "Carry on." He walked away with his hands clasped behind his back. Jason rolled his eyes, tucked the chart under his arm and headed to Chest Pain Two to tell the old man he didn't think he'd had a heart attack.

The voice inside his head, with its demand for answers, remained relatively quiet through most of the morning, and after awhile, he settled into the routine of the ER. The questions rattled inside him like background noise, rarely rising to a level that demanded attention. When he could provide no answers, they settled stubbornly and pouted like children.

The emergency room took on its own pace and rhythm, making the routine unique and, in fact, not at all routine. Jason thought that maybe this was what he liked about his job. No two days were really the same, which was not to say they were never dull, just different in little ways. This morning he ploughed through a lot of mundane problems. There were relatively few "emergencies" in the emergency room.

Before he knew it, his stomach told him it was nearing lunchtime. It refused to be quieted by coffee, no matter how he dressed it with creamer. A glance at the clock over the large patient board and showed that it was eleven-thirty and, more importantly, only two patients had "JG" in their provider column. They had nothing in the DISPO column and both had unchecked items in the PENDING column—a CT scan for HR (Ms. Rodgriquez and her probable diverticulitis) and an MRI that Neurology wanted on CP (Mr. Powell and his ten minutes of not being able to move his right side). He figured he had a good twenty or thirty minutes to grab a quick bite.

"Yo', Scooter," Jason called out to the short, dark-haired man in the stained lab coat at the chart stand. Rich Rizzutto had been Scooter since their orientation when one "clever" attendee had noted he shared a last name with a baseball player. Rich looked up with a "whatcha need?" arch of his eyebrows. "I'm gonna sneak away and grab a bite," Jason told him.

"I got the bitch," Rich responded with a thumbs-up and a nod. No one knew why Rich called covering the ER "having the bitch" but Jason chuckled every time he heard it.

"Getcha something?" he asked Rizzutto.

"Nah," he answered back. "I got something in the back I'll grab in a while."

Jason nodded and shuffled down the short hall to the push button activated doors into the back of the ER.

The cafeteria was crowded, as usual. There were several long lines for the various unhealthy venues in the hospital food court. He picked the shortest line, Subway, and waited patiently behind two loud girls in scrubs. They talked almost without breathing about a cute surgery resident that one or both of them apparently wanted to "get next to." He tried desperately to let his mind wander away from the piercing voices and found his mental route leading back to Jenny.

Jason realized, with some annoyance, that it had been months since he had been on a real date. Unlike his gregarious friend Dr. Dietrich, he found small talk with one person like practicing bleeding. The more someone tried to get to know him, the more he tried to turn a conversation superficial. For some reason this didn't seem to be a big formula for success with worthwhile women. This made the realization that he would love to sit in a quiet place and find out more about Jenny all the more shocking. *And I've never even talked to her.*

Maybe it was the way her eyes seemed so alive, so sincere. She was strikingly beautiful, no question about that, but it was something behind the exterior that was enticing. He wanted to caress her cheek, maybe kiss her. He felt drawn to her. She somehow seemed familiar.

"Next. Whatcha want, buddy?" The bored voice brought him back from his fantasy. He looked at the overweight, sweaty kid staring at him from beneath his blue hairnet and ordered a sandwich. Almost as an afterthought, he ordered three chocolate chip cookies from the hazy plastic box that claimed, "fresh-baked cookies." Every kid likes chocolate chip cookies.

After an annoying additional wait to pay for his food, Jason grabbed a plastic seat in the dining hall to wolf down part of his sandwich in time to take the cookies to Nathan. He chuckled, realizing he felt more excited about seeing the little boy than about catching up with Jenny.

* * *

He knew he was dreaming before the dream even started. Nathan promised himself he wouldn't get scared this time. Not because his mommy would want him to be brave. In fact, he felt pretty sure his mom would scream her head off if she saw what he knew he would see. No, he wanted to be brave because it seemed like being scared made the Lizard Men happy. It also seemed to make them stronger. Their being strong in his dream was a really bad thing.

He stood along the wall of the wet, dark cave. It was hotter than the hottest summer day. Probably as hot as the desert, except it seemed so wet that he felt steam in his mouth and lungs. The cave was totally black, but he could see anyway. He figured that was just the way dreams worked.

When he was younger his mommy used to tell him "Dreams are just like that" when he would tell her about scary nightmares. He guessed that was right. Dreams were just like that. He pressed himself against the damp wall and waited. They would come soon and he didn't want them to see him. He knew the dark wouldn't keep him safe but the less he was noticed here, the better.

Just like last time, he smelled it first. It smelled worse than moldy garbage, worse even than an awesome fart (his mommy called them poots, but all the bigger kids called them farts). Nathan thought it might be the worst odor in the world, except, of course, he knew he wasn't in the world. Then he heard them coming and pressed his small body tight against the hard wall. At least in his dreams his arm didn't have burns anymore, so it didn't hurt bad to reach up and pinch his nose shut. He breathed through his mouth—which didn't help 'cause he could kind of TASTE the fart smell—and waited.

They made wet growls, snarling as they scraped their long claws on the hard rock floor of the cave. The taste against his tongue got so bad he thought he might barf. Nathan couldn't make them out yet, not even straining as hard as he could, but the grunting got louder and the glowing embers of their eyes bobbed closer, getting brighter.

As they materialized from the emptiness, Nathan found he could keep his fear small by remembering he was really in bed in the hospital—his mommy holding his good hand and touching his hair. If he thought about it hard enough, he could even feel her soft fingers on his head, smoothing his hair. It seemed weird to feel his mom's touch and smell the Lizard Men at the same time.

"Dreams are just like that," he whispered to himself.

He could see them now. They were bunched close together and carrying something heavy between them. In the dark he couldn't be sure, but it looked like a body. And the body didn't move at all—a dead person? Were they carrying a dead body?

He felt his heart thumping in his chest, felt his fear grow in his throat and thought he might even cry. Nathan didn't want to see a dead person, not even Steve. The Lizard Men stopped. The one in the front, the taller one, seemed to sniff the air. As he watched, straining to see through the dark, he saw a long, red tongue slither out of the deformed dragon's head. It licked across a row of long pointed teeth and spit dripped from its dark green chin onto the ground. The creature hissed and turned in his direction, sniffing and pawing the air in front of it with a huge claw. The glowing eyes looked right at him but didn't seem to see him. The long, hideous snout sniffed the air again and the creature growled.

Nathan realized the creature was not seeing him but smelling him, smelling his fear. He closed his eyes tightly and concentrated with all of his might on the soft feel of his mother's hand in his hair. He could just barely hear her soft, sad voice, so far away that she seemed to talk to someone else in another room. But she told him everything was alright and that she was sorry. He held onto her voice, the feel of her fingers, and felt his heartbeat slow. The pounding in his head softened. His breathing didn't seem nearly so loud.

He opened his eyes to see the creatures grunt at each other, then move on, angling away to the other side of the cave. He felt sure they carried the mangled body of Steve. In his last dream they had dragged Steve behind them, only he had been alive and screaming. He could still remember the horrible screams as they dragged him down a long dark hallway by his ankles. He had writhed in pain and left a brown, wet trail of blood and vomit behind him. He had no doubt Steve's body would be a beaten, bloody mess.

He tried to be very still, tried to barely even breathe as they passed by. The gross fart smell burned his eyes, making them water, but he tried not to blink. It might be just a dream but Nathan knew it was also real. He didn't want the Lizard Me to know he could see them. As they passed, the shape they held between them became clearer and it was a body. But it wasn't gross or bloody.

And it wasn't Steve.

Nathan recognized the pretty face turned toward him, eyes closed, head bobbing as the Lizard Men walked. He knew immediately it was his favorite nurse. She had told him to call her Nurse Jenny and she always winked at him when she came by the room. She wasn't awake but he could tell that Nurse Jenny wasn't dead, either. Her face was contorted in disgust but not in pain—maybe from the smell. The Lizard Men held her arms and legs but they did so as gently as possible. None of that made Nathan any less terrified.

They're not going to do anything nice to Nurse Jenny.

He watched them place her carefully on the ground against the far wall of the cave. The taller one stood up and gave a slight nod to the shorter, who then bent over the crumpled figure of his favorite nurse. Nathan knew that something very bad was going to happen to her. He felt his pulse pound and he sucked a thick fart-filled gulp of air into his dry throat. His stomach turned and to his horror he heard a thin sound escape his throat.

"NNuuhh…"

It wasn't that loud, but loud enough. The tall Lizard Man turned slowly in his direction and its eyes held his. Then, so fast that he gasped out loud, the creature darted toward him across the cave floor.

Nathan screamed, or thought he did, and spun around to run away, but there was nowhere to go. Instead, he turned back and saw the creature had cut the distance across the cave in half already. He balled his fists tightly by his sides and squeezed his eyes shut. With all his will he thought about his mother's fingers in his hair and tried desperately to go to her. Her voice grew louder but was no longer soothing. It sounded scared. "Nathan, baby? What is it, honey? What's wrong? Wake up, baby, please!"

His mommy's voice boomed louder and louder, but it was too late. He could smell the breath of the creature, searing and hot, on the side of his face. He opened his mouth wide and screamed.

"Mommy! Mommy! Help me! Please help me!" His voice ricocheted briefly off the walls of the cave and then changed. He felt a claw on the side of his face. He swatted it away and opened his eyes, not wanting to see the long, red tongue and sharp teeth, but unable to keep his eyes shut any longer.

His mother looked at him, her face flushed, anxious. Nathan looked around the room in a panic, searching for the Lizard Man. He tasted coppery blood in his mouth and looked back at his mom as tears spilled onto his cheeks. Nathan threw his arms around his mother's neck, barely feeling the sharp pain in his right arm and hand. He held her tightly and cried loudly, muffled against her neck. He wanted her to hold him and make all the bad things go away. He didn't care if it meant he wasn't a big boy right now.

"What is it, baby? What's wrong?"

He heard his own voice tell her the Lizard Men were trying to get him and felt stupid because he knew she wouldn't know what that meant, but he kept saying it anyway, over and over. Mommy would make it all better. She would help him. She would make him safe.

He felt his raspy breathing slow as he sobbed against his mother's chest. She had crawled halfway into the bed with him now and cradled him like a baby. Nathan wanted to stop sobbing, but he couldn't. Every breath brought another startling noise. He let her soothing words wash over him like a warm blanket.

"Just a bad dream, baby. Nothing is going to hurt you ever again, son. Just a dream. You're safe. Mommy's little boy is safe here with me."

The words were magic and he started to calm down. The sobbing stopped. His stiff body relaxed, but he let her hold him anyway. He heard another voice from the doorway.

"Is everything, okay?" It was his nurse, the older one with all the Mickey Mouse characters on her jacket. He knew her voice but didn't look up. He nuzzled against his mother more intensely.

"Just a nightmare, I think," his mother answered, her voice heavy and tired.

"I'm sorry," the nurse said. "He's supposed to go to the treatment room for another debridement of his hand now."

Nathan felt a new wave of panic explode inside him. He didn't want to go, not again. He didn't want them to scrape the bad skin off again. It hurt so much and the medicine made him feel horrible—like he was in a different kind of nightmare.

"No, Mommy. Please!" He whined. He held her tighter, not wanting her to let him go. "I don't want to go." He knew he should be brave, but didn't care. He started to cry again.

"Can we wait just a little while?" He heard his mother plead. She was sobbing too and Nathan felt bad about that.

"Let me call the doctor and ask," the nurse answered after a moment, but she didn't sound very hopeful that Nathan would get a break.

"Why don't you let me call him?" a new voice asked. Nathan recognized it immediately. This time he did look up and managed a little smile at Dr. Jason. He felt relief that his new friend was here. He wasn't like the other doctors at all. Jason smiled back. "Hey there, little buddy." His friendly grin helped Nathan to relax a little more.

"Hi," he managed to squeak.

He listened as his mommy told Dr. Jason about him waking from the dream, how it seemed too much to have him go to the treatment room right now.

"I'll take care of it," Dr. Jason said.

A moment later, he came back into the room. Nathan looked at him and his heart raced. He was scared of going, but hopeful that his friend could make everything okay.

"Here's the deal, pal," Jason said seriously, but Nathan saw he was smiling and held onto that. "The other doctor said we can wait a little while but only if you let me do the treatment myself. Is that okay?" He sat on the edge of the bed and put his hand on Nathan's still-shaking shoulder. Nathan thought he seemed surprised when he threw his arms around his neck (he felt the pain in his arm and hand a lot more this time).

"Yes," he said. It wouldn't be so bad with Dr. Jason, he thought. But it would still hurt.

"Thank you so much, Dr. Gelman," his mom said.

"Who wants a cookie?" Dr. Jason said. He sounded a little uncomfortable.

Chapter
5

Jenny found it hard to sleep during the day, no matter how long or tiring her night-shift may have been. She darkened her apartment as best she could—hung towels over the curtain rods to block some of the sunlight that leaked through—and wore a "napping mask" over her eyes. Nonetheless, she usually struggled to fall asleep and found it hard to stay there once she had accomplished her goal.

Not today. She immediately fell into an exhausted slumber and woke from a dream around two hours later. It was a great dream. The quiet and handsome Jason Gelman had been making love to her, his luscious mouth kissing her face and neck.

She woke feeling giddy and slipped into her forgotten PJs. She had collapsed on her bed earlier wearing only her underwear from the night before. Then she donned her sleep mask (the towels really didn't quite do it), burrowed deep under her covers and fell easily back to sleep, thinking how great it was that she had only one night shift left to go in this cycle. After tonight she could cease the vampire life for a while. She tried to resurrect her sexy dream of Jason Gelman, but she knew that almost never worked out.

But she did dream again. She floated through the dark, suspended by strong hands, as she glided through what felt like a sauna. She kept her eyes closed, mostly because she knew she was supposed to, and let herself be carried through the wet heat. She felt very detached, emotionless. She remembered a book she once read by an author who claimed he had been abducted by aliens as a child, on multiple occasions. This seemed very much like what he had described but she felt no reason to be afraid.

I'm just having a dream, and not a scary one at that.
Then why don't you open your eyes, girl?
I'm not supposed to...

The steam-like heat soaked her pajamas. Beads of sweat ran down her face and neck, but she kept her eyes firmly shut. At one point a swell of anxiety built up inside her, a momentary panic, but it quickly disappeared. She let her head sway back and forth as she floated through the dark. Then she felt herself being gently set down on hard, uneven ground.

A horrible smell surrounded her and she couldn't shake the feeling that it was somehow familiar. A part of her brain screamed its importance. Another part, much stronger and eerily beyond her ability to control, soothed the feeling away, and in her dream she felt sleepy.

A cold, bony hand on her face sent a jarring alarm through her nerves. There was something there, something she should have remembered, but it eluded her memory. The cool touch should have felt soothing on her hot skin, but it felt wrong, frightening. The urge to sleep then became so powerful that she couldn't have opened her eyes even if she had wanted to. She no longer did.

"Dreams are just like that," she heard a child's voice whisper.

As she slipped deeper into the unknown, the cold became less uncomfortable. Inside her dream she had another dream, lying on the uneven floor of a hot cave. It was like a slide show of brief images, horrible pictures...

Memories, my dear. Your memories.

Horrible memories from somewhere—

Your childhood. Remember your poor brother?

—from her childhood. She saw her father silhouetted in the doorway late at night and fought the familiar fear exploding inside her. She could smell him, his liquor breath, as he got on top of her. She remembered her poor brother, lying on the floor in the kitchen with his face bloodied, his legs unmoving. He had cried, begged her to help him. She still felt the fist across her face that had dislocated her jaw when she had attacked the man. The man who had paralyzed her little brother...

The images played on and on. She sobbed as she lay on the hard, wet floor.

Then the familiar voice told her how to make things right. She couldn't change her past, but she could help stop the terror for another child.

Isn't that why you wanted to be a nurse, to help people? Is there anyone more deserving of your help than an innocent little boy?

She saw Nathan in his hospital bed with the bulky dressing on his arm. She heard him cry in the treatment room as the doctors peeled dead flesh from his mangled hand. She felt sad at first, but then became aware of a white-hot rage that grew inside of her. As the voice spoke she let her anger reach a hellistic crescendo.

She listened more carefully to the instructions telling her what she would do.

* * *

Steve must have passed out at the sight of the man called Clark. It seemed like only a split second, but when his eyes came into focus again, the thin, white face with its hidden eyes and slit of a mouth no longer stared down at him. So he waited. He wasn't sure for how long. Time spent staring at a white ceiling with its black lines was very hard to measure.

By the time Mr. Clark came back, a woman with a mask and blue shower cap on had put a rigid tube in his mouth, which sucked the vomit out. She had cleaned up his face.

The hissing had faded to background noise and the periodic pressure of his lungs being filled with air no longer freaked him out, though it felt no less miserable. The feel and taste of the plastic tube, which went through his mouth (it was cool on his tongue and had the rubbery taste of a balloon), drove him crazy. The more he tried to force his mind to something else, the more he found he could only think of that damn snaking tube in his throat.

He guessed it was attached to some kind of breathing machine. He couldn't get used to not being able to move, although he had gotten good at blinking, thank god. His eyes were so dry they felt like little particles of glass were peppered over them. He could move them a bit if he strained, although they would drift back to center after a few seconds.

Before Mr. Clark's return, he had heard an intermittent smattering of other voices whispering around him, saying things he couldn't understand. They talked about a medicine, he thought, *sucking*, or something like that, and about changing how it *dripped*. One voice kept mentioning how many *twitches* there were. They also talked about blood and *typing and crossing*, whatever that was—something to do with his blood, he thought. And then they disappeared as he stared at his tiled ceiling. He listened to the sickening hiss and tried hard to see *anything* other than that goddamn ceiling.

And then Mr. Clark entered again. Steve felt an icy set of fingers on the side of his face. Then the damned hat-covered head, with the thin smile and the shadows where eyes should be, leaned over into the center of his vision.

"Mr. Prescott," he said slowly. "I'm sure you are wondering what is going on." He paused, nodded so that his shadowed face bobbed in and out of Steve's field of vision. "Yes, I thought so. Well"—he disappeared but the voice continued—"you will figure it all out in due time. I am sure we will come to understand each other very soon." He paused and Steve heard a rustle of activity. Mr. Clark's voice changed, talking to someone else. "Is the succinylcholine back? Is he light enough to blink?" Another pause. "Good."

Mr. Clark leaned again into view, silhouetted in backlight from above. The thin lips parted and the dark, red tongue darted in and out as he spoke.

"Mr. Prescott, are you sorry for what you have done? If you are, I would like you to blink twice, please."

Still this bullshit!?

He assumed the pale freak meant Sherry and her little brat. Could it really all be about that?

Holy shit, how friggin' crazy is this? What the fuck is wrong with these people? It was an accident, goddamnit.

Steve's face flushed with anger. He wanted to clench his jaw, to scream at his captor, but he couldn't. So instead he stared at the wet, thin lips and seethed, breathed it with each mechanical *HISS* of the ventilator. Mr. Clark leaned back out of view.

"Well, Mr. Prescott," Clark sounded excited. "I see from your idiotic and ignorant expression that you are not sorry for the pain you have caused. So we'll begin."

Again Steve heard the sounds of muted activity from all around him. He heard the clatter of metal on metal, like tools being assembled. What in hell was going on? The muffled chatter and a flurry of activity around the room disoriented him. He heard more clinking of... *surgical instruments?*

Oh my god, No! Surely not. Oh God, please help me!

Steve stared at the ceiling, *his* ceiling as he thought of it now, and listened to the clatter of the unseen crowd. He occasionally struggled out a slow, hard blink when the dryness of his eyes became unbearable. A pale halo surrounded the white of the ceiling. With all of his concentration, he tried desperately to decipher the incoherent conversations. His face was hot and his heart felt like it might jump out of his chest. The beeping sounded very fast now, marching out the staccato rhythm of his elevated heart-beat.

Please...!

"What size gloves?"

"Seven and a half."

"Just one suction."

"Is there blood available?"

"We're going to need epi-soaked gauze at the donor site."

"I'll set up the electric cutter. Do you need the mesher?"

"No, but make sure the bovie is at 30."

"Go ahead and prep."

Steve felt a sudden shock of cold liquid on his right thigh and groin. Hands began to scrub his leg with the freezing solution. He felt it dribble down the inside of his thigh. There was a tug and then a burning in his dick. He tried desperately to shift his eyes downward, to see what was going on, but they only obeyed his command briefly. Nowhere near long enough to see anything. He really wanted to know what they were doing to his dick. The beeping sound of his heartbeat accelerated.

What the hell is happening? If I'm about to get an operation, why am I awake? Christ, I can feel everything! Don't they know that? How can I tell them?

The beeping banged into his head like a nail.

"Wow, he is really tachycardic."

"Well, go figure."

"Towels please."

"Towel clips?"

"No, thanks."

He felt warm towels laid across his crotch, then on his thigh, just above his knee. Then more on his inner and outer thigh.

"Ok, let's get it done. Two pairs of pick-ups please. Thanks."

Steve could not contain his terror but he had no way to release it. He heard a clinking of instruments and felt a hand pressing on his skin.

My god, this can't be happening. Please fucking stop. Please, please, please...

"Ok, hold the skin taunt right there. That's it." He felt the metal instrument pulling both up and down on his thigh, the skin between stretching tight. A tear trickled down his cheek into his ear.

"Electric blade."

Blade? BLADE? Please, god, NO! NO! NO!

A mechanical whirring sound, like a power tool spooling up, echoed in the room. He felt like he might vomit again; his stomach tightened. A flash of cool pressure on his leg startled him and then…

An explosion of pain jolted low on his leg. It spread upward as the pitch of the tool became lower, slower. When the whirring sound sped up again, the pressure stopped and the piercing torture relented, replaced by an unbelievable burning over his entire lower body. The sensation of being lit on fire was so overwhelming that Steve expected at any moment to smell smoke. Never in his life had he imagined anything so excruciating. Every nerve fired, trying to mobilize his muscles, to get him to move away from the source, but he remained still. He tried to scream, but the agony echoed silently in his mind instead. He looked in vain for any outlet.

"That's a good piece. Put that in some saline."

"There you are."

"Right here?"

"That's it, right next to the first cut."

Pressure on his thigh again. This time more to the inside. The horrible whirring sound.

Please, stop! For god's sake, not again!

The vacuous screams inside his head were followed again by the pressure and then by the sharp, ripping up the inside of his thigh and the terrible burning.

"Another good one."

"Man, he's really bleeding."

"Get some epi-soaked sponges on the site."

"Want me to hold pressure?"

"Guess you better."

A hand pressed roughly right where his leg burned. His pain ratcheted up two notches, the beeping boomed louder, and Steve felt sure that his brain would explode if he couldn't move immediately. But only his chest moved, outside of his control, with each *HISS* of the breathing machine.

"Here's the epi."

He heard a sound, like the pump of a squirt bottle, and then a cool wetness on his thigh. For a second it soothed the pain, but then the fire rose in intensity, and the room went black. Steve drifted. The voices around him became faint, the beeping softer and softer and softer...

* * *

Jason looked at the clock for the tenth time in eight minutes. His almost feverish desire to get out of the ER did nothing to make the damn thing go any faster. He stood next to the patient board and scribbled a final few notes in the last two charts of patients with pending items. He repeatedly looked down the hall for his relief; the infamous Dr. Dietrich. Jason didn't know if it was a desire to see (and maybe talk to) Jenny or his nearly desperate need to check on Nathan that drove his manic desire.

There was something very different about Nathan, something they shared other than scars. The afternoon had been tough on their new friendship (or whatever it was). It had been easy to talk Sheila Katzen, the General Surgery third year resident on the burn service, into letting him do Nathan's debridement. Hell, Sheila didn't want to do it any more than he did. Scraping and scrubbing dead skin off someone held no glamour or glory, and anyone who didn't feel agony when that patient was a crying child should probably not be allowed to mingle in a civilized society.

You couldn't give enough Morphine to make the pain go away without stopping their breathing. All you could do was hope that the little bit of Versed you gave would keep the little guy from remembering why he should hate you.

But Nathan had been a real trooper. He sobbed almost silently as Jason removed the dead skin on the sensitive palm of his hand and up the side of his index finger. Jason tried to talk to him at first, searched for consoling words, but it felt ridiculous. He finally tried to just finish as quickly as possible.

The hand itself looked remarkably good and could probably have a skin graft in another day or so (during which Nathan would get to have general anesthesia—thank god). When he finished he realized he had cried more than Nathan. He had nearly burst when his new buddy looked up at him between sobs and said, "Thanks for taking care of me, Jason."

Jason looked again at the painfully slow clock and his gaze caught Dietrich coming up the hallway from the magnetized doors. He walked slowly and whispered something to a pretty girl in scrubs, who looked familiar—someone from X-Ray, he thought. She blushed and glanced at her own feet, then put a hand on Dietrich's chest to push him away. The push held an intimacy that made it clear she had not shunned him earlier. Jason chuckled and shook his head.

"Hey there, big guy," Dietrich said as he breezed up beside him. "How's the nut house?"

"About average." Jason knew Rich wanted him to ask about the girl, so naturally, he refused. "Ready to get going?"

"Yeah," Dietrich said with an exaggerated stretch and yawn. "Pretty worn out this evening, I don't mind tellin' ya'," he baited.

"No doubt," Jason answered, feigning disinterest. "I have one sickie pending and another that might be a discharge."

"She might be Miss Right," Rich said and looked longingly down the hall at miss-right-now. She winked and waved with two fingers just before the magnetic doors shut. Jason felt a tug of jealousy, not at the parade of meaningless sex in his friend's life (he really didn't have more than a passing curiosity about that), but at the ease with which Rich talked to everyone, women included. Jason would have given about anything to be that comfortable.

Jason shook the thought off; they were pointless at best and distracting enough to keep him from talking to Jenny at worst.

"Ready?" he demanded, more irritably than he intended. Not Rich's fault he had what Jason needed.

"Yeah, sorry," Rich said and let himself get drawn into the somewhat boring tale of the very sick Mrs. Cathcart and the very annoying (and probably drug-seeking) Mr. Griffey.

Fifteen minutes later, Jason stood at the elevators, his back-pack over one shoulder, and stared at the button instead of pushing it. He didn't want to rehearse what he would say to Jenny and sound stilted and… well, rehearsed. But on the other hand, he couldn't just walk up unprepared and stammer at her like a choking victim (as he had done once already). He felt a familiar dread grow inside of him and rubbed his face with both hands.

"God, don't be such an asshole," he said to himself quietly. Then he looked up and saw an old man. The guy stared with a gaze usually reserved for a half-naked man on a street corner holding a "The End Is Coming" sign. "Good morning," Jason said, looking directly at him. The man only nodded in response and moved slowly away.

He mashed the up button with some irritation and one of the elevator doors swooshed open. Inside, he pushed the number six, then crossed his arms across his chest in defiance. He had to go up, for Christ's sake. He had to see Nathan in any case. For all he knew Jenny wouldn't even be there. He had no idea what her work schedule was.

Jenny sat at a round table looking through a chart. She looked beautiful. Jason stood at the doorway to the ICU for a moment and just watched her. She twirled her hair with one hand, the other resting on the clipboard. When she looked up and saw him, a smile lit her face. Instead of just smiling back, Jason walked over to her with a casualness he didn't feel, hoping he didn't look stupid. *Hi, I'm Larry...*

"Hi, I'm Jason," he said awkwardly and then felt so foolish he almost turned around.

"I know who you are, Dr. Gelman," Jenny said with a little chuckle. She held his eyes, his smile, and waited expectantly.

Jason took a deep breath and dove right in. "So how is our little guy this evening?" he asked and boldly sat down in the empty chair next to her.

"He's doing fine," Jenny said cheerfully. "I actually have him tonight, so I'll be looking after him. Listen..." She leaned forward, putting her warm hand on his wrist. Her hand felt smooth, soft on his skin and he worried he might actually give off a contented sigh. "I heard what you did earlier this afternoon, and, well, I just wanted to tell you I think you're great. I wish you were his doctor all the time instead of the Burn Service Team."

She looked down the hall at a group of retreating white coats with poorly veiled disappointment. "I'm sure they're all good, but they barely even talk to the poor kid." Her hand squeezed his wrist and he felt a little dizzy. "He's lucky to have met you," she said and then pulled her hand away.

"Well," Jason replied when he could speak. His face felt hot and he knew it was red. "Thanks. I mean—well, thanks a lot." He started to reach out to touch her hand and decided against it, though he desperately wanted to feel her skin again.

"I'm glad you'll be his nurse tonight," Jason said awkwardly. Jenny showed no signs of discomfort whatsoever. Probably because she was just being professional and polite and had no idea he was interested in being more colleagues.

"Oh, I asked to be," she said and he thought he saw a little blush, which to him looked more like hope. "I think Nathan is just great," she continued and looked down. She seemed to be gathering her courage for something. "And I like his doctor, too."

Jason felt a wave of nausea burning in his throat. Was it one of the Surgery Residents? Maybe an attending from the Pediatric ICU service? Holy shit, he was such an idiot. Why would a gorgeous woman like this be interested in him?

"You know I mean you, right?" Jenny asked. Her voice sounded nervous. When he looked at her, relief washed over him.

Wow. Shit, now what?

"Look," he said with a sigh. Being himself would probably be easier than trying to be Dietrich. "Jenny, I suck at this. But..." He hesitated. *But what?* "But, I would really like to get to know you." There, he said it. Go on. Get in there. No going back now anyway. "Do you want to grab some coffee or get breakfast or something in the morning after your shift?" He gazed expectantly into her beautiful green eyes.

"I would love that," she said and sighed, visibly relieved. "I thought I was going to look like an idiot here." She touched his wrist again. "I can sneak away for five or ten minutes in just a little while if you want. We can make plans for tomorrow?"

"That would be great," he said louder than he intended.

"I figured you were going to check on Nathan, right?" she asked.

"Yeah," Jason answered. He felt a twinge of guilt that Nathan waited in his room while he made time with his nurse. "Yeah, he had a tough day. I just want to spend a little time with him." He realized he really did.

"Great," Jenny said, but left her hand on his arm this time. He wondered if she knew that. "How about we meet in thirty or forty minutes when I finish my other assessments?" She handed him the chart she had been looking at.

The red tape on the front read "SMH Doe"—Nathan's chart. Jason realized he didn't really need the chart. He wasn't there as a doctor.

"Perfect," he said, remembering that Jenny still waited for a reply. They smiled at each other as Jason rose and headed to Nathan's room. He set the chart in the box by the door and quietly walked in.

Nathan sat up in his bed where he watched a video on a small TV set on a rolling cart. *Ice Age II.* He watched for a moment as Nathan stared at the screen with all the interest of a cross-country trucker forced to see

Cinderella when Monday night football was on. He wondered where his mind had taken him.

"What's up, kiddo?" Jason called from the door and screwed his biggest smile on his face. He noted that Nathan jumped a bit, startled away from wherever his thoughts had taken him. Jason hoped that Nathan had not been thinking about his earlier torture at the hands of Dr. Gelman. "How ya' feelin'?" he asked as he sat on the edge of his bed. To his relief, Nathan smiled a huge five-year-old grin.

"Hi, Jason," he said warmly. "I feel pretty good." He raised his bandaged arm a bit. "Hardly hurts at all."

Jason knew that if his hand felt better, it was because of the narcotics, not because of him. He nodded anyway. "Good," he said. "What are we watching?"

"*Ice Age II: The Melt Down,*" Nathan said. "I've already seen it but it's really funny. Can you watch it with me?" he asked hopefully.

"Absolutely," Jason answered and settled more comfortably onto the bed beside his buddy. "Where's your mom?" he asked.

"Went to get some food," Nathan said and Jason felt his heart warm when the boy scooted over so he would be right next to him. "She's gonna bring me back some ice cream, but you can share if you want." He seemed engrossed in the movie now, though he had been barely watching it when Jason came in.

Jason smiled at the warm feeling he had for this boy. He tried to watch the movie with Nathan and managed to laugh at Nathan giggling, but his mind remained consumed with thoughts about the boy's nightmares. He wanted so much to ask him about what he saw when he closed his eyes. He especially wanted to hear more about the Lizard Men. He saw a mental image of two tall men in trench coats in the alley, wide-brimmed hats low over their faces, and orange-yellow orbs peering from the shadows.

Remember me, Jason?

He shuddered uncontrollably. Nathan looked at him for a moment with uncertainty. Jason smiled back which seemed to be enough for his buddy, who returned eagerly to the movie.

"The big elephant is gonna help him," he chattered excitedly and pointed at the TV.

Jason knew he couldn't take Nathan to the nightmares. Not right now. He needed to just be a little boy for a while. He did his best to get into the movie, but mostly enjoyed hearing Nathan laugh and tell him what was going to happen next.

When Jenny tapped lightly on the door, he found himself a little disappointed to be pulled away. Then again, Jenny did smile at him beautifully from the doorway.

"Hi, Nathan," she said warmly. "Can I steal Dr. Gelman for a quick minute?"

"Okay," Nathan answered, but he held up the remote and pointed it at the TV. "I'll pause it for ya, Jason."

Jason smiled. "Sounds great," he said as he got up from the hospital bed, ruffling Nathan's mop of hair as he did. "I'll just be a minute," he said and slipped out the door with Jenny.

"Wow, you're so great with him," Jenny said warmly.

"Thanks," Jason replied. "You want a coffee?"

"No, thanks," she answered. "I like to wait until I need it in a few hours. Can we just sit in the staff lounge for a minute?"

"Sure," he answered. He followed her to the small kitchen-like lounge and enjoyed the pleasure of being beside her. They sat at the little table together and she seemed to gather her thoughts.

"Look," she said staring at her own hands. Her eyes seemed clouded.

Uh-oh. This doesn't look good. This could be a new personal record—a break up before the first date.

He swallowed hard and let her continue.

"I'm really excited about seeing you in the morning," she said.

But?

"But," she continued and then paused. To his relief she put her soft hand on his again and went on. "It's just that I have a rule about dating guys at work, or before that, at school." She stopped and looked to be in deep thought. "Actually," she said and smiled at him, "it seems I usually set up lots of rules to not date guys that would be worth dating. I just…" She looked at him as if searching for words.

Jason tried to let her off the hook. "Jenny, I think I like you but if you are uncomfortable with this…"

Yeah, no big deal at all. If you need me, I'll be at my apartment, hanging myself in the shower.

"No," she said. "I want to get together with you and I am excited." She sighed and looked embarrassed. "Listen, I am NOT some emotional, high-maintenance chick. I just have some stuff from my past that makes me like this—kind of—I don't know, awkward I guess— around guys." She looked at him to see his reaction and he smiled. "I'm a lot of fun, actually. I just have a hard time relaxing sometimes." She watched his eyes carefully.

Jason laughed. "It'll be cool not being the only one who's awkward and uncomfortable. Maybe I won't be at such a disadvantage." Jenny laughed with him. "I just want to find out who you are." He allowed himself to take her hand in his this time.

Again he thought her eyes clouded.

"That takes time," she said, looking at her hand in his.

"I have it," he said and she gazed at him, happily it seemed.

"Alright then," she said getting up. "It's a date." She put her hands on her hips at the declaration and they both laughed.

"I'll meet you at around seven-thirty," he said. "Where?"

"How about right in the lobby by the elevators?" she offered.

"Perfect." He turned to go.

"Jason," she said from behind him. He turned to look again at her incredibly beautiful face, eyebrows raised. "Thanks for making me comfortable. It's not you, just bad family stuff." He winced at that.

"Believe me, I know." He tried to sound reassuring and not creepy.

He headed back to Nathan's room. Inside, Nathan sat talking to his mom and eating vanilla ice cream from a Styrofoam bowl. When he entered the boy's face lit up.

Man, I am having a great day.

"Hey, Jason," Nathan tried to sound older than five. "Mommy... I mean, my mom, only got one spoon. Can Jenny get you another spoon?"

"How about I just let you eat while we watch the movie?" he asked and smiled at Nathan's mom. "How are you doing?"

"I'm doing well," she answered, but her eyes were dark and heavy. Jason knew she hadn't had a real night's sleep in a couple of days. "Thanks so much for spending so much time with him."

"I should be thanking you," he said sincerely. "I have a great time with my buddy here."

Nathan beamed as Jason took back his place on the edge of the bed and they started the movie again. He sat with him for a long while. They finished *Ice Age* and got halfway through *Shrek* before Nathan fell asleep, his head against Jason's arm. Jason tried not to move, letting the little guy get into a deeper sleep. Then he awkwardly extracted himself, laid Nathan on his own pillow and pulled the covers up around his shoulders. He watched him for a moment then kissed him on the forehead without thinking.

Sherry Doren slept deeply in the chair-turned-uncomfortable bed. He spread out a thin blanket over her as well and then turned off the TV. He watched Nathan again from the door.

He thought of Lizard Men and shadowy figures in trench coats with glowing eyes. He prayed silently that Nathan's demons would leave him alone tonight.

Prey on someone else tonight and let the little guy sleep.

Then he closed the door gently behind him to block out the noise from the unit.

Chapter
6

Steve knew he was dreaming, but he didn't want it to end. He couldn't remember why being awake was a terrible thing to avoid.

He stood on the pier with Toby and leaned over the railing, a fishing line dangling in the water. The air felt wicked hot and he had sunburned badly, though strangely mostly on his right thigh. Man, it hurt. He grabbed his Budweiser and tipped it up to his lips.

The beer tasted all wrong—warm as piss, and for some reason rubbery, like a balloon. He wanted to tell Toby about the beer. When he turned to him, the face was Toby's only now his eyes were black as coal, with a shimmer of orange.

I know those eyes. Those aren't Toby's eyes, but I know them.

He heard a weird beeping noise, but he couldn't place it.

"Dude, your leg's on fuckin' fire, man." Toby turned and stared off the pier, teased the line from his fishing pole, trying to bob his bait and attract the fish below.

Steve looked down and saw his thigh engulfed in orange-blue flame. It wrapped around his leg from just above his knee and he watched it turn his skin red, then white. Panic grew in his chest as blisters started to form. The searing pain ran up his thigh and into his groin, then spread around to his back.

Steve dropped his fishing pole and slapped at the flames on his right thigh with his hands, to stop the horrible pain, but his arms were ridiculously short nubs with normal hands on the end, too little to reach his leg. His stubs just flapped, slapping weakly against his chest.

Steve opened his mouth to scream, strained his chest, but nothing came out. Then finally he heard a scream, but instead of his voice it sounded more like a—

HISSS!

Steve's eyes opened. He stared up at the pale, thin-lipped face. He felt the pulsating burn in his leg. The thin lips turned into a smile.

"Ah, Mr. Prescott. Welcome back. You left us for a moment." Mr. Clark stood back up, pulling out of view.

"I was asking you a question, do you remember? No? Well I guess we'll ask again." He let a long pause hang in the air. Steve stared at the white ceiling with its black line and tried desperately to make his mind go somewhere, anywhere, away from the searing pain. Abruptly, Mr. Clark leaned into view again.

"Mr. Prescott, are you sorry for what you have done?" The head tilted back and his eyes glowed through the shadows. "No? Not yet?" The red lips pulled back in another tight smile. Steve suddenly knew that the creature wanted more than an apology. He saw an excitement in the quivering lips and something else—a hunger.

"Well, you will be." He straightened up and disappeared from view. "Good night, Mr. Prescott. We will see you in the morning. Yes, we will most definitely see you then."

He heard the shuffling of feet and a door clicking shut, then silence except for the low beeping and hissing that his mind barely registered anymore.

His eyes filled with tears. This time they flowed down his face for hours, soaking his hair and tickling his skin. He tried all night to force his mind onto the sensation of the salty streams running down his face, away from the thunderous ache in his right thigh, but it didn't work. The intensity consumed him, until he thought he would lose his mind.

* * *

The work dragged on as night shifts always do. Jenny decided to skip the assessment at two a.m. on Nathan Doren. She had checked on him and he looked so peaceful that it seemed wrong to wake him, just to chart his blood pressure and respiratory rate. For a few moments, she watched him from the door.

Something about this boy had captured the heart of the man she found herself so enamored with. It was intriguing, but oddly, there was something scary in that thought. She had no idea why on earth she felt that way. Maybe Nathan reminded her of her own shitty past. Whatever it was, she felt strongly about this little boy, too. If breaking the rules and letting him sleep a little more would be best for him, she would.

She closed the door softly.

The other patient she had was labor intensive but not very challenging. The fifteen-year-old had been hit by a car weeks ago and remained on the ventilator with a closed head injury. Ventilator patients were a lot more time demanding: frequent checks, labs, vitals, and in the case of this patient, lots of sucking the snot from the airway.

She spent most of the night working with the critically-ill teenager. When she needed a sanity check, she checked on Nathan. Nathan's mom had not stirred since Jason covered her with a blanket. She seemed totally exhausted and Jenny did her best not to disturb her either.

She spent her free time thinking of Jason. She felt nervous about seeing him in a few hours, but excited too. What the hell had she been thinking with her melodramatic confessions of "family problems?" Maybe she was trying to scare him away, like she had the handful of men in the past. Easier than letting them get close perhaps.

Thanks for that, Dad, you shithead.

Jenny's heart raced at the thought. Strange, but thoughts of her father felt wrong somehow. Forced seemed more accurate. Why did it feel so off (other than the obvious) to think of her dad and what he had done to her and her brother?

Screw it. He's gone. Mom is nuts and Patrick is in a wheelchair for life. How much more wrong do you need?

She pushed the thoughts from her head and tried to focus on her work, but a part of her mind refused to let it go, trying to make her see something important. "Not now, damnit," she muttered to herself. This sudden obsession with her past would do nothing to enhance her budding relationship with Jason. "Haven't you taken enough from me?" she said out loud.

"What's that, dear?" Jenny looked up at Carol Wernicke, the senior nurse on duty with her tonight and the one in charge. She liked Carol, who had taken her under her wing after her orientation. She was the kind of nurse Jenny hoped to eventually be, and she blushed a little at being caught mumbling to herself.

"Oh, nothing," she said. "Just trying to talk myself awake. I'm dragging a little tonight."

"Yeah, nights are hard. You're off tomorrow, aren't you?"

"Yes," Jenny answered. "Then back for days on the weekend."

"Well," Nurse Wernicke said maternally, "you should do something fun with your two days off—maybe with your new friend, Dr.

Gelman." She winked at Jenny. "Relax dear," the older nurse said with a hand on her shoulder. "I can read those residents pretty well by now and that guy is one of the few good ones. He doesn't seem to be looking for a place to just park his car for a few weeks, you know what I mean?"

"Thanks," she said. "I hope you're right."

Her charge nurse walked off and she tried to make sense of what she had been charting. What had she been thinking about that had seemed so important? Her mind grew suddenly heavy and struggled to keep focus on the words in front of her.

Holy shit, I'm tired. I should have taken that cup of coffee from Jason instead of bearing my soul.

Her head bobbed forward and she forced her eyes to open wide. She knew she couldn't nap at work but wondered if five minutes with her eyes closed would help her rally.

Not sleeping, just resting my eyes. Her mom looked amused from a distant, happy memory but the warm feeling it brought confused her. She felt her mind drifting away.

We need your help now, Jenny. Only people like you, those who have been through it, can understand enough to help us punish these bastards.

The voice was frightening and a part of her resisted its call. But she felt herself falling into its grasp. It felt a lot like drowning.

Images flashed through her mind at a rocket pace. At first they were a slideshow, just like before, of her father tearing off her nightgown and roughly pulling her panties aside. She cried and begged him to stop. Her brother writhing on the floor of the kitchen, legs motionless. Pictures of her mother, mouth swollen and bloody, black trails of mascara streaming down her face as she rocked quietly in a corner of the den.

Then there were other images, more confusing. Glowing lights in a dark stairwell, an impossibly pale face. A blood-red mouth splitting apart to reveal long, sharp teeth.

Images of her father holding her lovingly and reassuring her that everything would be okay after her pet gerbil died. Images of her and both of her parents watching Patrick at a high school soccer game. Impossible! Her brother had been in a wheelchair for years by then. After a few months in foster care, she had come home to her mother, broken, her father long since gone.

That's right.

Isn't it?

The loving images faded away and her sanity's pleading voice drifted with them, whatever its message might have been.

Then she watched the slide show, the dark pictures. Her fear and anger built in intensity.

We need your help.

She walked in a poorly lit cave with a man in a long trench coat, a top hat on his head. She couldn't see his face but sensed he was a friend. She still fought a terrible sense of dread.

"Dreams are just like that," she remembered some child's voice muttering. The memory reassured her.

As she walked, another stranger came to her. It sounded like the man in the coat, but he spoke to her, in her head, without really talking.

You have to help us stop the evil man that hurt your little Nathan. Only you can help stop him.

She heard the voice and knew what it said was true.

Here is what you must do.

* * *

Jason waited nervously by the elevators, pacing back and forth, trying to look casual. He had changed clothes three times and still looked wrong. His choices were admittedly limited but he wanted to look confident. After looking in the mirror the first time, he had given up on that pipe dream and settled for just having his socks match.

The chime of the elevator snapped him back from his fashion worries. He tried to look fun, happy, cool and casual all at once, but it hurt his face so he set his sights on a content smile.

The old couple that shuffled slowly from the elevator didn't seem very impressed but did manage a smile back in his direction. He sighed in frustration.

Hadn't he learned last night that Jenny felt awkward and uncomfortable too? As hard as he found that to believe, he took strength from the thought.

"Jason?"

He looked up at the beautiful blue-green eyes with a start. He hadn't heard the elevator ding. She looked so damn pretty. Then he noticed how heavy and clouded her eyes were.

Just tired?

"Hi," he managed to cough out. "Sorry, I didn't see you come down. How are you?"

"Tired," she said with a smile and a little sigh. "I'm not going to be very good company I'm afraid."

He felt his heart sink a little.

"Would you like to do this another time?" he asked.

Please, no. Please, no. Please, no.

"No," she said with another weak smile. "I want to have breakfast with you. I just have somewhere I have to be in a little while if that's okay."

He couldn't blame her for building an out into their date. You never know. At least she hadn't changed her mind all together.

"Okay," he said. "I know a little place about a block from here that's got great food. It's not very fancy or anything," he warned.

"Sounds perfect," she said.

He managed to contain his excitement when she took his hand as they walked out the door. Her fingers were warm and soft in his.

On the brief walk to the Sunrise Café, Jenny caught him up on Nathan's night. She flushed a little when she told him she had skipped his assessment at two a.m., so as not to wake him.

"I probably shouldn't tell his doctor that, huh?" she said with a nervous laugh. "You probably think I'm a bad nurse."

Jason squeezed her hand and chuckled. "I don't think you're a bad nurse and actually I'm not really his doctor. I'm more like..." He paused. Like what? "A friend I guess."

Jenny smiled. "Well you're a good friend, Jason," she said. "He sure as hell needs one, huh?"

"Yeah," Jason answered. "I don't know why I feel so pulled to that little guy. There's just something special about him."

Jenny yanked him to a stop and he turned to look at her, a little surprised. Her face looked very serious.

"There is, isn't there?" she asked. She seemed far away. Jason waited patiently for her to return and after a moment she seemed to focus on him again. "I feel it too. What is it about him that's so special?"

"I don't know." He felt a little uncomfortable. "I really don't. I'm just sort of, I don't know, drawn to him or something."

"Yeah," Jenny looked off again. "Yeah. Drawn to him somehow." Then she shook her head and blushed. She looked at him and smirked. "I sound like a flake, huh? I'm NOT a night person." She pulled him along again and he relaxed. "Working nights makes me loopy."

They enjoyed a nice breakfast. Jason wanted a bigger word for their first date but it was 'nice.' Fortunately, nice he could handle. Anything bigger would probably just scare the crap out of him.

Jenny seemed tired and distracted but they chatted anyway and he delighted in the observation that she touched his arm a lot when she talked. They went on about the hospital a little but both seemed content to try and avoid the gossip mill.

They talked about running, as both had been avid runners in the past, though neither made much time for it lately. Again and again, they would come back to Nathan.

"I hope the asshole that hurt him gets what he deserves," Jason said over a bite of eggs benedict. He watched her closely to see if she would react negatively to that, but to his surprise he saw a hint of rage flash across her face at the mere mention.

"Oh, he will," she said and Jason thought that for a moment she looked almost evil.

Maybe she feels similar…

"I wish I had your confidence in our legal system." He put his fork down and felt his appetite abandon him.

Jenny's eyes flashed again. "I didn't say anything about the legal system."

And then the odd expression vanished and they moved on to other topics. He learned that Jenny would love to one day have kids of her own but had trouble seeing herself in that role.

"No role models," she said simply and then rushed on before he could press her for more. Not that he would have. He felt perfectly content leaving the past untouched for awhile.

Like a dozen years. Maybe twenty.

Jason actually felt pretty relaxed as he walked her back to her car in the hospital parking deck. The mini-date had gone smoothly and he was relieved that Jenny's other commitment had set a time limit on them. No pressure about what to do next.

I know what I'd like to do next, but a kiss seems out of the question.

He admired her beauty, allowing his gaze to pass briefly over her body. The scrubs were not flattering on anyone but her athletic figure looked great even in those. He tried not to stare and felt his stomach drop when he saw her eyes were on him. *Caught.*

He started to stammer an excuse or an apology, unsure which would be better, but she relieved him of his need for either when she kissed his cheek and then squeezed his arm against her neck.

They waited in the parking garage for the elevator in silence but it didn't feel awkward. Jason summoned his courage as best he could. Maybe it would have been best to leave well enough alone, play it cool, but he found himself almost uncontrollably eager to see her again—like in an hour or less.

As they entered the elevator he heard a gasp. Her face seemed pale and he took her arms.

"Are you okay?"

Jenny shuddered but seemed to collect herself. "Yeah," she said and smiled at him weakly. "Sorry. I don't know what the hell that was."

"Are you afraid of elevators?" he asked.

Instead of answering, Jenny closed her eyes and leaned into him. Her lips touched his gently and he felt her hands on his waist. His pulse quickened and he was a little dizzy from her soft, gentle mouth meeting his. She pulled back and he lingered, staring at her for a moment.

"Wow," he finally managed to whisper.

"Yeah," she said and gazed down at her twisting hands. "I hope that was okay. I'm not usually such a… I don't know. So forward I guess."

Jason tilted her face up gently by the chin. "It was fine. I mean it was great. Look." He stopped for a moment. "Can I see you later? After you nap, I mean. We could have dinner."

Jenny's face clouded and he worried he had made the wrong choice. "I don't know," she said with a troubled voice. "I have this thing I have to do and then I really need some sleep."

"No problem," he said but he knew how disappointed he sounded.

Now it was her turn to touch his chin. "It's not that I don't want to. I definitely want to see you again. It's just this thing I have to do is, well…" She left the explanation unfinished. "Can you give me your number and I can call you if I feel up to something later? I mean, I don't expect you to wait around or anything…"

Jason laughed out loud. "That's not a problem," he said and wrote his cell number on a scratch of paper from his pocket. He handed it to her "Call even if you just want to chat on the phone. I got nowhere I need to be. My social calendar is a big blank piece of emptiness."

Jenny took the paper and smiled, then leaned up and kissed him again. "Can I see you tomorrow if tonight doesn't work out?" she asked and he thought she sounded hopeful.

"Absolutely."

He walked her to her car, a lone SUV on the top floor of the garage, and they kissed one last time. He watched her drive off and then headed to the elevators, back to see Nathan.

That went way better than expected.

* * *

Jenny drove around the bend and out of sight and then slowed as she descended the ramp to the next floor below. She suspected that Jason would head back in to visit Nathan and the thought of him sitting beside the little boy made her feel warm—and conflicted. It wouldn't do for him to see her returning, so she decided to sit for a minute before heading in. It would take some luck to not run into him, but she couldn't really do anything about that now.

I should have just told him I had a work meeting.

Too late, though she could always fall back on it if they did run into each other later.

Jenny drew in a shaking sigh. She decided to just hope that they didn't run into each other. If they did, she would deal with it. There were plenty of other things to worry about without making herself sick over how she would handle her budding crush.

Like what I'm doing here. And why it feels so perfectly right and horribly wrong at the same time.

It dawned on her that she now finally understood the word surrealistic.

The LED clock on the dash told her that only four minutes had passed. Surely Jason was well out of view and in the unit with Nathan by now. Just the same, she watched as the indicator clicked over two more times in what felt like a half hour. When the clock made its second silent click, she took her key out of the ignition, got out of her truck and headed for the elevators with a determined grimace on her face. A part of her mind demanded to know just how she knew where she was supposed to go and what she was supposed to do. A much stronger part shut the doubts up. She knew where to go and why.

How she knew didn't matter any more than the haunting lies of a happy childhood that couldn't possibly belong to her.

Chapter
7

Steve must have fallen asleep, because he didn't remember the woman in a mask and blue shower cap leaning over him. His mind wandered in and out of reality and she seemed to materialize out of nowhere. For a moment he thought he dreamt her.

Maybe she can help me.

Steve concentrated with all of his might and his eyes moved slightly to the left for several seconds—long enough to see a large, heavy door that looked closed and nothing else before they ticked center again. He didn't see anyone else in the room; he tried to focus on the surgical-mask girl who kept darting in and out of his peripheral vision. If he could catch her attention, get her to notice that he was awake, maybe she would give him some medicine. Or better, maybe she would feel bad for him, see what they were doing was horribly fucking wrong, and maybe she could stop it. If he could only catch her gaze.

Steve ignored the horrible, burning pain in his thigh. Finally, he had something else to focus on. He needed this woman's pretty green eyes to *SEE* him. Her face grazed his vision to the right and he could hear her adjusting some equipment. Steve strained to follow her movement, but saw she had turned away, her back to him. With all of his might he forced his eyes to remain where they were, feeling them quiver. The room seemed to shake, but his eyes stayed in the girl's direction. A wave of nausea swept over him as his view of the room rocked back and forth, but he ignored it and concentrated solely on his fight to keep his eyes fixated.

She turned. He rallied and strained harder. The quivering slowed, almost stopped. She leaned over.

"Well, look who's awake." Her voice sounded flat and hollow and her expression was stone. Steve saw none of the compassion he hoped for.

He tried to talk to her with his eyes.

Please, please help me! Please, I'm so scared. My leg hurts so bad, so, so bad. Please don't let them hurt me again. I'm begging you. Please help me. Get me out of here or at least get me some medicine. PLEASE!

The nurse stared at him, paused, seemed to understand.

Please let her understand!

She leaned closer and her stone eyes looked into his soul. He could smell her perfume.

"Hurts, does it? Well…" She patted his hand. Her skin felt warm.

Yes, god, how it hurts! Please, please, make the pain go away. Won't you please help?

The nurse put her lips right beside his ear, her breath diffused by her mask but warm on his face.

"Well I'm glad, you miserable little bastard. I hope they show you pain that you never imagined. I know what you did to that poor little boy, to Nathan, and I'm so glad someone is making you pay, you shit. The courts sure as hell don't do it. They didn't do a goddamn thing when my father raped me or paralyzed my brother. I hope they kill you!"

The nurse stood up, a little fire to her now. She patted his hand, less softly than before, and Steve knew he was fucked.

"Alright, sir, your doctors will be with you shortly." She laughed. Then she turned and walked away.

Steve's eyes drifted back to center, back to his white ceiling with the black line. But he couldn't see it clearly, not through the tears. He felt the pressure change of the door opening again, felt the bustling activity. There were voices and the clinking sound of instruments.

"Donor site?"

"Right upper extremity and chest."

"Oh?"

"Gonna move this one along. Got another one coming in, they say."

"Well, fine. We could use the tissue, god knows. The burn ICU is full right now."

"Get some towels?"

"Sure, doctor."

Arm and chest? The blades again? Please, no I can't stand it again! I'll die, I swear to God! My mind will explode and I will DIE!

Steve heard the beeping speed up, get louder. Then an alarm sounded.

"What's that?"

"Nothing, just the heart rate alarm. He went above 150."

"I guess he knows what's coming, huh?"

"Yeah, just reset the alarms. Better yet, just turn them off."

He heard a shuffle of activity and the alarm stopped.

The pressure changed as the door opened again. Steve tried to look that way but he was exhausted. A moment later, the pale face, the red lips, the eyes hidden in the shadows of a gray hat, came into view. Steve felt his tears erupt, the image of Mr. Clark blurring. Somehow it made him look even more demonic.

"Good morning, Mr. Prescott."

He felt a warm towel on his face and a cold, pale hand mopped away his tears. "There we are. I want us to be able to clearly see one another. Mr. Prescott." The red cut with teeth spread again in a tight smile.

Steve focused pleadingly on the ghostlike face above him. *Yes, I'm sorry. Whatever I did, I'm so fucking sorry. I'm sorry for being born! Just please, don't cut me again! Please, Please, Please! I'll do anything to make it all better! I'll marry the bitch and take care of her brat! PLEASE DON'T CUT ME AGAIN!!*

The pale man tilted his head to the left. He seemed to be considering, as if he had heard Steve's mental pleas. Then he rose up slightly.

"No. Sorry, Mr. Prescott. Not good enough." The gray face disappeared from view.

Steve felt dizzy. How was this fucking possible? He was sorry, goddamnit.

He doesn't care if you're sorry. That's just a show for the others. He doesn't want your remorse or grief. What he needs is your fear and your pain.

The voice sounded like his, inside his head, but he knew it wasn't. He also knew that it told him the truth.

"Prep both arms and his whole chest please."

"The whole chest? Jesus! We're gonna need some blood in the room then. Do we have the type and cross up to date?"

"That won't be necessary," Mr. Clark said. "Give all the fluids you need but we won't be giving any blood."

"Why not?"

Steve felt a wave of heat in the room and a terrible smell. He could barely focus on the debate over whether he would get a blood transfusion after they tore more flesh from his body. The ceiling blurred and the horrible shit smell in the room made his stomach turn.

"Let's give him a liter of crystalloid now," said a voice that sounded unsure.

Someone new leaned over him—Clark's shorter friend. The red scar up the side of the white cheek looked wet to him. The deep orange, almost red eyes peered at him from the impossibly dark shadow of the grey top hat. The thin red lips quivered with excitement, waiting to taste that first cool sip of liquid after a long hot day in the sun.

The lips parted and thin wet drool trickled down the pasty chin. Steve heard a loud, animal like pant and felt the hot, ass-smelling breath on his skin. He looked at teeth that were way too long and pointed to be inside a human mouth. A part of his mind understood that this creature fed on him somehow. The shit smell faded away, disappeared, but the acid-hot breath of the creature seemed every bit as nauseating. Then it slipped from view and he stared again at his familiar ceiling.

Steve tried with all his might to make his heart stop beating. To stop being alive, quickly, before the cutting started again—before the demons fed on his anguish. But no matter how hard he focused his desire, his heart just kept on beating, sending blood and oxygen to his brain, keeping him alive and awake for what was about to begin. He wanted to scream, to flail his arms, to at least close his eyes, but he could do nothing except stare at the white ceiling, listen and wait.

So he waited for the cold steel and the ripping pain of skin being torn from his body.

"Prep please."

Again the cold liquid, the scrubbing. A pair of hands pulled his arms out from his sides, crucifix style. They wrapped straps around his wrists to hold them in place. As they cleaned him the icy liquid ran down his arms to his hands. Drops of soap trickled down his fingers and dripped off onto the floor. The coldness on his chest flowed down his sides, onto his back. He was fucking freezing.

"Towels please."

Warm towels were splayed across his waist and neck, then across his arms at the elbows. Steve's brain fired burst after burst, signals to his nervous system, commanding his arms to move, his head to turn, his legs to kick. It demanded that his voice wail. But his body ignored the commands, somehow unsure of how to follow them, and he lay motionless.

"Two pickups and the electric blade, please."

The whirring sound cut into his thoughts like a bullet. Steve screamed loudly, again and again, in his mind, certain the terror would make his head explode. He prayed for death.

His chest exploded. Pain and searing heat erupted as the vibrating blade impacted his skin just below his rib cage. Flashes of white light blurred his vision and his internal shrieking reached a fever pitch. Everything happened in slow motion.

He could feel the vibrating blade lift the skin from his body, feel the hand-held saw as it ran up his chest, all the way to his neck. He felt the tearing as the long strip of skin pulled free. A blurry, gloved hand passed briefly through his vision, pulling a silver square past his eyes. Hanging from it was a long, six-inch wide strip of grayish-white skin.

His skin.

The flapping piece of flesh was mixed with red. Warm spatters of blood speckled his cheek and chin. A deep burning, intense, like he had been dowsed in kerosene and lit, joined the tearing flesh pain. His vision blurred further still.

God, please, let me die! Let me die! Just let me fucking die!!

"Wow, great piece! Wish I'd had that for grafting that guy from the car fire."

"Put that in saline. Let's keep going."

Steve again felt liquid on his chest, warm this time, and he knew it must be his blood. It felt like a *lot* of his blood. His muscles burned.

The whirring noise fired up again and then the vibrating blade bit into his flesh again. The tearing pain, the burning, the horrible noise, the spatters of blood on his face.

He stared at the ceiling, red discoloration splashing through his field of vision. His mind screamed as the whirring machine peeled strip after strip of flesh from his chest, his sides, both of his upper arms. It was like being burned alive, the horrible pain that wrapped around his body and mind.

The pain in his right leg faded to less than an itch. The burning-hot pain in his upper body consumed his brain. He could feel the warm pool of his blood on the table, running down his sides in streams now, following his body, trickling over his hips and thighs.

The whirring had stopped and he could hear the rhythmic *pat pat pat* of his blood as it dripped onto the floor beneath the table. He felt lightheaded.

Please, please, please let me pass out!

"That is a lot of bleeding."

"Epi-soaked gauze, please."

"You may stop. Give him more fluid but only give blood to keep him from dying."

The last voice sounded familiar: Mr. Clark. Steve could see his strange eyes blazing from the shadows of his mind.

"The rest of you may go. Thank you for your assistance, Jenny. You have been a huge help, my dear."

He felt only vaguely aware of the motion around him, the pressure change as the door opened and people filed quietly out. It seemed like a hazy dream, voices in the next room when you were almost asleep. The dizziness only added to the dream-like feeling, but the pain in his chest and arms remained very real. He would give anything to stop that pain.

Anything!

He listened with dread as the footsteps moved toward him. He stared at the ceiling and waited for the question. This time two pale faces came into view, both in gray hats. Mr. Clark spoke and Steve tried to close his eyes.

"Mr. Prescott, you have fed us well tonight. You won't last much longer, but there is more pain waiting for you tomorrow. Do you understand?"

Yes! Yes, I am sorry! Please forgive me! Please make the burning stop! I am SOOOOOO SORRY! PLEEEEEEEASE!

They turned toward each other and nodded in unison. Then as he watched, they began to change. Steve knew hallucinations when he saw them, had done enough mushrooms with Kenny. Even knowing that what he saw had to be a hallucination, or a dream, or whatever the fuck it was, did nothing to stem the terror he felt as the demons transformed.

The dizziness cascaded into a vortex and the room seemed to tilt. The ceiling crumpled as he watched it, turning dark and moist. Suddenly he found himself lying in a wet, hot cave. The creatures peering hungrily down at him no longer vaguely resembled anything human.

He stared at the reptilian monstrosities with their wet, long teeth dripping yellowish liquid onto their bare gray chests. He thought of the raptors in *Jurassic Park*. The things grunted at him and he screamed silently in his head. His eyes wouldn't close but it didn't matter. Everything faded away to blackness and his last thought was that he hoped he had bled to death.

*   *   *

Nathan tried his best not to want any of the medicine that they put in his arm through the tube. It made him feel too weird. He thought it might be the cause of his horrible dreams. Or maybe it made them worse.

They're not dreams.

He already knew that, so it was easy to ignore his own voice in his head. They weren't dreams at all and Steve was in really big trouble. He didn't care about that so much but he felt really scared of the creatures that tortured him, had maybe even killed him, by now.

He cared a lot about Jenny, though. She became his favorite almost immediately and he knew that Jason liked her too. Jenny and Jason were his friends, real friends, and he felt really scared for her. The Lizard Men had clearly done something to her. When he had seen her last night he'd felt happy and relieved that she seemed okay.

But she had also seemed different and Nathan knew that the Lizard Men had done something. Now she was gone. She had told him that she wouldn't see him until Saturday, two days away. He worried that he might never see her again though he didn't know what he thought would happen.

You know they're not done with her. You have to tell Jason. He'll believe you because he's special too. Be a big boy and tell him.

The pain in his hand grew so big that he thought he might have to ask for the medicine. He tried all the tricks he could think of. He tried to make up a dream that his hand was buried in cold snow to take away the burning. He tried to pretend that he could throw the pain away and tossed his hand toward the door over and over.

It had worked for a while but now the pain grew out of his control and even though he was a big boy, he really needed to have the medicine. So he told Mommy and she went to get the black-haired nurse to bring him some.

"Just a little," he told her. Maybe if he didn't take too much the Lizard Men wouldn't get in his head again. Part of him wanted to go to the cave, just to make sure Jenny was alright now that she had left work, but most of him just felt scared.

Scaredy cat, scaredy cat. Who will help her if you don't? Who else knows how?

For a minute, Nathan thought about telling Mommy, but he knew that she wouldn't understand. Even if she believed him—and she wouldn't— she couldn't help. But Jason could. He could make Jenny safe and stop the Lizard Men before something bad happened to her. Nathan didn't know if that was true but he really, really wanted it to be. He hoped Jason would come soon so he could talk to him before the medicine made him go to sleep.

His mom brought back the nurse, who smiled and told him he would feel better in a minute. Nathan forced a smile and lay still while she stuck the needle into his tubing and slowly injected the medicine while chatting with his mom about something on TV.

The medicine felt warm in a way that seemed good and bad together as it ran up his arm. It made his head feel bigger. Nathan felt his eyes grow heavy almost immediately and leaned over against his mommy's soft leg. Her hand felt so good in his hair. The burning in his hand faded away like he really did put it in the snow or something, but he felt woozy and a little sick as the room grew dark.

Nathan listened to his mommy's voice, hoping that he would stay there in the big bed, his head on her leg. He couldn't tell what her words meant anymore, but the sound of her voice comforted him, like music. It seemed far away now but he could still hear it.

The fart smell woke him. He could still hear the music of Mommy's voice, but without opening his eyes, he knew where he had gone. For a moment he kept them closed and tried to make his mommy's voice grow louder, traveling to her. But then he thought of Jenny, and with a fluttering of fear in his chest, he balled up his hands, tried to be brave, and opened them.

The cave seemed a little brighter but no less hot or humid. He realized he lay curled up right where he had been when the creature had come for him. The thought of the dinosaur-looking demon bearing down on him made a whimper sneak out of his throat. Nathan pushed his fist into his mouth as he sat up.

He could see a lot better this time and realized the cave seemed lighter. He could make out streams of thick dark liquid that ran down the walls, forming puddles on the dirty floor. He got carefully to his feet, leaned against the wall, and tried hard not to touch the purple streams that looked really gross.

He saw no one nearby, but could hear a sound, muffled and not too far away. It came from deeper in the cave. Nathan really wanted to go back to his mom now, but something inside him told him that Jenny might be here, down where the scary sound came from. With his lower lip trembling, he walked down the sloping dirt floor, deeper into the cavern, toward the creepy noise.

He realized that he was barefoot only when he stepped into one of the purple pools in the uneven surface. He pulled his foot away in revulsion, the hot sticky liquid dripping from his foot, and dragged his toes over and over through dirt, trying to get the nasty stuff off.

His foot felt tingly and a weird sensation raced up his leg. His heart pumped faster and his breathing sounded crazy loud. He shoved his fist into his mouth again to stifle a building scream. Nathan could only barely feel his mommy's fingers still on his head, though he could tell when they rubbed him more urgently. He wondered if he had made a sound in his sleep. Then he noticed that the sound from deeper in the cave had stopped.

He stood as still as possible and tried to slow his breathing with his hand still perched in his mouth. Last time, the creatures noticed him when he felt scared and so he tried desperately to think about his mommy's voice, willing it to get louder. The more he tried to not be scared, the more he worried they could smell him and the more scared he became.

Scaredy cat, scaredy cat. Don't you want to see if Jenny is okay? Jason would want you to help her.

Maybe he should go back to his mommy and wait for Jason. A grown-up should help a kid, and Jason would know what to do.

"Like Steve helped you? Don't be a baby. Jason probably can't come here anyway, even if he believes you. Let's just go look and make sure she's okay."

The sound of his own voice calmed him more than his mommy's far-away one.

Nathan could hear the sound again: a wet, grunting sort of noise. Maybe it meant they couldn't smell him anymore. He continued slowly down the sloping floor, deeper into the cave.

He tried to pretend the voice in his head was Jason's and that he walked beside him, held his hand. For a moment he *did* feel a hand in his but he thought it was probably his mommy's. Still, he could kind of see Jason beside him, smiling, making him feel brave. Then the imaginary Jason faded away.

"Dreams are just like that," he mumbled and continued on.

His feet felt dirty but at least not sticky.

He came to a little rise where he took a few steps up and then stopped, just short of the crest where the floor turned downward again. Nathan paused for only a moment. No sense in getting scared again—the voice in his head would just make fun of him and then he would do the same stupid thing anyway. His mommy said that stupid was a bad word, but right now he felt grown-up enough to use a bad word. It actually was just a not-very-nice word and anyway, he felt pretty stupid. He was standing in a dream cave with sweat running down his thin chest, barefoot, waiting to crawl over the crest to where creatures were.

The floor felt almost wet but not muddy on his hands so he crouched down and crawled like a dog up to the crest of the little hill. At the top he lay down on his belly in the dirt and peered cautiously down the path. It got quite narrow as it plunged into a big open room in the cave below. He didn't want to be scared and so he wasn't.

In the middle of the room, two creatures squatted in the dirt over a meal. Steve's legs didn't exactly kick but kind of shook back and forth, flopping sporadically between the beasts that fed on him.

Nathan heard a tearing sound, another wet grunt and one of the Lizard Men raised its head. A long strip of stringy skin hung from its sharp teeth. Blood ran down its chest. It gulped the bloody strip down. Instead of being scared or feeling sick as the creatures literally tore Steve's flesh from his writhing body, Nathan felt only relief that the shuddering legs were not Jenny's.

It's not her. Can we please go back to Mommy now?

Wait.

He saw her on the far side of the cave. She lay naked on the floor, arms and legs splayed out to the side. Her skin glistened with sweat. Nathan watched as her head rocked slowly back and forth. Her voice rose up to him, but not the voice he knew from the hospital. He couldn't make out the words, but he could tell that her voice shifted chaotically back and forth between a sobbing cry and a demonic laugh. The piercing laugh sent an electric shock up his back. It sounded loud, cackling and kind of crazy.

And mean sounding. Evil.

He watched as Jenny, his Jenny, obscenely naked in the dirt, closed her eyes and cried. She opened them and turned her head to watch the Lizard Men tear flesh from Steve's jerking body. Then she laughed the evil laugh again.

At least she didn't seem to be in danger from the creatures.

Not yet, little man. But she will be if you don't help her soon.

Nathan concentrated on making his mommy's voice sound louder and the feel of her hands in his hair more real. It seemed easier this time. With little effort he traveled back to his hospital bed, to his mommy and hopefully soon to Jason.

Nathan opened his eyes and looked up at his mommy's concerned face. His head was in her lap and her fingers ran gently through his hair. He looked around but didn't see Jason.

"There, there, sweetheart. Just another dream. Just a bad dream," his mommy's voice told him. She sounded sad, he thought.

"No it's not," he whispered and closed his eyes again.

Then he drifted off to a dreamless sleep.

Chapter
8

Jenny felt like she was waking up from a dream. Not a dream where you lie in bed and mull over the details, good or bad, but the kind where you wake up confused and disoriented, unable to make the fragments and images gel into something with meaning. It could be anything from a nightmare to a wild fantasy, but your mind wasn't letting you in on the details.

That's exactly how I feel. I don't know where I was or what I did, but I have a feeling it was bad.

Jenny woke, or became aware, or whatever...

You're not waking up, because it wasn't a dream, was it?

...and found herself sitting on a vinyl sofa beside the Starbuck's Kiosk in the hospital lobby. A cold, untouched cup of coffee hung in her hand (which she had no memory of getting) and her head pounded with a headache of biblical proportions. A foul odor lingered for a moment but it disappeared quickly. She wondered if it might be part of the dream, or a memory or something. She still wore her scrubs from work but they stuck to her skin with sweat.

Jenny looked around the lobby nervously, but no one paid any attention to her. She got up from the vinyl seat, which stuck to her skin and clothes, tossed the cold Styrofoam cup into the garbage can and headed to the ladies room.

The face in the mirror shocked her. Her matted hair was pasted to the side of her head. She looked pale and dark rings surrounded her eyes. Smears of mascara striped her upper eyelids and her lipstick was all but gone. Her lips seemed shrunken and purple, except for the globs bunched in the corners of her mouth.

Jenny splashed cool water from the white porcelain sink onto her face with cupped hands, rubbing briskly to remove the smeared residuals of makeup and the salty white streaks of dried sweat, or tears. She did her best to dry her face off with the thin brown paper towels spit magically from the dispenser when she waved her hands past the motion detectors underneath.

Then she balled another towel up, moistened it, and sponged off the rings of sweat from beneath her armpits and between her breasts. A subtle smell of sulfur permeated the air when she'd finished. She tossed the towel toward the trash can where it spun off the rim and landed with a splat on the floor. She left it and pushed her way out of the restroom.

Jenny kept her head down as she briskly walked the short hall that took her past the elevators, through the walkway and to the parking garage. She avoided looking up and prayed quietly that she wouldn't see anyone she knew.

Especially not Jason.

Her eyes welled up from pent-up emotional turmoil.

The elevator took her to the top floor of the garage but her car wasn't there. A small pearl of panic grew in the middle of her chest. Then she remembered that she had moved it down a level so Jason wouldn't know she was still at the hospital. She didn't know why that mattered so much to her. Much more frightening, she realized she didn't know why she had needed to stay at the hospital.

Where have I been? What the hell did I do?

You did what needed to be done.

The second voice sounded like hers, but wasn't. An unsettling laugh hid beneath the words. Jenny started to cry harder and rode the elevator to the floor below.

Thankfully the garage was empty and her car sat only a short distance from the doors. She desperately needed to get away. She wanted to wash herself in a hot shower and then collapse into bed.

As she slid behind the wheel of her SUV the blue LED clock glared back at her.

11:45.

She had been at the hospital for three hours and she had no idea why. Jenny started the car and wiped the moisture from her eyes to clear her vision. As she drove out of the garage she let go of any attempt to control the flood of random thoughts and voices.

I hope Nathan is okay.

That fucker got what he deserved.

I miss Jason. How is that possible? I barely know him.

Dad's birthday is Sunday. I need to remember to call him. I wish I was home with Mom and Dad right now.

You must continue to help us. We'll show you how.

Fuck Dad, that bastard.

There was a little boy there, right? A little boy looking after me in the cave? Scared for me?

I am so tired.

I wish I was making love with Jason right now.

You have to help Nathan.

Can he help me? Can he save me?

She stopped listening, but the words droned on as she robotically drove the short distance to her apartment.

* * *

Jason sipped the stale coffee he had scrounged from the staff break room and sighed. Nathan looked pretty peaceful at the moment—or deeply stoned, probably both—and his initial contentment to just watch the boy get a little sleep turned to boredom. He felt like a jerk but he wanted the tired kid to wake up.

Nice.

Sherry told him that her son had suffered another nightmare but it didn't seem as bad this time. He hadn't cried or hollered out but she could tell that his sleep was disturbing. He woke up mumbling something but slept soundly now.

It surprised Jason how relaxed he felt talking with Nathan's mom, now. He worried for her, about her. She looked tired as hell and her hands trembled as she stroked her son's hair.

"When was the last time you really slept?" he asked.

Sherry smiled tightly. "I sleep a little here and there."

Jason had a picture flash through his head: his mom, sitting beside him in a bed just like Nathan's, holding his hand, her eyes red and her face pale.

He looked at his mom's double as she held Nathan's hand. Jason felt a lump form in his throat.

"Sherry," he said softly and put a hand on her shoulder. Her bloodshot eyes looked up at him. "Why don't you go home for a little while and sleep in your own bed? He's doing great and you could really use some rest."

Sadness contorted Sherry Doren's face and he again saw his mom, this time lying in her hospital bed, thin and wasted as cancer devoured her from inside.

"I'm sorry I wasn't a better mom."

He had said nothing—had just let his mom lie there with that agony. Even at eight he knew he should have said something.

"I don't want to leave him." Sherry looked down. She seemed like a kid herself. "I never wanted anything to happen to him. I never thought..."

She trailed off and started to cry. Jason sat down beside her, put an arm around her.

"I know, Sherry," he said and wished someone had been there to tell his mom that. "He's going to be fine now. He has a great mom and I know you'll keep him safe."

Sherry sobbed loudly and leaned against him.

"Thank you so much," she said without looking at him. He knew guilt kept her focus diverted. "I don't know what we would have done without you. He likes you so much. You and your girlfriend are his favorites."

Girlfriend?

The word made him smile. Guess he was pretty easy to read.

"Nathan is really special," he said, but then didn't know what else to tell her. "If you want, I would love to stay with him so you can go home and rest, freshen up, and have a little time for yourself." Sherry looked at him with relief and fear. "I won't let anything happen to him," he said.

"I know," she answered, and her smile was real. "Thank you so much. Maybe I can just stay until he wakes up so he knows I didn't leave him?"

"Of course," Jason said and squeezed her shoulder again. "Maybe I can get him something special for lunch. What's his favorite?"

"A Happy Meal?" a little voice said. Jason looked over at Nathan who blinked to clear glazed eyes.

"Hey, big guy," he said and enjoyed a genuine warm feeling thinking about Nathan's happiness to come. "A Happy Meal, huh?" He tossed a hand through Nathan's hair.

"Yeah," he muttered, a little more awake now. "I don't know what the prize is but it's got to be something good." He sat up and grimaced slightly as he bumped his hand on the side rail. "You have to tell them it's for a boy, okay? Otherwise I might get the girl prize." He wrinkled his nose at the thought and Jason laughed.

"Are you hungry now?" he asked.

"A little."

Jason looked at Sherry with raised eyebrows and she nodded. He smiled and nodded back.

"Tell you what," he said and got up from the edge of the bed. "How about I go get you a Happy Meal and when I get back maybe we can have some boy time." He looked at Nathan who seemed to like the sound of that. "If I bring back a movie for us, do you think it would be okay if your Mom sneaks home for a nap and a shower?"

"Sure," Nathan answered.

"Great," Jason announced. "Don't talk about me while I'm gone."

It took way less than an hour. The food court had a McDonald's and he grabbed a movie off the big cart on the Pediatric Ward right around the corner from Pedi ICU. He chose *Sky High* because it seemed like a boy kind of movie for their man time. He strolled back in with two McDonald's bags in no time.

"I'm back," he announced with a flourish. Nathan's face lit up and Sherry forced a weary wave. Nathan leaned over and kissed his mom on the cheek.

"Bye, Mom," he said with little ceremony—so much for being nervous. Jason took a burger and fries out of the bigger bag and then handed it to Nathan's mom.

"I got you something too. I figured you were hungry. Not too healthy I'm afraid."

Sherry sighed gratefully. "Thank you, Dr. Gelman," she said and got up with her lunch in hand.

"Jason," he corrected her. "If the five-year-old can call me that, it's probably okay for his mom, too."

"I'm almost six," a squeaky voice pointed out.

"Thank you, Jason," Sherry corrected herself, then bent over and gave her boy a long kiss on the cheek. "See you in a little while, sweetheart. Are you sure it's okay for Mommy to go for a little while?"

"Yeah, Mom," Nathan answered, squirming a little at the attention in front of Jason. "You wouldn't like this movie anyway." He flipped the case over in his un-bandaged hand. "It's not really a girl movie."

"Oh, I see," his mom humored him. "Well, I'll see you two boys in a little bit."

"Okay, Mom," Nathan said opening the case.

"He'll be fine; don't worry," Jason reassured. Sherry left and he turned to his young pal. "So have you seen this movie?" he asked.

"No," Nathan said. He handed it to him to pop into the machine on the cart beside the bed. "It looks totally cool though."

The Happy Meal prize turned out to be some kind of little plastic guy on a skate board which Nathan got very excited about and Jason snapped together. Then they munched their junk food and fries and watched Kurt Russell as an aging super hero as he raised his high school son to be the same.

Jason actually found the movie enjoyable but with a full belly a nagging voice in his head prodded him to have a conversation with Nathan. There were things he needed to know—things about his dreams. They scared him for reasons he couldn't understand.

He bravely watched the movie but said nothing.

After a while (sometime after Kurt Russell's movie son found out Dad really did have super powers), Jason looked over at Nathan to say something about the movie and noticed him staring past the TV, deep in thought. "You okay?" Jason asked with real concern.

"Yeah," the boy answered, but looked down at his bandaged hand. Jason wondered for a moment if Nathan just needed more pain medicine.

"What's up, buddy?" He picked up the remote from the bed and hit the pause button. They would find out how the heroes stopped the villain's evil pacifier device in a bit.

Nathan nervously looked up at him.

"You know," Jason said, "when guys are good friends they can tell each other anything. I really am your friend, Nathan."

"I know," Nathan said simply. He looked a little relieved. "Do you know where Jenny is?"

Jason felt confused.

"Well," he said, "she's probably at her home in bed. She was up all night working, you know?" He looked at Nathan carefully. "Why, buddy?"

"Do you love her?" Nathan asked. Jason gave an uncomfortable laugh at the surprising question. "I mean..." Nathan looked down, a little set off by the reaction. "She's your girlfriend, right?"

"I like her," Jason said softly. "I like her a lot. But I don't really know her that well, you know? We just met when we both met you. We both like you a lot, too."

"I know," Nathan said. He looked up then, hard, determined—and old. "I have to tell you something."

A long and uncomfortable pause hung between them.

"What is it, Nathan? Is it about Jenny?" Jason found he couldn't really understand the sense of dread that grew in him at the little boy's ageless aura.

"Yes," Nathan said holding his gaze.

"Well, what is it?" he asked again impatiently.

"I'm afraid you won't believe me," Nathan said and sniffled. "It's about the Lizard Men."

Jason felt relief spread across his chest and he sighed.

The dreams.

Dreams? The ones you see too, in alleys in the dark?

He ignored the second voice and put a hand on Nathan's back.

"Is it about the dreams?" he asked.

Nathan leaned into him, eyes blazing with fear or knowledge or both. His voice took on a conspiratorial whisper.

"They're not dreams," he said and Jason felt a cold finger tickle up his back.

He realized, remembering his terror, that not only did he believe Nathan–

Remember me?

—but that he had known that all along. Deep inside a part of him started to remember something, something frightening. "Tell me what you saw," he whispered back, frightened for Nathan.

And now for Jenny.

"They're not just in the cave, I think," Nathan said and snuggled closer to Jason. "They're here…"

Jason listened as the little boy described his dreams.

He had heard this tale before.

* * *

Steve's mind cleared slowly. The veil lifted more quickly once he grew aware of the animals that fed on him. As he did, he remembered to be terrified, but in a vague and dreamy sort of way.

This didn't feel anything like dreaming though. It felt more like being totally drugged. He knew goddamn well that he wouldn't wake up from this but his head swam fuzzily all the same. He knew the creatures tore at his flesh, but he felt too wasted to really give a shit, so he just played his part, being scared.

A moaning sound made him open his eyes and he looked at the raptor-man eating him alive. Thin trails of blood ran down its long chin. The creature tilted its head back to swallow a large piece of muscle. Movement to his right caught his eye. The disgust of seeing the other creature bend over him and tear away a strip of flesh from his chest did nothing to lessen the excitement at being able to move his head.

Oh, fuck yeah! Oh God it feels good to move.

Steve blinked his eyes and giggled a little at the feel of his lids sliding gently and easily across his eyeballs. Then he felt pressure and a tug at his chest, heard the moan again. He realized the moan was his voice, but the thought just sat there. It didn't raise any alarms.

Maybe I did bleed to death. Maybe this is hell.

The pain rose in intensity and became more real but he decided to ignore it for another few moments. Instead he luxuriated in the feel of being able to see and move. His eyes traced along the dark ceiling of what looked like a wet cave. He turned to his right, surprised to see a naked woman lying in the corner.

The woman sprawled out on her back, her arms and legs splayed wide apart. Her creamy skin glistened with a film of sweat that made her young and athletic build even more erotic. She moved her head slowly from side to side, mumbling something he couldn't make out. Steve twisted his head farther toward her, trying to get a better look at her naked form. Man, she looked good. He watched her, hoping she would move her left leg a little. Man, what he could do to her.

Come on baby. Show me your hot...

A sudden, sharp pain tore through his chest and he grunted in anguish. Oh, Jesus, that hurt. Instinctively, he threw his arms up and felt them wrap around the creature's head. He turned and looked into the now-blinding glow of the bright red eye in the side of a scaly dinosaur head. The long teeth, the same long teeth that seemed so out of place in the mouth of Mr. Clarke's partner, latched onto a thick piece of flesh and tore it from his rib cage.

There seemed nothing at all dreamy about the pain now and he shrieked in agony. Wrapping his arms tightly around the large beast, he lifted himself out of the blood-stained dirt. When the piece of flesh tore loose, he stared in horror at the creature, the long strip of his bloody skin hanging from its mouth. Then a movement caught his attention, past the demon, in the background.

Steve tried to make sense of what he saw, up the sloping trail, past the creatures feeding on him. At the top of the little rise, a little kid peered down. Seeing the tussled hair and pink cheeks, even though he couldn't be sure in the dark at such a distance, he had no doubt. It was Sherry's little brat, come to watch him.

What are you looking at, you little asshole? You fuckin' did this!

Steve watched the kid pull away from the top of the rise as he let his head fall back into the dirt. *If I get out of here, I will burn the rest of that fuckin' little brat. I'll tear his chubby little arms off and beat him fucking to death with them. He'll feel this pain.*

I'm not sorry I hurt that little shit! I'm only sorry I didn't finish fucking him off!

Another set of teeth tore deeply into the flesh of his left armpit. He forgot all about the kid at the top of the hill. He forgot about the hot naked chick he wanted to brutally fuck.

All he thought about was the pain and the never-ending sound of his own screams.

* * *

Nathan snuggled under the stiff, scratchy hospital sheets. He pulled the softer blanket from his bed at home, the one with the Red Power Ranger from *Dino Thunder* (he still liked them better than *Mystic Force*), up next to his cheek and breathed in the warm familiar scent. He wanted to be there of course, but felt too afraid of being away from Jason. He had watched his friend carefully as he told of his dreams...

They're not dreams

...and he knew that Jason understood. His face had been sad, maybe a little scared, but Nathan could tell that he believed him and nothing else really mattered. In his heart he felt certain that Jason could help him.

Help you what? What do you want to do? Save Steve from the Lizard Men so he can hurt you or your mommy again?

"No," he whispered in a sleepy voice. "We have to save Jenny and stop them from hurting someone else. They won't stop with Steve."

He knew that for sure. The creatures didn't care about him or Mommy. They just wanted to feed. They would feed on him just the same as Steve if they could. Anyway, it was way too late for Steve. He would be dead soon. Maybe he was dead already.

"He's toast," he said in his best Red Ranger voice—but he still shuddered at the thought.

So how would he save Jenny? What could a single boy do, even with the help of a grown-up? He didn't know but he felt better now that he had told Jason everything. Jason loved Jenny and he would think of something.

Nathan yawned, snuggled deeper beneath his soft blanket and pushed away the rigid sheets even more. His hand throbbed but not so bad that he couldn't sleep. He knew somehow that there would be no bad dreams, at least no trip to the cave, so he wanted to rest for when he needed to be strong.

The doctors would be by later to tell him when he would have his operation, but he didn't feel scared about that. Jason told him it would probably be tomorrow but that he would get medicine to sleep through it, so it wouldn't hurt. He felt a lot more scared about the being asleep part.

But not right now. Right now he floated toward an easy sleep that he knew waited for him. No caves, no Lizard Men. Maybe he would dream about being a Power Ranger. Boy, then he would know what to do.

Nathan drifted into a dreamless, restful slumber.

* * *

Jason hadn't been honest with Sherry, but how could he tell her what he had heard from her son? Didn't she have enough to worry about already? Jason knew that missed the point though. He couldn't possibly tell Sherry because he believed Nathan.

They're not really dreams.

The eerie thought that this was somehow familiar spoke to him from across a few decades, trying to help him see something he had buried a long time ago. The fear of what lurked back there felt much bigger than his need to see it, so he left it alone for the moment. He forced his thoughts back to more pressing worries—Nathan and Jenny.

Jason knew he wanted to keep them both safe. From the sound of Nathan's dreams, Jenny was anything but. And a boy eluding Lizard Men in a cave by himself sure didn't seem much better. Jason was in awe at the courage of this kid. He had to help him and together they could help Jenny.

A sudden explosion of activity down the hall pulled Jason back from his thoughts. He looked up. Dietrich moved toward him at a much faster pace than he'd come to expect from his laid-back friend. When he noticed Jason, he motioned, tight-lipped and serious.

"What're you doin' here?" he asked as he hurried by. "Thought you were off today."

Jason stepped into pace with his buddy, who clearly wanted to get down the hall to the large double doors labeled ER as quickly as possible. "Visiting the kid from the other night," he said, watching his fellow resident's lab coat flutter behind him. "What's the hurry?"

"Gunshot wound. Supposed to be a cop," Dietrich answered. He stopped at the punch-key pad beside the ER doors and tapped in his code. The doors swung open. "I heard it's that shift sergeant we like. What's his name?"

Jason shrugged and watched Rich hang his stained lab coat on a peg outside the Trauma Bay.

"Come on, you know him. Big guy with kind of red hair with a lot of gray? He's a sergeant, remember? He came in special that day your kid upstairs came in."

Jason did remember. Maloney was his name. He always chided them in the ER. Great guy. He once told him if he ever had any problems to call him at the precinct, had even given him a card even, though Jason wouldn't be able to find it to save his life.

"Maloney?" he said.

"Yeah, yeah. That's it—Maloney." Rich pulled on a surgical cap and mask.

"Someone shot him?" Jason asked. He felt a little numb. He really liked that guy. Sort of like a big brother at work, though he knew nothing about him outside of the small world of his hospital.

"That's what they say," Rich said as he pulled a blue plastic gown over his head. "Hey, you wanna give me a quick hand? The Trauma Chief is up in the OR with their third year, so it's just me and two of their interns until they get someone over here."

"Sure," Jason said and started to dress out in his own gown. He felt a little dizzy. Someone had shot Maloney?

He was still struggling to tie up his mask when the doors burst open and a stretcher was thrust into the room. Two jumpsuit-clad medics maneuvered it and a third rode on top, straddling the patient, pounding out CPR as he rode. The medic at the foot of the stretcher barked out a quick report.

"Fifty-year-old police officer—single gunshot wound to the head— entrance looks to be through the right eye, large exit wound at the left occipital region—good vitals at the scene so we scooped and ran—coded as we pulled up just a minute ago..."

The medic hopped off the stretcher and the ER nurses helped the other two medics heave the man from the wooden backboard onto the ER bed. The nurse at the far side took over the chest compressions.

"We've got a good airway," the medic continued. "Intubated at the scene with a number eight endotracheal tube."

He continued his report but Jason stopped paying attention. He watched as Rich listened with his stethoscope and the nurse squeezed the green bag that forced air into the cop's lungs. He looked at the swollen face of the patient.

His right eye-socket looked impossibly large and Jason saw no trace of the actual eye. The whole right side of his cheek and forehead had swollen to twice their normal size and turned a deep crimson color. If he hadn't already known it was Maloney, he could never have told from the misshapen face. As the nurse pounded on the dead man's chest, dark purple gore mixed with chunks of grey snot spewed from behind the head. Jason looked down, closed his eyes and swallowed hard.

"Rich," he said softly.

Rich looked up at him, face all business, but then he followed Jason's gaze to the pool of old blood and brain tissue that now spilled onto the floor.

"Stop, man," Jason choked out.

Dietrich's shoulders sagged. "Yeah," he said. He sounded beat, though they had worked for less than a minute. "Stop, everyone."

The nurse who had been doing CPR stepped back and Rich felt for a pulse. Then he looked at the clock.

"Time of death—fifteen forty-three," he said, then snapped off his rubber gloves and threw them onto the patient's belly in disgust. "Fuck me," he said and headed for the door.

Jason stood and stared at the man he barely knew but had considered some sort of friend. He wanted to feel sad, angry, or something. Instead, he just felt numb. He looked over at the medic, who leaned across his run report, filling in the blanks. Past him a large group of uniformed police officers had formed, huddled together like a football team, talking in hushed voices. Planning their revenge, he hoped. Why the fuck not?

"Did they get the guy?" Jason asked the medic in a soft voice. For some reason it felt irreverent to let the other cops hear him.

"Who?" the medic asked without looking up.

Who? What the fuck is wrong with you, dude? Jesus!

"The guy who shot Maloney," he said with some irritation. "The fucker that shot this cop." He realized his voice had risen and the nurses looked over in uncomfortable silence then back at each other.

"Shit," the medic said as he tore the pink copy from the run report and stuck it in a box beside the podium. A nurse filled out her own paperwork next to him. "I thought I said it in my report – self-inflicted. Suicide."

Jason suppressed the bile and anger that rose in his chest. "Bullshit, not this guy."

The medic shrugged. "I don't know what to tell you, Doc. I was at the scene and this dude definitely shot himself. His wife says he's been acting all crazy the last few days—having horrible nightmares, that kind of thing. She said he kept telling her the Lizard Men were going to get him. I guess he kind of…" Jason's hand on his arm cut the medic off. "You okay, Doc? He a friend of yours?"

Jason struggled to find his voice but couldn't. The room started to tilt, spin madly and he thought he might pass out. The medic's hand at his elbow kept him on his feet. He saw the medic's mouth moving, his eyes full of concern, but he couldn't hear a thing. It felt like watching TV with the sound off. Jason shrugged the hand from his arm and headed for the door and down the hall to the ER exit, nearly sprinting from there to the ambulance bay. He maneuvered around the few rescue trucks parked there, smashing his knee painfully on the chrome step on the one at the back of the line. He ignored the pain, turned into the little alley beside the entrance and bent over, steadying himself with one hand against the blackened brick wall.

He vomited once then spit the remaining bit of breakfast out of his mouth onto the ground. Jason cleared his throat, spit again, then leaned back against the wall. He looked up and down the alley, hopeful that no one had seen him. He was alone.

The sudden memory of the men from the other night burst its way to the front of his brain—two bizarre men with glowing eyes, in long coats and top hats,. Jason felt the grip of certainty envelope his chest. He didn't know why he knew it, but he did.

The men with the glowing eyes were Nathan's Lizard Men. They had driven the police sergeant to kill himself and now threatened Jenny and Nathan.

And I know where I remember them from.

* * *

It's nighttime. The towels on the windows don't work this well.

She awoke to that thought feeling hot—still very tired—and scared. She kicked the blankets off of her body and discovered she was naked, coated in a thin film of sweat. She felt a chill course through her and shuddered, then pulled the sheet back up. Jenny cleared her eyes and saw the apartment was quite dark, save for a sliver of light from the partly opened bathroom door. She lay in the dim light, stared at the shadows on the walls of her bedroom, and tried to remember why she felt so anxious and frightened.

Did I have a bad dream? Is that it?

Her mind was bizarrely blank. She remembered she'd wanted to spend more time with Jason but she had an appointment. The emptiness returned as she realized she had no idea what that appointment had been for. She had a mental picture of the coffee kiosk at work and of feeling scared—of looking at herself in the mirror and sneaking out of the hospital. She wanted to avoid seeing Jason.

No, wait. That part must be a dream.

Images of the day felt weird and disconnected—like a dream. She searched her mind for some details but found only a few breadcrumbs that led nowhere. There had been a cave, hot and humid. She had been naked in the cave, and in danger from something so terrifying her mind wouldn't give it up, no matter how hard she demanded the details. But the boy had been there, had watched her from a ledge or something. He wanted to help her but couldn't. And there were monsters of some sort.

The phone beside her bed made her jump. A small yelp escaped her throat.

"Jesus, Mary and Joseph..." That had been as close as her dad had ever come to swearing when she had been a little girl. She held the clearest recollection of the first time she had heard him swear. He had called someone a "damn asshole" on the phone from his den. She had been seventeen, not shocked or disappointed, but relieved.

"Human after all," she repeated now, nearly a decade later. The phone rang a third time and she rolled to the side of the bed and picked it up, the sheet falling off of her. She shivered and cleared her throat.

"Hello," she said, surprised at how raspy her voice sounded. Her throat felt dry and sore. Jenny cleared it again and swallowed. "Hello?" she said a little more clearly.

"Baby, is that you? It's Daddy, honey. Are you okay?"

Her head swam. Her stomach tightened. Why did she feel so anxious and confused?

"Daddy?"

"Yeah, Jen. Your mom and I are worried sick. Are you alright? We haven't heard from you in a couple of days."

A bright light popped on inside of her head. A movie screen flashed a schizophrenic series of images, some horrible, some wonderful all of her family. She tried desperately to make the room stop spinning, to stop the nauseating barrage of memories, but couldn't.

"Jen, honey? Are you there?" Her dad's voice sounded deeply concerned. She had to say something.

Say something, damnit.

"I'm, uh...I'm sorry, Dad." Her mind raced for an acceptable follow up to that brilliant introduction. "I've, um, been working nights..."

There you go—now you're talkin'.

"...and I was sleeping. Sorry, I think I was having a bad dream." She sat up and leaned over to turn on the light beside her bed. It burned into her retinas and she rested her forehead on her free hand. "I'm sorry I worried you guys. I've just been real tired. I'm not a night person, as you know."

Her dad laughed. "Yeah, we do. Just a little T and G, huh?"

T and G—Tired and Grumpy. That had always been the big tease when she was worn out in High School. Her brother had used a less kind "B" word for it when they were away from Mom and Dad.

My brother? Why does that feel weird, too?

"Yeah, I guess," she said.

A voice called to her from the shadows, sinister and familiar. She pushed it out of her mind. "How's Mom?" she asked reflexively.

"She's great, Jen. Don't worry." He sounded a little sheepish. "I'm so sorry I woke you. I guess we still see you as our little girl."

More images assaulted her, like pictures on a screen, and a white pain shot through her temple. She nearly dropped the phone. They didn't make any sense, the nightmares of her dad doing unspeakable things. Where in the hell did they come from and why were they inside of her head? Her aching head.

He just wants to fuck you again, that son of a bitch!

Her voice, but not. A horrible thing to think. She wanted to scream.

"...you know how she is," her dad said. "Go back to sleep, baby. Call us tomorrow?"

"Sure, Dad," she choked out and managed somehow to keep the vomit in back of her throat from spewing onto the receiver.

"Love you, Jen," her Dad said from the receiver now pressed forcefully to her forehead. "Mom sends her love too."

Jenny pulled the phone near her mouth. She said, "Love you both," then nearly slammed it into the cradle on the nightstand. She struggled to her feet, legs aching, and weaved to the bathroom.

She fell painfully to her knees in front of the commode, leaned forward and vomited. Wretch after wretch of burning, bilious vomit filled the bowl until her sides ached and she thought she would pass out from the need to breathe. She intermittently felt on fire and shivered from the cold air on her naked skin.

Finally, the slideshow in her head, the rapid-paced barrage of conflicting images stopped. Jenny lay panting over the open bowl, staring at her own vomit. She reached an unsteady hand up and flushed the smelly mess, then leaned back against the cool wall.

After a moment, she struggled to her feet and propped her hands over the sink. Her sweat-streaked face stared back in the mirror and she saw a brief flash of herself from the hospital—the same sweat streaked hair, white lines of salt and dead-looking eyes.

That's not a dream. That really happened earlier today.

She began to cry softly as she splashed water on her face...

Just like before

...and rinsed her mouth. She brushed her teeth, still sobbing quietly. She avoided looking at her reflection and wrapped herself in a powder blue terrycloth robe that hung behind the bathroom door. In the kitchen, Jenny grabbed a citrus peach Fresca from the fridge door, cracked it open, skipped the glass, and wrapped herself in the soft blanket she kept on her couch; the robe wasn't quite warm enough now. She sipped her cool drink, soothing on her aching throat, and watched with the calm of those resigned to fate as a new image materialized in her mind.

Just like a home movie, the memory of lying naked on her back, on the dirty floor of a hot, wet cave materialized in her mind. Just past her, horrible creatures feasted on the still-live body of a blood-soaked man. He fought back weakly, kicking up his legs in pathetic protest as the monsters tore strip after strip of bloody flesh from his body. The bloody man looked at her, but instead of pleading for help his expression was filled with anger and lust.

Another face peered down at her from another direction; she recognized it immediately. Confused, she watched Nathan over the lip of a little rise in the path that lead down to the large room she was in. He looked scared but seemed oddly older than five. As she watched, he slipped away, and disappeared from sight.

"Please help me," she called after him.

The image dissipated.

Back on her couch, Jenny wiped away the hot tears burning her cheeks and sipped the cool soda. She wiped snot off her upper lip with the back of her hand.

I'm going insane.

The thought terrified her, but no better explanation offered itself up. So she lay there, vulnerable and alone.

A sudden thought gave her hope and she crawled off the couch. Her blanket fell to the ground and her can of Fresca missed the coffee table. It fell on its side to the floor where it slowly bled its peach-flavored contents onto her throw rug.

Her scrubs were on the floor beside her bed, where she'd left them in a heap, and she tore through them like a woman possessed, tears streaming down her cheeks. It was in the left side pocket of her scrub jacket.

Jenny looked at the little sliver of paper with Jason's name on it and scribbled below, his home and cell phone numbers. He had drawn a smiley face and "I had so much fun" underneath. Her heart warmed. What guy did that?

Jenny sat back on the couch in the other room with the phone and his number cradled in her lap. She rocked slowly back and forth.

What would she say? Could she really let him see her like this? She barely knew him, but the intense draw she felt to him, and Nathan too, felt almost like love.

Did she dare risk that for this insanity?

Do you dare risk being alone right now? You know they aren't dreams.

A violent shake of her head pushed that thought from her mind and she dialed the home number from the strip of paper. The phone chirped in her ear as she collapsed backward into the cushion with her eyes closed. She could picture him, getting up and looking for a cordless phone. He wore boxers with no shirt.

That made her smile a little.

Chapter
9

Jason stared at the ceiling fan that turned slowly above his bed. His eyes had acclimated after several hours of peering into the darkness at the spinning shadow. He knew that sleep wouldn't come anytime soon, if at all.

He didn't want to visit the nightmare that had peeked over the wall he had built some twenty some years ago, but he felt more afraid not to. There were answers there that he suspected would be needed soon.

I've been there before and survived. I have to go again if I want to help Nathan and save Jenny.

His mind still kept enough hidden that fear of the unknown nearly trumped the anxiety of what might be revealed. He closed his eyes and drifted.

Let me sneak up on this memory...

His first nightmare of the cave had been the night they had drilled holes in his leg and driven long steel pins into his thigh bone. The medicine had made him feel weird and the dream—

trip

—had been easy to write off to the morphine haze. He was entitled to a few nightmares. His father (he could never think of him as "Dad") had just hours ago punched his mother's face to a purple mass. He could still remember the feel of warm blood that spattered on his cheek when Mom's lip had split. And then he grabbed Dad's arm (a big hero at seven) and he remembered very little after that, except the feel of his femur snapping under the impact of a steel-toed boot and his head slamming into a counter.

Jason shook out a raspy sigh. He pushed the details of the beating away and tried to remember the nightmare instead. It happened right after the long steel pins had been drilled through his skinny leg just above his knee.

They had made it out of the ER and his mother leaned over his bed, her bruised and swollen face beside him, her eyes closed. He thought about how Mom's back must have ached in that uncomfortable position. He could see the blue threads they had used to sew her lip back together.

It occurred to Jason that she should have been in her own room, under observation for a closed head injury, instead of leaning awkwardly over her little boy. How had he never thought of that before? Had she refused treatment to be with him? All these years and he never wondered who had taken care of his mom.

You are one selfish fucking piece of work, Jason Gelman.

He wiped a tear from his face, this one just for Mom, and let the memory continue at its own rambling pace. Sleep had been pretty elusive that night too. He remembered having little pain, but he had been nauseous from the narcotics. There had been panic attacks where he imagined his father would come through the door, into his room, and finish what he had started.

Jason had no doubt the monster wanted them both dead. He could not fathom what he had done to create so much hate.

Then he had woken up in a dark cave.

His memory of the cave seemed quite different from what Nathan described—not the cave itself but the creatures. He remembered no one else being there with him. He had never seen them carrying anyone, much less the horrible picture Nathan had given of them tearing someone apart.

His little buddy believed that someone had been Steve, his own tormentor. Jason found it hard to picture the creatures he remembered preying on a shithead like Steve. They seemed more like Boogeymen after scared children. And that was what they had been. His recurrent dreams—

trips

—had been classic night terrors: monsters chased him in the dark and the feeling that he couldn't scream. Moving in slow motion no matter how hard he'd tried to run. He remembered the creatures fed somehow on that fear but never did they EAT anyone.

They're braver now, and stronger.

Jason shuddered at the thought. His horrible visions had been countless sprints through dark, humid passageways, the grunting creatures hot on his heels. He remembered the feel of hot, wet breath on his neck.

He had no memory of them ever catching him though. They had never actually touched him; he knew that with certainty. He would sure as shit remember being touched and had been haunted by that deadly possibility many times during his childhood. The thought of that had driven his fear, and maybe their hunger. No, this seemed different—and much, much worse. Nathan seemed convinced that his Lizard Men—

Our Lizard Men

—had actually KILLED Steve or would shortly. It just didn't fit.

The phone on his nightstand hollered a sudden, loud chirp and Jason nearly shit himself. His left fist smacked painfully into the headboard when he jumped. The impact made him swear under his breath.

The phone rang again and he leaned over to grab it as he looked at the clock—eleven fifteen p.m. Who the hell would call him this late? He pulled the phone out of its cradle, which crashed to the floor between the nightstand and his bed, and pushed the talk button as he put it to his ear.

"Hello?" he said a little louder than he meant to. There was a long pause but he heard a sob on the other end. For a moment, he thought it might be a wrong number or a crank call but then a soft response broke free.

"Jason?"

He knew the voice immediately, even through the strained breathing.

"Jenny? Are you okay? What's wrong?"

Jason listened to the contorted sniffles and wished he could reach through the phone to hold her.

"I'm sorry to call so late," she said softly. She sounded a little more in control.

"No, no," he said, fearful for a moment that she might try and end the call. "It's okay. I'm up." Jason swung out of bed and started pacing the room in his boxers, the nervous energy more than he could handle lying down. "What happened? Are you alright?"

"Yeah," she said, and he heard a nervous laugh. "So much for the low-maintenance-girlfriend thing, huh?"

Jason smiled.

"Look," she said. "I had this really bad nightmare and I'm just feeling kind of—I don't know—scared a little and"—she paused and he envisioned her closing her eyes—"lonely."

"I'm right here," he said simply.

She sighed again. "Jason, I don't want to ruin whatever we're starting here and I don't want to sound... I just..." She paused again—gaining some strength. "Look, if it isn't too crazy sounding, do you think you could come over here and just hang out for a little while? I'm just kind of scared." Her voice cracked.

"I'll be right over," he said. "Give me two minutes to pull on some clothes. Can you give me directions?"

He pulled on some jeans with the phone tucked between his shoulder and ear as she told him how to get to her apartment. Then he tossed it on the bed to slowly lose its charge, not nearly patient enough to set the cradle back on the nightstand. He pulled on a sweatshirt, grabbed his cell phone and his keys, and practically sprinted out of his apartment.

* * *

Jason reminded himself that her nervousness had nothing to do with him being there. He naturally defaulted to the assumption that a woman acting uncomfortable around him meant she almost certainly wanted to be somewhere else. But this time, no matter what the relationship cards held for them, he knew exactly what had her upset.

"Are you sure I can't get you something?" she asked for the third time and twisted her fingers together in her lap. She looked adorable in her jeans and long-sleeve T-shirt with a pair of fuzzy pink socks on her feet. Jason knew that she really needed to have something to do, so he relented.

"Sure, I'll have whatever you're having. Do you want me to get it?"

"No, no," she said, clearly relieved to have a task. She got up and headed over to the adjoining kitchen where she leaned across the breakfast bar toward him. "I kind of want a glass of wine," she said a little sheepishly. "Is that okay?"

Jason considered himself more of a beer guy, but he would drink anything if it would make this woman he felt so drawn to feel more comfortable. "Wine sounds great."

Jenny smiled and disappeared into the kitchen where he heard a drawer open and the sound of a bottle on the counter. The small, comfortable living room looked exactly as he would have pictured it—simple and feminine—a few girly knick-knacks, a large picture in black and white of a city street in Spain over the couch. On the built-in bookshelves beside her TV stand, he noticed several pictures that lay face down.

"Sure I can't give you a hand?" he asked.

"I'm good, just grabbing a corkscrew."

Jason figured he had a moment, went over to the bookshelves and quickly peeked at the three facedown pictures. All three held pictures of what he assumed to be her family. One showed a middle-aged couple, smiling in the way that only happy couples with a long history can, their faces pressed together closely. Another showed Jenny in a cap and gown, flanked by the same man, presumably her Dad, and another guy, who looked a few years younger than her—brother perhaps?

The last showed her and the same guy. *Definitely a brother*, he decided, sitting in front of her smiling parents, an overly decorated Christmas tree in the background. Jason felt the tug of sadness he always had when he saw happy families. Jealousy, he knew. But something else about the pictures troubled him and it took a second to grab it. The family in the picture seemed happy.

"Everything okay?" He turned around quickly like a kid caught with Dad's *Penthouse* and blushed. She looked at him without anger or irritation but did seem pretty curious about what he was doing. She held two glasses of red wine out in front of her.

"I'm sorry. I didn't mean to snoop," he said, taking one of the glasses. "Just sort of looking around and trying to get to know you. You can tell a lot about someone by what they have on their shelves." He shrugged awkwardly.

God, please don't be pissed.

"What did you learn?" she asked. She seemed relieved to have something to talk about.

"Not much," he said sheepishly as he joined her on the couch.

So now what? He watched her sip her wine and tasted his own. Not bad actually. Should he wait for her to bring up the nightmares? He couldn't very well dive right in.

Thanks for the wine... have you been transported to a dark, hell-like cave where Lizard Men tore a man apart while he was still alive? Oh, by the way, was Nathan there?

"You doing okay?" he asked instead.

"Yeah," she said and ran a hand through her hair. She smelled fantastic. "I'm really sorry that I called you so late. I'm a little embarrassed now that you're here." She sipped her wine again. "It's kind of hard to explain." She looked at him—gauging his response it seemed.

"Do you want to talk about it?" he asked after a moment. "I have bad dreams sometimes too," he added and then regretted it. What the hell difference did that make?

Jenny scrunched up her (very cute) face as she thought about something. Her hand found his on the couch.

"It's not just the dream." She squeezed his hand. "It's how I felt when I woke up. It's not just tonight either." She looked at him tentatively. "Lately, I have this weird, kind of... I don't know—this weird feeling—like things are sort of out of place."

She sighed and looked down at her hand in his. She studied their hands, their intertwined fingers, then smiled. She looked back up at him and held his eyes. "I swear this wasn't a trick to get you over here." She looked down again. "But I am afraid, Jason"—her hand squeezed his tightly—"of the dream and other stuff—and I would really like it if you would stay."

Jason was mesmerized.

"I'll be a perfect gentleman, and I would love to stay with you," he said. "I'm off all day tomorrow and I have no where I need to be."

Jenny laughed. "Well you don't have to be a total gentleman," she said nervously, then kissed him gently on the mouth. His heart swelled. He wrapped his arms around her, hugging her tightly.

"I'll keep you safe." It sounded pretty corny but he hoped she knew he meant it.

She leaned back, took his other hand and stood up. "Can we just go to bed?" she asked awkwardly. "I'm exhausted."

Jason nodded and followed her into the bedroom. The lights were out but she looked gorgeous and erotic silhouetted in the crease of light from her bathroom. She pulled off her jeans, left on her top and slipped quickly under the covers. Jason joined her and she slid over to make room.

Jason's hands trembled as he fumbled with the button to his jeans and awkwardly kicked them off, leaving them under the covers. The smell of her on the sheets drove him crazy as she snuggled up next to him. Her soft, bare legs sent a chill up his spine as she got closer. Jason shifted his hips away from her slightly. The last thing he wanted after his noble I'll-just-hold-you-and-keep-you-safe line was for her to feel the effect she had on him. He breathed her scent in and wrapped his arms around her tightly.

"Thank you so much, Jason," she said.

"You're welcome," he said, unsure what else to say. "Do you want to tell me about your dream?" he asked.

"In the morning, okay?" she said sleepily.

Jason lay with her, but his mind raced. He had lots of questions and he suspected a few answers that he wanted to share.

In the morning.

He held her close, lost for a moment in the softness of her hair, then he thought of Nathan.

He sighed and waited for morning.

Chapter 10

Nathan thought he woke up because he couldn't stop thinking about his operation. Well, not the operation, but the part where they would give him medicine to make him sleep. A sleep he couldn't wake up from. The lady doctor, the one that Jason knew, had come by and talked to him and his mom for a little while after it was already dark out. She seemed nice enough, but Nathan didn't trust her like he did his friend. He hoped Jason would come by before the operation began.

He wanted to talk to him. He had no idea whether he could go to the cave from that sleep or not and he wanted to ask Jason what he thought. He asked the lady doctor about dreams and she had made a funny face, said she was pretty sure people don't dream in the medicine sleep (she called it a long doctor word that started with an "a" that Nathan couldn't remember).

Still, these weren't *really* dreams, so Nathan felt uneasy. Maybe that didn't apply to him at all. All he knew was that if he went to the cave, he might not be able to get back on his own like he had before and that felt pretty scary.

Scaredy cat, scaredy cat.

Maybe so, but sometimes things really were scary. This wasn't like his bathrobe lying on his dresser that looked like a monster. The more you looked, the more it appeared to be some fanged beast. Even though you KNEW it was just your bathrobe, eventually you had to get up and turn on the light to be sure. No, that was just a silly game kids played in their heads. These really were monsters and Nathan felt terrified of what they could do if he couldn't get away.

You saw what they did to Steve.

Nathan sighed, a big grown-up sigh, and pulled the soft cover from home up around his shoulders. It was still nighttime but he had no idea how long nighttime was or when the light would come back on.

Maybe just a few minutes but probably not. He wished he was big enough to drive a car. He could go to Jason's apartment and talk to him. He still worried a lot about Jenny. She seemed fine when he saw her last but he felt like a lot could change in that cave.

Go check on her, scaredy cat. You can sneak up on them quiet-like again, like last time. Sneak up on them like Red Ranger and make sure she's okay. What are ya—scared?

"Yeah, a little," he admitted softly.

Maybe just a quick peek. If he did go now, he could come right back.

Nathan concentrated on the soft blanket rubbing against his cheek and the steady sound of Mommy's breathing from the hospital chair. Then he tentatively closed his eyes.

It came much quicker this time so he guessed he must be getting better—at least at going. He would see if he could be quick at getting back. He opened his eyes and found himself standing against the wall in the narrow passageway just a short distance from the ledge where he had seen Jenny in the room.

Good, now be quick.

Nathan shuffled quietly up the path to the ledge, his body coated in dust after only a moment in the wet heat. He squatted down on all fours like a kitty cat and moved slowly the last few feet to the edge. Then he cautiously looked into the room.

Relief washed over him. He didn't see Jenny lying naked in the corner anymore. He was more relieved that the Lizard Men weren't there, but then worried about where they might be hiding. He peered nervously over his shoulder.

A real Power Ranger wouldn't be scared. Anyway, you can always hear them grunting before they get close and they make that nasty fart smell when they first come around.

Huh. Nathan didn't think he knew that before but he thought it seemed right. He thanked his invisible friend for that. Then he glanced back down into the room.

Steve looked pretty gnarly. There were long squares on his chest and sides, even on his arms, that were deep purple and wet where the creatures had pulled his skin off with their teeth. Nathan shuddered at the memory. He seemed to be alive though, which surprised Nathan a little. His left leg rocked slowly back and forth and he could hear a soft steady moan.

There was no blood or anything where Jenny had been and he thought she might be okay. He knew he wouldn't really stop worrying until he saw her at the hospital. Or maybe if Jason just told him she was okay and that he had seen her.

A new shape was in the room as well. Another body sat half-upright against the far wall, the head slumped over onto the chest. He could see a ragged hole in the back of the head that looked wet and glistened in the nearly absent light. The hole looked like a mix of purple-red and a whitish gray. He wondered if that was what brains looked like.

I'll bash your fucking brains out.

That was Steve's voice, but it was a memory, he felt sure. The Steve he saw in the cave was in no condition to bash any brains out. He looked again at the big man with grayish-red hair and the big hole in his head. He guessed the Lizard Men had bashed his brains out—so now he totally knew what the expression meant.

He had seen enough. Jenny was gone and hopefully safe, Steve looked nearly dead and a new guy seemed dead with his brains bashed out.

Time to power down.

His own voice tried to sound like an SPD Power Ranger. He slid his body slowly back from the ledge and then thought hard about the soft blanket on his cheek and the heavy sound of Mommy's breathing. Nathan opened his eyes and looked around the dark hospital room.

If I had a window, I could tell if it was almost morning.

Jason would be there soon, he felt pretty sure. *Maybe he's with Jenny right now.* That thought made him feel better.

He drifted off to sleep hoping he and the other Power Rangers would bravely fight the crybots together with his SPD zord. That would be a way better dream than the stupid cave.

* * *

Steve floated, with his half-closed eyes out of focus. He didn't want to know whether he lay in the cave or was paralyzed in his torture room. His mind tried to remind him that it might be nice to know which nightmare was real and which was just a dream but he told his mind to just shut the fuck up for a minute.

For now he wanted to savor the floating, stoned feeling that kept his thoughts off the horrible pain in his chest and arms. That pain called to him, from down a long hallway, and he knew it would find him soon. He tried to stay lost for just a few more precious moments, like hitting a snooze alarm for the tenth time.

Just a few more minutes.

The pain didn't bring him back but the sucking swish, the pressure change in the room that announced a new arrival, did, and answered the question of where he was. With some difficulty he opened his eyes by not trying to open them—just letting the lids kind of slide back across his eyeballs on their own.

The intersecting black lines of his monotonous fucking ceiling confirmed what he knew. The horrible smell, like tasting a wet fart, told him that he had company. He listened to the hiss of his breathing machine.

I don't give a fuck. I don't care anymore. What the fuck are they going to do to me worse than what they've done? I'm not afraid of you anymore—not now that I want to die. Bring it on, motherfuckers.

He couldn't really make sense of the hushed whispers so he stopped trying. He felt way past giving a shit. He focused on the black lines, listened to his lungs pumped in and out with air and tried to think of the sweaty hot chick's cute titties, instead of the burning that wracked his body.

It seemed amazing how his mind could numb him to both the pain and fear. He knew his tormentors were there but they felt make-believe now. Steve concentrated on remembering every detail he could summon of the naked girl in the cave.

"Hello, Mr. Prescott," the familiar voice hissed at him. It sounded more like Smith, the little rat-fuck sidekick with the scar and the teeth that he knew were now stained with his blood. He didn't even try to move his eyes to see him.

Hello yourself, shit bag. You smell like ass. Did you know that?

There was a long pause and Steve tried to go back to the image of the naked girl, but his mounting anxiety kept her from him.

What are they going to do to me now?

Who gives a good wet shit? Try and picture the chick!

Hard shoes clicked on the floor and another voice joined the first as Mr. Clarke's pale face, eyes glowing from under his hat, came into view.

"Feeling a little better, are you?" The blood-red lips parted slightly and Steve saw the long teeth. "Well, we can fix that."

I don't think so, bitch. I'll be dead soon and you can fucking go hungry.

He wanted to smile but wasn't the least bit surprised that he couldn't. The thin, pale face leaned in closer.

"You'll be dead when I decide it's time, *bitch*." The voice hissed in his ear. Steve was not surprised that the demon had heard his thoughts. "Not feeling scared, Mr. Prescott? Well, you should be." The head pulled back and hovered just over his face. For a moment it seemed to shimmer and Steve saw briefly the raptor, though the eyes remained somewhat human. Then the thin red lips were back.

You will feel fear again, Mr. Prescott. The pain you have had is nothing compared to the unimaginable agony I am bringing you today. You will feed us with your terror, I promise you that...

The voice became real again in his ear as Mr. Clarke slid from view above him.

"Before you die today, Mr. Prescott," it hissed, "you will feed me. You will feel horror and terror as you watch us rip your organs from your belly. You will be awake to see us feed on your liver, your kidneys, your miserable little shit tube, and finally your heart and lungs. You think you are ready to die? Before we are done you will scream, begging for death."

A brand new terror was born. The blazing eyes came back into his view. His plan to deny the demons his anguish was a stupid, fucked-up pipe dream. He knew he would give them all the shit-yourself-terror that they needed. And he knew that death would be the highlight of his day.

Steve heard the staccato click of hard-soled shoes and listened to the voices of Mr. Clarke and Mr. Smith.

"We will need a new doctor. We are close to losing one I think."

"Get it done soon. We have another coming any time now. And get the girl back here. We need help keeping him alive for the feeding."

Steve thought he heard a slurping sound.

"And the boy?"

"We have time for one more. He doesn't yet know his power. We'll be gone before he does." A pause hung in the air and for a moment Steve felt twin pairs of hungry eyes on him. "Tell the team we have an organ harvest."

The shit smell returned for a moment, but then faded away and he realized he was alone again. Tears filled his eyes, blurred the ceiling panels and his mind fought furiously for a plan to stop being alive. He couldn't make himself stop breathing because the fucking machine forced air into his lungs. He couldn't move, could barely think.

So instead, he screamed in anguish, an animalistic sound, quiet, inside his head.

Chapter
11

Nathan wanted to be brave, mostly for Mommy. She did her best not to let him see her crying but he knew. As the man and woman in the green PJ-looking doctor suits settled him onto the smaller bed and checked his IV he smiled and waved to her, but for some reason it made her look sadder.

"I'll be okay, Mommy," he said, trying real hard to sound grown-up.

His mom raised a hand to her mouth. "I know, baby," she choked out. "Mommy is just silly sometimes, you know?" She smoothed his hair and kissed his forehead. "It won't even hurt, Dr. Katzen says. She says you get some special medicine and just go to sleep. When you wake up, your hand will be all fixed."

"It will still have a lot of healing to do," Dr. Katzen's voice cautioned from the doorway. "Another couple of days in the hospital I think." His mommy ignored her and unconsciously shooed her words away with her hand, which made Nathan snicker.

"You'll go to sleep and when you wake up, you'll be all fixed," Mom said again and kissed his cheek.

Nathan felt tightness in his chest, like someone squeezed him too hard and a big-swallow-of-peanut-butter feeling in his throat. He didn't say anything, because Mommy seemed so worried, but going to sleep was all that really scared him. He looked up again at the doorway as the man in the green pajamas tucked a bunch of papers under his pillow.

Please come, Jason. Please. I have to ask you something.

The bed started to roll and he jumped in response. His head felt kind of swimmy and he wondered if they put medicine in him to make him sleep already. The thought made him cry, but he turned his head so Mommy wouldn't see.

I don't want to go to the cave. Please don't let me go there if I can't get out when I want to.

"I love you, baby," his mom said as he rolled out of his room.

"See you in a minute, Mommy," he said, and thought he did a pretty good job of sounding brave.

Dr. Katzen said he wouldn't dream in the medicine sleep, so maybe he wouldn't go to the cave at all. Maybe he really would just drift off and wake up when his hand was all fixed up. He wanted to believe that with all his heart.

They're not dreams at all.

He knew that was true but still, if a medicine made it so he couldn't dream it might very well mean he couldn't go to the cave, either. He didn't know how it worked.

You're such a little scaredy cat. If you go to the cave, just hide like before.

But what if they found him? What if they saw him and ran after him like before? Nathan had thought about that time a lot and something seemed weird about it. Why hadn't the Lizard Man just bitten him with his sharp teeth? It almost seemed like he just wanted to scare him, make him leave the cave.

Maybe they're scaredy cats. Maybe they're scared of me. Did you ever think of that?

That didn't seem likely. Nathan closed his eyes and felt his lower lip tremble. Just wishful thinking (like Mommy called it). He couldn't think of a single reason why the Lizard Men, the creatures he watched tear Steve apart and leave him bleeding in the cave, would ever be afraid of a little five-year-old boy.

I'm almost six and I think they are scared of me a little.

You're figuring it out, now. The bad creatures on Power Rangers get scared and they are much bigger than a Power Ranger.

The second voice in his head sounded like him, but he knew it was the other-him that helped him hear things he needed. He wished Jason were with him again.

A finger touched his hand. Nathan jumped and struggled to open his eyes, certain he would see his buddy smiling down at him. Why did it feel so hard to open his eyes? He pulled them open so he could see Jason, standing above him.

Dr. Katzen looked down at him instead. His lip quivered badly now.

"It's okay, buddy," Dr. Katzen said and patted his hand. "The medicine is making you sleepy. Just go ahead and rest. When you wake up it will all be over."

Nathan struggled hard not to fall asleep. He opened his eyes wide when the narrow bed bumped to a stop. He looked up at three big round lights with handles, one of them blazing painfully in his eyes. He tried to raise a hand to block the powerful light, but felt too weak.

Stupid medicine.

"Sorry, little man," a deeper voice said. A hand grabbed the light handle and swung it out of his view. He started to not be so scared though. *That might be the medicine,* he thought. He panicked as they lifted him in the air but he saw that they were just moving him over to another bed, this one even smaller. A round face, full of kindness, looked down at him.

"You okay, Nathan?" a soft voice asked.

He tried to shake his head 'no' but he just lay there and looked up at the stranger. The man wore a puffy blue hat and a green doctor mask.

"Just the medicine, big guy. Nothing to worry about."

Nathan drifted off. He felt so tired. He could feel hands move his body around some, felt a warm blanket or something across his waist, but he couldn't make himself care anymore. Then he felt a really warm, almost hot, sensation run up his arm from his wrist and spread across his chest and neck. His head felt really dizzy.

"That's the other medicine, Nathan. Just relax and in a few seconds you'll be asleep." He looked up and tried to talk. He could feel his mouth moving, but he didn't hear his voice—only in his head.

Please don't let me go to the cave.

Darkness spread over him and Nathan couldn't remember what he wanted to say or why he felt so scared. He tried to make sense of the words in his head...

Jason! Jason, please come find me!

...and then he drifted into the middle of the circling darkness and disappeared.

* * *

Jason dreamt of Jenny's soft legs, her hips moving back and forth, until a voice interrupted. *Nathan's voice.*

He didn't wake up, but tried to switch dreams in his sleep; to hear the voice more clearly. He focused his mind, willing Nathan to speak. Just when he thought the boy wasn't really there, he heard him again, faint, far away.

Please don't let me go to the cave. Jason! Jason, please come find me!

Jason sat bolt upright in bed. For a moment he struggled, disoriented. Nothing looked familiar. Faint orange light from the dawn danced around narrow slits between towels hung over the windows. He searched for clues and started to think perhaps this was another dream, but then he caught the scent of Jenny, the soft flower-like smell on the sheets, and remembered exactly where he was.

Jason collapsed back on a big pillow and rubbed his hands across his face. He looked over as his eyes got used to the light and saw he was alone.

There were no sounds from the bathroom and the door stood fully open. The bathroom was dark. He stretched luxuriously in the soft bed, breathed her scent in. Then the thought of Nathan's pleading voice made him sit up again.

Real or not, the dream-Nathan's voice sounded frightened and urgent. He couldn't possibly ignore it.

Jason headed into the small living room while he pulled on his jeans and shirt. He hopped on one foot and tried to pull as he scanned around for a note from Jenny. It seemed pretty weird that she would just leave without waking him. Perhaps she had just run out for coffee or to the store to get stuff to make something for breakfast. The big clock on the bookshelf read seven-thirty. Could she have been called into to work?

In the bathroom he squirted some toothpaste on a finger (using her toothbrush felt dirty and wrong) and looked at himself in the mirror as he rubbed his teeth clean. He rinsed his mouth with tap water then headed back to the other room.

He scrounged in a narrow kitchen drawer for a pen and scrap of paper (they were always in the narrow drawers, right?) and scribbled a quick note to Jenny on a pharmaceutical-company notepad full of stickys.

I had to go to the hospital to check on Nathan. Meet me there if you can.
I miss you, even if that sounds silly. Hope you are okay.
-Jason

Jason jogged to the bedroom and put the note on her pillow (nice). Then he scanned quickly to see if her keys were in sight so he would know what to do with the door, then shrugged and he grabbed his keys. He would lock the door behind him. She would call on his cell if there was a problem. He wished he had her number so he could call her on the drive.

On the short drive to the hospital it finally hit him—Nathan probably had his surgery today. Shit! Why in the hell had he not checked with Katzen yesterday? He realized what a complete asshole he would be if he hadn't seen Nathan before he went to the OR. He pushed his foot a little harder on the accelerator and sped just above the limit the short distance to the hospital.

He pulled into the parking deck and found a spot on the second floor pretty close to the stairs. His car sat crooked in his haste, but Jason didn't bother fixing it. Jason sprinted down the stairs, nearly knocked into two middle-aged nurses, who gave long, exaggerated eye rolls in response to his mumbled apology, and then ran full speed through the glass walkway. The elevators felt like they took hours, but he walked into the Pedi-ICU only a few moments after parking.

"Can I help you, sir? We usually ask you to call in to see if it is okay for a visit." Jason looked at an older nurse who looked scoldingly back at him as she approached. He realized he knew very few people in the Pediatrics Unit and that in his present state he didn't look very doctorly. He started to explain whom he was when another voice interrupted.

"Oh, hi, Dr. Gelman." He turned and saw a heavier-set nurse who smiled at him warmly. The hall-monitor nurse walked away. Jason looked at the new nurse's ID, but the name didn't ring a bell. "I'm Carol," she said and put out her hand. "Jenny has talked about you a lot," she said and winked at him. "I'm afraid she's off today, though."

"I know," Jason said and felt a little awkward. "I'm actually here to see Nathan Doren—I took care of him in the ER."

"Oh, I know," the nurse said. "I'm afraid you just missed him. They took him down for his skin graft about thirty minutes ago." Jason's heart sank through the floor. "His mom might be in the surgery waiting room if you want to catch up with her."

"Thanks," he mumbled, feeling like a complete jerk-off. "I'll head over there and wait on him."

"Nice to officially meet you," the nurse said with another conspiratorial wink. "Jenny is a wonderful girl."

Jason smiled. "I know." He headed through the automatic doors and out of the unit.

In the hall, Jason stood for a moment, unsure what to do. His concern about Jenny certainly got a boost when he hadn't found her at work, but since he couldn't think what to do about that, he headed to the OR to check on Nathan. Maybe she was at the apartment reading his note right now.

The OR occupied a large portion of the third floor and he took the stairs, unable to wait for the elevator. He avoided the waiting room, not wanting to get hung up with Sherry until he satisfied himself that Nathan was okay. After a quick call to Jenny's apartment (no answer) he pulled on a pair of scrubs in the male physician locker room, tied on a blue hat and mask, and then headed down the short hall past Preop heading toward the main OR rooms. He walked up to a tech in scrubs on his way.

"Hey, bud—can you tell me what room the skin graft on Doren is in?"

The tech pointed at the big dry erase board without breaking stride. "Check the board."

Jason saw the name halfway down next to the attending surgeons name from the burn service. Room fifteen.

Through the narrow window of the door to room fifteen, Jason saw Sheila Katzen, who stood beside Nathan's outstretched arm. The arm and hand looked tiny surrounded by the blue drapes and he thought how it kind of looked mummified, painted all brown with the betadine prep. He couldn't see Nathan's face because of the drape pulled up to separate the operative field from anesthesia. Another small square of brown broke the field of blue a little farther down where his thigh had been prepped to take a small piece of skin for the graft to his hand—the donor site. Sheila closely examined his hand, which bled a little where she had debrided some more dead tissue off. Jason pushed through the door and Sheila looked up.

"Hey, Gelman," she said and returned to her inspection of the little bleeding hand. "What are you up to? Finally giving up on being the hospital gate keeper and considering the switch to a real doctor job?"

Jason enjoyed the endless and expected rivalry between ER and surgery. "Nah," he said. "I'll keep my life outside of work, thanks just the same. How's our boy?"

Sheila smiled with her eyes. "Doin' great. This should only take a half hour or so. You want to scrub?"

"No," Jason said and moved around the table to the anesthesia side of the drape. He looked at Nathan's face and felt a lump at the sight of him with a tube down his throat and his eyelids taped shut. "I'll just hang out with him up here if it's okay with everyone."

"Fine with me," Sheila said and the anesthesia doctor, whom Jason did not recognize, just shrugged and looked bored. "Let's get the graft," Sheila said to the team scrubbing with her and moved down by the exposed square over Nathan's thigh. Jason decided the last thing he needed was to see them slice a bloody piece of his little guy's thigh skin off with their electric cheese-knife. He bent over beside Nathan's head and whispered in his ear.

"I'm here, buddy. I'm so sorry I'm late." He felt a little rim of tears in his eyes, but they stayed off his cheeks. Nathan's cheek felt cool when he touched it lightly. The ventilator hissed and the little boy's chest rose. Jason looked up and saw the anesthesiologist looking at him curiously.

"He related to you?" he asked. He seemed a little uncomfortable now with Jason's presence.

"No," Jason answered, though it felt a little like a lie. "No, I just took care of him on admission."

"The ER guys are pretty touchy-feely," Sheila prodded. "Jason here does this with all of his patients, which is why he always looks like shit."

Jason chuckled but said nothing. He hadn't showered or shaved and he hadn't gotten a hell of a lot of sleep, either. He felt pretty sure that he did, in fact, look like shit. He thought of a couple of witty responses, but instead just gently stroked Nathan's cheek.

"I've kind of gotten attached to this one," he said—like that gross understatement explained it all. "He's been through a lot." The truth in that simple statement sobered the room and no one else said anything. The anesthesiologist checked his machine and monitors, nodded to himself, and settled back in his chair. Sheila tested the electric graft knife, which made Jason jump a little. Nathan's delicate chest rose and fell when the machine commanded.

"I'm right here," Jason said again.

* * *

The sound of Jason's voice and the soft, though far away, feel of his hand on his cheek made Nathan's pulse stop pounding in his ears. He knew where he was, could feel the wet heat on his skin and smell the moist dirt that he laid in. He had been afraid to open his eyes, but hearing Jason's voice made him feel a little bit brave. He would be okay. Maybe he would even be able to leave if he wanted, since he could feel and hear Jason.

Don't count on it, Ranger. Time to Power Up.

Well, even if not, knowing Jason sat with him made it a little bit not-so-scary. Nathan opened his eyes slowly and found himself right where he knew he would be—on his side in the dirty cave. He had not expected to see one of the sticky-looking purple puddles right next to his head, and seeing it made him sit up quickly. Nathan saw immediately that he lay right beside a little stream of the reddish-purple goo which ran down the wall and made the puddle near his face, and he scrambled to his feet.

As he looked around, he saw more little purple streams running down the walls and he wondered what that meant. It kind of looked like the cave had begun to bleed. The rise where he could look down into the big room, where the Lizard Men seemed to feed, was just a few paces away and Nathan wanted desperately to check and see if Jenny was there. But he felt a lot more afraid this time; the burning question of whether he would be able to escape back to Jason if the creatures saw him tugged at him, and he stood a moment, unsure what to do.

There looked like a little passageway just behind him that branched off in another direction, and for a moment he thought about maybe scurrying down that narrow path and just hiding until his surgery was over. But even before his in-his-head voice called him a scaredy cat, he knew he had to make sure Jenny looked alright. He hoped she wasn't there at all, but knew she would be.

Nathan walked slowly up the slope of the path and maneuvered awkwardly around the purple puddles, which seemed harder to avoid this time. Up on his toes he sneaked around what he now thought of as cave blood and tried not to get any on him.

At the rise he dropped down again on his naked belly, relieved and happy that he saw no blood puddles, and sneaked up the last few feet to the rise. Then he peered over the edge.

Again Jenny lay naked and sweaty, writhing slowly in the corner. The man with the bashed-in brains had fallen over and looked gray and old, a dark stain around his head in the dirt. Nathan heard the soft noises from the Lizard Men, who bent over Steve's barely moving body. Their dinosaur heads leaned over Steve's and now and again they grunted at each other. The eyes in those demon heads glowed a lot redder today, and he wondered if that meant they really had grown stronger.

The taller creature leaned over suddenly and pointed one impossibly long, black claw at Steve's bare belly then pushed the claw into Steve with a little spurt of dark blood. Slowly, the demon dragged the claw downward and Steve's belly split open with a little splash of bloody water. His guts rolled out of him and fell in a pile, like thick gray sausages, beside him in the dirt. The sound of Steve's cry bounced off the walls and pounded into his head and he balled a dirty fist up and shoved it into his mouth to stifle a scream.

Nathan tried to force away his fear, but the creatures didn't seem to notice the smell of him this time. Instead they focused only on Steve as they bent over and started to feed. Nathan felt sick and scared and thought he might spit up. He wanted to slip down from the ledge and hide, but he couldn't take his eyes off the horrible sight in front of him and he wanted to watch to make sure they didn't feed on Jenny next. He suddenly felt alone and way too little.

Help me, Jason. Please come here and help me.

* * *

They were back now. He had passed out for most of the cold, wet washing of his belly—his terror taking him away—and then checked in for a moment to see how things came along. Now the towels seemed all in place, tucked in a tight square around his exposed belly, and his eyes stared at the white and black checkered ceiling while his ears listened to the clink of metal on metal. Now and again the ceiling seemed to shimmer, slowly take on the darker image of the ceiling of a cave, then faded slowly back to his familiar checkerboard. He thought the pulse in his temples would explode his head right off his neck and prayed something would burst in his brain and he would die quickly.

The shimmering cave-ceiling came again into view and a horrifying dinosaur head leaned over him, red slit of a mouth open, long teeth wet and glistening. He heard a grunt that may have been him, but probably was the raptor-man. Then the head shimmered and the lights came up and he stared into the glowing red embers of Mr. Clarke's shadowy eyes.

"The pain you have felt until now is nothing," the monotone whisper told him. "We will tear you apart, rip out your organs while you watch and listen, and you will bleed to death as we devour you from inside. You will die only when I say so. Do you understand?"

The terror consumed him, and he heard Mr. Clarke moan with the pleasure of a man coming; his head tilted back and his mouth split impossibly wide around his long teeth.

"Yes," he hissed. "Yes, feed me."

He stood up and went out of view.

"Kidneys first." He heard Clarke say.

"Look," a stuttering voice said. "I think we need to give him a little something. Fentanyl or something—please." The voice hesitated. "You know he can feel everything, right?"

The creature's voice echoed off the walls. "IT'S TOO LATE FOR THAT. GET ME MY FUCKING ORGANS!"

He felt trembling fingers on his bare belly and his mind jumped at the touch because his body couldn't. The nurse with the cold blue-green eyes bent over him, her eyes on his, and for a moment she seemed to really see him, but then the moment disappeared and the stones turned cold again. She turned and looked away, adjusting an IV or something.

He felt a sharp blade on his skin, just below his breastbone and for a moment it hesitated. Then the voice bellowed again.

"NOW."

He felt a sharp, ripping pain move fast from his breastbone downward, stopping just above his dick. His brain exploded with a million signals—half screamed at his body to do something to stop the horrible pain and the other half failed to answer the signals to every muscle in his body to sit up, run, swing arms and legs—do some goddamn thing. Another searing pass of the knife and he felt a terrible pull, a tearing sensation as his belly split apart, and then he felt warm, wet things slide down over his right side.

His mind screamed at him again as he realized that it was his own guts he felt spew out of his belly onto the bed. The room got dark for a moment and he tried to scramble into the darkness, to pass out or die or anything that would take him away. Then a new pain, a vague and uncertain feeling that seemed hard to localize but came from deep inside of him, brought the light back and he stared through tear-filled eyes at the ceiling again.

"Can you pull the colon over out of the way?"

"How's that?" Another ripping pain accompanied the question. He felt his stomach lurch and his throat filled with warm, stinging vomit that spilled out onto his face. It trickled into his right eye and he felt a burning pain from the acidic liquid. Then the pain inside him took over again.

"Okay, hold that there—perfect."

"Can I have a dever retractor?"

"Here you are, Doctor," the stone-eyed nurse answered, only her voice quivered now.

Now that I'm dead, you give a shit? You fucking whore. If I could move I would fuck you to death, you bitch.

Another shock of pain, like someone drove a sword right through him.

"You see that bleeder?"

"Just leave it."

"Let me have a bovie. Here, help me get in behind here. See the hilum?"

"Clamp," the shaky man's voice said. "Put it across the vessels, there."

"Scissors."

"Got a kidney coming out."

A short, sharp pain inside and then it felt like a small animal was moving around inside of him. He could see nothing out of his right eye and his left looked blurry, filled with tears. The voices faded farther and farther away, and Steve knew where he was going. He felt incredibly weak, but became aware that his right foot rocked back and forth in response to every shock of pain from inside him. He balled up his fists, but his arms were too weak to rise. He strained with all his might and just barely lifted his head out of the wet dirt, his eyes wide, and looked downward in terror, knowing what he would see.

One of the dinosaur heads was buried snout-deep inside his belly. His intestines lay curled in a circle beside him and his belly lay split wide open, gaping up at the ceiling. He felt a terrible ripping pain and then the face came out of his belly, a dark purple, crescent-shaped hunk of flesh in its long teeth. He screamed as the beast tilted back its head and greedily ate his left kidney.

"NOOoooo!" His screams echoed away and he squished his eyes closed when the other creature bent over, hesitated a moment, then shoved its long face deep inside again.

He lay back, eyes closed, and let out scream after scream, just as the creatures had promised.

Chapter
12

The voice sounded so real that Jason looked around to see if the anesthesiologist might have heard it. The man still looked bored and flipped through a copy of "The Kiplinger Letter", occasionally looking up at the monitors to make sure his ward still looked stable. Jason looked again at Nathan's motionless face—the eyelids taped and the tube through his vocal cords obviously made any sound impossible. But the sound hung in the air around him anyway.

Please come here and help me.

"How?" he said aloud without meaning to. The anesthesiologist looked at him curiously over his magazine.

"How what?"

"Uh," Jason stammered. "Oh, uh, never mind," he said, trying to sound like he had figured some mystery out on his own. The other doctor shrugged, looked at the vital signs on the monitor, and returned to his reading.

Jason peered over the blue drape that separated them from the surgical field. Sheila had taken and prepped the piece of skin from Nathan's thigh, leaving a little square of red blood in the field of brown prep, and now scraped away at his hand and finger to prepare the surface to accept the graft. They had maybe another fifteen or twenty minutes to go and then they could start to wake Nathan up.

Hurry, Jason. I think they see me.

The voice sounded terrified and Jason stood up. He didn't know what he could do but some far away memory told him he couldn't do it from here.

"Hey, Sheila," he said as he strode as casually as he could to the door, "can you page me when you're done and waking him up? I'd like to be there in recovery when he comes around."

"No problem," his friend said more softly. She seemed to sense it was a bad time for a joke. "Nearly done—I'll call you in a few."

"Thanks," he said and pushed through the heavy door.

Outside Jason tore his mask off his face, suddenly feeling like he couldn't get enough air. He fast walked out of the OR and headed down the hallway to a locked door labeled "Resident Call Rooms." Jason's hands shook as he punched in the code, fumbled, and had to start over. Finally, he heard a magnetic click and he pulled the door open. The parallel hallways had row after row of doors labeled with the various specialties that took in-house call. He found one that was cracked open (it happened to be labeled cardiology) and went inside, pulled the door closed harder than he meant to, and then spun the lock, knowing it would turn a green tab to red near the handle, letting anyone who came along know that this room was occupied, probably by an exhausted resident trying to steal a few minutes of sleep.

Jason sat on the edge of the narrow bunk and rubbed his face with both hands. He listened for Nathan's voice and searched desperately for the memory that would tell him how to get to the cave. He remembered only going there—just lying down and going—but how?

He lay back on the bunk, crossed his arms on his chest, and tried to slow his breathing. Forcing himself to concentrate on a slow inhale and a slow exhale, he closed his eyes and tried to picture what he remembered of the cave in his head. Twenty years of cobwebs started to melt away and he began to see it more clearly in his mind. *Nathan needs me. And anyway, they can smell fear.*

Yeah, don't be a scaredy cat.

The second voice felt déjà vu familiar. He slowed his breathing more and warmth began wrapping around him.

I'm coming, little buddy.

* * *

Nathan heard Jason's voice and for a moment felt terrified that the Lizard Men would hear it too. Then he remembered that he probably just heard the voice in his brain. The creatures had already looked his way once; one of them sniffed the air, and he felt certain that they could smell him 'cause he felt so scared. After a moment, though, they went back to tearing Steve apart so Nathan crouched lower and sobbed as quietly as he could.

Jason will be here in a minute. He'll know what to do.

Will he? He needs you to figure it out, scaredy cat. You need to Power Up.

Nathan made himself as small as possible, his eyeballs barely above the ledge, and looked down again. The creatures rested back on powerful, thick legs. Their faces glistened with blood and spit and their eyes glowed so red it almost hurt to look at them. Steve looked very dead. His belly gaped open, the cavity an empty, dark hole, all of his guts scattered in a circle around his motionless body. Dark smears of blood stained his pale skin and face and his arms were pulled out from his sides like the Jesus-man statues. Yep—dead.

Nathan felt his stomach turn and thought he might spit up, but he swallowed back the feeling before the other-him voice could make fun of him and tell him to Power Up like a Power Ranger again. The smaller creature gave a look and a sniff in Jenny's direction, but the bigger one smacked him and they grunted at each other. He felt pretty sure that Jenny was okay.

'Cause they need her for something. She's okay, but just for now.

Nathan looked back down the path to see if maybe Jason was coming up, but he saw nothing but big cave blood puddles. A sudden nasty fart smell filled his nose and he looked back down into the room. The Lizard Men were gone.

Maybe they're looking for you. Did you ever think of that?

Nathan scrambled back down the path in a growing panic. The creatures were nowhere in sight, so he ran as fast as he could to the little passageway he had seen. His bare feet splashed through a couple of blood puddles, but he realized he no longer cared. He just wanted to hide as fast as he could. His feet tingled for a moment after he splashed in the purple goo, but the feeling disappeared quickly.

I think they're looking for me. Where is Jason?

The passageway was little more than a low hole, but Nathan scrambled inside anyway. Instead of being scared of the tight, dark fit, he thought that maybe the Lizard Men would be too big to follow him in and he would be safe. He moved deeper into the small cave. Just past a little turn where the light from the entrance disappeared from sight, he plopped down in the moist dirt and felt a tickle of sweat roll down his back and onto his butt. He tried to slow his breathing, which sounded really, really loud in the little cave.

Nathan leaned his head back and tried to make the far-away sounds louder. He could hear the lady doctor talking, but he didn't understand what she said because it all sounded like doctor words. He also heard a hissing sound over and over and every time he heard it his chest felt kind of full and a little cold. The comforting feel of Jason's hand on his cheek had disappeared and he realized he hadn't heard his voice in awhile.

Why isn't he here?

Just help yourself. You can do it. Try and leave if you can.

Nathan closed his eyes tight and felt warm tears roll down his cheeks. He concentrated as hard as he could on the few sounds he still heard—the lady doctor, a metal sound, and the hissing. He didn't feel anything else and had no other sounds to think on. He wished that he felt Jason's hand on his cheek 'cause that would probably help. He tried and tried to go to the sounds, to make them louder and more real, but he didn't even feel a little different.

Nothing's happening. I really am stuck here. What if they find me?

His breathing got loud and raspy and a little whimper came out of his throat.

They won't unless you are a scaredy cat. They only want you if you're scared, right?

The other-him voice didn't sound so teasing this time. It sounded more like it tried to help. Nathan did the three slow, deep breaths like Mommy used to make him do when he got too upset to tell her what was wrong. It worked a little, and he felt himself start to shake a lot less and his breathing sounded quieter.

Now just stay still and quiet. Jason will come and even if he doesn't, you will be able to leave very soon. Be a brave, Power Ranger, for a little while more and then you can go back.

That sounded really good. Nathan leaned his head back against the cave wall in the dark and sent one more thought to Jason in his brain.

I'm okay, but please come and get me.

Chapter
13

Jason heard Nathan much more clearly, but the anxiety it produced just made it harder for him to relax. The call room ceiling shimmered for a moment and the light seemed to fade, but Nathan's scared voice made him anxious and the lights came back up as if they were on a dimmer switch. Jason took a deep breath and tried to picture the cave as he remembered it from so long ago. He closed his eyes again and tried to imagine the hot wet feel that his memory told him to expect.

"I'm coming, buddy," he mumbled and gave a long exhale. The room around him started to feel warm and heavy and the picture in his mind of the cave solidified. A small, little-boy voice from deep in his mind called out to him.

Don't go. The creatures are there and they are waiting for you.

Jason ignored his child voice and the picture in his mind became clearer. He pushed the childhood terror away like kicking off a blanket. He felt a cool, sweaty film form on his naked body and opened his eyes.

The low ceiling of the cave seemed much closer than he remembered and he reminded himself that he was a lot bigger than the last time he had been here. He sat up in the dirt and looked around.

The cave stretched out in both directions and disappeared into the dark. Scattered about on the dirt floor he saw several puddles formed by dark purple liquid which dripped in little streams from the walls. It looked a lot like old blood and seemed to ooze from the cave itself. Nathan failed to appear in either direction and he stood up, his head only inches from the irregular ceiling. Then he headed off slowly to the right, picking his way around the blood puddles. He listened intently for the grunting sound of the creatures from his childhood nightmares.

"Nathan," he whispered softly. "Where are you, buddy?"

I'm hiding. I'm in a littler cave hiding from the Lizard Men. Please come find me, Jason. I'm scared and I don't want them to smell me.

Jason picked up his pace. As he moved the passage seemed to narrow and after a slight bend he saw it rose up to a ledge about fifty yards ahead. Jason almost missed the small low hole to his right, but saw it at the last moment. He crouched down and peered into the darkness. In the inky blackness he could see nothing and the thought of belly crawling into the little hole terrified him. He stuck his head in, down on all fours, and called softly into the dark.

"Are you in there, buddy?"

"Jason," Nathan's scared but excited voice whispered back. "It's me. I'm in here."

The fear disappeared, replaced by an overwhelming need to get to the boy—to hug him and make sure he was alright. Jason was relieved to find he was just small enough to stay up on all fours, keeping his belly out of the moist dirt. A short distance inside the hole it took a slight bend and just past the turn he saw him. Nathan sat back against the wall with his knees pulled up to his chest and rocked slowly back and forth.

"Jason!" he called out, a little louder than Jason would have liked. He moved toward his buddy and awkwardly wrapped one arm around him. He supported himself with some difficulty with the other, his shoulder jammed against the wall. Nathan wrapped both skinny arms around his neck and Jason noticed without surprise that the bandage was missing from his hand, though he still held it up, the fingers curled in a ball.

"I gotcha, son," he said and felt tears from the boy's cheeks on his shoulder. "Are you okay?"

Nathan pulled back and wiped the tears from his face. He looked embarrassed that he was crying. "I think so," he said in a trembling voice. "Steve is dead. They tore him apart and ate up his guts. It was so gross." Nathan's voice cracked a little and Jason wanted desperately to take him away. "Jenny is there, too."

The words felt like a knife through Jason's heart.

"Jenny? Is she okay?" he asked.

"I think so," Nathan said and looked down at his knees. "The Lizard Men didn't want to mess with her, I think. They just ate up Steve and then disappeared."

"Can you show me?" Jason asked, his hand now on Nathan's cheek.

Nathan looked at him and hesitated, then seemed to summon his courage. He nodded silently and pointed back out of the narrow hole. "It's back that way."

The two of them crawled back into the larger passageway of the cave. Jason stood up. His back ached, but Nathan took his hand and pulled him up along the rise toward the ledge. He moved quickly, like he moved around in his own house, and Jason felt a tightness in his throat that the little boy had been here enough to be so familiar. As they approached the ledge, Nathan slowed and dropped onto his hands and knees. Together they crawled the last few yards.

"They might be back," Nathan said without looking back, more to himself than to Jason. "I didn't smell the fart smell, though."

That brought a flood of old memories and then a fresh one—the horrible smell in the alley when the creatures had disappeared. Everything clicked back into place.

The poop smell when they come and go? Remember? Remember smelling it when they took your mom?

Jason pushed the thought as far away as he could. Nathan arrived at the ledge, his head low, and peered down. Jason slid in beside him.

"She's gone," Nathan whispered.

Jason looked down into the cavern. The horrible sight of Steve's dead and mutilated body didn't bother him much—he had seen lots of horrible shit in the ER. What choked him up was the realization that Nathan had watched it happen. Then Jason saw another body slumped over in the corner of the room, a black puddle of old blood like a halo around the head.

"Who's that?" Jason asked with some fear. He felt like he should know.

"Don't know," Nathan answered. Jason realized the five-year-old's voice sounded steadier than his own. "He came yesterday."

Yesterday.

Jason suddenly knew exactly who the body in the corner belonged to, but he needed to be sure. He also wanted to see where Jenny had been and make sure that he didn't see any blood or other evidence that she had been hurt, at least physically. He could see an area of disturbed dirt.

"Is that where Jenny was?" he asked and pointed.

"Yeah," Nathan whispered.

Jason thought a moment. He sure as hell didn't want to be down there when the creatures came back, but he couldn't leave without being sure about the cop and Jenny. He would slip down real quick, check it out, and come right back.

"Stay here," he whispered to Nathan, "I'll be right back."

"No." Nathan's voice trembled and Jason felt his tiny hand on his arm. "Don't leave me. I want to go with you." The voice was full of tears. Jason suspected that Nathan hovered near his breaking point.

Jason stood, but stayed hunched over and squeezed Nathan's hand in his.

"Stay right with me and hold my hand," he said, as if they were going to cross a street to get ice cream.

Together they descended the steep path into the larger cave. Nathan's hand tightened in his as they approached Steve's corpse and Jason held his arm back behind him, to put himself between Nathan and the body.

"Don't look, buddy," he said paternally as he turned to see how Nathan was doing. Nathan shrugged. His eyes looked old.

"Already seen it," he said simply.

Steve's body looked like the scene of a botched, amateur autopsy. The belly had been torn apart more than cut, and now lay gaping open and eerily empty. He wondered how the body looked back home on the other side. For a moment that thought, which came to him so naturally, confused him—then he remembered what it meant. Jason didn't really understand the difference or the connection between the cave and the world they had come from, but he knew that all of them, including what remained of Steve, somehow existed in both places. He felt a tug on his hand that brought him back and looked down. Nathan looked back at him anxiously.

"We should hurry in case the Lizard Men come back," he said.

Jason tried to flash a reassuring smile, but felt a little more like he made the face of an infant with gas. They left Steve's body behind and headed toward the slumped body that lay face first in a pool of its own black blood and gray matter. The back of the police officer's head was nearly gone and Jason knew that if he rolled him over (which he had no friggin' intention of doing) there would be another hole where the right eye should have been. He looked fatter all bent over and naked, but he had never thought of Maloney as trim and fit. Jason looked at his 'friend,' who he'd sometimes kidded about eating donuts, and swallowed hard.

"Come on," he whispered to Nathan, who pulled back at his arm and stood on tippy-toes, trying to keep his feet out of the puddle of brains and blood. "Show me where Jenny was."

Nathan took the lead and pulled Jason behind him. He walked a yard or two to the left of Maloney's corpse, then stopped and pointed down into the dirt without saying a word. Jason looked at the small area of disturbed wet ground. His imagination helped him create an outline of where Jenny had lay and thrashed about, but really it just looked like an oblong depression. There was a small area of wetter looking dirt, and Jason wondered if it was where her sweat had pooled or if his girlfriend had pissed herself. He felt tears trickle down his cheeks as he imagined her there, naked and scared, writhing in confusion. What did she see in her head? Was it her trips here that she saw as nightmares? Jason closed his eyes. Nathan squeezed his hand tighter.

"She's okay, I think," he said—a parent reassuring a scared child. "I think we gotta go, Jason."

Jason looked at his friend and smiled sadly. He decided that Nathan was the bravest child he had ever heard of.

And if you were that brave, we might not even be here now. If you had stopped them, Mom would still be alive.

Jason pressed the heel of one hand to the bridge of his nose, physically stifling the obnoxious asshole of a voice. Then looked back at the dirt where Jenny had been. What did she have to do with this? The only connection seemed to be that all three of them had been abused as kids (though for Nathan, childhood had ended only days ago) and even that seemed wrong somehow. Why? It was the pictures right? The ones in the apartment? The thought seemed so important that he couldn't put it off, but he couldn't quite put it together either. And where the hell did she go? Why not come here from her own bed in her apartment, where shifting back and forth would be as easy as dreaming? The answers felt really important but eluded him.

"Jason, please." Nathan's voice tugged at him with the same scared insistence as the grasping hand on his arm. "Please, we gotta go."

Jason snapped back. "Alright, big guy," he said. "Let's get the hell out of here." He led Nathan back up the sloping path to the ledge. As they approached the top, Jason felt a weird push, like a slight pressure change; his heart pounded in his chest. Without looking back, he scrambled the last few yards to the ledge and heaved Nathan roughly over the low rise and both of them collapsed in a painful heap in the dirt. Just as the dust cloud settled around them the horrible smell, like someone pulled a hot bag full of shit over his head, engulfed him and he struggled not to vomit.

"They're coming," Nathan sounded terrified. He whimpered slightly. Jason put an arm around him and held him against his chest, their faces only a few inches apart.

"Shhh," he whispered. "It's okay, buddy. I'm here and I won't let anything hurt you."

Nathan's blue eyes held his in desperation, full of a need to believe him. Jason watched as the boy shoved a dirty fist into his own mouth and then nodded.

Jason doubted there was a goddamn thing he could do to keep his young friend safe, but he also knew that he would die trying if he had to. He kept his arm around the boy, then slowly lifted his head just enough to see above the ledge and down into the cavern.

The creatures sauntered around Steve's corpse; Jason felt terror grab him by the throat at the sight of them. They looked exactly as he remembered and the memory explosion nearly made him gasp aloud. The cascade of images, of his dad, of the hospital, of his frequent trips here, running and crying as he tried to hide from those creatures, battered him and nearly paralyzed him with fear. He resisted, with great effort, the need to jump up and run crying back down the path behind him, the Lizard Men snapping at his legs.

"Ow," a voice hissed from beside his head. He realized his grip on Nathan's arm had become ridiculously tight and he relaxed it, looking wide-eyed at the boy beside him. "They can only smell us if we're scaredy cats, I think," Nathan whispered in his ear. "You gotta not be too scared or they'll find us."

Jason nodded and risked another peek down below. The creatures stood very still in the middle of the cavern, right beside where Jenny's body had been. He saw that their heads were tilted back, mouths open to show long, yellowish teeth, their snouts up in the air.

They're smelling for you, you big scaredy cat. If they find you you'll look just like Steve. Control yourself or you and your boy will both be in big-shit trouble.

Jason slid his head back down beside Nathan's and closed his eyes. He took several long, deep breaths and felt his pulse slow a little in his temples. After a moment his breathing no longer sounded so ridiculously loud in his head. He opened his eyes and looked to see Nathan staring at him expectantly.

He's waiting for you to take care of him. How funny is that?

"Hold my hand and stay with me," he said. "We're gonna head back to the little hole and hide there until we can get out of here, okay?"

Nathan nodded. "I think I can hear the voices a little louder. I think we can leave real soon."

Jason listened for a moment but heard nothing. Then he realized that he lay alone in a quiet call room. There was no way he would hear the OR voices that Nathan heard. He took Nathan's hand and slid almost silently a few yards back down the path, then got up to his feet in a low crouch and started moving faster and faster back toward the dark bunny hole where he had found Nathan. Nothing about the little hole seemed scary, now.

Nothing scary about the dark once you've seen what's in it.

He stole a quick glance behind them as the dropped to all fours. No creatures came up over the ledge and he prodded Nathan gently to scurry into the hole ahead of him. Then he ducked his own head and scrambled like an animal behind his cub.

They stopped just past the little bend where he had first found Nathan, out of sight of the entrance to their tight burrow, and they collapsed together back against the wall. Jason realized that their breathing sounded wicked loud in the little cave, but tried not to think about it. Not like they could hold their breath for ten or fifteen minutes, right?

"Do you hear that voice? It's telling me I can wake up," Nathan said from his shoulder.

It took a moment to force that to make sense and then Jason realized what it meant. Nathan must be in the recovery room, or else waking up in the Operating Room. The voice he heard would be the anesthesiologist waking him up. They would only need another couple of minutes.

"Do you feel the breathing machine blowing air into you?" he asked. He realized that those were kid words from his past, not the grown-up Doctor Jason talking.

"I don't think so," Nathan answered.

So the breathing tube had been removed already. They were really, really close.

"Okay," Jason said. "Just try to go to the sounds and voices in your mind."

Nathan gave little kid head shake that meant No Duh. "I know how to do it," he said and Jason smiled as he felt, more than saw, Nathan close his eyes beside him. Then grunting close and loud made his heart explode out of his chest.

Jason suspected that the creatures were right at the entrance to their burrow. He could almost smell their hot breath and felt Nathan grip him tightly.

"Hurry, Nathan," he hissed. "They're coming."

Nathan's voice stayed remarkably calm. "I'm trying," he said.

The grunts echoed off the walls and he knew that the creatures were trying to burrow their way into the tight passageway. They had found them. Almost unconsciously he pulled his own legs closer and scooted the two of them another foot or two into the hide.

"It's working," Nathan said excitedly. "It's all getting louder."

Jason understood that Nathan meant the sounds from the other side, not the grunting that seemed to build to a roar and ripped through his head. The boy felt lighter in his arms and light sparkles seemed to fill the air around him in the dark. It worked. Nathan started to leave.

"I'll be there in a minute," he said as Nathan faded away in his arms. "I'll come to your bed in recovery as soon as I get back." But Nathan was gone and he found himself hugging only dark, empty air.

Jason pushed farther into the little cave, which quickly got even smaller and tighter. He realized he could go no farther unless he could tear his own arms off at the shoulders. Eyes closed tightly, he concentrated with all his might on—what? There were no sounds in the quiet call room that he could focus his mind on.

Oh fuck! I'm trapped here. I'm not going to be able to get back.

Jason felt movement behind him and realized that one of the creatures had somehow pushed into the small space. They were coming for him and he had nowhere to go. He let out a scream as he felt a cold, hard claw tickle across his right foot.

"No! No!' he hollered and pulled his foot the few inches he had left, his body now contorted and twisted, wedged into the tiny space. He felt the flesh tear from his shoulder where it pushed against the rock and blood ran from the wound down over his bare and sweaty chest. Pain shot through him as the cave wall ground dirt into the fresh cut and his fingers clawed at the ground, trying to pull himself just another few inches away from the Lizard Man. He could hear the creature stretching out its claw for him, thudding into the dirt floor only an inch or two behind his foot. Puffs of dirt sprinkled his legs each time the claw fell just short. Jason pushed hard against the unyielding wall, felt his foot push off a cold claw behind him. He could barely fill his lungs with air in the tight space, but screamed again.

Then he felt something cool. It was on his left cheek and he concentrated on it with all his might. The soft edge of the cheap foam pillow in the Call Room bunk gelled in his mind. Jason tried to go to the feel of it, to make it real in his mind, and he heard the thump of the reaching claw behind him begin to fade. The air became cooler, almost cold with the air-conditioning vent blowing across his sweat-covered body. The crushing tightness of the cave walls around him relaxed and then faded away completely. Suddenly, his body exploded out in all directions as he stretched out of his contorted position and filled the small bunk. Opening his eyes, he gasped deeply of the cool air for a moment and then sat up with some difficulty.

His left shoulder shot a lightning bolt at him as he shifted his weight to swing his legs out of the bed. He saw a large, dark stain grow rapidly on his shirt from his shoulder and spread downward over his chest. He pulled the neck of his T-shirt aside and saw a deep ragged gash in his shoulder, which bled freely. He awkwardly pulled his shirt over his head one-handed, balled it up, and held tight pressure against the wound. Jason lay back against the wall on the bunk, held his T-shirt tightly against his torn shoulder, and closed his eyes for a moment. He had a lot of shit he needed to sort out.

* * *

When Jenny awoke alone in bed her first thoughts were about Jason. It seemed weird that he would leave without waking her, especially since he had seemed so protective last night. She remembered the feel of his arms around her and smiled at the memory of how he had shifted his hips away. She had come very close to rolling over and attacking him, putting his arousal to good work, but in the end her need for comfort had overwhelmed the other aching need. She had finally let herself drift to sleep in his arms.

Then memories of her dream returned to her and her appetite for sex evaporated.

In the dream she drove to the hospital, the sun just peeking up over the horizon. She remembered the walk in and taking the elevators down to the basement, way past the morgue and down a long hallway to a kind of exam room, only much larger. After that the images became very jumbled and disorganized.

Dreams are just like that.

She thought she remembered dreaming of the cave again, where demons taunted her and around her hung the smell of death. Like before, she remembered Nathan peering down at her, but it felt more like he had looked after her instead of just watched her. The memories of the cave sporadically jumbled amongst memories of the exam room, which as she thought about it seemed more like an operating room. She remembered assisting surgeons and they had taken organs from a dead guy for transplant surgery. Her mind also held torn fragments of memory of her family. She decided to let the whole damn dream just float away like smoke.

Dreams are dreams—can't control them, so why dwell on them? Just stress sneaking into my sleep.

They're not dreams.

The second voice sent a chill up her back that made her shake and she pulled the warm blanket around her. Jenny closed her eyes and tried to think only about Jason and what she could do with him when he got back. The dream faded farther away, but left with one last scream.

The man's scream. The man on the table and in the cave.

Jenny's eyes popped open wide. The man had screamed—the man in the operating room. They had done an organ harvest, she felt sure of that. So why would the man be screaming? First, he should be brain dead to take his organs and second, he had been intubated and on a ventilator. A sudden, vivid picture of the man's eyes looking up at her, tears running down his cheeks, filled her mind and she felt sick to her stomach. The eyes looked very much alive and awake. But he still couldn't scream, right?

The screams came from the cave. There you can scream, or writhe in the dirt and piss yourself.

It's just a nightmare.

So why did it give her such a chill? Why did her stomach tighten and bile fill her throat? Jenny's eyes welled up and she closed them, letting the tears run down her cheek onto her pillow and tickle across her nose. The screams, the impossible screams from the dead organ donor, echoed in her head.

Dreams are just like that.

No—you know better than that, girl. You know what you did.

Jenny squeezed her eyes tighter and pushed the dream the rest of the way out of her head with a final shove. *Please come home, Jason.*

Jenny let her mind carry her to a new dream; she fell back into a fitful sleep.

Chapter
14

The scrub top Jason found in the call room floor locker smelled musty, but not B.O. smelly, so he pulled it on with some difficulty. Funny, after where he had just come from, that he could possibly give a shit about wearing someone else's shirt. The bleeding had pretty much stopped, but he knew it would start up again and he would probably need a couple of stitches. For now he decided to just make a quick stop in a supply closet and tape a couple of gauze 4x4's over the wound so that it wouldn't bleed through his stale scrub top. He wanted very much to get to Nathan, though he knew that the boy was fine for now.

Apparently, he can call out to you from pretty much anywhere, so you've got that going for you. Which is nice.

A few minutes later, Jason hurried down the hall toward the recovery room, his bloody shoulder bandaged, anxious to see Nathan in one piece with his own two eyes. He walked up to the imposing double doors to the recovery room, the big red Staff Only sign in the middle, and pushed the silver plate beside the door. Nothing happened. For a moment he felt confused, but then remembered — the door was swipe-card protected to keep people out. Naturally his ID and swipe card were hanging on his lab coat — down in the ER residents room.

For a moment he thought about running down and grabbing them, but the thought of waiting another five minutes to see Nathan felt unbearable. Jason pushed a gray button in the middle of a black speaker-looking square and heard a buzz and an electronic tone. Then a Hardee's Drive Thru voice squawked at him.

"Recovery Room. How can I help you?"

"Hi," Jason said, leaning awkwardly toward the black box. "This is Dr. Gelman from Emergency Medicine. I have a patient in there and I don't have my ID with me. Can you let me in?"

There was a long pause and he wondered for a moment if they had heard him. Maybe he wasn't supposed to push the damn button when he talked. He leaned over to speak again, but then the static-filled speaker barked at him.

"Patient's name?"

"Nathan Doren."

After a moment the voice answered.

"He's not here."

Jason felt the now-familiar band around his chest and throat. *What the hell are they talking about? What had happened? He had to be in recovery by now.*

"Whadya mean he's not there?" he demanded as he pushed the button hard enough this time to bend back his thumbnail. He noticed with detached interest that the nail had filthy dirt from the cave under it. "He just got out of surgery a few minutes ago, for God's sake." The next pause felt eternal and he nearly left to jog over to the OR and make sure Nathan wasn't still in the room having a problem.

"Mr. Doren is an ICU patient, sir," the clown voice said. "ICU patients are recovered back in the ICU, sir." Jason spun around without bothering with an answer and headed for the elevators. "Have a nice day, sir," the box taunted after him. Jason flipped the wall box a middle finger, then blushed at the eighty-year-old volunteer in her red smock, who raised a hand to her mouth at the gesture.

"Sorry," he mumbled.

He skipped the elevators and jogged up the three flights of stairs to the sixth floor. At the door to the ICU, he pressed his fingers to his temples in frustration. He still had the same frigging swipe card problem. Another gray button on another goddamn fast-food speaker laughed at him from beside the door and he pushed it gently trying in vain to slow the rise of a miserable headache.

"Yes?" a nicer voice said.

"It's Dr. Gelman," he said as patiently as he could and started to launch into his explanation when the doors swung open.

Thank God.

"Good morning, Dr. Gelman," a nurse he had never met said as he entered.

"Thank you," he said. "Good morning."

"How's Jenny?" the young nurse asked with a sly smile and a knowing insider's wink. "Is she enjoying her days off?"

"She's great," Jason said with a forced smile and hoped it was true.

Nathan's eyes looked heavy with sleep, but they were open and he looked happily at Jason when he entered. Sherry Doren held her boy's good hand and smoothed his hair with her other. She smiled when she saw him.

"Hi, Dr. Gleman—I'm sorry—Jason," she corrected.

"Hi, Sherry," he said. "And how are you doing, big guy?" He winked at Nathan, the world suddenly becoming not such a terrible place, at least for a moment.

"Good," Nathan said, his voice still thick with anesthesia and narcotics. "Thank you for coming."

Jason suspected that they both knew what he meant, and it had nothing to do with his surgery.

"Were you with him in there?" Sherry asked.

"For most of it," Jason answered. His shoulder burned to remind him of where they had been. "Everything went great."

You have no idea, lady.

"So when do you think he can go home?"

Jason felt a heat spread over him. That issue had danced around in his head for the last day, but now that he had been to the cave and knew that Jenny was in real danger; the importance of the issue exploded in size.

"The Burn Service doctors are gonna want to watch the graft closely for at least a few days," he said. "He can probably leave the ICU soon, but I would count on another couple of days in the hospital."

Sherry nodded. She seemed quite content to keep Nathan in the safe and secure environment. He wondered if she would feel as content if she knew where he went when his eyes closed. Jason sat on the edge of the bed across from Nathan's mom and looked affectionately at the groggy boy.

"You sure you're okay?"

"Yeah," Nathan answered. He looked over at his mom. "Mommy, can you get me some juice, please?"

"Sure, baby," Sherry said. She seemed relieved to have something to do to take care of her boy. She kissed him on the forehead and then stood up and smoothed her shirt with both hands. Jason noticed that her eyes were puffy and guessed she had been crying. "You want apple or orange?" she asked.

"Apple, please," Nathan answered.

"Okay—apple it is." She gave Jason another sad smile and headed out the door. As soon as she was gone, Nathan took Jason's hand.

"You got out okay," he said and immediately sounded much older than the child who had just asked his mommy for some juice. "I was worried you could get stuck and I knew the Lizard Men were tryin' to get you." He squeezed Jason's hand.

"I'm fine," Jason said. A wet trickle under his jury-rigged bandage reminded him he wasn't exactly unscathed, but he would get to that in a little while. "I'm really proud of you, Nathan. I can't believe how brave you are."

Nathan smiled, but his eyes still looked heavy and Jason no longer believed it was just the anesthesia.

"What are we gonna do, Jason?" he asked. "They won't stop now, 'cause I think they got a taste for it." He stared off for a moment and Jason felt helpless that he couldn't keep the boy away from the horrible images that must have been replaying in his mind. He had no idea what to say, but he knew Nathan was right—they had to stop these creatures somehow. They had done enough harm.

"I don't know what we're gonna do, buddy," he said and put a hand on Nathan's shoulder. "But we'll do something. I promise. And I will definitely keep you safe."

Nathan looked at him quizzically. "I'm not worried about that," he said simply. "We gotta save Jenny and then stop them from hurting other people. What if they start to hurt people who aren't bad? What if they try to hurt Jenny?" Jason saw a rim of tears pool in the boy's eyes. He bent over and gave him a hug.

Nathan let himself be held for a moment, but then pushed back out of the embrace. "You gotta go and check on Jenny, okay?"

"Okay," Jason agreed and then panic grew inside him. "Do you think something bad is happening right now?" he asked. "Is she in trouble?"

Nathan shook his head. "I don't know." Jason thought he looked at a miniature old man. "I don't think so, but I'm not sure. I think if she's gone from the cave she's safe for now," he concluded.

Jason nodded. He realized, though, that he needed desperately to get to the apartment.

"Okay," he said. "I'll go find her."

"Can you bring her by here?" Nathan asked. His voice sounded scared and more like a little boy's now. Jason was relieved that for a moment he could be the grown-up.

"Sure, buddy, and if you need me, do you think you can call me again in our heads?" Jason had a sudden sense of how insane this conversation sounded.

"I can try," Nathan said. "I don't know if it works if I'm not in the cave." Their eyes met and Jason's heart broke for the umpteenth time. "I don't wanna go there without you anymore."

"I know," Jason said. He couldn't think of anything else.

"Apple juice," Sherry announced from the door, ending any additional conversation. "I brought one for you, too." She handed a plastic cup to Jason.

"Thanks, Mommy." Nathan reached out for it. He sounded like a five-year-old again and for some reason that made Jason feel better. "Jason is gonna try and bring Jenny by later," he said enthusiastically.

"Oh, that's nice, She's you're favorite, huh, sweetie?"

"They both are," Nathan answered with a child's honesty and sipped his juice through the bent straw.

Jason rose off the corner of the bed. "Well, I better get going so I can come back by later, okay?"

"Okay," Nathan said happily.

"You have my numbers if you need anything, right? If anything happens?" he said to Sherry.

"Yeah," Sherry answered nervously. "What's gonna happen?"

"Oh, nothing," Jason answered. "I don't mean to worry you. He's doing great." He bent over and kissed Nathan on top of the head. "I just want you to know you can call if you need anything at all."

"Thanks so much, Dr. Gleman." Sherry shook his hand warmly.

"I'll see you both later," he said, waving from the door. "Get some sleep, buddy." He immediately regretted it.

"Bye," Nathan waved back.

Jason hustled out of the ICU with a quick I-know-what-it-is-you-know smile at the nurse who had greeted him, then jogged down the hall for the stairwell door. His shoulder burned and definitely needed attention, but right now he wanted to get home to Jenny. Then he slapped his own forehead.

It's not the eighteenth century, dumbass. Call her on the phone.

He didn't have her cell number, but he thought he could still remember her home number from the call he had received last night. Jason snuck in the back entrance to the ER through the Resident's Lounge, grateful that this door had a push-button lock instead of a swipe. He felt even more grateful that he found the lounge empty. He grabbed the phone off its hook on the wall and pushed the number in from memory. A lump filled his throat when there was no answer after the third ring, but then he heard the click of the receiver and closed his eyes in relief.

"Hello?" a sleepy, beautiful, sexy voice said. "Jason, is that you?"

"Hey," he said. For a moment he couldn't think what else to say. "Are you okay?"

He listened to silence for a minute and felt uncomfortable. "Yes," she finally said. "Where are you? Did you go to get coffee? Are you coming back?" Her voice held more than a hint of need, but she sounded fine otherwise.

"I had to do something real quick," he said. "I'll explain when I get home." He screwed up his face at the mistake. "Sorry, I mean when I get to your apartment, if you still want me to come back."

"Yes, please," she said with glee he could hear. "I'll wait right under these warm covers for you."

"I'll hurry," he said with his own big smile.

Jason hung up the phone and decided to quickly repair his shoulder in the locker room so he wouldn't have to do it in the bathroom at Jenny's. For a moment he thought about asking one of his fellow residents to sew his wound for him; suturing it himself in a mirror would be a huge pain in the ass. Jason decided that would still be less painful than coming up for an explanation for the filthy gash.

The ER looked crazy busy and no one even acknowledged him as he snuck into the supply room and grabbed some sterile water, betadine scrub, lidocaine to numb his skin, and some sutures. He took the supplies back to the men's locker room and shower area and ten minutes later his wound was clean and closed. The stitches were a little crooked—it turned out to be harder than he thought to suture backward in a mirror and he had to kind of do it one handed—but it was good enough. He put a fresh bandage on and hurried out of the hospital to get to Jenny's.

As Jason entered the walkway to the parking garage, he noticed the figure in scrubs slumped against the glass wall. The man looked either exhausted or racked with grief, neither of which was at all uncommon for doctors at the training hospital—especially residents who still worked the impossible hours of doctors-in-training. As he got closer, he realized he knew the guy.

"Doug?" he said, a little unsure, as he approached. The man looked over with hollow eyes. The unshaven face stared back at Jason without recognition. Jason realized it was definitely Doug Driscoll—one of the Surgery Chief Residents—and he looked like absolute shit. "Doug, it's me—Jason Gelman. We did the Trauma Service together last year, remember?"

The hollow eyes stared back at him in silence.

"Dude, are you alright?"

"Jason?" The face looked confused, then the man's mouth finally closed and he swallowed hard. His eyes seemed to clear only slightly and he smiled. The smile sent a chill through Jason. He saw no joy in it. Instead it seemed the manic smile of a man with some serious-ass problems. "Hey, Jason. Whassup?" An even more disturbing rattling laugh escaped from the guy's mouth.

"Let me help you, bud." Jason put an arm around Doug's chest, pulling him to his feet. At first his friend felt like dead weight, but Doug finally tossed an arm around Jason's neck and got his feet under him. "Maybe we should get you to a call room for a couple of hours of sleep before you try and head home. Whatdya' say, man?"

The surgeon pushed hard against him and scrambled back against the wall as if Jason had suddenly turned into some terrifying animal.

"No!" he said, backpedaling away from Jason and toward the door. "No, you don't get it. They can get you in your sleep. That's when they come for you. I don't want to do it anymore."

Jason realized his fellow resident had cracked up. "Well, maybe we can just turn your pager off for a while. How's that sound? We can get one of the other chiefs to hold it, okay? They can't wake you if the beeper's off, right?"

The man's eyes cleared a little more and he seemed to really recognize Jason for the first time. He looked around as if he just then realized where he was. Then he seemed to calm down.

"Wow." He sounded embarrassed. "Sorry about that."

"Long night?" Jason asked, watching the surgeon closely. "You okay?"

"Yeah," Doug answered. "Long night. I'll be okay now." He gave another grin that Jason found disturbing. "I'm fine in fact. It's really gonna be over now." He straightened himself up and started toward the door that exited the walkway to the street.

"You sure you don't want me to help you home?" Jason called after him. "You look exhausted."

"Nah," Doug answered with a little wave over his shoulder. "I need to do this alone."

Jason watched as his friend pushed through the door and started down the block between the hospital and the parking deck, out toward the main road.

"Okay," he mumbled. He watched after the Chief Resident for only a moment and then hustled down the hall toward the garage.

Jason stopped dead in his tracks at the jarring blare of the horn, the squeal of locked-up car wheels skidding across asphalt, and a horrible, crunching thud. He turned slowly, and then sprinted toward the exit door and down the block.

The silver Lexus Sedan's driver screamed as she saw the same thing Jason did, but to Jason the scream sounded far away. He stared in horror at his friend's crumpled body, pinned beneath the left front tire of the car. The entire torso had twisted around backward—the upper body faced up into the cars smashed grill and the hips and legs faced down.

Above the neck there remained nothing but mangled flesh and part of the lower jaw—the rest of the head a dark, wet smear behind the car. Dark blood soaked the green scrub suit and formed a rapidly growing puddle around the neck and shoulders of the corpse. Little jets of red blood still pulsed out of the neck, the heart having not yet realized the futility of beating. An older man in a suit cried uncontrollably.

"He looked right at me! What the hell? He looked right at me and smiled and then he dove right under my car," the woman driver sobbed. "Oh, my God! Oh, my God!"

Jason closed his eyes, covered his ears with his hands and then turned away and sprinted for the parking garage. He had no idea why the sight of his fellow resident smeared all over the road suddenly filled him with dread for Jenny's safety. He needed desperately to be with her, to hold her, and to know she was okay.

There was nothing more he could do for Doug.

Chapter
15

Nathan drifted, but felt no real worry that he would head back to the cave. Something made him feel he would be safe for now, so he let himself go toward the comfort of sleep. He thought about Jenny, mostly, and whether Jason would find her like they both hoped. He didn't worry because he thought that if she was in trouble she would have still been in the cave when they had checked, either suffering or dead. He knew that they had to do something to keep her out of the cave, though.

Yep. You gotta Power Up, Ranger. She's gonna need you more than you think, and really soon.

He guessed that was right, but hoped that Jason knew what they had to do, 'cause he sure didn't.

I really am just a kid, even if I am almost six.

His hand didn't really hurt, not yet at least, but it had started to tingle and he figured it would start to hurt pretty soon. He thought about pushing the little button that the nurse had put beside him in the bed, the one that gave the stronger pain medicine. He was pretty sure he wouldn't go to the cave unless he chose to now, but he didn't want the funny feeling he got with the medicine. He would wait a little longer, until he really needed it.

The heavy breathing beside him told him his mom finally slept; her hand across his chest a warm comfort. The pictures of Steve in his head— Steve with all his guts torn out and lying beside him in the dirt—kept him from real sleep. He could see the blank, empty eyes in his brain, looking up but not seeing, the pale face spattered with drying blood. He wanted the pictures to go away, but they just kept coming back every time he closed his eyes.

He heard something, far away, kind of, but still like it was in his head. It sounded like a stirring, followed by a tremendous wet thump, and he knew immediately what the sound meant.

Someone just got dumped in the cave. Wanna go check it out?

"No," he said softly and pushed the voice away. He couldn't go right now, and not without Jason. He knew, somehow, that it wasn't Jenny who got dumped and Jason would call him in his head if he went there.

He decided to dream-build like his Mommy taught him when he got scared at night. He just needed to picture a happy place and then relax and fall asleep. Then, if he did it right, he would dream about the story he made up. It worked pretty well when he was little. He pictured Jason and Jenny and his Mommy all playing with him at the park.

In his imagination he ran around and Jason chased him and played tickle-me tag. Everyone looked so happy. Mommy and Jenny watched them and drank juice from juice boxes. Every now and then they would see him look over and they would smile real big and wave. He would giggle and wave back, then dash away from Jason, jumping down the slide. In the dream his hand had no bandage and didn't hurt or anything.

He smiled as he drifted off to sleep and into the dream he'd built. He hardly even heard the grunt of the Lizard Men as they returned to the cave with the new person they had taken there.

Hardly heard it at all.

* * *

Jenny couldn't fall back asleep and didn't really want to anyway, so she stared at the ceiling and waited for Jason. She thought about getting up to get a drink—her throat burned with dryness—but she really wanted to be snuggled under the warm covers when he arrived.

Jenny stretched her back and let her eyes travel around the dancing lights on the ceiling and walls. She watched them sway across the room in rhythm to the gentle motion of the towels that moved across the windows. She would be back on day shift tomorrow so the towels could come down. Lately, her laziness resulted in them being up all the time, but now that she might have company in here regularly… she smiled at that thought.

Her gaze fell on the nightstand on the far side of the bed where a picture frame laid face-down for some reason. She rolled on her side and pulled the five-by-seven picture over to her and then lay on her back and clutched it to her chest. She knew the picture well—it showed her parents, her brother, and her all smiling in front of the giant Mickey Magician's hat at Disney's MGM studios. They went only a few years ago, when she still had only college to worry about. They had laughed all week at being a family with grown kids who could think of no better family vacation than Disney. They had been surrounded mostly by families with kids fifteen years younger, but she doubted any of them were having more fun.

The week had been wonderful. They had spent hours and hours at all four parks, and at night, laughed and played board games or dominos, sipping wine in their rented condo. The picture held so many great memories—so why had she placed it face-down and why could she now not look at it? She took a deep breath and pulled the picture from her chest and held it up. She looked at the happy, smiling faces of her family—and then burst into tears. Dark images again exploded in her mind, and she shook her head violently back and forth to shake them out.

What the hell is wrong with me? Am I losing my mind?

She reached for the phone, suddenly overwhelmed by a need to talk to her mom. Then the other voice came to her and spoke, but she knew couldn't possibly be her own.

Why would you talk to that whiney bitch? Where was she when her bastard husband raped you until you couldn't walk? Where was she when your brother had his spine shattered?

"God, just please shut the hell up!" She threw her hands to her face. The right one still clutched the picture frame, which struck her forehead hard enough to cause white flashes of light in her closed eyes. She felt the pain, but not enough to let it rise above the anguish that spread out like heat from the center of her chest. She wanted her mom and dad—no, for now she really wanted Jason.

A knock at the door, just barely audible through the screaming in her head, brought her back and she opened her eyes. Jenny stared at the ceiling, her breath stuck in her throat. For a moment she thought perhaps the Lizard Men –

What the hell is a Lizard Man?

Oh, come on, girl—like you don't know.

–but then the sound of her door chime followed the knock and she knew Jason had finally come.

"Coming," she hollered louder than she meant to. The hysterical sound of her voice bothered her a lot.

Halfway into her sprint across the living room, she remembered that she wore only an American Heart Association Fun-Run T-Shirt and a pair of thong panties, but she couldn't make herself care. She tore open the door and wrapped her arms around Jason's neck, who looked both ways down the hallway of her apartment building to see who might catch a glimpse of his girlfriend in her panties. His arms hugged her back and she felt warm relief as he half carried her back into the apartment and closed the door.

Jenny clung to him tightly and breathed in his scent. She realized that Jason seemed the only reality she could be certain of right now. She felt him lean into her embrace and it seemed like maybe he needed it every bit as much. She pulled her head off his chest and looked up at him. His eyes were dark and heavy and she felt her relief slide away and the cloak of dread replace it.

"What's wrong?" she asked and put a hand on his cheek. "Are you okay? Is something wrong with Nathan?" The panic inside her grew. "You don't have to leave do you?"

"No," he said. "I'm not going anywhere and Nathan is fine. It's just— there are things we have to talk about."

Oh, God. Please don't leave me right now.

"Is it me?" she asked. Her voice cracked and her throat burned. "Do you want to be with me?"

"Oh, God, yes," he said and his voice clearly told her he meant it. "Yes, I want to be with you, Jenny." He dropped his hands around her waist and looked at her deeply. She let herself float away in his gaze. For a moment she felt safe. "It's about all of us—you, me and Nathan. It's about what's going on."

Jenny felt herself grow heavy in his arms, but his grip on her tightened. She didn't think she could take anything else right now. Tears filled her eyes and blurred his face.

"Can we just have a few minutes together first?" she pleaded.

Jason answered by kissing her, gently at first and then deeper and more urgently. She let her lips part and felt his tongue on hers. Jenny pressed her body against him and pulled him inside the apartment as she walked slowly backward toward her bedroom.

Jason realized they had slept, legs wrapped around each other in the sweat-soaked sheets, for much longer than he had intended. He'd needed the distraction of their passion at least as much as she had, but there were things that needed to be discussed. Twice now she had run away from his attempts to talk about what was happening. Jason doubted that she even knew how hard she avoided it. For them, all of them, to have a chance he needed to cowboy up and make the conversation happen. He had seen with his own eyes what had happened to Maloney and now Doug, and he had no doubt that this woman he found himself irresistibly drawn to was in immediate danger.

Jason shivered at the memory of Doug's lifeless body, the head a gory smear behind the car wheel. He hugged Jenny tight against him, felt the smoothness of her hip against his and the cool wetness of her thigh beneath his own leg. He kissed her neck softly.

"Jenny?"

"I'm awake," she said.

"Can we talk now?"

Jason felt her stretch out beside him. She pulled him tighter, held his wrists, and wrapped his arms around her like a blanket against the cold. "Yes," she said. He heard pain and fear in her voice and he kissed her neck again.

"First, I want you to know that I'm absolutely crazy about you," he said. "No matter what, I want you to know that, and that I really want us to…" He paused. To what? "To have something, you know? A future I mean."

"Me too," she said warmly to his relief. "It seems weird because we've been together so little time, but I feel there's something real here." She pulled his hand to her mouth and kissed it. "I don't want to lose it either."

"That's great," he said with more gushing than he intended. Then he dove in. "Jenny, I need you to tell me about your dreams."

He felt her entire body tense against his. "What do you mean?" she asked.

"I want you to tell me about the cave, Jenny. I know it's scary, but you need to tell me what you remember."

"I can't," she said and started to sob. "How do you know about the cave?"

Jason rolled her over to face him and pulled her hands from her face. He caressed a tear away from her cheek and she opened her eyes and looked at him. "Jenny," he started. "This is gonna sounds nuts, but I don't think the cave dreams are really dreams." She scrunched up her face. He kept his hand on her cheek and continued "I've been there, too, Jenny. It's real. I've been there with Nathan and he's been there a few times—he saw you there."

Jenny's face turned white, but she looked like something had clicked. The fear in her eyes disappeared, replaced with what looked like a desperate need to understand.

"Yes," she whispered. "I've seen him there, I think." Her hushed voice held a conspiratorial tone. "What the hell is going on, Jason?" Her fingernails dug into his arms, but he stroked her face gently anyway.

"I'll tell you everything I know and heard from Nathan, and then you have to tell me what you remember, okay?"

Jenny nodded, tight lipped.

And Jason told her. He held nothing back. He started with his strange draw to Nathan in the ER and continued on to his vision, or whatever it had been, of the creatures in the alley. He told her how Nathan had confided in him about the cave and how that had stirred up all of the memories from his past. He skirted around the issue of Steve at first, but then he explained how they had seen Steve—dead and disemboweled—in the cave. Jenny's face flushed and filled again with tears.

"Oh my God," she hissed.

"What is it?" he asked, both hands on her face now, frightened at the look in her eyes.

"I think I know how I play into all of this now," she said. Her eyes, sharp and clear, held his gaze. "I think I might have something to do with what happened to Steve." Her brow furrowed in confusion. "I can't clearly make out the memories," she said. "But, I don't think it had anything to do with the cave. It's like a different memory—something at the hospital, I think."

Jason considered that a moment. What had happened at the hospital and caused all the pain and death in the cave? Nathan believed that the Lizard Men—the creatures would always be Lizard Men to him now that Nathan had called them that—smelled their fear somehow and that they liked it or needed it or something. Might they be doing something at the hospital to feed that need? He had a flash of his mother's terrified face in the hospital room and for a moment he nearly had it—something she had said the night she died. But then it disappeared again, like someone dangled a needed piece to the puzzle in front of him and then jerked it away every time he grabbed for it.

You know what they need. They chased you that night—so many years ago. You tried to help her but you were too scared. Scaredy cat, scaredy cat—and now Mommy's dead.

"What is it?" Jenny asked, and this time she touched his cheek.

"Nothing," he said and looked away. "There's something back there—something in my past—but I can't get to it." He looked at her with a sad smile. "Tell me about your dreams. Not just the cave, but all of them."

Jason listened with the dull chest ache of empathy at the anguish Jenny felt from fragmented memories of the cave and the hospital. She told him of waking by the coffee kiosk and the strange feelings she'd had in the parking garage. Then she stopped for a moment. Jason watched her face as she searched for something.

"There is something, I think," she said. He waited patiently for her to try and get a grip on whatever it was. She looked at him and continued. "The night we first met—I went to my car the next morning and I think something happened." Again her eyes searched in vain around the room for the answer. "There was this horrible smell—and then—damnit, why can't I get to it?"

Jason hugged her. "It's okay," he said. "I have that too. It's like they put a wall around the memories somehow."

Jenny looked more than a little frightened. "Do you have any idea how insane this all sounds?"

He sure as shit did. Jason wrapped his arms around her and pulled her soft, naked body back against his. She laid her head on his chest and sighed. Jason remembered the picture, face down on the bookshelf.

"Can you tell me about your family?" he asked.

Her arms tightened around his chest and he heard her sob. "I don't think so," she said. "It's like I have two sets of memories, or something. Like a terrible fight is going on in my head, two voices trying to tell me which memory is true." She cried harder and Jason could do nothing but hold her.

"Can you tell me about both?"

It tumbled out of her in confusing bits, much the way he guessed it must be inside her head. Two competing pasts—one of a happy, close-knit family and the other a horrible story of rape, assault and broken lives—spilled out of her. As he listened, one more piece seemed to sort itself out in the puzzle of their shared nightmare. He remembered the pictures of the happy family, of a young man who must be her brother, smiling at the camera from beside her, both parents hugging her and beaming with pride at her graduation. They sure as hell looked happy. And her brother didn't look in any way crippled.

"They must create memories, somehow," he said softly, more to himself. "They insert nightmares of a past into your head—maybe to control you." For a moment he wondered about his own memories. Were they made up as well? He unconsciously rubbed his thigh, touching the scars where the pins had been driven through his little boy flesh. No—that had been real.

He looked over at Jenny who studied him closely now.

"Can you call them?"

"Who?" she asked.

"Your parents—your brother," he said. "Call them and see which reality seems right when you're talking to them. Call your brother and just ask what he's up to. See how he sounds."

"We don't really talk," she said and her face clouded. Then she stopped. "Do we? I mean I think we do—or don't." Her face scrunched up again, almost like she was in pain. "I just don't know."

"Call them," he said simply.

She laid her head back on his chest. "Okay," she said. Her voice seemed more resigned than agreeable. "I'll do whatever you think."

A few minutes later, Jason lay alone in the bed and listened to Jenny as she talked to her brother on the phone. Her voice sounded strained and her brother must have thought so as well, because Jason heard her tell him that she was just tired from working nights.

"Really, I'm fine," her voice said from the other room. "Just tired—I love you, too. I will, I promise. I'll call you this weekend."

Jason listened to silence for a moment and then he heard her voice again.

"Mom? Hey, it's me. No, no, I'm fine."

Jenny small talked in the other room with her mom and Jason's mind drifted to Nathan—a grown man in a five-year-old body (almost six—a Nathan voice reminded him). Little Nathan whom he now believed held the key to the whole thing.

Unless he turns out to be a scaredy cat like you were.

"Whatever, dude," Jason mumbled. He would protect Nathan and Jenny from whatever the hell this was if he could.

Like your mom?

Jason pressed the heels of his hands hard into his eyes which set off little lightning flashes. He saw his mother's face—thin and pale. She looked at him from the hospital bed and tried to smile. He remembered a stale smell about her. After a few years in medicine, he knew that smell very well—that death smell.

"When they come for me, I think I'll just go," she had said.

Even then, Jason thought he had known she meant the Lizard Men. He just hadn't been able to admit it to himself.

Jenny plopped down on the bed beside him and put the cell phone on the end table. Jason took her hand.

"Everything alright?" he asked.

"Fine," she said, and she seemed a little more confident. "They're fine—and I know them. The real them, I think. The other pictures are still there, not the cave ones but—the others. I'm pretty sure I know they're lies." She looked at him and smiled weakly. "At least for now I feel that way. Can you help me understand what this all means?"

Jason shifted uncomfortably. "I'll try real hard."

Jenny laid her head on his shoulder and he wrapped his arms around her. He knew they should head to the hospital soon and check on Nathan, but he would give Jenny a few more minutes. After only a moment, Jenny's breathing turned heavy. *I'll just let her sleep for thirty minutes.*

Jason stared at the wall beyond her and held on tightly.

Chapter
16

Nathan didn't exactly decide to go; he just got to the point where he felt it might be okay. The other-him voice told him to head to the cave, taunted him really, and Nathan gave in, like when your friend on a play date had a game they really wanted to play and even though you didn't think it sounded fun, you did it because that's what friends do. He didn't feel sure the other-him voice was a friend, but "kind of sort of," like Mommy liked to say.

Nathan knew that a new body would be in the big room but he didn't worry about it. It might be gross, but after seeing Steve with his guts torn out and the other fat guy with his brains bashed out, he thought those types of things might not bother him so much.

Nathan crawled to the top of the path and looked down. It seemed weird to be in the cave and not feel super scared—maybe a little nervous, but definitely not super scared. Maybe he'd grown stronger. Maybe he would be able to Ranger up when the time came.

The time is coming, Ranger. You can count on it. Scaredy-cat days need to be behind us now. The time is almost here.

"I know," he mumbled, and he really did.

He looked down into the big cavern of a room and felt no surprise at the body on the dirt floor. Nathan swallowed hard, made a soft "Oooh" sound and then covered his mouth. He felt pretty sure the Lizard Men were not home, but wanted to be extra quiet just in case. The body looked more than just a little gross. The head was mostly missing except for a little part of the bottom of the face, and that looked all squished up.

The man looked like he had put his pants on backward, only he wore no pants—his butt was in the front and his weenie was in the back. All around his waist where he must've got twisted up, a thick line of black and blue spread out. At first, Nathan thought one arm had been torn off but then he saw it had been crunched up underneath the body. It looked even grosser than Steve. Nathan wondered just how the Lizard Men had torn him up so bad.

Let's go, Ranger. You gotta go down there.

"No way," he whispered harshly. "Not by myself."

He felt a big lump in his throat like he had swallowed a piece of steak without chewing it enough and he felt himself shake.

We gotta use the other way out—the way the Lizard Men come in.

I can't. Not alone. We have to wait for Jason.

No time for that, Ranger. Next time you're here together it'll be too late.

I'm scared.

I know—let's Power Up.

Nathan closed his eyes and pictured himself as a real Power Ranger. He crossed his arms at the wrist then pulled one arm back like on the show and imagined he had a real Power Ranger Morpher on his arm—a red one like the best Ranger. He kept his eyes closed and mumbled softly—

"Power Rangers—Power Up—Yeah!"

In his head he pictured himself surrounded by light and magically transformed into the powerful Red Ranger, a blaster on his belt and the cool red helmet and mask on his head. When he opened his eyes, he knew he still looked small and naked, but he felt bigger and braver.

"Okay," he said to himself with a Ranger-like voice. "Let's do this."

Nathan crawled on all fours and went over the ledge. On the way down, he stood up and looked around nervously. He half expected the bad guys to come out of nowhere and kept his right hand on his imaginary blaster, just in case.

The Lizard Men seemed always to move off to the left and so he turned that way, smart enough to keep his eyes off the body with the smashed-away head and backward legs. As he moved toward the left side of the cave, a soft but hot breeze licked his face and he thought he must be headed the right way, but it sure looked dark that way. The pinpoint of light he saw was probably just made up in his head, so he tried to make the dark corner he headed toward lighter. The corner stayed dark no matter how hard his mind tried to force light in front of him, but he gripped his imaginary blaster and moved into the shadow anyway.

"No problem," he mumbled, trying to sound brave.

The hot breeze felt more like a wind now and started to smell bad—similar to the smell the Lizard Men had when they came back forth to the real world.

Kinda-sorta.

Nathan wondered how the other-him voice sounded like Mommy. He moved more quickly into the shadows and the walls seemed closer as the passage squeezed down and became narrower. He felt himself crouch a little without thinking about it, but he knew he had plenty of distance to the ceiling—the Lizard Men were much taller than him.

Far ahead the darkness seemed to melt away, replaced by a soft glow. The fear came back and suddenly the dark seemed heavy. Nathan stopped, unsure. He wanted to go back. In fact he wanted to go back to his hospital bed right now. The smell got worse and the hot wind pushed his hair back on his head.

"I wanna go back," he said and knew his voice sounded all trembly and like a scared little boy. He didn't care.

I'm a little boy. I'm scared. I want my mommy.

You're more than you imagine. You're not a scaredy cat and you can be powerful, but you have to believe it.

I want my mommy.

Okay. Can you come back this way when it's time?

"When is that?" he asked, aloud this time.

You'll know.

"Okay," he said. Then he stopped for a moment, his thoughts suddenly pulled in another direction. "Who are you?"

Nathan listened for the other-him voice to answer inside his head but it didn't. He stood there, alone in the hot wind and nasty smell.

You already know.

"Are you inside of me?"

No. But I'm a part of you, and of Jason. And the others.

"Others?"

It doesn't matter. Remember this passageway. Let's power down, Ranger.

Nathan closed his eyes tightly and the bad smell changed almost immediately to the funny smell of the hospital and the soft smell of his mom's shampoo. He opened his eyes and stared up at the dark ceiling and breathed deeply of the cooler air.

Stay ready.

"I will," he said softly so as not to wake his mom. Then he closed his eyes and sighed. He pictured the park again and in his mind his mommy and Jason and Jenny all sat together with him on a picnic blanket, the playground in the background. Nathan pictured every detail and tried to hear their laughter and see their smiles, building a nice dream for himself.

* * *

Jenny snuggled backward toward Jason and felt his breath on her neck. She could feel sleep coming and wanted to plunge into it, but knew they should go check on Nathan. She just felt so damn exhausted. Maybe just a few minutes with her eyes closed, a short power nap. Jenny pulled Jason's hand to her mouth and kissed it gently.

Then she dreamed.

She knew it really was a dream, not just the weird, dreamlike fugue that had taken her to places where she worried she had done horrible things, or to the cave where maybe things had been done to her. No, she dreamed like real people dream, loopy little snippets, some funny and others weird.

At least at first.

Instead of the hot, filthy cave, Jenny went to a quiet pond where she sat alone in the tall grass and watched two deer sip gently from the water a few feet away. It felt more like an interruption of her dream, like when someone tries to shake you awake and so you just start dreaming that you're riding on a bumpy road.

She knew the voice that called her and for a moment she had a flash of her car, alone in the empty parking deck, her faced scrunched up against the horrible fart smell. She still sat by the pond and watched the two deer drink, but the voice called from somewhere else and she heard it in the dream. The deer seemed to hear it too, because they raised their heads and sniffed the air, suddenly alert to some potential danger.

Are you going to believe these lies, Jenny? Don't you see he just wants the same thing your daddy stole from you? He just wants what's between your legs, and you're giving it to him!

No, that wasn't true. The memories of her dad, the horrible memories—those were the lies. Jason rescued her from the evil lies. Jason, her hero.

Really? Can you feel that? Feel it against your back? It's his dirty cock and you let him put it inside you. He's raped you just like daddy—only you're easier to rape now, aren't you?

One of the deer by her little pond dashed off, spooked by the voice that intruded into the peaceful scene. The other one stopped sniffing the air and looked at Jenny, its eyes suddenly glowing embers. The mouth opened and the deer smiled with impossibly long teeth.

"It's not too late to help us stop them. You can help us make sure they all keep their dirty little cocks to themselves. You can help us make sure no one else gets fucked like you."

The doe stared at her, almost through her, and the orange glow of the eyes deepened to a dark red. She noticed movement on the far side of the pond and looked past the devil-deer and there stood Nathan. He squatted on the edge of the pond and seemed to poke at something with a stick. Then he saw her and stood up, his body so thin and frail, and waved.

"Listen to me!" the devil deer snarled. "He can't save any of you now."

Jenny raised her head from her pillow and stifled a scream in her throat. The deer and the pond and the horrible voice disappeared like a mist sucked from the room. But the feeling stayed inside her and for a moment she started to push Jason's arms off her so she could squirm away from his dirty cock. Then she saw his face in the soft light from her bathroom, soft and real. He looked at her and she rested her head back on the pillow and turned her body toward him, their eyes and noses only inches apart.

"Hi," she said with a real smile.

"Hi," he answered and kissed her gently. "Are you okay?"

"Yeah," she said and kissed him back. He wrapped his arms around her and she melted into him.

Just five more minutes.

* * *

They ran no risk of running into anyone between the parking garage and the hospital, since they arrived a good hour before the standard shift changes began at six-forty-five. Jason didn't want to talk to anyone, even to answer questions about how the most socially impotent resident on staff seemed to be scoring with a really, really hot nurse.

The halls were abandoned, the hour too early for visitors and the staff all scrambling to finish up work before their relief arrived. He held hands with Jenny and pushed the elevator up button. She looked at him and he gave her his most dashing it's-all-gonna-be-okay smile, but doubted he looked very reassuring. But she smiled back.

"You okay?" he asked and squeezed her hand.

"Yeah," she said and kissed his cheek. "Tired and grumpy."

He laughed.

They rode up the elevator in silence, still holding hands.

"You've got the numbers?" he asked.

Jenny patted the pocket of her scrub jacket, this one covered in bears holding balloons. "Right here," she promised. He had written down her cell number and the unit number and put it in his pocket, then given her the ER number, his cell, and his pager number. He didn't know what he thought might happen while they were at work, but he wanted to make sure they could get each other, just in case. They would also meet for lunch if they could both get away. Jason felt a little like an over-protective father, and as they approached the doors to the Pediatric ICU his thoughts went to the reason they were up early—Nathan.

"Well, my, my. Whatever do we have here?" Jason was jarred from his thoughts by Nurse Wernicke and her happy, I-caught-you-kids chuckle. He looked up and saw she stood with her hands on her generous hips and mischievous joy on her ruddy face. "And just what have you kids been up to?" Jason felt himself blush.

Jenny squeezed his arm and laid her head briefly on his shoulder. Surprised, Jason grinned at the charge nurse like a seven-year-old kid who just scored his first basket in a real game. He tried to think of something clever to say, but instead just let Jenny pull him along toward Nathan's room.

"You guys look great together," the charge nurse called after them.

As Jenny reached for the door to Nathan's room, Jason put his hand on hers and she turned and looked at him with the same far away but real smile. "Are we?" he asked.

"What?"

"Great together?"

She kissed his cheek and smiled. For a moment she looked like what she should be—a young woman with the exciting butterflies from a new relationship.

Together they entered Nathan's room.

Nathan looked a little tired, but beamed when he opened his eyes and saw them.

"I was just dreaming about you guys," he said.

The words gave Jason a chill and his mouth went dry, but Nathan looked content so he shook the feeling off.

"How'r ya doin', bud?" he asked and sat beside Nathan on the edge of the bed.

"I just told my mommy—I mean my mom—about this great dream I had. All you guys were there and we were havin' a picnic and there was a playground and everything."

"Was there a pond? Were there deer there?" Jenny's voice sounded flat in a way that made Jason even more uneasy. He felt a growing sense, not of *déjà vu* exactly, but more of foreboding. Nathan must not have felt it because he continued on happily.

"No, Miss Jenny, but they had a water fountain and Jason splashed me with water from it. There was a fountain, but not a pond. I think I saw a squirrel."

Nathan continued on and Jason watched Jenny closely. The cloud that had engulfed her at the mention of the dream dissipated, but she still seemed distant.

Something's wrong. You know that, right, bro? You better keep your shit together and be ready to rock if you think you're gonna keep these two safe.

Yeah, like you did for your mom, scaredy cat.

Jason made a little "tsk" sound that no one heard and ignored the voice, again. Nathan talked about playing tag around the jungle gym in his dream.

"It was awesome, you guys." Jason noticed that Nathan unconsciously cradled his bandaged arm and wondered if he had much pain. "We should totally try and go to a park like that when this is all over." The boy looked over at his mom, like he had said a bad word or let out a secret. "You know—when I get out of the hospital, I mean." He looked at Jason and smiled; his face held the kid version of a wink.

"We will definitely do that, buddy," he said and squeezed Nathan's shoulder gently.

They chatted for a few more minutes and Jason tried to answer some of Sherry's questions. The Burn Service doctors had already told them that Nathan would leave the ICU today and go to a regular room.

Jason made a mental note to try and cash in some favors and get them a private room if there were any available. The time went by quickly until Jenny squeezed his arm gently.

"I need to get to shift report," she said.

"Ah, Jeez," Jason said looking at his watch. "I need to get down to the ER, too." He looked over at Sherry who seemed pretty content. "You've got my cell number, right, Sherry?"

"I do," she said with a smile. "You guys have both been so great."

"Can you call me and let me know when he moves to a new room so I can find him? We might try and stop by at lunch," he said and cast a glance at Jenny who nodded enthusiastically.

"Absolutely," she said. "And I'll try and get Nathan as part of my assignment so I can be the one who transfers him."

Jason kissed Nathan on top of the head, which seemed to embarrass the boy a little. Jenny gave Nathan a big hug.

"I'll see you in just a little while and I'm here all day if you need anything," she said.

"Thank you, Jenny," Sherry said with a warm smile.

Jason checked again that Jenny seemed okay and had the phone numbers, just in case.

"I got 'em—you're like a worried parent." Then she kissed his cheek and Jason headed to the ER.

I think we just might get through this day.

Stay sharp. Today things will begin—

He shuddered at the words of the other-him voice in his head and wondered just what the hell he could possibly do if anything did go wrong.

Chapter
17

He checked, for the tenth time, the nine millimeter tucked into the back of his baggy jeans. He had put on an old pair of jeans this morning, from before it was cool to wear 'em loose, just so's he could carry his gun in the small of his back like he'd seen Tick do so many times. He didn't feel nervous, just jacked. Tick would think he was a badass when he brought him all this green. Nah, not nervous. Just jacked. This would be easy.

The white kids weren't street, not really. They wanted to score some junk and be cool, try to impress their friends. They wanted to look street, but they didn't come from no shit-ass neighborhood. You wanna be street? Okay, no problem.

Jazz gonna bring you some street, assholes.

He'd never been able to actually get anyone except his little brother to call him Jazz, which he thought would be a slick street name, but that was gonna change today. Those white punks would bring the cash for dope he had no intention of giving them, and he was gonna take it from them and give it to Tick. Then they'd call him whatever the fuck he wanted. If he had to cap one of the bitches, even better. That would be some real serious street cred.

He felt warm in his hooded sweatshirt, even though the morning still seemed pretty cold. Must just be excited, 'cause he sure as shit wasn't nervous. Not him. He needed it to cover his piece in the back of his jeans (which he now checked one more time) and to cover his head and face when he ran away with the cash.

James (Jazz, goddamnit—James was a faggot name) rounded the corner and walked the short alley behind the tire store that would take him to the dead end behind the grocery. He forced himself not to check his piece again 'cause if they were here already, they would see him, and anyway, he could feel it rubbing uncomfortably on his back. Two guys in jeans and work boots with dark jackets waited for him at the end of the alley. He took a big breath and sauntered in.

"Where that other boy, the one with the shitty skin?" he called to the two boys standing crossed arm in front of him.

"Don't worry about him. You got our junk?"

"Yeah, man, don't sweat nothing," he answered and reached behind him like it was in his back pocket. Instead, he wrapped his hand around the butt of his gun. "Show me some green first."

The taller kid reached down into the front of his pants and pulled out a huge wad of bills. James felt his heart race and his eyes widened at the sight of it. Shit, these boys had really brought three thousand dollars. No fuckin' shit! He realized his arm shook a lot and tried to make it stop.

I ain't scared. Just excited.

He pulled the gun out and pointed it at the two, rotating it sideways—gang style, he thought to himself. He laughed a higher-pitched laugh than he meant to.

"How's 'bout you assholes put my money down on the ground there and get your silly white asses the fuck outta here?" He liked how tough that sounded. Shit, this was easy. The boys looked scared—but not really. He tightened his grip on the gun and felt his arm shake a little. What was wrong?

James felt a flurry of motion behind him and spun around just in time to see the zit-faced kid whip the big metal bar over his head. He tried to move out of the way, but the bar caught him at the base of the neck and he both heard and felt the sickening crunch of bones giving way. For a moment he saw white light and felt like he floated, but the sensation disappeared abruptly when he landed with a jarring thud on the street and his head exploded in pain. Through the flashes of light he tried to look up and see what had happened and saw the shadowy image of the boy spinning the bar over his head for another blow. James raised both of his arms above him.

"Crush his nigger head." He heard one of the other two scream. Then he felt the metal smash into his raised arms and again felt bones shatter. James heard a howling scream and realized it was him. His eyes started to clear, but tears blurred the image that towered above him. He realized the figure bent down beside him. James shook his head to clear it and the motion brought excruciating pain from his shattered collarbone.

He heard a clattering sound and, in terror, realized the figure had picked up his gun. He squeezed his eyes shut and opened them again and saw the kid with the bad skin look down at him from behind the nine millimeter. The boy's acne-scarred face looked scared and Jazz had a glimmer of hope that the boy wouldn't be able to do it.

"Try and rip us off, you black piece of shit."

The hate in the voice stole away his hope. He closed his eyes and waited for his head to explode like a pumpkin.

The bang of the gun sounded much louder than he expected and it felt like the boy had kicked him hard in the chest—but that was all. He felt nothing else and opened his eyes.

The boy looked down at him in terror instead of victory, then dropped the gun and dashed out of view. Holy shit! He had missed. Point-fucking-blank and he had missed. He listened to the boys scurry out of the alley and couldn't believe he was alive.

"HOLY FUCK, DUDE. YOU FUCKING KILLED HIM. LET'S GET OUTTA HERE."

You didn't kill shit, man. I can't believe you fuckin' missed. I will find you bitches and we will fuck you up for this.

James felt incredibly tired. He knew he had to grab his piece and get out of there before the cops came, but his body weighed a thousand pounds and he couldn't possibly get up. Maybe he would just rest a second and then he would jam. He took a deep breath and felt a hollow tug in the right side of his chest and then a hot, shooting pain. He painfully reached his hand to the spot and new anguish shot up his arm. A warm wetness met his tingling fingers as he felt the side of his shirt. Panic started to build in his chest, right alongside the new full feeling, and he raised his hand to his eyes slowly, the pain in his arm now irrelevant.

The hand was coated in blood and he realized what that meant.

"That fuckin' guy shot me," he whispered and heard a raspy gurgle. It was hard to suck in the air he needed and he began to feel real fear now.

"Help me," he whispered. "I don't wanna die."

Sirens screamed in the distance and for once they gave him hope instead of fear. They would take him to the hospital. They would get him there and he would be okay. The hospital would be safe and they would save him.

And when I get better, I will fuck those guys up.

Chapter
18

Jason usually loved the trauma cases. Today, anything that took his thoughts away from his search for a plan to stop the nightmare he found himself in served as a distraction and nothing more.

Still, anything that makes the day go faster is good, right?

The residents from the Trauma Service, mostly surgeons plus a couple of students and Brent from his ER program, already scurried around donning their gowns and masks. His job was really to help out and assume care if the patient turned out to not need surgical admission to the hospital. That seemed pretty unlikely since the dispatcher for EMS told them the patient had a gunshot wound to the chest and multiple fractures. Jason pulled on his own stuff just in case they needed a hand and felt a little relief that he could think for a moment about something other than caves and Lizard Men.

Jason stood back against the wall as the medics came in, rolling the stretcher in front of them.

"African-American male, about nineteen or twenty years old, single gunshot wound to the right chest. Hemodynamically stable after one liter of IV fluids. Very poor breath sounds on the right—getting a little tachycardic the last few minutes and breathing fast now—also has obvious fractures with deformity to both forearms, which we splinted and a big 'ol hematoma at the base of his neck on the left—probably a clavicle fracture—looks like someone beat him with a bat or something before they shot him."

"I'm sure he was mindin' his own business and two dudes shot him for no reason," someone chimed in from the Trauma Bay. The familiar old joke referred to what it seemed nearly all of the victims said when they were likely bad guys themselves. The medic ignored the comment and continued with the patient's vital signs, which Jason noted were not too terrible.

The patient's heart beat a little faster than normal, he breathed too fast and Jason guessed he had either a blood or an air leak in his chest. Probably both. He wished he could do the chest tube, which the patient definitely needed, but he knew someone on the Trauma Team would get to do that procedure. He busied himself setting up the chest-tube tray so they could pop it in quickly once the team finished their initial assessment.

"Brent, pop in a chest tube on the right, will 'ya?" the trauma chief ordered.

Jason handed off the chest-tube tray to his friend from the ER and stepped back. He found himself rapidly losing interest and decided to just wait until they placed the tube to find out how much blood came out; anything less than a liter and a half and the guy probably didn't need surgery. This patient was definitely being admitted to the ICU either way, so Jason's role in his care was dwindling fast.

"What's your name, sir?" The chief resident asked.

"Jazz. What the fuck is your name?"

"Jazz. Right. Perfect." The chief rolled his eyes and turned to Brent. "What ya got?"

"About six hundred milliliters and a little rush of air," Brent called after a moment.

"Pressure looks stable and his heart rate is coming down," someone else said.

Jason snapped off his gloves and tossed them in the big red trash can. Enough of that—the guy would definitely be admitted to the Trauma Service. He decided to start whittling down his patient list so he could get out on time. He had no idea what the evening might hold, but the weird, uneasy feeling hadn't left him.

"Spidey sense is tingling," he mumbled.

You'll need more than that, trooper. You better start looking deep for things you'll need. It isn't just you that suffers if you fail this time.

He pictured Nathan—little Nathan, all boy and more of a man than him—and the pretty face of Jenny who he thought he might love even though he barely knew her. "Chest pain patient in six, Dr. Gelman," a nursing triage tech said and shoved a chart in his hand.

If he could just get a minute to think.

Chapter
19

His chafed ankle, handcuffed to the rail of the ICU bed, hurt nearly as bad as where the fuckin' white, college-boy doctor had stabbed him in the chest with the tube. Didn't even give him no fuckin' medicine. Rich assholes. He knew they did that shit on purpose. That tube thing did take away the smothering feeling and made it easier to breathe, though, so he guessed they got that right. It still ached any time he shifted.

"Let me meet you on my street, bitch," he mumbled.

"What's that you say there, James?" The big cop sat with his knees crossed in the oversized beige chair beside him. "You talkin' shit, boy? Better keep that to yourself." The cop glared at him for a moment and then went back to his newspaper. James knew enough to say nothing.

His belly ached and he wondered when the hell he would get some food. Probably they kept that from the brothers too. He shifted in bed again and tried to lay his left leg so that it didn't pull on the handcuffs.

The door opened and an even bigger cop came in. He cast a look of more than hate, of almost a blind rage, at him before pulling his eyes away. He leaned over and whispered something to the cop in the chair.

"You sure?" the first cop said.

"Yeah, it's not a problem. I'll stay here with him while they chat."

"He's a Fed or something?"

"Can't really talk about it, Danny. But it's fine. I'll stay here I promise."

The cop in the chair frowned but got up and folded his paper. "Whatever you say, Sarge. I'll go grab a cup of coffee." He glared back before he left. "You try not to be an asshole while I'm gone, James."

James looked away and said nothing.

"Oh, he won't. I promise you that," the new cop said. Something in his voice sent a shiver up James's spine, but he couldn't be sure why.

Fuck these guys. They just tryin' to scare me. I ain't sayin' shit to no one.

The older cop stood against the wall with his arms folded across his chest. James found it hard not to look over at him, but managed somehow. Then the door opened again and he looked up.

The figure that walked through the door should've looked funny, but he didn't. In another circumstance James would have hassled the man in the long trench coat and low-riding hat. But something about the pale skin and the eerie trick of the hospital lights that made his eyes appear to be glowing orange, made his chest feel tight in a place nowhere near the big tube that hung from his side.

He strained his own eyes to make sense of the image before him, the head tilted down and the hands clasped in front. At first, James didn't notice the shorter version behind the first man; same low hat and long coat, his pale hands up close to his hidden face and holding a small notebook and a stub of a pencil.

"These men have some questions for you, James," the older cop said without moving from the wall.

"Name's Jazz," James said, trying to sound tough. He tried to clear his throat but made a squeaking noise instead. His mouth felt so dry that it actually burned and he thought his throat might close up.

The taller figure tilted his head slightly back.

"I'm Mr. Clark and this is Mr. Smith," he said. "We have some questions, James."

Mr. Clark's mouth seemed to grow until it split open like an infected wound, revealing impossibly long and pointed teeth.

* * *

Nathan lay alone in his bed. His mother had left to hunt down some apple juice for him (they only had orange in the ICU right now) and at first the being alone felt kind of nice. But now he felt anxious and didn't know why. His stuff sat in a pile at the foot of his bed—some clothes and a few toys from home stuffed into a Buzz Lightyear rolling suitcase. It didn't matter much since he only took up about half the length of the bed.

Miss Jenny came in a lot to check on him and she seemed to be doing a little better. Her smile seemed more real, he thought. The last time she came by, Jenny told them that Nathan's room on the other floor—the place where people went when they were nearly better she told him—was ready and helped his mom organize all his stuff for the ride to the new place. New places could always make you a little nervous.

It's not the new room. Things are going on, Ranger. You are on high alert.

I'm ready.

But he could be more ready if he knew what things were happening. No pictures showed up clearly in his head, but Nathan felt sure the Lizard Men were up to something bad. He wished Miss Jenny would come in again. He closed his eyes and tried to listen, strained to hear the far-off sounds of the cave without really going there.

Name's Jazz.

The voice sounded nothing like the other-him voice from his head. It sounded scared. He could hear the raspy sound of the Lizard Men breathing, the hunger in them. Nathan felt even more scared when the room felt swimmy and he worried he might open his eyes and be in the cave by himself with the creatures. When he opened his eyes, he was relieved to see his hospital room, but it made the conversation and the shuffling noises seem much farther away. Nathan took a deep breath and got ready to close his eyes and listen again, but the door opened and Miss Jenny came in.

"Hi, Nathan," she said warmly. He liked that she always called him Nathan, just like he liked it that Jason almost never did—to him he was always buddy or bud or sport or something.

"Hi," he said.

"Are you okay?" Jenny asked. Her face knitted up like Mommy's did when she thought he might be sick.

"Yeah," he said and looked past her to be sure his mom wasn't right behind her. "I think something bad is happening—in the cave." He nearly whispered the last part, but she heard it and Nathan knew she heard it because her face got all pale.

"Is it Jason?" she asked. "Is he okay?"

"No," he said and saw her mouth drop open. "I mean yes, yes he's okay—no it's not Jason who's in trouble."

"Thank God." She breathed and hugged him. Then she sat on the side of his bed and took Nathan's hand.

"I think they're takin' someone else," he said. "I think we gotta tell Jason."

The door opened and his mom came in with some juice. She looked at the two of them and they must have looked like something bad had happened, because she got her worried look.

"What is it? What's wrong?" she asked and stopped in the door like she could stay away from whatever the problem was.

"Oh, nothing," Jenny said and got up, but she kept his hand in her own. "He's just got a tiny little bit of pain so I'm going to get him some medicine," she said and looked at him with a *please go along with it* look. "I'll go get that, sweetie, and I think Jason will be up in a little while to check on you. Probably you'll already be in your new room."

"Okay," he said and rubbed his arm to make it look like it really hurt. "Thanks, Miss Jenny."

Jenny left and his Mommy sat where she had been and opened his juice for him. A part of him felt glad that he couldn't really close his eyes and listen to the rest. He already knew that the Lizard Men were taking someone new to the cave. He didn't need to hear the screams to prove it.

* * *

Jason changed quickly out of his scrubs and into the jeans and T-shirt he had worn in from Jenny's apartment. He had to stop at his apartment sometime tonight and get some fresh clothes and a toothbrush, he decided, but his shirt passed the sniff test at least. He headed to the fifth floor and the Pediatric Observation Ward. The busy shift meant that time had passed quickly, but he had not been able to come by and see Nathan or have lunch with Jenny.

Jenny had left at three-thirty, after her shift ended, offering to come back and pick him up later when Jason's twelve-hour shift was over. Jason had kissed her cheek and told her he would walk to her apartment, the question of whether they would be together tonight apparently answered for both of them. Perhaps the walk would give him a chance to think.

The Pedi Ward looked exactly like it should—bright colors, pictures of animals and balloons stenciled on the walls, soft music—but none of it could overcome the hospital smell and the feel of sick people around him. The nurses all wore brightly colored scrubs and jackets with animals and toys on them, but they were still the strange grown-ups that woke you up at night and rammed a glass rod up your butt.

Nathan's room (a private room, he needed to remember to thank Sheila for that) sat conveniently beside the oversized cubicle jammed with toys, little chairs and beanbags for kids well enough to play. The lights were on in Nathan's room and he could hear the music from Disney's *Aladdin* blare from the TV. He smiled. He liked reminders that there really was a normal five-year-old in that brave little man.

"Hi, Jason," Nathan said as casually as if he had walked into his living room at home.

"Hey, kid," Jason said back. "Did I miss much?"

"Yeah, kinda," Nathan answered and kept watching the screen. "I seen it before though."

"*Have* seen it before," his mother corrected, looking amused.

"I HAVE seen it before," Nathan said and rolled his eyes a little.

"You ready for a little time out of bed?" Jason asked.

"Sure," Nathan said, his face full of excited curiosity. He glanced over at his mom and she just smiled. "Where we goin'?"

"Thought you and I could go spend a few minutes in the play room—get you out of bed a bit and give your mom a break for a little while." He looked at Sherry and winked.

Just wanna help out—not going to talk to your five-year-old about demon caves and Lizard Men—

"Is it okay, Mom?" Nathan pleaded.

"Sure, sweetheart," Sherry said. "Just listen to Mr. Jason and do what you're told," she added.

"I will," Nathan said and literally bounded out of the bed.

"And be careful of your arm, please," his mother added with a grimace at how he bounced around.

"No problem," he answered and took Jason's hand with his un-bandaged good one, practically dragging him to the door.

"We won't be long," Jason promised over his shoulder. "And the play room is right next door."

"Have fun," Sherry said with a nervous little wave. But she didn't get up. She trusted him and that felt pretty good.

They went into the oversized cubicle of a room and Jason collapsed into a furry, purple beanbag chair while Nathan scurried around and looked at the toys. He settled on a couple of plastic action figures and brought them over.

"Wanna play Power Rangers?" he asked.

Just a normal little boy.

"Sure," Jason said and accepted the black and gray figure that Nathan passed him.

"That's a crybot. He's a bad guy," Nathan said matter-of-factly. "This one is the Yellow Ranger and she's a good guy, although she's a girl." The last part was like an apology and Jason fought down a snicker. "They don't have any boy ones that I saw, so I guess I'll be this one. Her name is Z." Nathan sat beside him in the beanbag and winced a little when his hand bumped Jason's knee. They played for a while, the crybot in Jason's hand never quite getting the best of the Power Ranger—even if she was a girl. After a few minutes, Jason leaned in closer.

"You doing okay for real, buddy?"

Nathan shrugged. "I guess," he said. "I'm nervous because I think something is going to happen soon." He looked at Jason with his older eyes.

"What do you think is going to happen?" Jason asked.

"I don't know," His brow wrinkled in thought. "Something bad, I think." He looked at him again. "They took someone else, you know."

Jason felt his mouth go dry, not just because he knew what Nathan meant, but because of the casual way Nathan told him.

They're gonna tear another human being apart alive. Do you want to play Power Rangers with me?

For the umpteenth time, Jason found himself worried about how all of this would affect his young friend in the coming years. Right now he had more pressing worries, however.

"Who did they take, Nathan? Is it someone you know?"

"No," Nathan said and started putting his figure into another action pose. "I don't think so. I didn't see them, just heard them. Like from far away, you know?" Jason did know. The memory slowly became more and more real. "I think his name is Jazz. I think I heard him say it."

Jazz. He had heard that name today. But where? He thought hard for a moment and then it came to him— the Trauma Bay. The kid with the gunshot wound. He'd said his name was Jazz.

"Did you say they already took him? Are you sure?"

"Pretty sure," Nathan said without looking up. He now held the action figure tightly in his hand but no longer looked at it. "It sounded like they got him a little while ago." Nathan looked up at him and Jason saw both pain and fear. "Is he a bad guy, Jason? Is Jazz a bad guy like Steve?"

"Yeah, buddy," he said and put his arm around Nathan's shoulders. "He's a bad guy like Steve." He understood why that mattered so much to Nathan. It did to him, too, though as a doctor he wasn't supposed to make those distinctions.

How about as a human being? They are torturing and killing people.

"Everything's going to be okay." He kissed the top of Nathan's head.

"Unless we can't stop them before they hurt someone good, right?" Nathan's eyes now looked hard. "We gotta stop them, don't we Jason?"

"Yeah, we do," he answered. "And we'll figure out how, I promise."

"I know." Nathan gave him a big hug.

Jason explained how important it was that Nathan call him if anything happened, no matter how little.

"Just call me in your head like last time and I'll hear you okay?" Nathan nodded. "If for some reason that doesn't work, just tell your mommy you really need me and have her call me on my phone. She has the numbers, okay?" Nathan nodded again. Jason carried the little boy back to his room and tucked him into his bed for the rest of his Disney movie. He made a point to check again that Sherry had his cell phone number, then high-fived his buddy and left the ward.

The Trauma ICU sat two floors down and Jason took the stairs two at a time. He hurried not just because he needed to know if Nathan was right, but because he now wanted very much to get out of the hospital and check on Jenny.

Something is going to happen soon—something bad.

In contrast to the Pediatric ICU, the Trauma ICU nearly vibrated with activity and noise. No bright colors and happy pictures adorned the walls here—the Trauma ICU was all business. Jason had spent plenty of time here over the last three years and it felt... not exactly comfortable, but familiar.

"Hey, Jason," a friendly voice called out.

Jason looked over at the counter by the nurse's station where his ER colleague had a chart spread out over a large area. "Oh, hey, Brent. Didn't see you there. How's it goin'?"

"It's ass, dude. This rotation is killing me. I mean, I'm learning a lot, but, Jesus, I don't know how the surgery residents do this shit for five years."

Jason laughed. "I know how they do it—I just don't know why they do it."

He turned and started to scan the large patient board trying to find the trauma patient from the ER. There were at least eight DOE names on the board, each with a first name based on the next letter in the alphabet from the one before. He had no way to tell which was which.

"Hey, Brent," he called over his shoulder without turning around. "What was the DOE name for the gang-banger trauma from earlier—you know, the gunshot wound?"

"Yeah, that was 'Classical DOE'—get it? He wanted us to call him Jazz so the chief made his DOE name 'Classical' because the letter C was up next. Get it?"

"Yeah, I get it, dude. Where is he at?"

"I got his chart right here. You need it?"

Jason felt a little sense of relief. Nathan must be wrong. Ol' Jazz was right here in the Trauma ICU. He turned and walked over to Brent and felt his pulse slow and his shoulders drop from the painful, scrunched-up position he hadn't even noticed they were in. "Yeah, can I have a look?" Nothing for him to see now, of course.

Might as well relax. Maybe nothing bad is coming after all.

He realized Brent was talking and something he said struck Jason's unconscious as really important. He felt his pulse quicken again.

"What did you say?" he asked.

"I said I just gotta get the thing organized so I can do his death summary dictation, but it shouldn't be too hard since he was only here a few hours."

"Death summary? What the hell are you talking about? He seemed stable in the ER, just needed a chest tube. What the hell did he die of?" He realized his voice had gotten a little high-pitched and loud and struggled to look more casual.

"Take it easy, dude," Brent said and gave him a strange, sideways look. "The guy just stopped breathing. He was doin' fine, kinda bein' a pain in the ass, and then the alarms went off and he was just dead. Code only lasted a few minutes and he was gone."

"Who ran the code?" Jason asked, his voice more controlled with some effort on his part.

"I don't know, some surgery attending who happened to be in the room when he boxed. What the hell difference does it make? Either way I gotta do the friggin' dictation..."

His friend continued to drone on about the ER resident always getting the scut work or something, but Jason couldn't hear him.

Nathan had been right. Somehow (*you know how*) he had known.

Jazz had been taken.

And something's going to happen--something bad.

Jason turned and darted out of the ICU, his friend still babbling about the work and seemingly oblivious to his departure. He had to get home to Jenny. He had to make sure she was okay and then he would call and check on Nathan.

Get ready, trooper—start figuring this out. He's gonna need what you got locked up inside your scaredy-cat head real soon.

* * *

Jenny tried again to shake the uneasiness that tugged at her. She found herself unable to stay seated on the sofa, not just because she couldn't concentrate on the mindless babble from the TV, but because her body needed to be in motion. She paced back and forth and looked again at the clock. She really, really wanted Jason to be here.

Get a grip, girl. This isn't you. You're acting like a scared little girl.

The other voice saw its opportunity and jumped in before she could stop it.

Just like when you were a scared little girl, remember? How did that turn out? What did the man in your life back then do to help you? Pried you skinny legs apart, didn't he?

"Goddamnit, just shut the hell up!" She squeezed her temples tightly between two fists. "That's all lies. I know it's all lies. We checked— we called them—ALL LIES!"

Doesn't matter what the man prying your legs apart now says. These people are animals—preying on weaklings like you, and we can stop them. We can do it if you help us. Help us stop the slaughter of more little boys, Jenny. We need you to come help us tonight.

"No, please." Her voice was little more than a gentle sob, a pleading. She dropped slowly to her knees in the living room. "Please leave me alone." She raised her head and looked around. "Please, I have to get away from the voice..." Her eyes darted around the apartment and for a moment she looked at the sliding glass door onto the fourth-floor balcony and had a terrible, crazy thought. Crazy, but it would stop the voice, wouldn't it? And then she would be sure she didn't hurt anyone. She looked again at the door like a starving man would look at a T-bone steak. She got up slowly, her eyes fixed on the glass. The crazy, terrible thought started to look less crazy. Jenny walked toward the door and her hand reached out and grabbed the cool metal handle.

The loud chirp of her cell phone caused a gasp to escape from her chest and almost made her pee herself. She looked at her trembling hand on the handle of the door and pulled it back in revulsion. Bile filled the back of her throat as her stomach heaved.

The phone gave a third, insistent chirp and Jenny jogged to the table in her dinette to pick it up. The pale blue screen flashed the name she desperately needed to see.

"Jason," she read aloud and then fumbled to flip the phone open. "Hello?" Her voice had lost the tremble and she felt glad that she wouldn't make Jason worry. "Jason, is that you?"

"Hey, baby," the voice said. To her the sound was soothing music. "You doin' okay?"

"Yeah," she lied. "Great. Are you done? Can I come pick you up?"

"I'm on my way," he said. His voice sounded strong. He would keep her safe, she knew it.

Until he gets bored with what's between your legs.

She squeezed the voice out of her head with her fingers, pressing deeply into both temples.

"I'll be there shortly. I'm walking, but I'm already on my way. I can be there by the time you even get to your car, so just relax and I'll be at your door in ten minutes."

She loved his voice, strong and confident, but no arrogance and no bullshit. "Okay," she said and then couldn't help adding, "Hurry, okay?"

"Are you sure everything is alright?" Jason sounded worried now.

"Yes," she lied again. "I just miss you."

"I'll see you in a minute." His voice disappeared with a click.

Jenny looked at the clock on her bookshelf. Ten minutes—she could make it that long.

Chapter 20

Jason picked up his pace, double-timing it across the corner. Something in Jenny's voice made him anxious, and he tried to plug it into the equation with all the other crap—the gang banger getting taken, Nathan saying something bad was coming, his own other-voice—but he couldn't make the math spit out an answer.

Remember me?

The voice in his head sounded so clear and loud that he didn't believe it was in his head at all. He slowed his pace and checked nervously behind him: nothing. The voice from his head and the voice from the alley—

And from before, Jason. Now you really do remember me, don't you?

Jason turned and looked down a short dark alley, just wide enough for the garbage truck to make its run behind the businesses he passed. The lone street light with its painfully harsh whitish-blue glare made a loud buzzing noise, flickered once, and went out. A strange red glow lit the now dark alley from behind. Jason stood almost paralyzed, his feet cemented to the ground, and strained to see into the darkness. A small flash of blue startled him backward for a moment and then he smelled the horrible shit smell and squeezed his eyes tight against the memories and emotion that accompanied it. He saw flashes of his mother's face, of Nathan smiling at him, of a mutilated body that seemed to be in black and white but which he remembered in crimson red from a long, long time ago.

Jason opened his eyes and saw two glowing embers stare back at him from the alley. The dark figure in the long trench coat stood motionless and for a moment Jason tried to convince himself that the image was just a creation of his tortured mind. Then the voice spoke to him, an impossible whisper that seemed loud enough to be right beside him, hissing in his ear, yet the figure remained halfway down the alley, too far away to hear.

We are not the enemy, Jason. We have the same goals, you and I. We want only to protect the innocent, like you so many years ago, like Nathan now. Help us, Jason. Help us stop them from hurting any more children.

The sudden explosion of images in his head obscured his view of the figure in the alley and he nearly dropped to his knees. Jason's hands clutched the sides of his head, but they did nothing to stop the flood of graphic images—his father beating his mother until she couldn't stand, the feel of his young thigh bone snapping under the stomp of the heavy boot, Nathan clutching his mother with his deformed, charred hand, a young girl screaming under the thrusting body of her father—Jason felt a scream from his chest more than heard it and then finally did fall to his knees. When he opened his eyes, the shadowy figure towered above him, the voice filling him.

We are here to stop the torture of the innocent and you can help us. You can help Nathan. Help us just as Jenny has and we can stop them from hurting more children.

The images returned, but flashed by so fast now that he could no longer focus on the individual pictures and instead saw only a horrible stream of suffering—some young faces twisted in screaming anguish and others pale and silent in death. Jason pitched forward at the feet of the overcoat-cloaked figure, caught himself on one outstretched arm and vomited violently at its feet.

No! You're evil. The Devil maybe.

Jason looked up, his face now set in rage as much as pain. He saw the face of his mother, weak and pale, and her mouth moved silently with words he thought he needed but couldn't hear.

"You killed my mother, you son of a bitch. We'll stop you and your friend. Demon bastard!" He thought the scream came from his voice and not his head. Blue light exploded from the center of the Lizard Man and for a moment Jason was completely blinded. He felt sure he would die from the pain of the light and was engulfed in that horrible smell just as the buzzing sound returned and vibrated from somewhere deep inside him. Then, just as suddenly, it stopped—the smell and light disappeared and he fell over onto his face in the dark.

It took Jason a moment to open his eyes and struggle to his knees. When he did he found himself back on the sidewalk; he stared into the alley, trying to peel back the darkness to find the demon he feared might still be there. Then the streetlight hiccupped with soft static and popped back on, revealing, emptiness.

As he watched, the soft-red backlight faded and disappeared. Jason coughed once and tasted the coppery bitterness of blood and spit a red glob onto the sidewalk. He ran the back of his hand across his mouth and looked at the brick-colored saliva that stained it. Then he set off toward Jenny's apartment with a new sense of urgency.

Nathan was right.

Something's going to happen. Something bad.

Jason's legs ached from his long jog as he walked up the stairs to Jenny's apartment. The images from the alley hung on him like cigarette smoke, but he wanted nothing right now but to be sure that Jenny was okay. Jason leaned his head against her door and rubbed his aching right thigh before he knocked.

Jenny threw open the door and nearly crawled into his arms. "We really ought to get you a key," she whispered into his ear. Her voice held a strained urgency that bothered him.

"I missed you, too," he said with a forced chuckle then pulled her back so he could see her face. "You sure you're okay?" he asked.

Jenny blushed and her eyes looked red, but her smile seemed genuine. "I am now," she answered and pulled him by the hand into the apartment. "How's Nathan?" She walked to the kitchen, not giving up her tight grip on his hand. Jason saw the refrigerator stood open and there was an eclectic assortment of food spread across the counter top. She saw his look and blushed again. "I wanted to fix you dinner," she said sheepishly, "but I didn't really have much to piece something together."

Jason felt warm enough at the gesture. "What a great thought," he said. "I'm kind of a Mac and Cheese sort of guy when I'm at home." He took her other hand and kissed her. His anxiety softened a bit. "We can just go out a grab a bite," he suggested.

"Can we order out?" she said quickly. "I, um, well—I guess I would feel better just staying here with you."

"That's fine," he said. Food was the furthest thing from his mind. "I need to call and check on Nathan real quick and then we can brainstorm up something that can be delivered." He felt weird at how not-so-weird he felt. Only minutes ago he had encountered the creature in the alley and had felt the evil pull of their control, the very pull he knew still tore at Jenny.

Somehow, he seemed able to chat comfortably about what they should eat for dinner. Surreal, that was the word for it. Only in dreams did normal people have a battle of wits with demon Lizard Men in a dark alley and then hug their girlfriends and casually discuss dinner plans.

Jenny let go of one of his hands and handed him the phone from the counter. Jason punched in the direct line to Nathan's room. After only two rings, the phone clicked to a connection.

"Hello?" Nathan's small voice said. "Jason?"

"Yeah, buddy it's me. Jenny and I just wanted to check on you. Is everything okay?"

"Yeah." Jason heard a rustle like he had adjusted in bed. Nathan's voice took on a conspiratorial whisper and he imagined the kid moving away from his mom so as not to be overheard. "Are you okay? Did something happen?"

"I'm fine, buddy," he answered with a cautious glance at Jenny. "Why? Did you feel something or hear something?" He had already decided not to tell Jenny what had happened in the alley. She seemed to be teetering on the edge as it was.

"Kinda," Nathan said softly. "I just kinda thought that maybe the Lizard Men tried to hurt you. It just felt that way I guess."

"I'm fine, Nathan. I promise," he reassured. No sense in worrying him either. "And Jenny is here and fine too. Are you gonna be okay tonight? You know how to get me if you need me or anything happens, right?"

"Yeah," Nathan said as if the question was silly. "I can talk to you in my head whenever I want."

"I'll come see you real early in the morning again and then we'll talk about a plan okay?"

"Okay, Jason," Nathan said and seemed content. "Bring Miss Jenny, okay?"

Something's going to happen—something bad.

"I will," Jason promised. "Get some sleep, alright?"

"Sure," said Nathan with that same what-a-silly-thing-to-say voice. "See ya tomorrow." The phone clicked off and he was gone.

The creatures were sure to be busy with Jazz, and Jason could think of no way to help him. The fear in him told him he shouldn't want to. The two people that mattered were safe. Tonight, that would have to be enough. He needed some sleep and now that Jenny had planted the seed, he realized he needed some food as well. Tomorrow would be the day, he suspected, one way or another. Jason looked at Jenny, the other half of what he thought of now as his dysfunctional family, who stared back expectantly.

"You like Chinese food?" he asked.

*   *   *

James had tried a big mix of drugs over his short life, but had always preferred liquor. He loved the mellow buzz of weed, but even that left him wanting a drink. The hard shit never made him feel anything but scared and his one trip with mushrooms had been like living in a cartoon, not fun at all.

This felt nothing like any of that. He figured it must be some kind of shit he hadn't tried and whatever the doctor gave him definitely felt like no trip he wanted to take again. It didn't suck, except for the weird feeling in his chest that he got used to pretty quick, but it didn't feel good either. It felt like floating or something—like floating inside a dream.

He could feel pretty much everything, only more. The sheets on his skin and the sensation of the bed against his back became more real somehow. James could feel and taste plastic in his mouth, but whatever they gave him made it not bug him too bad. And he heard voices, lots of them. He knew they spoke in English but the words were mostly big doctor words and he felt so fucked up from the drugs he couldn't follow what they said.

And who gives a shit anyway?

The only bad part was the dream. He dreamed that he had died in the ICU and that the doctors talked about him being dead right in front of him. In his dream he tried to sit up and tell them he was still alive and nearly shit when he couldn't move. Alarms were going off all around him and the doctors and nurses scurried around.

In the dream he felt a terrible stab in his chest and choked when they lifted him nearly off the bed by his jaw and jammed a plastic tube in his throat. Then someone, a doctor he figured, said to stop, that he was gone, and that was when he really freaked out. In the dream his body really was dead, because he couldn't move anything, not even his eyes which looked up into a bright light that he couldn't focus on.

Someone leaned over him, the face huge, and they had pulled up his eyelids and shined another light in his eye. Then the voices mumbled more about him being gone and how it maybe was a "bee-eee" from a clot or something. They had even pulled a sheet over his face which actually felt good because it blocked out the blinding goddamn light.

He remembered rough hands that picked him up and moved him to another bed and his head got real swimmy then and he thought he couldn't breathe. The sheet had slipped off his face and he looked up at someone, a brother, but big and fat and in scrubs like the doctors, who looked back with a scrunched-up face then pulled the sheet back over him. Then he passed out.

Fuckin' dream. But them drugs is sure okay.

"He's had too much narcotic," a raspy voice that sounded familiar said. It sounded pretty pissed off and he guessed the voice was the doctor in charge. Something in the voice made his brain tell him to be scared, but he couldn't figure out why so he decided not to give a shit.

"We had too. Without it he would have had a big sympathetic response and we could never have pulled it off. We needed lots of hypotension so there would be no pulse that could be felt. We can't fake that by disconnecting leads."

"When will he be light?" the voice asked.

"Soon," another nervous voice said. "I can give him some Narcan to speed it up if you want—even run it as a drip until the Fentanyl is gone—but it'll clear on its own in about fifteen to thirty minutes."

"I'll be back in ten," the scary voice that he couldn't quite get scared of said. "Have him ready by then, however you have to."

James felt motion just above him and then cool, waxy fingers grabbed his eyelids and yanked them up. The image that hovered above him stayed slightly out of focus but his mind recognized it from somewhere and alarms went off in some part of his brain that wanted to give a shit. The eyes beneath the hat glowed orange from the shadows.

"I'll be back, James," the familiar voice said. "And then we will talk, you and I, about what the future holds for you." Red lips split apart enough to let a blood-red tongue push out. It stroked across the impossibly long teeth and then sucked back into the slit of a mouth in the ash white face.

Deep inside James hollered and a layer of haze lifted. Then the cold, bony fingers let go of his eyelids so they slid wetly back in place. He sank into the rust-colored darkness and heard the voice in his head rise to a scream. He decided he probably better start to give a shit.

* * *

Jenny felt the voice of the man in the long coat and top hat, but she didn't really hear it. It felt like she imagined mind reading would be like; no sound or even words, just thoughts and feelings pounded into your head against your will. She didn't let it bother her because she knew she was dreaming. The dream broke itself into a million senseless fragments, each piece meaningless alone, but the kaleidoscope of pieces formed a kind of abstract art that meant a lot. But she knew it would be a worthless jumble when she woke up.

Dreams are just like that.

Yes, they are. They really are.

The images floated around her, the same disturbing images as before, and she refused to look at them. She knew exactly what they were without looking, so what the hell difference did it make? She floated through the dream she couldn't describe, ignored the images, snuggled against Jason and pulled his arms tightly around her.

Just a dream, you know.

No, pay attention. Don't let them in.

The child's voice sounded like a whisper, the words more like feelings and tied to the images she wouldn't look at. The fragments were ugly and violent, but they didn't hurt like before. Like when you got your teeth drilled after they gave you novacaine. You know it hurts—it has to hurt of course, and you can feel the tugging and pushing—but you're numb.

The new images showed a thin and angry-faced black man—a boy really. He sneered at her as the images wiggled into her brain, still just feelings, but with pictures. He had done terrible things, this boy James. Had raped and murdered—but young children not adults—and that mattered she knew. He wouldn't stop. Not ever.

Run back to Jason, girl. You're in the cave and you don't even see it.

Help us stop him, Jenny. It's okay. It's right.

Jason nodded to her from the cave and smiled. He would understand—maybe even do the same thing if he were in Jenny's shoes. She felt fear grow insider her, but something else in the dream stifled it. None of that made sense, but that was okay in dreams.

Dreams are just like that.

She realized the child's voice was not really Nathan, not this time. Like Nathan, but deep and false. But that was okay, dreams really were like that.

Just help us in the dream. Just this time and we'll leave. You can be with Jason and even with Nathan. We'll take the evil people like James away with us and we'll leave you together in peace. One last time and just in a dream. Jason would want you to if he knew it could save you all from this nightmare. Help Jason and make this all go away. Just help us finish and we'll be gone.

Dreams are just like that.

She dreamed that she slowly and carefully unwrapped herself from Jason's embrace and slid gently out of bed. She padded barefoot across the bedroom floor, careful to avoid the squeaky board near the closet door as she scooped up her dirty scrubs and jacket from the closet floor and grabbed her Crocks from the wall beside the bathroom.

Even in her dream she couldn't just slip away from him, and so she tiptoed gently back to the edge of the bed, bent over and kissed Jason softly on the corner of the mouth. She looked at his gentle face for a moment, softly illuminated by the street light that snuck in between the bath towels over the windows.

"I love you, I think," she said.

The corner of his mouth ticked up a bit, a half-smile, like he had heard her. It looked to her like "I love you, too." Then she creeped silently out of the room, steered around the loose board again, and dressed in the living room. Jason would worry if he woke up and shouldn't she really go, especially if this would make the nightmare stop?

Dreams are just like that.

True enough.

She locked the door softly behind her and then headed to her truck and the hospital.

Chapter
21

He didn't crave a drink at all, but prayed for the drug that had made him not give a shit about the nightmare he found himself in. He could see some of what went on in the room, like if your TV was black on the top half of the screen and you could just see people's legs. The nightmare didn't feel like no dream no more, and he had tried for what felt to be an hour to wake up, so he felt pretty sure about it being real.

The burst of air in his chest every few seconds no longer seemed like no big deal, either. The most terrifying part was that he couldn't move, not at all. The half-up eyelid thing was the most movement he had managed since the doctors had given him the other medicine that sucked the high out of him in seconds and left him with pain, terror, and half a view of the room he lay in, paralyzed and helpless.

He sensed a change, like a suction almost, and felt his ears fill with pressure. Much of the movement in the room stopped and he could hear hard shoes clicking on a tile floor. He seemed to be able to focus his eyes a little better now, and the bottom half of his vision revealed a long overcoat as a figure approached him.

He knew that coat—it was that pasty mother fucker with the red eyes and long teeth. He had convinced himself that he had been a prank the asshole cops played on him. Maybe it still was. Maybe this was just more of that same grab-ass bullshit. But then he remembered the long teeth and red tongue and knew it wasn't no prank. They had asked him a bunch of bullshit and then left—had told him they'd help him be sorry for the shit he done. What shit, goddamnit? Them white bitches had beat him half to shit—had shot his ass, not the other way around.

The coat stood right beside him now and he couldn't focus as good up close.

"Hello, James. I'm here to help you repent."

The bony fingers pulled his eyes open again and he stared up into that deformed face. James felt his heart beat in his chest and in his temples, even in his eyes. The cold hand grasped his hair, and pain shot through the top of his head as he felt it lifted from the table he lay on. He saw clearly now: a surgery room. Two people in masks and shower caps with long blue gowns arranged surgical instruments on a blue, covered table.

Beside them a woman, out of place in brightly colored scrubs and a jacket covered with clowns holding balloons, stared at him with large, beautiful blue-green eyes. Her look was stone, like she might be in a trance or something. Then his head dropped suddenly onto the table again and a burst of air exploded in his chest. Tears filled his eyes and broke over the bridge of his lower lids, tickling down the sides of his face.

"Start the Narcan drip—no narcotics of any kind."

The girl with the pretty eyes and the colorful scrubs came forward and he watched her hang a smaller IV bag on his pole and jamb some tubing into it.

"I want you to enjoy every moment of your repentance, James," Mr. Clark said, only his mouth didn't move. James felt glad 'cause he thought if he saw the long teeth again his heart might explode. "Let me tell you what we're going to do to you, James," the voice said only this time the blood-red lips did move.

The face, still in shadows under the brim of the hat, leaned close, and as he watched, it shimmered and started to change. So did the room behind it. For a moment, he stared at a dinosaur-like head, the eyes burning lumps of coal—black surrounded by a halo of red. Darkness replaced the harsh lights and he thought he saw the dirty roof of a cave. Then the image shimmered like a tar road in the heat and he looked again at the shadowy face in the top hat. The lights burned his eyes and made them water.

"We're going to cut you open, James," the voice said in his head, the mouth a partly open, but motionless, blood-red slit. "We are going to tear you open and rip things out of you while you are awake and powerless, and you will feel everything we do."

The ridiculous words cut through him. He heard alarms sound and a furiously fast beeping that had been slow background noise moments ago. James's own voice screamed in his head. This was impossible. They couldn't do this. He had rights. The cops would come and stop this shit. The mouth above him split wider into a horrible grin and then Mr. Clark stood slowly and addressed the blue-suited doctors by the table full of instruments.

"Take a kidney, only one for now, and don't feel you have to rush."

James's eyes wouldn't move, but his corner vision caught a man in blue moving toward him. He felt cold wetness on his skin followed by fingers pressing harshly into his belly above his navel.

"Knife, please," a new voice said.

His screams rose to a fever pitch inside his head and he heard a hissing sigh from the creature in the hat, like he was coming in his pants.

"Yeeesss....."

* * *

The other voice inside Jason's head called to him and he reluctantly decided to listen. It felt more like a taunt than a calling.

Double dare you, scaredy cat.

"Bite me," Jason whispered in his sleep, but he went just the same. He remembered that the other-him voice, the one with the sing-song, little-boy quality, wasn't him at all. It never called him to do anything that didn't have a purpose. He doubted he had understood that before, so long ago, how could he have? He had been barely older than Nathan. His fear for Nathan and Jenny had grown enough now that he couldn't ignore the call, and so he went.

You learned about ignoring, didn't you? And Mom paid the price.

He opened his eyes and looked around. As silly as it seemed that he would find comfort or safety in the presence of a five-year-old, he realized that it felt much, much worse being here alone. Partly because of the memories and the little-kid terror it brought back, but also because last time he had been so focused on taking care of Nathan that he'd had little time to be scared for himself.

Well, not this time, bro. I may actually piss my pants — if I was wearing any friggin' pants.

He felt some comfort in the dreamlike quality this time, and he wondered for a moment if he might not be dreaming. He didn't think so, but couldn't be sure. The darkness and the wet heat felt real, and he already felt a tickle of sweat running down the middle of his back and into his crack.

Real, I think.

Doesn't matter, Jedi. Get moving. Lots to see and lots to do.

Jason felt an intense sense of déjà vu when the other-him voice called him Jedi. He remembered now that he had been heavy into *Star Wars* back then, and the voice had always called him Jedi or Young Jedi. The memory hit him hard. A closet full of heavy and painful memories might come crashing down on him if he cracked open the door to his brain a tiny bit more. He closed it firmly and started up the path toward the ledge where he and Nathan had looked down on his mom.

You mean Jenny, don't you, Jedi? Mom was last time—long before Nathan, unfortunately for her.

He shook the voice silent and kept moving. The dark puddles of purplish blood seemed to be everywhere now, like the cave bled slowly to death. He stood on his tiptoes to make his feet small and hunched over, trying not to touch the ceiling. His back ached as he zigzagged around the puddles and up to the top of the rise. Cautiously, he peered over, though he felt nearly certain that the creatures weren't here. What he did see nearly made a scream escape; he tasted Chinese food in the back of his throat.

Jenny lay on her back, naked in the dirt, and her filthy body glistened with sweat. Her hands were balled up and her fists clutched wet dirt so tightly that even from this far he could see her fingers and knuckles turn white. A large pool of cave blood, from a steady glistening stream on the far wall, snaked a narrow tongue in her direction. It curved toward her like a small river, twisting around mounds of dirt like it went to her on purpose. Already it had started to form a little puddle beside her head and her hair looked wet with it. At first Jason sprang to his feet, ready to scoop her up and carry her away, but he froze at the sound of the voice.

Won't work like that, Jedi. She's not all the way here yet. You know how it works.

"No, goddamnit, I don't know how it works," Jason hissed and crouched back down.

Think, my young Jedi. You can't help her here unless she comes all the way here on her own or—well, the other way. She is still doing things on the other side.

As Jason watched, Jenny writhed around in the dirt—not in physical pain, he didn't think, but she clearly struggled against something. Her mouth lay open in a dark "O" and now and again little grunts escaped. Tears fell down Jason's cheeks.

For the first time, he noticed the other body, naked and supine on the dirt floor of the cave. He felt no surprise to see the long, thin body of the boy who called himself Jazz a few yards from Jenny. His arms stretched straight out from his sides and his feet sat close together, like he had been crucified to the floor. His eyes were open, but stared unseeing at the ceiling. Jason tore gaze away and focused again on Jenny. In another circumstance he might have given a shit about the kid whose fate he knew to be horrible. But not now. He watched as Jenny's head tossed back and forth in the dirt and the halo of cave blood started to move toward her shoulders.

"I have to help her," he sobbed.

You can. Use the real force, Jedi. The power that you used to have and can help Nathan find. Nathan is the one, now.

Jason didn't really understand what that meant, but he knew he had to help Jenny and soon. Being all the way here sure as hell didn't sound good. He closed his eyes and listened—probably she squirmed around right beside him in her bed—but he heard nothing. Then he decided what he had to do.

He scurried back down the short rise and leaned his back against the cave wall, careful to avoid the purple that ran down the walls everywhere. He didn't know what the cave blood really was, but it looked like there was more now than even a few minutes ago. He filed that away in case it became important and then closed his eyes and concentrated on the feel of the sheets, the soft and subtle sounds of apartment living, and the little stream of light across his eyelids from the breaks in the towels over the windows.

He felt the air cool suddenly on his wet skin and opened his eyes and stared at the fingers of light, which danced mockingly across the ceiling of Jenny's bedroom. A sharp pain stabbed through his neck when he turned his head to the right too hard. Jenny's side of the bed lay empty.

"Jenny," he called in panic, but he knew there would be no reply.

He leaped from the bed and pulled on jeans over his sticky legs with some difficulty. He tried to walk as he struggled, took two steps then hopped up and tugged, and felt sure he would fall on his face. By the time he reached the living room, he could button his fly. Jason slipped on his shoes, grabbed his keys, and dashed out the door.

He stopped in his tracks and then spun around just before the door slammed shut, grabbing it. He heard his keys hit the floor. Where was he going? He had no idea where Jenny would be on this side—it could take forever to find her. He needed help.

Nathan.

But it would be much quicker to go to him another way.

Jason went back into the apartment, closed the door behind him, and collapsed on the sofa. He sucked two long, deep breaths into his aching chest and then blew the last one out between pursed lips. He forced himself to relax and tried to concentrate. In his mind he called out to his only ally.

Nathan. It's me. I need your help.

He heard his thought echo and more warm tears spilled out onto his cheeks.

Nathan.

Chapter
22

He drank in the powerful energy of the terror that emanated from the motionless body on the operating room table. The meal filled him with hot energy and an intoxicating sense of invincibility. The new boy and the old boy would be too late. He had worried when they had failed to take the grown-up boy, but as his blood surged with new power from the meal, he realized that they could not possibly stop them in time. The boy would never discover his true power before they drank the last of the energy from this meal and moved on.

He watched the dark-skinned belly split apart under the flashing knife of the surgeon. His control over the doctor had waned badly, but after his meal he would spend a little of his new power to fill his mind and reassert his power—it would be enough. To the creature's now bright glowing eyes, the terror and pain in the dark-skinned boy poured out from his head and chest as a visible, swirling light; he opened his wide mouth and sucked the light in.

It filled him in an almost sexual way. Beside him, his partner stood with his arms dangling by his sides, his own mouth open as golden light poured past the razor sharp teeth. He saw the glow of his eyes deepen in intensity as he ate. The power of this meal seemed better even than the last. Perhaps the youth of the victim or his ability to imagine his death intensified his terror. When he saw and felt the swirling light begin to diminish, he knew that the mind of the meal had set up the protective wall that humans always could. He knew they would be best served to wait for a new surge with the next feed. He drank a few more sips then looked over as the doctor dropped a greyish-blue clump of bloody tissue into a shiny silver dish.

"Get that on ice for the transplant team," his strained voice said.

He walked over and peered into the open belly where dark blood pooled onto the two pairs of stained, white-gloved hands.

"Stop that bleeding quickly," he said. "We are a long way from done here. You can pack his belly open to save time for the next procedure, but give him blood if he needs it."

The doctor said nothing, but began to hunt for the source of the bleeding. The creature turned and saw the hollow blue-green eyes staring at him as if in a trance.

Thank-you, my dear, he said with his mind. *You have been most helpful. Together we will stop this animal from hurting other children. Now please hang another liter of fluids to stabilize him.*

The girl took a step forward as if to obey, but then stopped, and her eyes widened as if she saw him for the first time. Her eyes rolled back in her face and she collapsed at his feet.

Most inconvenient.

He stepped over the motionless body. They would have to remove her from the room. He suspected she would no longer be of any use to them, but they would be able to proceed without her. There would be little use for her anyway, since their next meal would likely be their last. He flashed with momentary rage that the grown boy had taken her from him, but it would not stop them. Perhaps he could get a short meal from her before she was gone.

If not, he knew where he could—and either source he chose would slow the boys down. His mouth to split wide over his long teeth and he licked his dark tongue across them.

Just like before.

* * *

Nathan travelled against his will. He gave in to the visit mostly to shut up the other-him voice. He closed his eyes in the dark hospital room, listened to be sure he brought the soft sound of his mommy's sleep-breathing with him, took one big breath and went.

The dark, craggy walls of the cave and the dirty floor no longer held much surprise. What he didn't expect was how much more cave blood pooled on the floor and trickled down the walls. The puddles had increased in number and size and, in many places, had met each other to form a few really big puddles. The other thing he didn't expect was the feel of Jason's lingering presence. He knew that his buddy had been here, and not long ago. He wished that they were here at the same time, but he didn't plan on staying long. The voice wanted him to see something so he would have a look, then power down and head home.

Just a little scouting mission, Power Ranger.

The other him voice tried to sound like the big dog-looking Ranger on SPD, and actually did a pretty good job. Nathan started to pick his way around the puddles and climb the slope to the ledge. He knew that the creatures weren't here—while one part of his brain clung to the sound of Mommy's breathing, yet a third could hear the far-off sounds of the creatures as they sighed and fed somewhere else—so he didn't really try to be quiet. He concentrated instead on not stepping in any of the cave blood. At times he had to stretch his legs out so far that it hurt the muscles near his butt and he worried he might fall over and plunge headfirst into the goo.

As he neared the top of the rise, Nathan could hear movement down in the big room. He knew it couldn't be the Lizard Men 'cause he could still hear them on the other side, and anyway he would smell the nasty fart smell if they came. Still, he stayed on his hands and knees to be safe and peered over the ledge.

The dark-skinned man looked a lot younger than Steve. He lay still and quiet on his back, stretched out like the Jesus-man pictures. Jason said he was a bad man like Steve, but he looked kind of young and Nathan didn't want to look at him long. A writhing figure in the corner caught his eye and Nathan suddenly felt sick and scared.

Jenny looked like she might be angry, the way she squiggled around, but the grunting noises bothered him the most. She struggled like some invisible rope tied her up or something. Just as he started to scurry over the edge to help her, her groaning and wiggling stopped. Nathan hesitated for a moment and he expected that she might disappear and go back to the other side all the way, so he sat still and watched.

You must help her. You and Jason.

Jenny sat suddenly bolt upright, and Nathan hollered out in surprise. Her head tilted back, and she let out an animal scream. Then her eyes popped open and for a moment she looked around, her face contorted in fear. Her eyes fell on the dark-skinned guy; she looked for a minute at his motionless body and began to cry. Nathan started to call to her, but the sound stuck in his throat when she turned her head slowly toward him and looked right at him. She really saw him, her face clearly showed she recognized him, and a hint of a smile crossed her lips. Jenny shifted her weight to steady herself on one arm, and then reached the other out toward him and her mouth moved.

"Nathan," she croaked. "I'm so sorry."

Then she collapsed in a heap.

Nathan wanted to scramble down to her, but wondered what he could do, only being almost six and all. He knew he had to do something. Jenny was way too big for him to carry or even drag, and anyway, where would he take her? She had to be awake to leave here. *I'm too little to help her. I'm not really a Power Ranger—I'm just a kid.*

You are more than you think. You have the power you need but you will have to have Jason's help. Find him. Call him.

He needed Jason. He could call him in his head and together they could move her. First he had to be sure she was okay, so he scrambled down the little dirt path into the big room.

Nathan walked slowly. No cave blood puddles blocked his way, because the room was so big. But he felt really scared and wanted to be careful. The young man lay perfectly still, but his eyes moved back and forth, not seeming to see anything, but wide with terror. Nathan scurried past him, knelt at Jenny's side, and reached a hand out to touch the hair that had fallen across her face. He could hear her breathe, fast and kind of loud, but he wanted to see her face.

What he saw made him pull his hand away and make a little bird noise in his throat. Her face looked normal except for the dirt and being all sweaty, but her eyes were all wrong. They were wide, so wide it looked like it might hurt, but they had changed from a pretty blue-green to a murky grayish. It looked like someone had poured gray finger paint into her eyes—he could still see the faint greenish haze behind the milky gray. He felt pretty sure she couldn't see him.

"Miss Jenny," he whispered. He looked around, terrified he would smell the fart smell of the Lizard Men. "Miss Jenny, please wake up. We gotta get outta here." Tears filled his eyes and his lower lip began to quiver, just like it did when he was a little kid and he didn't want to cry about something. Jenny gave no sign she heard him. She stared off across the room and her body shuddered as air moved in and out of her. Except for that, Nathan thought she looked dead.

Then he did hear a voice.

"Nathan. It's me. I need your help." Nathan looked up and half expected to see Jason beside him. Then he realized the voice called him from his head.

"Nathan."

"I'm here," he whispered, "I'm here with Miss Jenny. She's all sick or something and I can't get her to wake up. I need you here."

"Where are you?" Jason's voice sounded strained and frightened. "Where are you, buddy?"

"I'm in the cave," he answered. "In the big room. Jenny is sick and there's something wrong with her eyes." Nathan realized that tears streamed down his cheeks like rivers, but he didn't care. Let the other-him voice call him a scaredy cat all he wanted. He needed Jason and he wanted his mommy.

"Hide in the little cave again, buddy. I'll be right there."

"I wanna stay with Jenny," he called back. He no longer used his voice at all. "She's sick and I don't want to leave her." He looked around the cave which suddenly looked scarier than ever. "Please hurry," he said and even his thought voice cracked.

"I'll be right there," Jason said with a new strength that made him feel better.

Nathan smoothed Jenny's hair and leaned close to her ear.

"He's coming, Jenny," he said softly. "He's coming to get us out of here, okay?"

* * *

He hadn't expected Nathan to be in the cave and pushed away his fear at going back. He felt a renewed sense, not just of purpose, but responsibility. His mind wanted to examine whether it was love, or atonement, or just old-fashioned guilt, but he had no time. He shook off the fear and concentrated.

If a five-year-old can sit by her side and wait in that hell, what does that say about you? You better cowboy the fuck up.

He had no idea what they would do for Jenny when he got there. Whatever. He needed to get to his family.

Eyes still closed, he imagined the stifling, steamy air of the cave—imagined it filled his lungs and coated his skin in sweat, and then he tasted the ass-smelling air in his mouth for real.

He leaned back against the cave wall in the same seated position from the sofa and noticed a little river of cave blood only an inch or less from his right shoulder. As he watched, the little river seemed to bend toward him, like his body held some magnetic attraction. He scurried to his feet, crouched over again in the low passageway, and scrambled the few yards to the top of the rise.

He didn't even stop to peek down into the room this time—just leapt over the ledge and half-ran, half-slid down the dusty hill and into the room. Nathan bent over Jenny's motionless body, his forehead touching hers, and for a moment Jason felt a panic that she might be dead. He jumped over Jazz's inert body like a hurdler and skidded to a stop beside the two people that felt more like family than anyone he had known since long before his mom had died.

"Nathan, I'm here," he said just as the boy turned around, startled and fearful. Nathan crawled up into his lap, arms tight around his neck, and sobbed in his ear.

"I didn't know what to do, Jason," he cried softly. "I wanted to help her, but I'm too little and she's too heavy. I wanted to take her to the little cave, but I ain't strong enough." Nathan sniffed loudly in his ear and then pulled away. "I'm sorry—I mean I'm *not* strong enough."

Jason smiled and hugged Nathan back.

"It's okay, pal," he said. "We can do this together." He pulled back again and smoothed Nathan's wet hair from his face. "Nathan, you have a power that you can't even believe. You're the strongest and bravest kid I've ever known. If I had been as brave as you…" Jason's voice trailed off and he forced the memory to fade with it. He turned to Jenny and said, "Let's get her out of this room and then we can figure out what to do."

"Her eyes are all funny," Nathan said. "I think that something's wrong with her."

Jason bent over and smoothed the hair from Jenny's face. At the sight of her milky eyes, a sudden cold washed over him. He closed his eyes and in his mind a blue light flashed. He watched, like in an old movie, a young Jason, only a little older than Nathan, lean over the thin and wasted body of his mother in the same hot cave.

"Mommy, please wake up. We have to go before they come again and get us."

His mother lay deathly still except for the occasional raspy breath that shook her body from the inside. She stared at him without seeing, through milky-white eyes. The young Jason shook her and cried, his naked body trembling with fear. Then he heard a voice far off in his head—his mommy's voice from some other place.

"I have to stay here now. I can't do it anymore. Leave me, son. Get out and leave me here."

In his head he watched the little boy Jason tug once at his Mommy's arm and then look up in terror. He had smelled that awful shit smell, he remembered. He watched as the boy left his mother and scurried back up the rise, leaving her behind. As he cleared the rise and slid down the path, he heard the grunting of the creatures and the heavy shuffle of their clawed feet in the dirt. He never looked back, not even when he heard the spine-shocking scream of his mother being torn to pieces…

Jason felt a tight grip on his wrist and his eyes popped open. Nathan stared at him with unconcealed worry.

"Jason, are you okay?" the boy asked. "I think we really gotta go."

Jason looked at Jenny and tried to decide what to do next. He felt a lot of memories gel together. He saw his mother's dead body in the hospital room as they pulled a sheet over her face and told him the cancer had gotten her—but he had known better. She'd died because he left her behind. He wouldn't leave Jenny behind, or Nathan.

"Not this time," he said and pulled the dead weight of Jenny into his lap.

"I don't think we can take her out of here and back to the other side," Nathan said, a tremor in his voice. "I think she's gotta be awake to do it on her own."

"I don't think she can even do it then," Jason said and rose painfully to his feet with her limp body hanging from his arms. "I think we have to pull her back from the other side, but we need to get her out of here first. We have to take her somewhere safe."

"Where's safe?" Nathan asked and gripped his forearm tightly. Jason saw him look nervously off to the left.

Not that way, Jedi. Not yet.

"Not that way, Jason," Nathan said in an eerie whisper. "Not yet."

"This way," Jason said.

Together they struggled up the short rise and slipped over the little ledge. Nathan clutched at his arm and Jason realized it was impossible to avoid the cave blood puddles entirely with the awkward dead weight of Jenny and doing his best to keep Nathan close. Now and again his dirty feet tickled through one and he would feel pins and needles where the puddle touched his skin. It didn't feel nearly as gross as he thought, but he didn't like it either.

Find somewhere safe and easy, Jedi. The storm troopers are coming, but they aren't looking for you yet. You'll have to get to her on the other side quickly or it will be too late. You have a lot of work to do tonight.

Jason looked down at the boy beside him. Nathan stared straight ahead. Jason prayed quietly that together they would succeed where he alone had failed.

Chapter
23

Jenny felt a strange, detached sort of awareness that she traveled somehow through a dark void that engulfed her. Far off she heard the buzzing murmur of voices that she knew to be Jason and Nathan, and though a part of her wanted to rush toward the sound, she knew that was not be an option.

Too late. I have to just stay here. I don't want to hurt anyone else. I have to get away from the demons.

So she floated in the void. If she came back from the dark, she felt certain that bad things would happen, not just to herself or to people she didn't know in the basement surgery room, but to people she loved. She had to keep her parents safe. She had to keep her brother safe. She needed very much to know that Nathan and Jason were safe, too. So she burrowed down into the darkness and let it engulf her.

I have to escape the demons and their voices. I'm sorry, Jason. I really do think that I loved you.

Other sounds penetrated the black cocoon she hid in—the sounds of surgical instruments clinked and clanged amid the muffled voices of an OR team at work. She felt a tremor of disgust and guilt at those sounds, very different from the fear and remorse she felt at the voices of her two boys. She needed to escape from what went on there even more, perhaps, than from the terror of the cave.

I am not brave enough to kill myself, but maybe I can just stay here and let myself die. Forgive me for being weak, Jason. Forgive me, Mom and Dad. I have to make it all stop.

In some reality, she had died slowly in the cave.

That felt okay to her.

* * *

Jason stared uncomfortably at Nathan, who leaned back against the dirty wall in the impossibly tight little cave in which they had hidden before—a lifetime ago. He felt deeply moved by the boy's insistence that he stay with Jenny, whose lifeless head he cradled in his little lap. Jason had done his best to curl his girlfriend's limp body into the small space as best he could. With the two of them back as far as they could go together, Jason could fit only his upper body in behind them and felt terribly vulnerable with his own lower half jutting out into the larger passageway.

"Are you sure you're okay, Nathan?" he asked.

Nathan nodded his head but his eyes were filled with fear. "I think so," he whispered. "Just hurry back."

"Look," Jason said. "If I can get her back to the other side, then I guess she'll just sort of disappear, right?"

Nathan nodded his head. "I guess so," he said.

"Okay, if that happens I want you to come back immediately to your room and I'll meet you there. Got it?" Nathan nodded again. Jason hesitated a minute. He certainly didn't want to give the boy anything else to worry about. "Look, Nathan," he began and watched the boy closely. "If anything else happens—anything at all—I want you to come back over right away. We'll figure out what to do next, but come back okay?"

"You mean just leave her here?" Nathan asked. His eyes grew wide.

A picture of himself as a young boy, running up the rise and away from his mommy, flashed in Jason's mind. He felt horrible guilt and inadequacy looking at the little boy for whom such an act seemed unthinkable.

"We can help her better together and I'll need your help," Jason told him. "Do you understand?" The boy nodded but still seemed confused. "I can't lose you both," he told him and felt tears in his own eyes.

"Okay." This time he seemed to understand. "It'll be okay, Jason. We'll save her."

"I'll be right back," he promised.

Then he closed his eyes and concentrated hard on the feel of the sofa beneath him and the sounds of the city outside the apartment. He found it difficult at first, distracted by the sound of Nathan's heavy breathing, but he forced that from his mind and the city sounds got louder. He felt the coarseness of blue jeans on his legs—a feeling he would normally be oblivious to—and opened his eyes in the dark apartment.

Jason took one long, sighing breath and then jumped to his feet, noticed that his keys were still clutched painfully in his balled up fist, and headed for the door.

The ride to the hospital took only a few minutes but felt like nearly a day. He had no idea where to look for Jenny, but felt certain she would be at the hospital somewhere. As he pulled into the parking garage, he started to panic at the thought of how many places there were to search. What if she wasn't even at the hospital at all? He picked up the pace as he twisted upward in the deck, and heard the wheels of his car squeal as he rounded each corner on his way to the top floor. He remembered Jenny telling him how she always ended up on the top floor.

Sure enough, in the middle of the otherwise empty lot he saw her grey Ford Escape, poorly parked in a center space. Jason jerked to a halt beside her truck. He pulled out his keys and sat silently for a minute, then checked in on Nathan.

Nathan? Can you hear me, buddy?

Yeah. We're here. We're okay right now and I don't smell the fart smell or nothin'.

Jason couldn't help but smile and decided this would not be the time to correct grammar.

Do you have any idea at all where Miss Jenny might be at the hospital?

He waited through an uncomfortably long pause and started to worry that something had happened. Then Nathan's voice returned to his head, smaller and more frightened.

I don't know. I tried to see inside her head but it looks so dark in there.

The voice sobbed a little and Jason thought about telling him to come back but didn't.

It's okay, bud. I'll find her.

She's somewhere where she can lay down and people won't think that's funny.

Brilliant. Of course Nathan was right—there were only so many places where she could be and not draw attention. The ER wouldn't work, because someone might know her, and the same would be true for patient rooms. The morgue, perhaps? That gave him a chill and caused his stomach to tighten.

Waiting rooms!

He didn't know if that had been his own thought, Nathan's, the other-him's voice, or someone else's, but it made a great deal of sense. Family members asleep on the long couches of waiting rooms were incredibly common, especially this time of night. The OR and ICUs would be the best spots to not raise suspicion.

I think I might know, Nathan. I'll let you know when I find her, but call if you need me and I can come right away, okay?

Okay.

Jason sprinted across the parking deck and pushed through the door to the stairwell—no way would his anxious body contain the adrenaline if he had to stand and wait for the elevator. He bounded down the stairs two at a time and by the time he reached the bottom his thigh, with its steel screws and plate from so long ago, screamed at him. He forced himself to slow his sprint as he entered the glass walkway to the hospital. He didn't need questions or attention from folks that might see him run through the hospital in street clothes. He needed to get to Jenny and get her and Nathan home, but he could make that happen faster by being calm.

Jason stopped first on the third floor and checked in the OR waiting room. It was still the weekend and the traumas had no doubt rolled in for hours; as expected, the waiting room looked packed full of family members, some huddled together and others stretched out for a long wait on the uncomfortable vinyl couches. No Jenny, however.

He had similar luck in the Burn/Trauma ICU and the Pedi ICU waiting rooms and started to lose hope. The Cardiac ICU sat on the fifth floor and Jason again took the stairs. His leg ached.

Did you find her?

Nathan's voice sounded no worse than before, but Jason imagined he must be terrified. He stopped in the stairwell so he wouldn't crash into a wall or fall down the steps. For some reason he needed to close his eyes to talk to Nathan.

Not yet, pal, but I got a few more places to check.

Hurry, Jason. I think I'm getting too scared.

Is Jenny okay?

Maybe he could give him something to think about other than imaginary sounds of the Lizard Men returning and hunting them down.

I guess so. She's making kind of snoring noises every now and then.

Okay, buddy. Keep checking on her. I have one more place to check and then I'm coming back if I don't find her.

Nathan didn't answer, but Jason knew he had heard, so he continued up the stairs and hurried to the Cardiac waiting room—which he found to be empty. He leaned back against the wall in bitter disappointment. What had he not thought of? Where was a waiting room that would be quiet?

Jason's eyes sprung open. The outpatient center, where people had minor procedures and tests and then went home. It had a huge waiting room with a big TV and everything. It would be empty this time of night after the SurgiCenter stopped for the day. Jason couldn't help but run to the fourth floor and then down the long, winding hall that led to the fourth floor annex. He could see blue light through the narrow window set into the heavy wood door of the waiting room. He passed the modern, floor-to-ceiling glass walls and door that led into the darkened procedure area of the outpatient center and then peered into the waiting room.

A large man in the dark blue pants and light blue shirt of an environmental services employee sat in a chair and munched on a cheeseburger from a Styrofoam container. His eyes were riveted to the TV screen where the late night re-run of *Entertainment Tonight* told him all the juicy details of the rich and famous. Jason looked past the long legs, propped up on the mop bucket–turned–ottoman, and saw the familiar colorful scrub jacket on a figure curled up on a corner couch. The janitor seemed completely oblivious to her. Jason leaned his forehead against the door for a moment, suddenly exhausted, though thrilled

Found her.

Great. Hurry up.

Jason pulled open the door to the waiting room and the janitor jumped a little, startled at the late intrusion.

"Aw, shit," he mumbled, but caught his container of fries just in time. "Sorry," he said looking up at Jason. "Don't usually get much company this time a' day." He stood up, apparently embarrassed.

"No problem at all," Jason said. He wanted desperately to run to Jenny, but that would clearly not do. "My wife seems to have wandered to the wrong waiting room," he said and gestured toward Jenny's motionless body across the room. "She has had such a hard time since our daughter got so sick."

"Yeah, I saw her, but I didn't want to disturb her," the man said and closed the lid on his unfinished dinner. "Let me give ya'll a little privacy."

"Thanks so much," Jason said as the man pushed his mop bucket awkwardly past him and through the door. "Everyone here has been so wonderful," Jason added as the man closed the door behind him.

Jason hustled over to the couch and knelt on the floor beside his girlfriend's motionless body. Gently he stroked her hair from her face and then, tears in his eyes, kissed her cheek, which felt hot to his lips. He pulled back and examined her face. Flushed and moist with sweat, she really did look like an exhausted family member, asleep after an emotional day. Her breathing was deep, but not labored. So now what? Jason leaned in closer to her ear.

"Jenny," he said into her ear. "Baby, it's me, Jason. Can you hear me?"

Her body responded by pulling in long breaths. Jason felt a new anxiety grow inside him. He had told Nathan he would try and pull her back across to this side, but now he realized how stupid that sounded. He didn't even know what it meant to pull her or what this side or that side meant. He gently shook her body at the shoulder which did nothing but make her head lull to one side. Her eyelids were half open and while at least here her eyes didn't have that milky-white, dead look, they were every bit as lifeless. Her face had the same slack and unseeing appearance of the handful of brain dead patients he had seen. Jason didn't think she really was brain dead, but she certainly appeared comatose. In a panic he shook her a little more vigorously.

"Jenny, wake up. Wake up, goddamnit." He realized his voice had risen to a shout and tried to calm himself down.

Doesn't work that way, Jedi. Can't do much from here, not now.

"Bullshit! You said I had to come here."

That window is closed. She's too far gone now.

"Is she dead? Is she going to die?" he asked the voice in his head.

Maybe. Don't know yet. But you can't save her and certainly not here, not anymore. You need the power of the other one and he needs your courage to find that power.

"The other one?" But he knew the answer.

Nathan. He holds the power that you abandoned, but you have to help him find it.

"How?" he moaned to the empty room. "What do we have to do?"

Nathan will have to figure that out. All you can do is help.

Jason stared at the motionless body of the woman he felt pretty sure he was in love with. He couldn't leave her here in the waiting room. Someone might discover her and take her to the ER where they would start doing pointless procedures to her. Or worse, take her somewhere else for their own procedures.

Jason tucked her head gently into a more natural and comfortable position—

Like she gives a shit

—and dashed for the door. He saw what he needed beside the plain wooden door—the less dramatic employee entrance to the outpatient center—a few yards away. He grabbed the wheelchair, brought it into the waiting room and positioned it as close to Jenny as he could.

Jason. You have to come back here.

He stopped and looked around the room, then wiped tears from his eyes and closed them. Nathan's voice sounded so clear, as if he stood right beside him.

Are you okay, buddy?

Yeah, but you have to come back. It doesn't work that way anymore. The other voice told me you have to come back.

I know. I have to move Jenny and then I'll be there. Just a few more minutes.

Jason bundled up Jenny's body and, with considerable effort, moved her dead weight into the chair and slid her down low so her head wouldn't toss around. He wished he had a blanket to cover her with, but decided he would likely not run into anyone if he hurried. He would take the back way into the resident call room area to minimize the risk of— God forbid—being seen by another resident as he rolled an unconscious nurse through the halls.

Yeah, no questions there.

He peered out of the waiting room door, saw no one, and dashed into the hall, heading toward the main hospital.

He would have to go back to the cave.

He would have to trust that a five-year-old boy could save her for him.

And then you will have to find him some answers or none of it will matter, Jedi.

Chapter
24

The tight space and the hot air began to make Nathan feel like he might suffocate. He tried again to go to a happy place, to close his eyes and see himself with Mommy and Jason and Jenny playing in the park and having a picnic. But the pain in his back and left arm, where he tried to gently cradle Miss Jenny's now-heavy head, interrupted and reminded him how much the cave sucked. That was a big-boy word, he knew, but it must mean a place just like this.

He thought about crawling out into the passageway to wait for Jason, but he didn't feel right laying Miss Jenny's face down in the dirt and he couldn't really move her by himself. Jason might think he was doing a good job at being big, but Nathan felt more like a little kid than ever. He took in a deep breath of hot, wet air and sighed, then shifted uncomfortably and waited.

He sort of heard him, but it really felt more like he just knew Jason arrived. He listened as Jason shuffled around the cave blood puddles and whispered to him. Nathan's arms and shoulders sagged in relief. He had never been happier to hear any voice—not even Mommy on Christmas morning.

"Nathan? Nathan, it's me… Jason."

Who else would it be? He wondered why Jason whispered—there was no one in the cave right now except them and the skinny brown-skinned guy who definitely would not be bothering them.

"I'm still in here," he called back in a normal voice.

He heard more shuffling around and then a little grunt as Jason wiggled into the small space. A moment later he saw his face in the dim light.

"Hey, buddy," he said with a weak smile. "You okay?"

"Yeah, I think so," he answered. He realized that he felt more scared now. There was something he had to do—something for Jenny—but the other-him voice had not given any idea what it would be.

You'll either know and do it, or you won't and it won't matter.

That did not make him feel any better and he worried he would let down Jason and Jenny and they would be hurt for good, maybe even die.

I'm just a kid.

Not anymore, Ranger. Be ready—when the time comes you'll have to Power Up quickly.

"Okay," he said aloud.

Jason wrapped his arms around Jenny's waist, which was about as far into the little hole as he could reach without climbing up on top of both of them. He gently scooted her, a little at a time, off Nathan's lap and out toward him. When she got closer to him, Jason wrapped his arms around her tightly and kissed her wet cheek. Nathan shuddered at the way her pasty white doll's eyes stared over her shoulder back at him.

"I'm so sorry, baby," Jason mumbled and he thought that he saw tears. Then Jason scooted Jenny out of the tight cave and Nathan followed quickly behind them. In the larger passageway, he stood up and stretched. His left arm felt all like bees from falling asleep under the weight of Jenny's head and he shook it up and down and waited for the little sparks before it woke again.

"What are we gonna do?" he asked Jason.

Jason held Jenny awkwardly in his arms, his head hunched down, though he had plenty of space between him and the ceiling.

Nathan started to feel scared again. Jason was all grown-up. He was supposed to take care of things, right?

Not anymore. You are the Red Ranger now. Do you know what that means?

Nathan thought for a minute. On all the Power Ranger shows, the Red Ranger was always the leader and the best fighter.

Does it mean I'm in charge?

It means you have to lead your team. You have the most power, but you must all work together. Can you do that, Ranger?

"Yes, sir," Nathan said and stood just a little straighter.

Jason looked at him funny for a minute and then seemed to understand. He nodded slightly and gave him a tight-lipped smile.

"Did he give you any answers?" he asked.

Nathan shook his head. "Not really," he said. They looked at each other a moment and he saw a flicker of a scared little boy in his grown up friend. "I guess I thought you could do it for me, but you can't." Nathan said and looked at his feet.

"I failed at this once already, Nathan. You should know that." Jason's voice sounded strained, not just with the weight of Jenny, but with something else really bad. Nathan looked at him. He wanted his friend to feel better and to believe in him.

"You were alone then," he said simply. "Now we have a team. Even Miss Jenny is part of the team—like the Pink or Yellow Ranger." He didn't tell Jason that he had to be the Red Ranger. He didn't want to hurt his feelings.

"Do you know what you have to do?" Jason asked nervously. "Do you know how to help Jenny?"

"No," Nathan answered honestly, but he didn't feel worried anymore. With Jason on his team he felt pretty sure he could do anything. "I'll know when it's time."

"How?" Jason asked.

"I just will, I think. Or else the other-me voice will give me a hint, maybe." He put his hand on Jason's arm, not able to hold Jason's hand because of Miss Jenny, and looked up at him. "I kind of wish you were my dad," he said.

Jason's eyes filled with tears but he smiled really big. "Me too, buddy. That's the nicest thing I've ever heard in my life. How about we just be best friends instead?"

"Okay," Nathan answered. That sounded good to him. "I think we need to head back to the big cave room." He didn't know why—he just felt it.

You'll have more room there.

"Alright," Jason said.

Together, his Power Ranger team maneuvered through the maze of cave blood. It had become impossible to miss all the puddles now, and occasionally his bare feet would touch one of the hot pools of purple and tingle for a few minutes. Sometimes the feeling spread a little way up his leg. He tried hard to stay beside Jason and to keep a hand on his arm, but Jason struggled under the dead weight of Miss Jenny. Sometimes Nathan would dart ahead a few feet so neither of them would have to step directly in the puddles.

"Tingly," Jason said softly when his bare toes touched some of the purple goop.

"Yeah," Nathan agreed. "Like when you sleep funny on your arm."

The two of them continued up the rise to the crest. At the top, Nathan vaulted down the other side without hesitation, but it took Jason a moment to work his way down with the precious load he carried. While he waited, Nathan looked closely at the thin young man who lay sprawled on the dirt floor. He remained motionless except for his eyes, which danced madly under his closed lids. He wondered what the boy could see on the other side and what the creatures were doing to him, but decided it probably was better not knowing.

Jason came up beside him, his breathing fast and heavy.

"Now what?" Jason asked.

Nathan heard strain in Jason's voice and for a moment it felt a little unfair that Nathan had to be the grown-up.

It's not fair, but that's how it is. You're the Red Ranger. Lead your team. Jason will be there for you when you need him. You have the power, Nathan. It's in you like how a flashlight holds the light until you click it on—and then it shines bright. Jason used to have it, but he's too old now. He held it longer than most, still has some of it, but he is just too old.

Dreams are just like that, I guess.

Jason stared at him patiently. He seemed to get it, how the other-him could take a minute to understand sometimes. Nathan didn't know what to do, but he felt a great big sense of "here it comes." And he thought he could feel a bit of that light inside him.

"I hope I know how to turn on the switch," he mumbled.

"Huh?" Nathan ignored Jason's confused look and walked over by the wall. He stayed far away from where the guy had his brains bashed in, but everywhere streams of dark cave blood ran down the walls. He stepped out a few yards, aware of Jason's curious gaze, and found a place without any puddles—easier to do in the big room with lots of space away from the walls.

"Do you want to set her down here? She looks heavy." Nathan looked at Jason and his friend looked back.

Jason held on tightly to Jenny, not trusting the ooze on the wall wouldn't reach her. "Can you tell me what is going to happen? How do you think we can save her?"

"I don't know yet," he answered. He could almost feel a buzzing, like the air vibrated gently in the room. "Maybe we have to kill the Lizard Men—I'm not sure." He closed his eyes and tried to listen for them on the other side but heard nothing. "Something is going to happen now," he said softly, his voice nearly a whisper. "We gotta be ready to Power Up."

Nathan balled his fists up tight and stared down the long path he had journeyed into before. He wondered when he would have to know to go down there and how he would know and what he would find. He hardly noticed Jason's hand on his tense shoulder.

"It's going to happen right now."

Then he nearly gagged as the horrible fart smell filled the room.

* * *

Mr. Clarke stood quietly against the wall and waited for his next drink. They had learned long ago that the best feed came if they let the victim slip away when needed and then brought them back up to another crescendo of fear and pain. It was the difference between eating a milkshake though a straw or with a spoon.

Two doctors hovered around the body on the table. They would not need the nurse. She had become a luxury and her absence was only a minor inconvenience. He was nonetheless enraged that he could no longer get in her mind. The little sips of fear and pain had been most pleasant and his alone to enjoy. No matter.

He watched as they repositioned James on the table and prepared to take some skin from his left side. The boy's belly still gaped open and only few wet blue towels and a large square of brown, transparent plastic kept the air from drying out his organs. They would take what he had left to give them over the next few hours and then it would be best to move on.

He felt the vibrations at the same time as he felt his partner's clawed hand on his arm.

"The boy," his partner hissed.

"Yes," he answered in rage, "and the older boy too. We'll stop them quickly and then come back."

They could not hurt the younger boy. They could not even touch him if they wanted to remain well. But they could sure hurt the older boy now—his power was but a faint glow. And that would scare the powerful younger one off long enough to finish. It had worked before.

If that failed they still had one more plan to stop him.

The room shimmered and danced and then began to disappear.

* * *

Nathan felt the fear inside him, but in a far off sort of way that didn't matter. The poop smell filled the room and he knew the Lizard Men would appear from down the passageway with the glowing light. He felt ready. He felt a power—the light the other-him told him about—grow from the center of his chest and his skin nearly tingled with it. Nathan shifted back and forth as much with excitement as fear.

A crisp, blue light exploded outward from the middle of a little ball of yellow and then the Lizard Men stared back at him from a few yards away, just inside the entrance to the passageway. He started to move toward them and the glowing light in the path behind them.

No—that's for later, Ranger. You won't need that now. They can't hurt you, so don't be afraid. Protect your friends, bring back Jenny, and get out of here for now.

Why not kill them?

You need to be alone so the others won't get hurt. Save Jenny and Jason first.

The Lizard Men moved forward slowly toward him, their claws in front of them and their mouths split open over long and razor-sharp teeth. Nathan suddenly understood that they moved slowly not out of confidence, but out of fear.

Fear of me.

"Jesus Christ—Nathan, run! Let's get out of here."

"Stay still," he commanded and his voice sounded old to him—like a real Ranger. He let the creatures get a little closer and then grabbed his right wrist with his left and pulled his arm back like a karate move. "Power Rangers," he shouted at the ceiling—just like in the real TV show. "POWER UP! YEAH!"

He titled his head back and imagined his body flipped backward and that his red suit and helmet magically appeared over him.

He felt a tremendous heat spread out from the center of his chest in all directions, fast like lightening. He held his vibrating hands in front of him and watched as long pencils of light exploded from the tips of his fingers. He opened his mouth and howled brilliant white light out of his throat just as his vision changed, growing tinted with a harsh blue.

I found the switch for my flashlight.
Yes you did. Now make them leave.

Nathan felt only a vague awareness of Jason screaming behind him. His friend believed something terrible had happened to him; that the creatures were hurting him somehow. He had no time to explain.

He moved toward the Lizard Men in a way that felt like floating and he saw them cower as he approached. Occasionally, the light beams would dance across their skin and he could hear the hiss and pop like bacon frying on the stove. The smaller creature pulled back his reptilian head and let out a bellowing squeal. The taller creature moved suddenly to the right, and Nathan saw that he meant to get around him and get to Jenny and Jason.

The rage that grew inside him felt like hunger and his light got brighter. He rose off the floor and looked down on the large creatures from well above. He shot a hand out at the taller one, who moved with incredible speed toward Jason, one huge-clawed hand raised to strike. The beams of light organized somehow, and wrapped around the creature's arms and shoulders like thick neon ropes. Smoke rose from the greenish-grey skin where the light-rope ensnared him and Nathan heard a blood-curdling scream of raw agony as the creature arched its back in pain.

The claw had lost its momentum, but still struck Jason high on the forehead, causing him to stumble backward. Jenny's inert body flew from Jason's arms.

Nathan tightened his finger lights. The sizzling sound got louder, and more animal screams came from the Lizard Man. He opened his mouth again and shouted out another, thicker beam of light that struck the creature on the side of the face and knocked him to the ground.

Nathan looked over his shoulder and saw that the shorter lizard man had retreated into the passageway. Then he turned his gaze back to the creature on the floor whose eyes had paled to a dull orange. For a moment, he thought the creature would rise and try to strike again, and he could feel more power vibrate inside of his own chest at the thought, but instead the Lizard Man screeched one more loud protest and then, in a flash of blue light, disappeared. The blue light crackled like a live power line and followed after the creature. A dull, burned-oil smell joined the nasty fart smell.

Barely noticing in his relief, Nathan tumbled roughly to the dirt floor several feet below with a thud and a moan as the air was forced from his lungs. He sat up and looked over at Jason who sat beside Jenny, a hand on her shoulder.

"My God, Nathan. Are you alright? Did they hurt you?"

Nathan started to answer, but he didn't want to lose the ebbing power before he could use it again. He got up and shuffled over to Jenny, then knelt in the dirt beside her. He looked at Jason, trying to communicate reassurance, then lightly placed his hand on her head. He saw his hand start to glow, pulsing like a heartbeat. He closed his eyes and went into her mind.

At first he saw only darkness and he called to her. Her voice answered back from far away. She sounded like a very little girl.

Chapter 25

She floated in the dark, warm pool and felt neither fear nor relief. She simply existed in the blackness and though a part of her mind knew just what it escaped from, most of her couldn't possibly care less. She thought for a moment that it must be like this in the womb, dark and warm and safe.

She felt a tug of sadness at what must be left behind and she saw fleeting images in the dark—her parents, her brother in his cap and gown, Jason looking down from on top of her, Nathan—but those things had to be left to escape the bad things that she chose not to remember. It would be best for her to stay here—to keep the images safe from the dark creatures and their poisonous thoughts. She had floated here long enough now that the good and bad things started to feel abstract and she thought maybe she would just let herself dissolve in the darkness...dissolve completely and go away forever.

Then she heard the little boy's voice that seemed familiar.

Jenny? Jenny, answer me please. It's Nathan. I need to find you before it's too late.

Both the name and the voice felt important in a way that ached, but she just didn't have any energy left. She had decided to go and should finish her journey.

Jenny, please. Jason and I need you so bad. Please answer me.

Another name that felt important and she matched it to the picture of Jason smiling down at her in her bed.

"Jason?"

It's Nathan. Let me help you find the light and come home.

"Nathan? Where are you?" Her own voice sounded like a child's to her.

I'm in here with you. I brought some light. Can you see it? Come to it, Jenny.

She did see the light. At first it looked like a tiny pinpoint that grew into a bobbing flashlight. She floated toward it and the blackness faded to a soft grey. She willed herself to float on, to head toward the glowing ball of light. As she approached, it got brighter, almost blinding, and then she saw that a boy stood in the middle of the light. The light emanated from him.

"Nathan?"

It's me, Jenny. If you take my hand we can go back. Jason is waiting for you.

She reached out a tentative hand and felt the soft hand in hers. A warm vibration spread out from her hand, chased quickly up her arm and then out into her whole body. It felt a lot like an orgasm, only better.

"Oh my" she whispered.

And then she felt as if she were pulled to light speed and accelerated out of the darkness.

Still holding Nathan's warm hand, she flew out of her mind. She closed her eyes tightly, not in pain or fear, but to try and hold onto the light for just a moment more.

She opened her eyes slowly and looked up into two faces looking back at her. Nathan looked like the little boy she had always known and Jason looked like her future.

"Hi," she said and smiled.

* * *

Jason cradled Jenny and felt a flood of relief that she hugged him back. Tears streamed down his cheeks as he kissed her dirty hair. Then he reached up and pulled Nathan over into their embrace.

"Thank you, Nathan. I don't know what the hell you did, but thank you so much."

Nathan beamed back at him, all little boy again. For a moment Jason saw the terrifying image of the thing Nathan had become—the blindingly bright light creature that had shot energy beams, or whatever they were, and defeated the Lizard Men. He could almost still hear the shrill sound when he had opened his glowing mouth and screamed out the energy that had chased the beasts away. It seemed unbelievable that now he just looked like Nathan.

"You're welcome," Nathan said with a shrug. "I just want us to all be okay."

"Are they gone?" Jason asked.

You know better, young Jedi.

"I don't think so," Nathan answered and he looked dark. "But I think we're okay now and I think Miss Jenny is gonna be fine." He hugged the two of them tightly.

"We need to get out of here," Jason said. He rose and pulled them both to their feet. Jenny looked over at the inert figure a few yards away from them and pulled in closer to him. Jazz's body lay completely still. Even his eyes were now motionless. Jason wondered for a moment if he might be dead, but thought he saw his chest rise and fall slightly.

"Did I do that?" Jenny asked, her fingers digging into his arm.

"No," he answered quickly. "No you didn't, Jenny. And it's over now." He hugged her tightly. "God, don't even think about leaving again."

"I won't," she promised. "But I think we have to save him somehow. We can't just let them kill him."

Together they decided to meet up in Nathan's room as soon as they all got back. Once they were together and everyone was alright, Jason would find the room where Jazz was kept and take him out of there, to the ER or something.

"I'll go with you," Jenny said. "I can find it easier than you and I kind of need to do it." Jason reluctantly agreed. They huddled together in the corner, far away from the walls and the cave blood puddles. Jason held Jenny's hand and told her to just hang on tight. Then he checked on Nathan, who had bowed his head gently and already faded beside him.

He closed his own eyes and listened to the far off sounds of Jenny's breathing beside him on the call room bed and searched with his skin for the feel of the sheets. He felt a small shudder, like an unexpected sigh, then realized he lay on his side and opened his eyes. He stared deeply into the beautiful blue-green eyes a few inches from his face and smiled at Jenny, who lay wrapped in his embrace on the call room bed.

"Hi," he said.

"Hi," she answered and kissed him deeply. "Thank you."

They hugged and then sat up together awkwardly on the narrow bunk. Jenny had no shoes on for some reason, but that would be an easy fix. Jason felt that once they made sure Jazz was safely in the care of the ER, assuming he was still alive, they might be free from this. He knew that the creatures weren't dead—didn't know if "dead" even applied to them—but he felt pretty sure they would be moving on after their encounter with Nathan. He felt a stab of guilt. If he had been strong enough to do twenty years ago what Nathan had done today, maybe none of them would have had to go through this hell.

And maybe Mom would still be here.

He took Jenny's hand and they slipped out of the call room.

"Nice, guys," a voice said from behind them. "Very nice."

He turned and saw one of the anesthesia residents grin broadly and give them a thumbs-up and then a little golf-clap. "Strong work guys," he called after them.

Jason blushed, ignored him, and headed hand in hand with Jenny toward the door.

* * *

Nathan opened his eyes and looked without surprise at the hallway lights that danced strange patterns on the ceiling of his hospital room. In the corner Mom's sheets and pillows sat on the empty chair-turned-bed. She must have gone to the bathroom or to get something to drink. The bathroom door stood open and the light remained off.

"Mom?" he called out softly.

No answer.

He felt relieved. He needed a minute to settle down before he had to pretend that everything was right and normal. Already the memory of the lights that struck out of his fingers and beat back the Lizard Men had taken on a dreamlike quality. For a moment he wondered if he *had* dreamed the whole thing.

You know better than that, Ranger. He'll be along in a minute and then you'll see.

That sounded more like his own voice then the other-him, and he started to have more doubts. It seemed so real, though. He went to push his hair off his forehead where it tickled a little and clumped himself in the face with the bulky white bandage on his arm, the splint that kept his cracked bones together, certain to raise a red mark.

"Ouch," he said.

But the arm didn't hurt at all where the bones were supposed to be broken. More amazing, his hand where they had scraped the dead skin off and just recently stapled new skin on didn't sting either. Even with a bunch of pain medicine in his IV, bumping his hand should hurt like crazy.

Nathan pushed the button on his bed rail to turn on the soft reading light behind the head of his bed. He pulled down the sheet and looked at the clear plastic dressing on his upper thigh where they had taken the good skin to fix his burned hand. The dressing still looked stuck to his leg, right where it had been, but the skin underneath the see-through plastic no longer looked red and bloody. Before it had looked like the worst raspberry you could imagine, but now he saw normal skin, and none of the yellowish liquid and blood that always collected under the plastic. Nathan used his good hand to gently peel the plastic off and then lightly ran a finger over the site. Completely normal, like nothing had happened there ever. It even tickled a little 'cause he rubbed so soft.

A little excited, he peeled the tape off his arm dressing and started to unravel the yards and yards of gauze. When the bandage lay in a tall pile beside him and the splint fell away, he looked at the fluffy four-by-fours on the palm of his hand, took a deep breath, then pulled them away quickly like revealing a magic trick.

The trick worked.

"Tah-duh," he said with a giggle.

The skin on his hand looked completely normal, even on the two fingers that had looked all black—the ones the first doctor had told his mother he might lose. He balled his hand into a fist and it felt normal, except for a little tug of pain where a dozen little staples, placed to hold the skin graft in place, stuck up uselessly from normal skin. Nathan bent his wrist back and forth, a movement that the splint would have prevented, and felt no pain where the bones had been broken.

"Wow," he whispered.

He looked around the room, suddenly worried that he would get caught and have to explain why his burns and broken bones had healed like magic. He grabbed a stack of fluffy four-by-fours in his magic hand and then awkwardly wrapped the gauze around to his mid forearm and tucked it in. It didn't really look at all neat, but if he kept his hand under the covers, he doubted anyone would notice. He could ask Jason what he should do once he came.

Nathan craned his neck to see out through the door into the hallway. He wondered where his mom had gone, but also kind of hoped that Jason and Jenny would hurry up and come before she got back. He slipped out of his bed and padded across the cool floor in bare feet to the door where he cautiously peered into the hall.

Way at the end he saw a nurse with a big cart that he knew held medicines, but the hallway looked otherwise empty and the lights had been dimmed for the night shift. The nurse at the end of the hall saw him and held up a finger at him in a silent "just a minute and I'll be there."

Nathan slipped back into bed so he could hide his poorly wrapped hand under the covers. He wished Jason would come through the door instead of the nurse. Something was wrong, he was certain now.

Something is going to happen. Something bad.

"I thought it already happened. I thought I did good." He felt his lower lip start to quiver and tears welled up in his eyes.

It's still coming, Ranger. You have more work to do. Your mommy needs you.

The words gripped him by the throat, and for a minute, he couldn't breathe. Where was she? He needed her to come back right now. He closed his eyes tightly.

I need you to come here, Jason.

The words echoed around in his head but no answer came. Now he felt more than a little afraid.

He can't help you now, Nathan. You have to do this.

"I thought we were a team. I thought you said I have to lead my team. I'm the Red Ranger," he sobbed. "I want my mommy!"

Some things the team can't help you with, Nathan, and this is one of them. Only you can do this. The others would get hurt if they tried to help. I know you want your mom and she needs you too. I can help a little, but you really have to power up now, okay?

The door opened and the tall nurse came in with a big smile on her face.

"Hi, there, Nathan Doren," she said without looking at her card. "Are you doing okay?"

"I want my mommy," Nathan said, feeling hot tears run down his face and drip off his chin.

"Oh, she'll be back real soon, sweetie. She left with someone—a family member, maybe? Kind of a tall man in a long coat and top hat? He had scars on his face."

It took Nathan a moment to realize he felt dizzy because he had stopped breathing. It seemed like some invisible giant squeezed him way too tight. He needed Jason—needed him right now.

No Ranger—you have to do this alone. You can do it, Nathan. Remember how great you did in the cave just a little while ago? You rescued

Jenny and Jason and you can rescue your mom. You will have to defeat the Lizard Men. You have the power.

I might be too scared.

"Are you okay, little guy?" The nurse touched his face. "Are you having pain?"

Nathan struggled to swallow his fear. He had to make this nurse go away. He had to find his mommy and he had to kill the Lizard Men.

"No," he said softly and lay down on his pillow, pulling the covers up on his shoulder. "I'm just tired. I wanna go back to sleep and my mommy will be here when I get back."

"I'm sure she will, sweetie," the nurse said and turned off his light. "Is it okay to turn this off?"

"Yes please," he said and faked a big yawn.

"Call me if you need anything." The nurse pulled the door nearly closed behind her.

I want to talk to Jason. I want to tell him where I'm going.

No, Nathan. He'll want to go with you and that would be too dangerous. I'm sorry, but you have to do this alone.

Nathan swallowed hard and closed his eyes. He grabbed his good wrist with his healed, but bandaged, other hand and pulled it back, karate style.

"Power Up," he said.

* * *

"Excuse me—can I help you?"

Jason wondered how it had not occurred to him that it might look strange for them to arrive on the Pediatric Ward in the middle of the night. He wore street clothes and Jenny sported her ICU scrubs and jacket, but with floppy, oversized rubber clogs stolen from the OR locker room. She looked like she had bright blue clown feet. They both looked worse for wear, Jenny's hair dirty and plastered to the side of her head and Jason's standing at impossible angles. Jason guessed they looked like they woke up under a bridge and then put on clothes they had stolen from a clothesline somewhere. He struggled for a response when Jenny saved them.

"Hey, Janice, it's me—Jenny from ICU?"

"Jenny?" the nurse clearly found it hard to believe this hobo was someone she knew. Then her eyes widened. "Jenny! My God, are you alright?"

Jenny forced a smile and took Jason's hand. "It's been a tough day," she said without elaborating. "Dr. Gelman just wanted to check real quick on one of his patients before we head out of here."

"Oh, I'm sorry, Dr. Gelman. I didn't recognize you in street clothes." Janice the nurse looked him up and down. It was clear to him that she had no idea who Dr. Gelman was, but wanted to cover the bases in case she should know.

"No problem, Janice," he said with a smile. "I'm sure I've looked better." He pulled Jenny along to end the conversation before the nurse could ask anything else. When he reached out for the door to Nathan's room, he heard a sigh of recognition.

"Oh, you're seeing the Doren boy. That's great. I just saw him and he's up. Is there anything I can tell you or help you with?"

"No, we're good," Jason answered.

"Well, he'll be glad to see you. He woke up and his mother had stepped out and I think he got a little nervous."

"Thanks, Janice," he called back and they pushed into the room and closed the door behind them. Where the hell had Sherry gone in the middle of the night? It was probably a good thing that she felt comfortable leaving him for a while and it certainly helped them out tonight. Still, getting her to head home for a shower had been like pulling teeth.

Strange.

"Nathan?"

Hand in hand he and Jenny went to the bedside. Nathan lay on his side with the sheet pulled up to his neck and his face half buried in the pillow. Poor guy had to be exhausted.

Yeah. Must take a lot of energy to light up like a firecracker and float to the ceiling, huh?

For a moment he thought about letting him sleep, but knew if Nathan woke up and hadn't seen them he would be scared. Best to let him know everything was okay before getting him back to sleep.

Then we can go take care of Jazz, if he's still alive.

Jason sat on the edge of the bed and Jenny put her hand on his shoulder. He smoothed the boy's hair and lightly touched his forehead, which felt cool to his fingers. Something felt wrong and Jason tensed up.

"Nathan?" he said, a little louder than he meant to. No sense startling him awake. God knows what he might do by accident. Nathan didn't even stir.

"What's the matter?" Jenny asked with a quiver in her voice.

Jason took Nathan by both shoulders and rolled him on his back. "Nathan come on—wake up." He could hear the panic in his own voice. Nathan's lifeless body rolled over, face pale, mouth slack and eyes open and unseeing. He stood up and fumbled for a pulse in the boy's neck, unconsciously feeling along his breastbone with his other hand for his xiphoid, ready to begin CPR.

But the pulse was there, strong and fast.

He pulled one of Nathan's eyelids up farther and the eye continued to look without seeing. He looked like a comatose patient—in fact he looked like Jenny had looked only a couple of hours ago in the waiting room.

"What's wrong with him?" Jenny asked. One hand dug into Jason's arm and the other went to her mouth.

"I don't know," Jason said shortly. "Give me a minute here."

He must not have made it back from the cave—but why? Everything had seemed fine. In fact he had seen Nathan shimmer and disappear moments before he and Jenny had left. Jason waited for the other-him to answer some of the questions, but now that he needed to hear something, the voice remained silent so only the questions echoed in his head. He turned to Jenny, who had become very pale. He took her arms and gently eased her into the big chair with Sherry's covers still in a ball beside her.

And just where the hell is Sherry? Hell of a coincidence that she's not here the one time something is terribly wrong.

Jason felt his tenuous grip on control slip a little more. He smiled at Jenny and tried to look reassuring. "Everything is going to be fine," he said. "Just give me a minute. I need you to be real quiet for a minute or two."

Jenny nodded and he closed his eyes tightly. He listened as hard as he could, but heard nothing from Nathan. He hollered out in his mind.

Nathan? Nathan, it's Jason. Where are you, buddy?

Jason kept his eyes closed through the pause that felt like forever. He was just about to tell Jenny he had to go back to the cave when he heard the voice from far off. At first he thought it might be a trick of his imagination, like a subject pushing the little button in the hearing test and finding out they stopped putting the little tones in your headset ten minutes ago.

Jason?

Nathan! Where are you, buddy?

I have to save my mom.

The words cut Jason deeply and he fought off the flood of memories—images of his own mom, thin and wild eyed in the hospital bed. Darker images of the Lizard Men tearing apart Steve. He saw a flash of his mother's dull eyes when he left her in the cave to run and hide. He felt his throat tighten and stifled a sob. It was way too late to undo his failure—but he could help Nathan save his mommy.

Where are you, Nathan? I'm coming to help you.

No!

The boy's voice held panic that Jason didn't understand.

You can't. Please find my mommy on that side—like you did for Jenny. My voice said I have to do this part alone.

Why did the little boy have to be all alone in that shitty place? He had to help somehow.

I'll be right back, Nathan.

Jason opened his eyes and saw that Jenny stared at him in confusion and fright. "What's wrong?"

"He's okay for now," he told her. He didn't have time to explain how that worked—even if he could. "We have to find Sherry, his mom."

Jason searched his pocket for his cell phone to see if he had programmed the number in, but his pockets were empty. He needed the number so he could call the house. Maybe she would answer and be fine and he could bring Nathan back.

You know a lot better than that, Jedi.

He ignored the voice and searched again in the pockets of his jeans. Nothing.

"Can you go and get me his chart?" he asked Jenny. It would probably help her to have something to do in any case. Jenny headed out the door to the nurse's station.

Jason looked at Nathan's small shape beneath the covers. He smoothed his hair and pulled the covers back up over the cool body. The skin felt waxy.

Jenny returned a moment later with the chart.

"They wanted to know if you would be writing any orders," she said. That gave him an idea. He *would* write an order.

Jason looked at the face sheet in the front of the chart and found the Doren's home phone number. He dialed nine on the bedside phone to get an outside line and then punched the number in. He might have waited longer if he really believed she might answer. Still, he listened to at least ten ring tones before he hung up.

You know where she is, Jedi. If you want to help Nathan, then help him here. Find his mom.

Jason wrote a quick order to cancel all of the vital sign checks and that Nathan should be undisturbed until Dr. Gelman checked back. The order would only be followed until shift change, but that gave them a few hours. If they couldn't have Nathan back by then, they would have much bigger problems than the nurses not being able to wake him. He closed his eyes.

Nathan, it's me. We're going to find your mommy okay? I'll find her and make her safe and then I'm coming to help you.

He didn't care if Nathan's other him voice told him he had to do this alone. Ridiculous. He had been alone in the cave before when he was little like Nathan, and look how that turned out. That asshole voice had told him that Nathan needed him—needed something that was buried inside him—and he sure as shit was going to be there for him.

Okay.

Nathan's voice sounded quite far away. Jason waited for more but heard only his own breathing and the pounding pulse in his temples. He opened his eyes and exchanged a quiet look with Jenny.

Jason took a blank sheet of progress note paper from the chart and flipped it over. With the pen Jenny had brought him, he wrote, "Do not disturb. Please see Nurse," on the back. He clipped it to the door and then returned the chart to Nurse Janice. She smiled at him with saccharin sweetness.

"The little guy is completely exhausted," he told her. "Let's just let him sleep the rest of the night. I wrote an order to hold all checks on him and put a note on the door. I also spoke with his mother who will be back soon, so can you help me out and keep everyone out of his room?"

"Sure, Doctor," Janice told him.

"You too, okay? Let's let him get a little sleep."

"No problem, Dr. Gelman," she said.

Jason hustled back to the room where he kissed Nathan on his cool and pasty forehead, then smoothed his hair one last time. He positioned him back on his side facing away from the door just in case. Then he grabbed Jenny's hand.

"Let's go," he said softly.

"Where?" She looked like she had very little left to give.

Jason kissed her cheek. "We gotta save Sherry and I guess Jazz, too, while we're at it."

She followed him out the door and together they hurried off the ward and toward the stairs.

Chapter
26

Nathan felt better knowing that Jason would find his mom. Images of Steve with his guts all torn out and the other man with his brains bashed in made him shudder uncontrollably. He had to stop the Lizard Men before they could hurt Mommy.

I have to kill them.

Nathan slid down the dirty path to the large room, intent on not being afraid when he had to go down the smaller tunnel with the scary glowing lights. He had no doubt that this would be the time he would need to go there. He was half way down the slope, watching Jazz who now stirred and mumbled, a long cut down the center of his belly oozing dark blood, before he noticed the other figure near the wall. She lay perfectly still, curled up on her side and facing away from him, but he knew immediately who it was.

"Mommy!" His voice sounded shrill and scared as it echoed off the walls. He ran to his mother's side, nearly tripping over Jazz's thrashing legs. "Mommy, Mommy," he cried as he collapsed beside her in the dirt.

His mom didn't move, but she seemed unhurt. Nathan couldn't bring himself to look at her eyes, just in case they looked all white and dead like Jenny's had, but he smoothed her hair from her cheek. Her face felt hot and wet and he leaned over to kiss her.

You have to get to work, Ranger. Time to Power Up.

I can't leave her here. They'll get her and hurt her.

They already have her. If you want to save her you have to defeat them. It's the only way. She is too big for you to move by yourself.

Then Jason can come and help me.

The thought of leaving his mom naked and unprotected on the dirt floor was more than he could bear. He wanted to move her to the little cave they had hidden in before.

She's no safer there, Nathan. Safety is an illusion here. You know what you have to do.

Nathan stood up, his small fists balled up at his sides.

"Power Up," he mumbled. He made no attempt to mimic the movements of the characters from the TV show. He looked back at his mommy and tears streamed down his face. "I'll be back in a minute, Mom," he said.

Nathan took a few steps and then stopped for a minute and stared at Jazz, who now writhed in agony on the floor, his mouth open in a scream, his voice little more than a gurgle. Loops of intestines had spilled out of his open belly that now danced around in the dirt. Nathan stepped over him, his small jaw set firmly and his usually blue eyes turning deep crimson.

He headed for the passageway with its strange yellow glow.

* * *

The burning itch of the thick red wounds on his face did little to dampen the near sexual pleasure of feeding from the boy on the table. The surgeons had torn several large pieces of skin from James's hip and side and worked now at stretching the skin taunt over the lower part of his chest—a tricky place to harvest skin because of the ribs that made the area all uneven, especially in a thin person like James. The dull light that poured out of his victim tasted like warm water at a holiday feast compared to the bright and pulsating light that he swallowed greedily earlier.

Mr. Clark caressed the still-wet wounds on his face, neck and shoulder gently and without awareness. His focus stayed completely on absorbing the power of his meal. The deep acid-like burns had become little more than background noise and he suppressed his own fear at the power of the boy who had wounded him. He needed the energy from this meal—needed it to be able to finish their work here and move on, but sensed the power he ingested now may prove less important than having the woman in their possession.

The older boy had been defeated years ago when his fear had been turned against him using his mother—and her death. That loss had been unfortunate. The older boy's mother had been an unbelievably rich fuel source, her guilt and fear powerful and always close to the surface. He pushed the thoughts from his mind and sucked deeply in of the light that poured from James's bleeding body. He knew, to the others in the room, he looked to be simply standing in the back and watching as they stripped the body of bleeding skin—the light would not be visible to them. He felt his skin tingle with the energy that filled him and his partner and closed his eyes in pleasure.

Soon they would go back in the abdomen and take the other kidney and then they would split open the chest to take lungs and heart. He needed to remember to interrupt his feed long enough to let James know that was coming—to bring his tapering terror back to a crescendo. For now he gulped greedily in his rapture. He failed to notice the door behind him open.

* * *

Jason squeezed Jenny's hand in disbelief as he peered into the large operating room. After his recent trips to the other-world cave with its resident Lizard Men, it seemed odd that it would be the secret room in the hospital basement that his mind had the most trouble accepting. The taller Lizard Man in his long overcoat and low-riding top hat stood only a few feet in front of him, head tilted back as he sucked in pulsating light gushing out of the motionless body on the table.

Still, he found the sight of the operating team as they peeled another strip of skin from Jazz's chest more astounding than the Lizard Man who fed on the boy's raw terror. These were physicians, likely physicians he knew at least casually, who tortured this boy to death.

Jason scanned the room quickly and caught sight of the other one, the shorter one, farther to his left, also facing away from them. Like the taller creature, his head tilted back and his mouth gaped open as pulsating swirls of light poured into him. How could the operating team see such a thing and not be terrified by it?

He slipped the rest of the way into the room and moved quietly to the right. Another gurney had been pushed against the wall and on it he saw Sherry, a sheet pulled up to her shoulders. Plastic IV tubing snaked under the sheet from a bag that hung from the bed's pole. On the bag someone had plastered a red sticker on which "SUX" had been written in black marker.

Succinylcholine? Holy shit.

The drug, a powerful paralytic used in anesthesia, was supposed to be combined with an anesthetic during surgery. By itself it would paralyze a patient, but they would remain completely awake and aware and would feel everything. Jason couldn't imagine the horror that Jazz must be experiencing—that Steve had experienced—as the surgical team tore them apart. The IV bag that hung on Sherry's bed pole didn't seem to be running, at least not yet, which explained why she wasn't on a ventilator.

The creatures seemed completely absorbed by their feeding, and the two surgeons remained intent on their work, so Jason pulled Jenny behind him and quietly approached Sherry's gurney. Gently, he turned her face toward him and raised her eyelids. The eyes stared back at him, unseeing, and he wondered whether she had been given a sedative or if she had been knocked down by the powerful images that the creatures somehow forced into people's minds. Either way, she looked to be down for the count.

Jason stared now at the back of the taller creature only a few yards away from him.

Keep them from Nathan, Jedi. He needs more time to prepare.

Jason pulled Jenny beside him closely and whispered softly in her ear. "Stay behind me." Her eyes were wide, her mouth slack and open, but to his relief she nodded weakly and moved behind him. With some difficulty he pried his hand out of hers and felt her hand move to his belt.

Use the force, Jedi.

Jason rushed forward, surprised at his own speed and balance, and slammed into the trench-coated back of the tall lizard man in front of him. Just before impact, as he passed through the pulsating light that swirled around the creature and then poured into his huge open mouth, he felt a strange tingle throughout his body and his mind filled with images of being torn apart alive, of a weak and sobbing voice.

Jazz.

Then his shoulder crunched painfully into the Lizard Man and the swirling light became disorganized and tumbled off into the room. His enemy screeched, not with pain, but anger and frustration, like a still-hungry infant when its bottle was pulled away.

Jason wrapped both arms around the creature. The trench coat fluttered in his face and blinded him as his momentum propelled them both deeper into the room. His right knee crashed painfully into the tile floor and he grimaced as the pain shot up his leg all the way to his hip, no doubt conducted by the steel rod that he still carried in his thigh bone.

The breath hissed out of his chest as Jenny tumbled on top of him from behind.

Jason rolled quickly to his left and pulled Jenny with him, more worried about her than what the creatures might do. He turned his head back toward the Lizard Man, expecting to see the long, razor teeth heading directly at him.

Instead, the creature squirmed away with remarkable speed, the body twisting across the floor in impossible gyrations that reminded Jason of a frightened snake. As he struggled to his knees, he watched in fascination as the creature made it to the far wall—and then continued up the wall with the same reptilian gyrations of his body, apparently not subject to gravity at all.

When the motionless feet got just above floor level, the creature twisted around, floated a moment in space, and then—arms out and face turned up—he stopped hovering and dropped the few inches onto the floor. The head tilted back down and glowing red eyes narrowed in on Jason.

Jason scurried to his feet and forced Jenny backward. He had no doubt that the creature would charge him in a moment and felt just as certain that he would not survive the attack. He hoped only to buy Jenny enough time to get away.

"Take Sherry with you," he shouted as he braced his body. Jenny squeezed his hand and then let go and moved away.

The red eyes pulsated. Instead of charging forward, the creature began to shimmer. As Jason watched, even the air around him seemed to waver; as the coat and hat disappeared slowly at the same time, that eerie face stretched and changed. For a brief moment he looked at the image of the Lizard Man he knew from the cave—long snout with dark skin and pointed teeth, caressed by a blood-red tongue—and then a blue light flashed in the room and the creature disappeared.

Jason's nose wrinkled at the terrible, wet-shit smell. His peripheral vision caught another flash of blue and he turned to see the shorter creature disappear as well. The room fell silent and Jason became aware of the eyes of the two surgeons at the table that stared at him in silence. He looked back, unsure what to say. Then a sharp sound made him jump as one of them dropped a stainless steel instrument to the floor. The surgeon's head fell back and he collapsed beside the OR table. The other man's shoulders sagged and he leaned forward and steadied himself on the table.

"What the hell just happened?" Jenny choked out from beside him.

"It doesn't matter," Jason answered, unsure that he knew anyway. "We've gotta get these people out of here."

And then I'm going after Nathan.

You can't help him, Jedi. The force is weak in you now. Your time is past.

"Bullshit," he mumbled.

He went to the OR table and grabbed the still-standing surgeon by the shoulders. The eyes that looked back at him were those of a junkie on a binge and Jason shook him hard.

"Come on. Wake up," he said in frustration.

The eyes cleared a little but filled with confusion. Jason pulled the surgical mask off and recognized the man as one of the more junior staff transplant surgeons.

"You need to get the hell out of here—now!" he commanded. "Go home. This was just a horrible dream, but I promise it's over now."

"Dream?' the dazed man asked.

"Yeah," Jason answered. "A terrible, fucked-up dream."

The man seemed to understand and went to the other side of the table to collect his partner. He helped him from the floor and they headed across the room.

"It's over?" he asked as he hesitated at the door.

"Yes," Jason answered.

The man nodded again and tears spilled out onto his cheeks. "Thank God," he mumbled, and the two of them left the room.

Jason looked down at the boy on the OR table. His eyes stared at the ceiling without moving, but Jason knew they could see. The ventilator hissed, but otherwise the room remained silent.

The wound in Jazz's abdomen gaped up at Jason from his breastbone to his pubic bone. The thin, shallow pool of blood mixed in with the shiny rolls of intestines. Jason saw that the liver and spleen were intact, but there stood a bloody ragged hole stuffed with stained laparotomy sponges where the left kidney should have been. Jason hoped that the other kidney had not been harvested already—he could live with one.

He grabbed a pair of gloves off the back table, snapped them on, and then packed more of the sterile gauze into the gaping abdomen to keep dust and air out and to maybe stop the slow bleeding. Then he wet several more strips of the dressing material in the blue basin on the table and lay them across the stark white tissue that remained in the long strips where the skin had been stripped off. He wished he had some morphine to give, but he saw none.

Jason walked over to Jenny who stared at him.

"What just happened?" she asked again.

"Listen to me," he said shortly. "I have to go help Nathan, but we have to get this kid to the ER and Sherry out of this room. I have to hurry, because I think Nathan may be in real trouble. Can you help me?"

Jenny nodded and wiped tears from her cheeks. "What do you need me to do?"

Jason hugged tightly against him. "I love you," he said,

"I love you, too," she answered.

"Here's what we need to do," he began.

* * *

Nathan hesitated. He had moved deep into the passageway with the weird glow and strange smell, well past where he'd ventured the first time when the other-him voice had asked him to check it out. He worried a lot about what caused the glow and the smell, both of which grew stronger as he moved deeper into the cavern, but that wasn't what slowed him down. He looked at his bare and dirty feet.

The blood puddles had grown bigger and bigger and now joined to form a flowing stream than ran into the glowing passageway the same way he headed. He had been able to stay out of the purple liquid for the most part, and the few times his toes had tickled into it he had felt the same tingling as before. His tummy felt a little bad like he might spit up. Now the stream nearly touched the walls, which bled from every surface and filled the stream with the gross stuff. Soon the stream would be a river and he didn't know if he could stand the thought of having to wade through cave blood.

When will I be there?

Soon. I know it's hard, but you have to keep going to save Mommy. The cave blood will make you feel a little sick, but it can't hurt you.

What is it?

There was a long pause and for a moment he thought the other-him voice might not answer.

It's the bad stuff that the creatures can't use. It's going to where they come from.

What will I do when I get there?
Stop them.
How?

This time the voiced stayed silent. Whatever he had to do, Nathan knew that his mommy's life depended on it. He took a deep, shivering breath and moved on, pressing himself into the wall as best he could. He felt the nasty tingling of the cave blood up his left ankle and leg and his stomach tightened. "This sucks," he said loudly as he continued on into the slowly brightening passage.

He felt he had earned the right to use big kid words today.

Chapter
27

Moving Sherry to the Pediatric Ward had been the easy part. Jenny checked down the hallway of the Pedi Ward and then Jason had carried her limp body into Nathan's room and placed her on the big chair. He tucked the covers up on her shoulders to make her look to be sleeping, and then left her beside her similarly comatose son.

Now Jason pushed the stretcher with Jazz's inert body while Jenny used the green plastic ambu-bag to force air into his paralyzed chest. They had pulled a sheet up to cover his gaping abdominal wound and long, bloody strips of missing skin on his chest and flank.

Jason planned to get the boy into the Trauma Bay and then push meds in him quickly. In the elevator he hit the button for the first floor; a moment later the doors opened onto an empty staff hallway. Jason jogged the fifty yards to the code-key panel by the double doors, pushed in seven-one-zero-zero and the doors swished open together. He pushed the stretcher through, nearly lost Jenny as he turned the corner, and moved toward the Trauma Bay. As he approached a large and unhappy-looking woman in blue scrubs peered over her glasses at him in disapproval.

"Just what's this?" she asked with an exaggerated frown.

"No time, Jan. Call the Trauma Team stat. And bring me some morphine, etomidate, and succinylcholine right now." He wheeled past her and turned left into the large Trauma Bay just beyond her and across from the large admissions desk. The woman stood motionless, her mouth open. "Goddamnit, Jan—now! And get me some help in here."

They pulled the stretcher into the first bay and pulled the curtain between them and the next bay where an old man lay with his hands over his face and his left leg pulled straight between two narrow rods that kept his broken femur stable. Jason looked at Jenny who stared back at him impassively as she squeezed rhythmically on the ambu-bag. He winked at her, hopeful that the gesture might reassure her.

She's hanging on by a thread.

Two nurses burst into the bay, a man and a woman in matching blue scrubs.

"Sux, morphine, and etomidate," the woman said and handed Jason three syringes with red-label tape on them. An ER resident shuffled in behind them. Jason felt relief to see his buddy Rich Rizutto in a stained white coat over green scrubs. The unspoken fraternal code of ER required that he look bored and unhurried, but his voice sounded anything but bored.

"Whisky-tango-foxtrot, bro? Where the hell did this guy come from?"

"Hey, Scooter," Jason answered as he pushed a bolus of morphine into the IV tubing. Jazz had all the succinylcholine he needed so he casually wasted it onto the wet sheets, hopeful no one noticed. "Shit if I know. Jenny and I were coming in through the ambulance entrance when some medics pulled this guy out. Some kind of transfer from another hospital—some sort of fucked-up surgery gone bad, I think. They went tearing out of here when I offered to help them—something about a chemical explosion somewhere, so you guys may have a bunch of patients coming."

"Mass casualty?" Rizutto asked with arched eyebrows. "Tasty— how's this guy?"

"Seems stable," Jason said and moved away so Rizutto could take over. "I don't really know anything else. Just tryin' to help the medics out."

"Well, shit, dude," Scooter said and rubbed his chin. "I mean what was the surgery, who was the doctor, which hospital—is there any fucking paperwork on the stretcher?" He pointed at the male nurse who shook his head. "Great—fuck me—okay, let's hang some ringer's lactate until we know how he got here. And where are the surgeons?"

Jason grabbed Jenny's hand and pulled her away as a respiratory tech rolled a ventilator in to hook up to Jazz's breathing tube. "I'll let the triage desk know what I heard about the mass casualty thing," he called to Rizutto. Scooter waved his hand and continued to look over his patient.

"What the hell? Someone just gave up, packed his abdomen, and transferred him without a receiving surgeon? What kind of cosmic fucking bunny hole have I fallen through? Is it a full moon out? Anyone? Is it?"

Jason let the door close on his friend's rant and then dragged Jenny back down the hall and out of the ER. "What are you going to do?" she asked.

"Help Nathan," he answered simply. He didn't know anything more than that. Jenny nodded like that was enough.

"In the cave," she said. It sounded more of a statement than a question, but he nodded and she hugged him. The ding of the elevator's arrival interrupted their embrace.

On the fifth floor, Jason forced himself to slow down and not look so suspicious as he entered the Pedi Ward. The tall nurse from earlier waved at him from the other end of the hall and he raised a hand back. Together they slipped into Nathan's room.

Sherry and Nathan lay just as he had left them. He heard loud snoring sounds from Sherry's bed and gently adjusted her head so that her airway stayed a little more open. Then he pulled the covers down off Nathan's shoulders and stroked his hair. He felt a tear well up, but didn't know why.

"I'm coming, little buddy," he said and then leaned over and kissed Nathan's soft cheek. Jason turned to Jenny and took both of her hands. "I have to go," he said softly.

"I know," she said. "Both of you come back, okay?" She looked around the room. "I'll mind the store, I suppose, and keep everyone out of here as long as I can."

Jason looked at his watch—nearly four a.m. The Burn Team residents would be here for rounds no later than six or six-thirty. It would all be over one way or another by then. "Thanks," he said awkwardly. She kissed him and he settled onto the vinyl bench seat by the window. "I'll be right back," he said and smiled. She looked like she tried to smile back, but couldn't.

Jason closed his eyes.

This is a mistake, young Jedi. You won't survive.

Watch me.

Remember how you failed before?

I was just a boy. I'm a different person now. I have others to be brave for.

That isn't what it takes. There are other things that matter. That's why we sent the boy.

Well I'm going to help him or die trying.

Why?

Because. I love him.

The voice said nothing for a moment and Jason tried to imagine the wet feel of the cave. Then the voice came back.

Listen carefully, then, and take with you what you learn.

He had no idea what that meant, but he could feel himself shift or dissolve or whatever it was they did. The air got heavy and he opened his eyes.

What he saw made him want to cry or scream or both.

* * *

Jason stood at the foot of his mother's bed—her deathbed in fact—and wondered if he had finally lost his mind. Whatever had brought him here (insanity or something worse) it couldn't be real, because it looked exactly like it had nearly twenty years ago.

I'm hallucinating, right? Or remembering somehow, a really vivid memory? It doesn't matter. Pay attention.

"Jase?" His mother's voice sounded weak and gravelly. The arm that stretched out to him looked wasted. Her face appeared so gaunt that she might have been a skeleton except for the pasty skin that stuck stubbornly to her skull. Her mouth moved again, but no sound came out and then her body shook with a cough that seemed to come from her center. She spit a wad of bloody goo into a paper cup she held in her other hand. "Jase, baby, it is you, isn't it?"

"I'm here, Mom." Tears streamed down his cheeks.

"Come here, baby," she said and her thick, dry tongue tried to lick the paste from her teeth and lips. "Oh, Jason, honey, come here to Mommy."

The words sounded exactly the same, and his mom looked the same, but before someone had been with him right? A social worker had stood with him. He looked around, but saw no one—in fact he didn't really even see a room. He stood in a half room, like a stage that had been partially built, just the sides that face the audience. Behind him he saw blackness; even the two walls that came out at right angles to the wall behind her bed, came only a short distance and then disappeared.

But his mom looked exactly the same. And he knew immediately, without searching his memories, that her words were being repeated. He tried to remember what he'd said next.

"What's wrong, Mommy?" he choked out. "What's wrong with you?"

Jason felt no surprise that the voice that came from his throat was an eight year old's. Right now, somehow, he was eight-year-old Jase again. He reached out and took his mother's bony hand. As he approached her, he got a faint whiff of the smell he had grown to hate since that day, the death smell that hangs on people in their last days.

"Mommy has to go, baby," she said and tears fell from her eyes, but pooled in the gully formed by loss of muscle and fat beneath her skin. "I can't fight them anymore. I'm worried they'll hurt my baby. Oh, my poor brave little man."

Twenty years ago he had thought she might be delirious and talking nonsense.

He asked the question now that he had been too afraid to ask then.

"Who, Mommy? Who do you have to fight?"

"Why the creatures, of course," she said and her eyes glazed further. "They're here in my head even now, you know. They put things there, horrible things, and I have to go. I have to go, so I won't do the things they want me to do." Her voice cracked and Jason understood for the first time. The Lizard Men had been afraid of him, just like they were afraid of Nathan now, and had tried to get his own mother to stop him. She had given up and gone away to protect him.

The tightness in his throat nearly choked him and he heard himself sob out loud.

"Oh, my big boy," his mother said and pulled his face onto her frail, bony chest. "My brave boy. You have to be strong for Mommy, okay?"

Why had they not just hurt him themselves? They had chased him through the cave just before all of this, had damn near caught him and he had no doubt they would have killed him had they gotten their claws onto him. Why try to make his terminally-ill mother hurt him instead? It made no sense.

"Why, Mommy?" he bawled in his eight-year-old voice. "Why do they want you to hurt me?"

Her bony fingers felt cool and almost like plastic. She pulled his face off her chest and stared at him with the last bit of fire her eyes would ever hold. They looked crystal clear in that moment, bright and full of life.

"Because they know you're too young for them to stop," she said, voice teetering on maniacal. "I see that now. They can't hurt the young. You still have the power of the other place, the before place, and they are afraid of you."

"Why, Mommy?" he sobbed again.

"Because, to the young mind, anything is possible. Children—they can still find the power because they can still believe. They believe in Santa, and the Easter Bunny, and the Tooth Fairy, not because they're stupid, but because they still know that everything really is possible. Tell a child he can fly like Peter Pan did and he will fly away to Never-Never Land." Jason saw a little glow, a candle flicker, deep inside his mother's eyes. She spoke again, her face the same nearly dead one from that hospital room so long ago, but the voice now sounded like the other-him voice. "Only a child can believe like that. Only a child can fear without regret—but also believe in not being afraid. And only a child can remember the power that all of you come here with."

His mother's eyes glazed over again and she collapsed backward onto the bed. "I have to save my little boy...I have to..." He listened to her repeat it over and over, just like he remembered she had done that night, the night before he had abandoned her in the cave.

And then a bolt of blue light exploded out from her and she disappeared. He squeezed his eyes shut at the brightness of it and then gasped as the cool dark air turned hot and wet. He opened his eyes and looked around the large cavern in the cave.

Jazz lay where he had been, but his body seemed to shimmer slightly, like tiny little fireflies surrounded it. In the corner, Sherry lay on her side, motionless.

Help him then. But don't forget.

Where is he?

He is on his way down the glowing tunnel to your right. You will have to hurry. He's nearly there.

Where?

The place you couldn't go because you stopped believing.

Jason had no memory of that. He scrambled to his feet nonetheless, dusted the moist dirt off of his bare legs and ass, and headed down the passage at a slow jog.

I'm coming to help you, Nathan.

His thought-voice traveled down the passageway.

Chapter
28

Nathan fought the overpowering urge to turn around and run full tilt out of the tunnel that seemed now to close in on him. The glow he remembered from earlier had grown to a hazy light not yet bright enough to hurt his eyes. The air itself gave off the light and it penetrated through his skin. He could feel a constant irritation, like when he got a sun burn at the beach and the soft cloth of his shirt would just make it—not really hurt—just feel funny.

The tingling in his feet and ankles felt much worse. He now waded and splashed through the cave-blood river that sloshed over the tops of his feet at times. The tingly feeling moved up his legs now, gave his butt and privates a very unpleasant tightness, and made his stomach feel like he needed to spit up.

But he kept going. Every time he nearly turned around he pictured Mommy lying naked on her side in the big room. He knew if he pulled her hair away from her eyes that they would look like old milk, just like Jenny's. The Lizard Men would kill her if he didn't stop them.

"I gotta keep going," he mumbled and waded on through the awful purple yuck. He had no idea where he would end up and certainly no idea what to do when he got there.

You'll know, Power Ranger. You discovered a new power before, didn't you? One you never knew you had?

I guess so.

He didn't feel powerful right now. He remembered the feeling of the power when he saved Jenny, but like remembering a dream, like watching a movie.

That power is real, Ranger. No dream, I promise. You can use it only if you believe it, though, and your fear will make it evaporate.

How can I make myself not be afraid?

That was like saying you wouldn't cry when you got a shot at the doctor—you really wanted it to be true, but when the time came you either cry or you don't. Not much you can do to change that. The idea that he had to make himself not be afraid or he would lose his power made him really afraid—which sort of meant...

This sucks.

It does. It sucks and it is not fair, but there it is.

The other-him stayed quiet for a moment and Nathan waded on through the goo and the nasty feelings it gave him. He tried to think about his mom and how much he loved her and how much he wanted to save her. Maybe the trick was just to be mad enough—then you didn't get scared 'cause you didn't care what happened to you, right?

Stop for a moment.

Nathan stopped. He moved to the edge of the passage near the wall, close enough that the cave blood seemed a little less deep, but not so close that the little streams of it on the walls might splash on him. He knew he wouldn't be able to stand it on any other part of his body. He waited a long time.

I'm coming to help you, Nathan.

Jason's voice.

He felt a little panic now, not fear for himself but for Jason. He started to call out in his head, to make him go away, but the other voice stopped him.

It's okay. Let him come. He may be able to help you.

You said he would die. You said I had to do it alone.

He may be able to help you.

Nathan bit his lip, uncertain what to do.

Will he get hurt?

I don't know, but he has to help you. It has become his mission, too. Let him come, Nathan. Let him help you if he can. He will come no matter what, because he loves you.

There was a long pause and Nathan stayed still. He had no idea what to do. He thought he should probably go on by himself, but he thought maybe if Jason was with him he would have a better chance of not being scared.

You have a better chance to save your mom with his help—no matter what happens.

Okay.

He turned and looked back the way he had come. He reached out to his friend in his head.

Jason. Jason, I'm way down here inside the tunnel.

Wait for me, buddy. Don't go anywhere. I'm coming.

Okay.

He waited. The worry he had for Jason seemed like nothing compared to the relief that in a minute he would no longer be alone in this awful place. He waited at the end of the tunnel.

* * *

Jason felt nothing short of amazement that Nathan had come this far on his own—amazement and terrible guilt. He continued his jog up the passageway and tried to ignore the tingling in his bare feet every time they splashed through one of the blood puddles. The purple streams ran together into the depths of the tunnel as if pulled there by some gravitational force. He couldn't afford to slow down to avoid them and they seemed to coalesce into an unavoidable river in any case.

His back ached from his hunched-over jog, but he ignored it. Even though he cleared the ceiling by a foot, the closeness made him feel gross and so he bent awkwardly without meaning to. As he got deeper into the tunnel and the glow became a light floating in the air, he called out.

"Nathan! Nathan, are you there? Can you hear me?"

"Up here."

The voice sounded close, but the echoes in the tunnel made it hard to tell. Jason cupped a hand over his eyes to shield them from the light, but since the light seemed to come out of the air, it didn't help much. It felt a lot like looking at a streetlight after hours in a chlorinated pool, a kind of eerie halo, except filling the room. He stated the obvious.

"I'm coming."

A little farther up, a small shadow seemed to interrupt the glowing air. He picked up the pace as he saw Nathan's hunched form near the wall, not touching it. Nathan stretched out his arms to him and Jason picked him up and hugged him tightly.

"I gotcha buddy—you're okay."

"I'm glad you came," Nathan said and began to cry. He buried his face in Jason's neck and then wiped his eyes. "Sorry," he mumbled.

Jason smiled and rubbed the boy's hair. "I think you're allowed a few tears," he said.

Nathan hugged him again and then squirmed out of the embrace. He splashed into the cave blood and took Jason's hand.

"We have to hurry," he said and began pulling him along by the hand.

Jason couldn't think of anything to say so they continued on in silence. He thought he needed to explain some things to Nathan, but maybe the lessons of his memories were only for him. He thought he knew what the other-him tried to tell him. Up ahead he saw the tunnel begin to widen and the glow in the air grew even more intense. He tugged Nathan to a stop.

"Nathan, listen," Jason said. The boy turned and looked at him with fire in his eyes.

"We have to hurry, Jason," he said. "My mommy doesn't have much time."

"I know," he answered. "I know, but listen a sec, okay?"

Nathan stared back patiently, the grown up indulging his child.

"Two things, real quick," Jason said. "First, whatever you have to do there, just do it, okay. I mean don't worry about me. I want to help you but you can't worry about me and fail your mom, alright?" The boy nodded. "Okay, second," he paused. He didn't know what to say exactly and maybe Nathan knew all of this better than he did. He continued anyway. "Second, the creatures can't hurt you, Nathan. They're afraid of you and they know the power you have. But, you have to know it too. You can't be afraid, not even a little. You can do that, though, if you believe in yourself. You have to believe in yourself, like I believe in you. Nathan, I think the power is from the believing."

Nathan looked at him with a slightly cocked grin as if an idiot had just tried to convince him that fish lived in water. "I know, Jason," he said. "I needed you to help me be brave, but now you have to stay behind me okay?"

Jason arched his eyebrows in surprise. He was not the rescuer he had imagined. He nodded and Nathan turned and led him by the hand a few more yards until the tunnel ended and they entered the large room and the source of the light.

It felt like he had walked into the center of a light bulb. Despite the brightness, it didn't make him squint—didn't hurt his eyes at all, in fact. The light seemed pale, almost liquid, and shimmered outward from a pulsing, watery ball in the middle of the otherwise-ordinary room. Even though the light ball sat on a slight elevation, the cave blood flowed to it and splashed in a little swirling circle at its base—an upside-down version of water, swirling down a drain. Here a water spout stood on its head and the ball of light sucked the purple liquid up into its center.

The light he had seen from Jazz's body—the light the creatures had sucked into their open mouths—had been harsh white. The light that had erupted from Nathan's fingertips and face had been almost blue. This light seemed much duller, a dirty yellow. Nathan pulled Jason's hand to step them out of the cave-blood river. He couldn't pull his eyes off the bizarre sight, though vaguely aware that the horrible tingling in his feet and the tightness in his groin and stomach stopped immediately.

"Wow," he whispered.

Nathan said nothing and led him in a wide circle around the orb. On the far side of the light ball Jason saw that no other tunnels or passageways led into the room.

One way in and one way out. Now what?

The other-him stayed stubbornly quiet and Jason decided he would do best to just shut up and see what happened.

Then he smelled the shit smell and felt his pulse quicken and his throat tighten. He looked around the large room for the Lizard Men, but didn't see them. For a moment Jason considered snatching Nathan up and sprinting to the tunnel.

"No, stay still," Nathan whispered to him as if he had read his mind. His voice seemed too large for a little boy. "I have to destroy the light."

It took every bit of strength he had to obey the boy and stay still. Then he heard a voice in his head, but not the guiding, other-him voice.

Remember me, Jason? At last we have you. Now you can go and meet your mother while we feast on you like we did the others.

It was the voice from the alley, and the cave and his nightmares. Panic consumed him and he looked down at Nathan.

The fire in the boy's eyes filled him with shame and hope.

"Stay behind me, Jason," he said and pulled his small body between Jason and the tunnel.

The two Lizard Men appeared from the passageway and moved swiftly, their mouths open, yellow liquid dripping from their long, razor-sharp teeth.

* * *

Nathan stepped backward and angled himself between Jason and the creatures. He didn't feel afraid. He felt mad. His mind flashed on images of Steve as he had picked Nathan up by his broken arm and shoved his hand into the blue flame. He felt the fear of the doctors when they came to peel skin from his deformed fingers. Then he pictured Jenny, curled up with the milky-white, dead eyes—and his mother. He couldn't have been afraid even if he'd wanted to.

You can't hurt me.

"Power Rangers—POWER UP!"

The power exploded outward from deep inside of him and he again floated upward in the air. He held up his hands and watched as they began to glow, flickers of sparkler-like blue light fizzled from the tips of them. He smiled and felt hot inside—and angry.

You can't hurt us.

Blue light flew out from his hands and eyes. Nathan focused on the dull yellow orb in the middle of the room and watched as his own light sparked out toward it like lightening. When it hit the dirty little sun, sparks flew in the air and the light ball pulsed weakly and began to fade. Around the light ball the cave blood began to boil and pop, stinking like old garbage.

Nathan sensed a sudden movement and looked away from the electric scene. When he did he felt his power weaken. He saw the taller creature move with remarkable speed toward them from the tunnel. No, not toward them—toward Jason.

We can't hurt you, but we can certainly tear him to pieces.

Behind him a white light begin to bleed out from Jason. The creature's lizard mouth smiled and sucked it in. Nathan heard Jason scream in terror and he spun around in the air in time to see the creature's claw tear through the flesh on Jason's chest. Blood showered the Lizard Man as Jason crumpled to the floor.

"No," Nathan screamed, and redirected the blue light from his fingers and eyes. Lightning struck the creature in the neck and chest. Thin trails of foul-smelling smoke twisted from the green skin as an animalistic cry filled the room.

Beneath him, Jason shook his head clear, looked up at Nathan and nodded. Then he noticed the shorter creature circling around the other way from the tunnel.

"Nathan," Jason hollered up at him over the sizzling of the Lizard Man's skin. "Nathan, you have to destroy the light."

Nathan already knew that, but he didn't think he could keep the Lizard Men from killing Jason and destroy the light at the same time. He tried to move his power back over to the light ball, but when he did the taller Lizard Man gave out a terrible howl, the sound of an attacking animal, and moved again toward Jason. He started to feel frightened as he realized that he could save his mother or Jason, but not both. As his fear grew he saw his blue light fade in intensity.

"Nathan, destroy the light!" Jason called out again.

Nathan sent another bolt at the Lizard Man and propelled him backward, then sent another at the shorter creature who rounded the top of the circle and reached out for Jason.

"I can't," he cried as the shorter creature fell backward against his strike. "They'll kill you."

"No, they won't." Jason's voice sounded different—stronger somehow. "They can't, Nathan. I believe too." Jason struggled to his feet and dashed toward the tunnel. Both creatures whirled around and followed him. "I'll take care of the Lizard Men, you destroy that goddamn light so we can go home!"

With that, he disappeared into the tunnel and the Lizard Men followed him. Nathan hovered near the ceiling and tried to catch another glimpse of them, but they had disappeared. For a moment he thought about following them.

No, Ranger. Your mission is here. Your team is helping you, so finish your job.

What about Jason?

That is for Jason to decide. Destroy the light and set your mother free.

Nathan took a deep breath; the air felt cool and dry in his lungs. He closed his eyes tightly and summoned all the power he could. His skin began to tingle and his eyes filled with cold heat.

"I love you, Mommy," he whispered. Then he opened his eyes and opened his mouth. A huge and brilliant blue cone of light erupted from the middle of him and slammed into the light ball with a tremendous flash. This time the animal howl was his.

Chapter
29

Jason knew he probably would die, torn to pieces by the creatures, but he didn't care anymore. The important thing was only that Nathan could finish his work and be safe. He believed that meant that Jenny and Sherry would be safe also—always safe. He had to give the boy as much time as he could.

I'm sorry, Mom. I'm sorry I found my strength too late for you.

The cave blood splashed up all the way to his thighs as his bare feet pounded through the puddles. He could hear his breathing, raspy and shrill, and the animal grunts of the creatures behind him. Salty sweat burned in the ragged gash on his chest and streams of hot blood rolled down his side. If he could get out of the tunnel, maybe he could make it across the large room and up the rise to the other passageway. From there he could scurry into the little cave he'd hidden in with Nathan—and alone so many years ago.

Or you could stop and fight. Be a man for once. Be at least as much a man as the five-year-old you left in the other cave.

Not yet, Jedi. Keep running. Give him a little more time.

Jason pushed into a full sprint. He held his elbows up, pumping his arms furiously and using them to bounce himself off the walls, tearing through the never-ending, winding tunnel.

Suddenly, the grunting of the Lizard Men faded behind a new sound, a rising animalistic howl that seemed to penetrate through his torn and bleeding chest. Then a tremendous blue light exploded from behind him and the force of it picked him up and propelled him forward. The shock wave continued past him; he watched swirling tornados of blue bounce their way down the tunnel beyond him and he tumbled headfirst to the floor. His face and throat tingled from the cave blood. Jason rolled onto his back as he continued his slide down the tunnel and watched one last pulse of bluish light disappear. The dirty, yellow glow disappeared with it.

Nathan.

Jason shook his head and felt tears spill out onto his cheeks. He could not imagine any way that Nathan could have survived that explosion of power, especially not at ground zero. His throat tightened at the realization that the little boy he had come to love so much had just given his life to save them all.

* * *

Jenny jumped nearly out of her skin as Sherry let out a sudden, shrill gasp and sat up on the chair-bed, covers clutched in her white-knuckled hands. Once she realized where the sound came from she jumped up and snapped on the light behind Nathan's bed, then went quickly to Sherry's side.

"Oh, my God!" Sherry breathed. "Oh shit. Oh, God, what a terrible dream."

She looked around the room and then looked at Jenny, her face twisted in confusion.

"What are you doing here? Oh, my God. What a nightmare." She grabbed Jenny painfully by the wrists. "Where is Nathan? Where is my boy?"

Jenny broke her wrist free and held Sherry by the shoulders. "It's okay, Sherry. Everything is alright. Nathan is here." She gestured behind them at the figure curled up under the bed covers. "He's right there. He's sleeping."

"I have to see him." Sherry broke away and went to the bed, where she half crawled in beside her son and pulled the covers back.

Jenny squeezed past the outstretched legs of Jason, who slumped backward, mouth open, on the bench seat where she had cradled him moments ago. She placed a hand on Sherry's shoulder. Sherry put a hand over her mouth.

"What's wrong with him? Why won't he wake up?" She looked around the room and her gaze fell on Jason. "Why is Dr. Gelman not waking up? What the hell is going on?" Sherry's voice became a piercing shriek and Jenny worried that someone would come and check on them.

"Shhhh... Sherry listen to me." She pulled the woman's face away from the lifeless shape of her boy. "Listen. Everything is going to be okay. You have to trust me. Jason and Nathan will be right back."

"What do you mean, right back? They're right here. I..." She paused and drifted off. "I had this awful dream. There was like a sort of operating room and somewhere else. A..."

"Cave?" Jenny finished.

"What?"

"Sherry, listen. You have to calm down."

"How do you know about the cave? How can you know about my nightmare? What the hell is wrong with Nathan?" Sherry's voice rose again and Jenny looked anxiously at the door.

She took Sherry's hands gently in hers and took a deep breath. How did she explain this? "It's not a dream, Sherry. I can't explain it to you, but the cave is not a dream. It's real—I've been there too."

Sherry swayed and Jenny worried she might pass out.

"What? How? This is crazy..." She started to cry. "The creatures? The dinosaur creatures? Are they real too?"

Jenny wrapped her arms around the crying woman, pulling her close. "I'll tell you everything I know, but we have to be quiet." She looked at her watch. The resident doctors would be coming soon. Then what? "I don't understand it all, but I'll tell you what I can."

She rocked Nathan's near-hysterical mother in her arms and explained the nightmare as best she could.

* * *

Jason lay on his back wracked with grief until he heard a grunt behind him followed by a stirring in the darkness. The creatures were still behind him. Whatever power Nathan's death may have stolen from them, it had not killed them. Surrounded by the inky blackness, he struggled to his feet. The cave blood felt more like mud to him now, thick and sticky. It clung to his chest and neck, but the tingling and tightness in his stomach were gone. He pushed both arms out in front of him and continued to run down the tunnel. His hands and arms dug painfully into the drying walls of the cave as he fled back toward the room where he imagined that Sherry and Jazz would still lie on the ground.

The darkness began to thin and Jason felt he should be very close. He thought for a moment about all the movies he had seen where the characters fumbled in the dark, but a weird grayish light let the audience see them.

He could make out the ragged walls of the tunnel now and at his feet he could see dark irregular circles where the cave blood slowly dried up. Ahead he could just make out where the tunnel walls ended and a softer hue of gray marked the cave room. The grunt of the creatures behind him seemed to have fallen farther back, but he could still hear the pounding of powerful legs as they drove large, clawed feet into the dirt.

He pushed himself to speed up more, to widen the gap. Then he broke into the large room and skidded to a halt.

The dirt floor remained disturbed where Jazz's body had been, and he saw the dark brown of blood. But the body was gone. Jason nearly tore a muscle in his neck spinning his head to check.

Sherry had disappeared.

Nathan had done it. He had saved his mom.

He succeeded where I failed. He gave his life for her, for Jenny and for me as well.

Jason heard the grunt as the creatures entered the room behind him. He looked up at the rise, but felt no desire to sprint for the other tunnel and safety.

I love you, Nathan.

A peculiar tingle went up Jason's spine as he turned slowly and faced the Lizard Men. The two creatures weaved back and forth beside each other, two predators sizing up their prey. Their skin had turned a mottled gray and deep wounds striped their faces and bodies, but they still looked powerful. The two looked at each other with dull yellow eyes and nodded. He felt the tingle spread like heat to his chest and an electric ache that contracted his muscles in a painful but wonderful way. A bluish halo tinged his vision. The taller creature stopped his side-to-side shuffle as if it sensed something very wrong. The shorter one sniffed the air.

The heat inside him grew so great he knew he could no longer contain it and he tilted his head back and spread out his arms. Then his mouth fell open and he screamed out blue light which rose above him in the cave and began to swirl. The swirl solidified into a brightening globe. Finally, when he felt he might implode, the energy completely drained from the very center of him, and the globe of blue light began to shudder.

The Lizard Men seemed to understand they had made a terrible mistake and turned back into the tunnel just as the blue globe exploded in a shower of sparks. A blinding column of light poured from it, the diameter of a small tree. It struck the creatures and they disappeared into it. Jason fell backward, his hands in front of his eyes.

The light vanished.

And the creatures vanished with it.

Jason coughed painfully as his eyes adapted to the darkness. The faint glow of light revealed an empty cave, but at the entrance to the tunnel two thin spirals of smoke twirled upward toward the ceiling and disappeared. Jason struggled to his feet and an old man grunt escaped him. He stood nearly motionless and stared at the now-dark tunnel.

"Nathan," he whispered. He took a step toward the tunnel and then stopped.

Jason fell first to his knees and then fell forward, his hands over his face. Anguish engulfed him and he cried a long, deep cry for Nathan. He let himself rock back and forth and wailed his pain and loss.

"Nathan. Oh, God, no, little Nathan." He sobbed over and over.

"Jason?"

Jason froze, his hands still clutched over his face. The voice in his head sounded close, and young, and well.

Nathan? Nathan, are you alright?

He sent the thought out and prayed the voice had not been his imagination. He waited for what seemed an eternity, hands still clutched over his face and eyes shut tight. He always did better with his eyes closed.

"Jason?"

This time the voice was joined by a small, warm hand on his shoulder. Slowly he opened his eyes and looked up.

Nathan smiled back at him. His face looked happy—and clean somehow. His eyes shone with the brightness of the very young.

"Nathan," he exclaimed and wrapped his arms around the boy as a loud yelp escaped. They fell together to the ground, both of them laughing like idiots.

Jason pulled the boy away so he could look at him, still afraid he might be a dream.

"You did it? You destroyed the light?"

"Yes," Nathan answered, looking sheepish like a kid that just got his first Little League hit. "What happened to the Lizard Men?" There was not a hint of worry in the young voice.

"Gone," Jason answered with his own proud smile. "For good, I think."

Nathan hugged him again and rested his head on Jason's shoulder.

"I want to go home," he said in a sleepy voice. "I want to see my mommy."

Epilogue

Nathan crawled up the rope ladder as fast as his legs could take him. He giggled and knew it didn't sound cool, but he didn't care—Jason was in hot pursuit. He pulled himself up onto the wooden platform of the huge jungle gym with his right hand, rolled painfully onto his back and laughed upward into the blue sky when he felt Jason's hand on his leg. He squealed when Jason tickled his knee.

"Gotcha again," Jason said with a chuckle. "Man, are you sure you're the Red Ranger? You laugh more like the Pink Ranger!" He tickled Nathan's sides, which brought another girly squeal.

"Stop, stop," Nathan coughed out between giggles.

Jason collapsed beside him on his back, their two heads touching as they looked up at a few little clouds through the thick trees with their pretty white dogwood blooms. Nathan sighed and felt older than six.

"Do you ever feel like it was just a really bad dream?" he asked. He turned his head a little so he could see Jason's face. He saw him unconsciously rub his fingers across the place where his shirt covered the scars on his chest. Nathan flexed his right hand and wondered why he didn't have to have any scars. He wished Jason didn't either.

"Yeah," Jason said. "I feel like that a lot when I'm not with you. I think my mind tries to make me believe it so I won't be scared, you know?" Jason looked over at him and Nathan nodded. Jason looked back up at the sky. "I'm glad it happened though."

Nathan's eyes got wide. "Really?" he said. "Why?"

Jason sighed and rubbed his chest again. "I learned a lot about myself, Nathan. I learned a lot of things that made me okay with my past. I think I learned a lot about good and evil." He turned and looked at Nathan again. "I learned those things from you, Ranger."

Nathan blushed. Sometimes it bothered him when Jason called him that now, but not this time. He smiled back but couldn't think of anything to say. Jason squeezed his arm.

"Boys," Jenny's voice called from across the park. Nathan looked over and saw her and his mom waving at them. "Lunch, guys. Come and get it." Nathan waved back and they both sat up. He loved Saturdays more than he ever had.

"Do you ever build dreams?" he asked.

"What do you mean?" Jason asked.

"You know, build dreams. You try and imagine yourself in a story or something when you're trying to fall asleep and you're feeling scared. Then when you fall asleep you get to have a dream about what you thought about."

Jason smiled. "Yeah, I guess I've done that."

"Well," Nathan took his hand as they hopped down the big wooden steps. "When I was in the hospital and feeling really scared about the cave and all, I would build a dream about you and Mommy and Miss Jenny and me in the park." He looked contentedly up at his friend. "And it was just like this."

Jason stopped and picked him up.

"I love you, Jason," he said and put his head on his friend's shoulder.

"I know, buddy," Jason said with a big squeeze. "I love you too."

Jason set him down and got a twinkle in his eye. Nathan knew what was coming.

"Race ya!" Jason said.

And they tore off together toward the picnic tables and lunch.

CPSIA information can be obtained at www.ICGtesting.com
Printed in the USA
LVOW131326080113

314869LV00003B/116/P